THE PARROT GANG

&

WILD WEST GHOSTS

THE PARROT GANG & WILD WEST GHOSTS

Hideout Kids Book 5

by

Mike Gleason

Illustrated by Victoria Taylor

FARM STREET PUBLISHING

First published 2018 by Farm Street Publishing
www.hideoutkidsbooks.com

Paperback ISBN 978-1-912207-12-1
Hardback ISBN 978-1-912207-13-8
eBook ISBN 978-1-912207-14-5

A CIP catalogue record for this book is available from
the British Library.

Design and typesetting by Head & Heart

To Michelle and Luke,
who inspired me to write these stories
of the Wild West.

TUFF

SADIE

CONTENTS

Dear Reader,

Did you ever stay away from a place because you thought ghosts might haunt it? The Wild West was full of such places.

In *The Parrot Gang & Wild West Ghosts*, the fifth in the series of Hideout Kids books, the vicious outlaw "Big Nose" George Parrot and his gang try to get Sheriff Tuff Brunson and Deputy Sadie Marcus to leave Muleshoe for good.

The powerful enchantress Judge June Beak has finally had enough of the gang's tricks. She sends Tuff and Sadie to The Parrot Gang's Hideaway to arrest them. The gang uses an old tree house as their Hideaway. Everyone believes that ghosts haunt the tree house so the Parrots think they are safe from discovery.

If you want to curl up with a good story, start curling and turn the page.

Mike Gleason

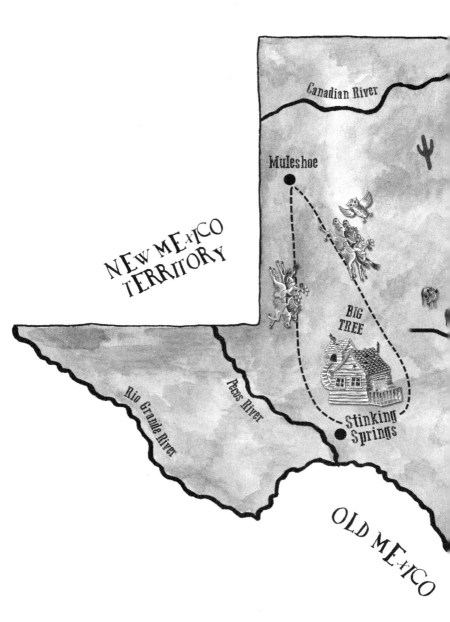

TUFF AND SADIE'S JOURNEY TO ARREST THE PARROT GANG

INDIAN TERRITORY

AUSTIN

Colorado River

TEXAS

Rio Grande River

GULF OF MEXICO

THE PARROT GANG

&

WILD WEST GHOSTS

CHAPTER ONE

SHOWDOWN AT THE HAPPY DAYS SALOON

A cold winter wind swirled down dusty Main Street in Muleshoe, Texas. It was the last day of December, New Year's Eve. Sheriff Tuff Brunson wrapped his buckskin coat around his shoulders as he and Deputy Sadie Marcus patrolled the street on their horses Silver Heels and Jenny. *Hope there's no trouble today,* he thought. *It's been a pretty good year.*

"If this wind gets any stronger it might

1

blow us to the next town," Tuff said as he looked over at Sadie. Her black ponytails blew straight back. "Let's duck into the Happy Days Saloon for a hot sarsaparilla."

"It's too windy to keep our hats on," Sadie said as they tied up their horses, grabbed their broad-brimmed white hats in their hands and hurried off the street.

As Tuff led the way up the steps to the saloon a small figure on the veranda caught his eye. "Look, Sadie, it's the singing cowboy poet," he whispered.

As usual the tiny cowboy was rocking in his old wooden rocking chair. He sang:

> *When Tuff & Sadie arrived*
> *In this pretty town*
> *Big Nose George was king*
> *And claimed the outlaw crown*
>
> *The pack of Parrots nest*
> *In their red tree house*

But when the ghosts show up
They'll hide like a mouse

"Let's go in, Tuff," Sadie said with a shiver. "I don't like songs about ghosts." They pushed through the batwing doors into the Happy Days.

"Where is everybody?" Tuff asked in a quiet voice. The four wooden tables and the few stools at the shiny wooden bar were empty. The smell of delicious s'mores was absent.

"I wondered that myself," Sadie replied. "Let's look around."

"Even Toothless Tom, the bartender, has wandered off," Tuff said. "This is strange. It's New Year's Eve. There should be a big party. But we've got it to ourselves."

"No you don't, Sheriff," a gruff voice said from the far corner of the room.

Boots shuffled on the wooden floor. Outlaws in black hats and red bandanas appeared from dark corners.

"What the -?" Tuff said.

"Pop, pop, pop," went the sound of bubblegum exploding from outlaw mouths.

"Nice of you to drop in. You remember me, don't you?" said "Big Nose" George Parrot, the meanest outlaw in the West, as he walked toward Tuff. "My brother 'Little Nose' George is here too. Ha, ha, ha."

"Ha, ha, ha. Thanks for droppin' in," sneered Little Nose George.

"Yeah, I remember you," said Tuff. "I might forget a face. But I never forget a smell, especially one as bad as yours. You smell like a rotten catfish. You must be one of those teenagers who has a bath once every ten years."

"Not funny," yelled Big Nose George. He glared at his sister, "Tiny Nose" Peggy, as she snickered behind him. "Stop gigglin', Peggy."

"Sorry," she said, still giggling.

"Yeah, don't laugh, Tiny Nose Peggy," said Sadie. "You smell even worse than your big brother."

"Grrr –" said Tiny Nose Peggy. "Let me pop her on the head. I wanna, I wanna, I wanna."

"What are you doing here, Parrots?" Tuff demanded. "Muleshoe is a kids-only town. No teenage outlaws allowed."

"Uh, I guess I forgot," said Big Nose George. "Now you listen up. I've got my sidekick with me, 'Short Arm' Sam. His finger gets real twitchy 'cause his arm is too short so don't try anythin' funny. He'll bash you if he can reach you. Ha, ha, ha."

Tuff saw "Short Arm" Sam standing in the corner and thought *Boy, is he ugly.*

"Ha, ha, ha," giggled Little Nose George.

"Your brain must be the same size as your nose," Tuff said to Little Nose George. "All you can do is copy your brother."

"Shut up, Sheriff," shouted Big Nose George. "I know my little brother's brain is the size of a pea but I'll be doin' the talkin' around here. All you and Deputy Ponytails got is a couple of bullwhips. But there ain't no bulls around here, just outlaws."

"Ha, ha, ha," laughed Little Nose George and Tiny Nose Peggy.

"Now, Dep-u-ties," said Big Nose George, "since you're nice and quiet, here's a last chance for you."

"A what?" Tuff said.

"A last chance. This is it." Big Nose George pulled out his super soaker water gun. "Get your hands in the air."

CHAPTER TWO

BIG NOSE GEORGE's THREAT

Tuff and Sadie lifted their hands above their heads.

"I don't feel like a shower right now, do you?" Tuff asked Sadie, rolling his eyes.

Sadie shook her head. "Nope."

"We've chased all the children of Muleshoe out of this saloon so we can have a little private chit-chat," Big Nose George said. "Since Judge June made you sheriff, you and your dep-u-ty have been crampin' our style."

9

"Yeah, yore crampin' our style," said Tiny Nose Peggy.

"Quiet, sis!" whined Big Nose George. "I just said that. Sheriff Brunson, before you got to Muleshoe we could rob the children any time we wanted. We took their kittens and puppies. We stole their toys. Since only children can live here it's easy pickings. This town belongs to *us*. You two need to get outta Muleshoe, *now*. This is your last chance."

"Guess what, stinky," Tuff said. "We're not leaving. We like it here. A gang of bullies like you won't scare us."

"Won't scare you? Ha, ha, ha," roared Big Nose George. "Ha, ha, ha," laughed Little Nose George, Tiny Nose Peggy and Short Arm Sam.

"Ha, ha, ha," neighed the outlaws' horses, which were tied up outside the saloon.

OK, you asked for it, Tuff thought. *Hope this works. I can hear Silver Heels and Jenny snorting outside.*

"Silver Heels, now," Tuff hollered.

"BAM!"

Big Nose George and his gang jumped. Silver Heels and Jenny had kicked down the saloon door.

"NEIGH!" they snorted.

"Quick, Sadie, go," Tuff shouted as he and Sadie grabbed their whips.

"Look out, you dirty outlaw, here comes Sheriff Tuff Brunson!" Tuff cried.

"CRACK!"

"Here comes Deputy Sadie!"

"CRACK!"

The two bullwhips lashed out. The ropes quickly wrapped up all the outlaws in the room.

"How did you do that?" yelped Big Nose George. "Nobody's that fast with a whip."

"Maybe we're lucky. Get out of town, bird brains," ordered Tuff, "or these whips will wrap you up so tight you'll turn red, like sausages. We'll feed you to the prairie wolves. They love to nibble on pretty Parrot sausage."

"Crime doesn't pay," Sadie said. She and Tuff loosened their whips so the outlaws could leave.

"We'll get you, Sheriff Brunson," Big Nose George bleated as he and his gang skedaddled for their horses. "Our final battle has started."

After they saw Big Nose George and his gang jump on their horses and ride out of town, Tuff and Sadie took Silver Heels and Jenny to the stables. When they got back to the saloon, a few of the children of Muleshoe had drifted back in. "Let's get some life in this place," said Jelly Roll Jim. "Crank up that player piano."

"Those loudmouth Parrots are dreadful," Toothless Tom said as he came out from his hiding place behind the bar. "I'm sick of the way they rip-roar through the town. Sheriff Brunson, somebody needs to put a stop to them."

The Happy Days filled up with children who sipped their hot chocolates and sarsaparillas.

Judge Junia "June" Beak appeared at the saloon entrance. "What was all that squawking about?" she asked. "It sounded like the Parrots."

"Big Nose George and his gang were just here," Sadie replied. "They threatened us and told us to leave Muleshoe. After a few lashes though they ran off."

"Tuff, Sadie, can you please come with me?" Judge June said. "Let's go over to the hut. This awful problem with The Parrot Gang has lasted long enough."

CHAPTER THREE

I SPY

Tuff put his white hat over his messy brown hair and tucked in his sheriff outfit against the cold. At least the wind had dropped a bit.

"Brrr," he said as they dashed across Main Street to Judge June's hut.

"Don't forget me," said Mr. Zip, Tuff's pet beaver, who was shivering outside the hut. "It's too frosty out here, even for beavers."

"C'mon, Mr. Zip," Tuff said. "I won't leave you outside."

A bright yellow door led into the old two-story wooden building. Tuff felt the warm, soothing air as Judge June closed the door behind them. The hut was filled with stacks of dusty books and ancient maps. A wood fire crackled in the fireplace.

Tuff glanced at one corner of the room. There stood a massive stuffed black bear, with sharp claws and gleaming white teeth. "I'm glad he's stuffed," he said to himself. *Wait, did that bear just smile at me?*

"Who invited the beaver?" growled Wild Thing, Judge June's pet pink fairy armadillo, as she woke up from her nap. "Get out of here, Mr. Zip. Mountain Men should have skinned you and turned you into a hat I could wear on a cold day like this."

"That's not nice at all, Wild Thing," Judge June scolded. "Tuff and Sadie, tell me about this latest visit from Big Nose George."

"We dropped into the Happy Days to get out of the cold," Tuff said. "Big Nose George and his gang appeared out of nowhere."

"They gave us a 'last chance' to get out of

Muleshoe," Sadie said, her black eyes staring at Judge June. "Big Nose George said 'our final battle has started'."

"I see," Judge June said. "I'll give you a short history of the terrible Parrot Gang. Big Nose George, Little Nose George and Tiny Nose Peggy showed up in Muleshoe when they were children. They ran away from their home in the desert. I knew they were trouble."

"How?" Tuff asked.

"They were the worst-behaved children we've ever had. Stealing, bullying, fighting, lying and cheating," Judge June said. "But since any children without a home can live here I had to let them stay. I thought after some time with me they would turn into good kids. I never lose hope but I'm afraid they might be under the spell of a bad witch somewhere."

"That's terrible, Judge June," Sadie said.

"The Parrots finally left when they got to be teenagers. But since they still know how to find us they want to take over the town. Don't forget," Judge June said, as she continued with her history, "Muleshoe is an oasis in the middle of a dry desert. We have our own food and water."

"I get it," Tuff said. "Since Muleshoe had no sheriff to protect the children these teenage bullies have terrorized the town. They want us to leave so they can take over."

"We must capture them once and for all," said Judge June.

"How about a spy?" Tuff said. "We can plant a spy in their midst, learn their plans, then arrest them."

"Great idea, Tuff," said Judge June. "Who can we get? It will be dangerous. If our spy gets caught the gang will feed him to the turkey vultures."

"I'll do it," shouted Wild Thing. "I'm good at pretending. Watch, I'll pretend to be a tooter. How about this, Mr. Zip?" She backed up to Mr. Zip and let fly with a massive toot, which blew the beaver across the room and slammed him into the wall.

"Stop it now, Wild Thing," Judge June ordered, "or I'll throw you in the stream. Sorry, Mr. Zip."

Mr. Zip slowly got to his paws. "Ouch, that hurt," he said. "You don't have to pretend, Wild Thing. Everyone knows you're a champion tooter."

"Enough you two," Judge June said.

"I volunteer," said Tuff in a cool voice, as he straightened his shoulders. "I'll disguise myself and pay a visit to the villains' den."

"Good." Judge June reached into her gun cabinet and pulled out a pair of silver, pearl-handled Colt 45 six-shooters. "These are fake guns. Usually outlaws don't carry bullwhips."

"Wow," Tuff whistled. "They look real enough. I'm still going to take my whip though."

"I understand, Tuff," said Judge June. "The pistols are part of your disguise. Also I'll send my familiar, Hooter, to help you. He's scouted The Parrot Gang Hideaway. He's also a genius with disguises and can help get you ready."

"Ok, Judge June," Tuff said.

"Sadie, you go with Tuff. Help him any way you can," Judge June said. She raised her arms and cast a spell that would help the

Deputies on their mission.

Tuff and Sadie looked up into the gaze of the magical Judge June's blue-gray almond-shaped eyes as she told them, "Your job is to arrest The Parrot Gang and bring them to justice. Please remember the most important thing. It's easier to *stay* out of trouble than to *get* out of trouble. Be careful."

CHAPTER FOUR

HOOTER, BLUEBIRD & SKEETER FINCH

Tuff and Sadie dashed out of Judge June's hut and hurried through the freezing cold wind to the jailhouse. The dark wooden building had six jail cells with black iron bars across the front. It smelled like old boots that had been left in the rain and mud for a few weeks.

"The jail cells are all empty, for now,"

Sadie said. "Soon we should have a few house guests."

"That must be Judge June's familiar," Tuff said as a knock came at the door. "It's about time we got to know him."

Sadie opened the door. A broad-shouldered animal with a large round head walked in. He had a friendly oval face and his hooded, yellowish eyes were set deep in his gray skin. He was dressed in gray and white buckskin, with brown deerskin moccasins.

"He looks like an owl," Tuff whispered to Sadie.

"Thank you," said the animal. "I should look like an owl because I am one. Owls have excellent hearing."

Tuff noticed the owl's large ears below a wisp of black hair.

"Oh dear," Tuff said. "I didn't mean to say anything wrong."

"Don't worry, Tuff. My real name is Wise Hooting Owl but you can call me Hooter like

Judge June does," said Hooter gently. "It's nice to meet you."

"It's good to meet you too."

"I'm Tuff's deputy," Sadie said. "Happy to meet you, Wise Hooting Owl."

"My pleasure, Sadie," the owl said. "Please call me 'Hooter' as well. I believe we have all seen each other before. I'm glad we have finally met."

"Hooter," Tuff said. "Judge June told us that you scouted The Parrot Gang Hideaway. What can you tell us about it?"

"Not surprisingly," Hooter said. "The Parrot Gang Hideaway is a tree house. It's built in a tall cottonwood tree above Stinking Springs."

"Stinking Springs," Tuff said. "Nobody goes near there. It's haunted by ghosts."

Hooter laughed and said, "That is what the Parrots want you to believe so people stay away. I have spent a lot of time in Stinking Springs. I haven't seen a ghost there."

"How do the Parrots get to their tree

house?" Tuff asked.

"They fly up a rope ladder," Hooter said. "Judge June told me that you'll pretend to be an outlaw and join their gang."

"Yes," Tuff said. "I have to be able to get up to the tree house."

"What is your fake outlaw name?" said Hooter.

"I've decided on a bird's name as well," Tuff answered. "Skeeter Finch."

"Oh, in that case, being a Finch, you can easily soar up to the tree house," Hooter said as he smiled. "OK, let's change your look, Tuff. Time to turn you into an outlaw."

"This is strange, Sadie," Tuff said, as Hooter went to work on his disguise. "I can't stand the sight of outlaws."

"There," said Hooter after a few minutes. "You look as mean as a vulture."

"Yuck!" Sadie said with disgust. "Go look in the mirror, Tuff, but you won't like what you see."

Tuff stepped over to the mirror. "Oh dear. I look horrible."

Tuff was an outlaw. His hair and hat were black. His red eyes looked like frozen toad eggs. He had gray beard stubble around his scowling mouth. His teeth were yellow. A red bandana hung around his neck, over his filthy outfit. His scuffed chaps and boots were caked in dust and gooey mud.

"Eww," Sadie said. "What's that smell?"

"Sorry, Sadie," Hooter said. "I had to

make 'Skeeter' smell like an outlaw. I rubbed him with my special mixture of armadillo poop plus jackrabbit guts, mixed in a bucket of goat spit."

Tuff smiled a mean smile. "I like the way I smell," he said with a growl. "Now where's my horse? I wanna ride with the bandits."

"Go right ahead, Tuff, you stink," Sadie said.

"Sadie," Tuff said. "I think you should also get into disguise. You and Hooter can set up a camp near the Hideaway. That way you'll be close to me."

"How about I pretend to be a Hopi Tribe Indian?" Sadie asked. "There are many Hopi in this area."

"Great idea," said Hooter. "We can build a tipi among the cottonwood trees by Stinking Springs. I'll disguise myself as a Hopi as well."

"Can we keep the campfire going all night?" Sadie asked. "Just in case you were wrong about the ghosts? I would sleep better."

"Hooter," Tuff said, "Let's make up a secret language of bird calls and songs. We should use it when we're near the outlaws."

"How about this?" Hooter said. "One call means 'Is all OK?'. Two calls means 'No'. Three calls means 'Yes'. Four calls means 'Run away'. And five calls means 'Help me'. Does that sound OK?"

"Exactly right," Sadie said.

"They don't call me Wise Hooting Owl for nothing," Hooter said shyly.

After Hooter had disguised Sadie, Tuff said, "You look just like a Hopi to me. Let's go." He led the way through the jailhouse to the stables in back.

"Neigh," Tuff's horse Silver Heels stomped and roared. "I wanna gallop with the outlaw horses."

"What about my nickname?" Sadie said.

"How about Bluebird?" Hooter said.

"Perfect," Sadie said.

"Is that your horse, Hooter?" Tuff

asked as a short,
broad-chested bay
colt trotted up.
"He looks fast."

"Yes," Hooter
said. "He takes
me everywhere, all
in good time. His
name is Speedy."

"Hey, Skeeter,"
Sadie asked.
"What about
your bullwhip?
I've got mine."

"It's looped
in my belt,
hidden under my
outlaw outfit,"
Tuff answered.
"Ready?"

"Wait just a
moment," Sadie

said. "I need to grab one more thing."

"What is it, Bluebird?" Tuff asked as Sadie stuffed something into her saddlebags.

"Oh, just an extra bullwhip. You never know when it might come in handy," Sadie replied.

"Sadie, was that Jelly Roll Jim's bullwhip?" Tuff said. "It looked just like it."

"Um, yes. I borrowed it from him."

"Does he know you borrowed it, Sadie?"

"No. But it's just for a day or two. He won't miss it. Let's go."

Tuff looked at Hooter and rolled his eyes. "She just can't help taking things that don't belong to her."

They all mounted their horses and tucked their boots into the stirrups.

"Let's ride, Bluebird. Let's ride, Hooter," Tuff said as he showed the whip to Silver Heels.

"We're with you, Skeeter," Sadie said. "To the den of outlaws!"

CHAPTER FIVE

STINKING SPRINGS

The brave trio galloped their horses out of Muleshoe into the high plains desert. Prickly pear cactus and thick mesquite trees lined the trail.

"Hooter," said Tuff, "You and Bluebird ride ahead and set up your tipi and camp. Send up a smoke signal of three puffs to let me know you're ready. I suggest in the secret language, Hooter, you speak with 'Hoot' like an owl. I'll speak with 'whistle' like a finch. Sadie can speak with 'chirp' like a bluebird."

"Gotcha, Tuff."

Hooter and Sadie rode ahead on their horses.

Tuff waited until he couldn't see Sadie and Hooter anymore then rode on. He guided Silver Heels to a small rocky hill where he could look out over Stinking Springs. After a while, he saw three puffs of white smoke rise up.

Are there really ghosts there? he wondered.

He saw Silver Heels' ears prick up.

"Whatcha doin' there, fella?" snarled one of two filthy horse riders who appeared on either side of Tuff. "Don't think I've seen yore ugly face in these parts before. You gotta name?"

"Yeah," said Tuff coolly. "I'll tell you my name just as soon as you back off. You've got nothing to worry about from me."

"We'll stay close for the time bein'," said the rider, who Tuff thought he recognized from Big Nose George's gang. "What are you called?"

"My name's Skeeter Finch. I'm from California," Tuff answered.

"California," laughed the rider. "That's darn near off the edge of the earth."

"Who are you?" Tuff asked, in a gruff voice. "I didn't invite you to come talk to me."

"My name's Short Arm Sam. This here's Borin' Bob. We're in The Parrot Gang. Our boss is Big Nose George Parrot. He's king of this territory. Since you rode on to our land that means he's the king of you."

"I've heard of your boss," Tuff said. "That's why I'm here – to see if he'd like to come help me out."

"Why would he want to help you?" Short Arm Sam asked.

"I'm known as 'King of the Train Robbers' out in California. I get more gold and silver

bars than everybody else," Tuff said. "But I need help. I've got more shiny metal bars than I can handle but not enough outlaws.

I hear Big Nose George might be up for the job. If he's not too scared, that is."

"Too scared!" a voice roared. Tuff turned around to see Big Nose George.

"I rode over here when I saw my patrol stop you. I've been listenin'," said Big Nose George. "Those are some nice Colts you got holstered. Don't think I caught your name."

"Skeeter Finch," said Tuff as he thought *I hope he doesn't realize these are pretend guns.*

"Well, Mr. Skeeter Finch, why don't you come over to our Hideaway and we can see about teamin' up with each other," said Big Nose George. "Did I hear you mention gold and silver?"

"You did," Tuff said. "Lots of it."

"C'mon, then, to the Hideaway," said Big Nose George. He led the way as they galloped the short distance to Stinking Springs. As they drew close Big Nose George sharply reined in his horse and looked toward a clearing among the cottonwood trees.

A tipi was standing in the clearing, with a campfire in front. Hooter and Sadie sat by the fire.

"Who's that?" Big Nose George asked.

"A coupla' travelin' Hopi Tribe Indians set up camp," Short Arm Sam answered. "I found 'em earlier. Their names are Hooter and Bluebird. Their horses are tied to Big Tree. Want me to chase 'em off, boss?"

"Nah, leave 'em there till mornin'," Big Nose George said. "Then take all their stuff and run 'em off Buffalo Cliff.

They've got bird names so let's see if they can fly."

Tuff gave a quick "whistle" toward the tipi.

"Chirp, chirp, chirp," came the song back, followed by "hoot, hoot, hoot."

Big Nose George turned around. He gave Tuff a mean stare.

If I can, I must warn Sadie and Hooter by morning, Tuff thought. *They're in great danger from The Parrot Gang.*

CHAPTER SIX

BIG NOSE GEORGE's HIDEAWAY

"Hop off your horse here," Big Nose George ordered Tuff. "You can tie him up to Big Tree, with those Hopi horses."

In front of them was a huge cottonwood tree, with a rope ladder hanging down its thick trunk. A sign attached to it said:

BIG TREE
PROPERTY OF THE PARROT GANG

KEEP OUT!
IT'S HAUNTED BY GHOSTS!

At the top of the tree was a massive tree house, painted bright red. Tuff tied Silver Heels to the tree, next to Jenny and Speedy.

"Keep me posted on anythin' goin' on down here," Big Nose George said to Short Arm Sam as he handed him the reins of his horse. "Watch those two Hopi."

"Are these ladder steps wooden? They don't look like it. They look like bones," Tuff said.

"They are bones," Big Nose George snarled. "The bones from mountain lions that I killed with my bare hands. Now grab your saddlebags. Up we go, Skeeter Finch."

He really is mean, Tuff thought. *Better be extra careful.*

They scrambled up the rope ladder till they came to a trapdoor. The trapdoor swung open and after Big Nose George went through Tuff followed him in.

Sprawled out on blankets on the floor of the tree house were Little Nose George and Tiny Nose Peggy, sound asleep. Tiny Nose Peggy was cuddling a doll. The doll was dressed in a deputy outfit and had needles stuck into her arms and legs.

Oh dear, Tuff thought, *that doll looks just like Sadie.*

In one corner was a rusty metal cage. Inside were two huge diamondback rattlesnakes.

"I see you noticed my pet rattlers. Here you go boys," chuckled Big Nose George as he tossed a couple of mice into the cage. "I usually feed 'em armadillos on cold days but we ran out."

"CHOMP!" went the rattlers.

Tuff looked past the rattlers into another corner. There stood a huge stack of old rifles. Boxes of bullets were scattered about.

"I haven't seen rifles that old in a long time," Tuff said.

"They're not ours," Big Nose George said. "We found 'em here. They must have belonged to a gang from long ago."

Next to the rattler cage were two large boxes labeled:

**EXPLOSIVES
ENOUGH TO BLAST YOU TO CHINA
DANGER!**

Long black fuses stuck out of each box.

"That's a lot of explosives," Tuff said. "Must be a bunch of trouble around here."

"The only trouble we got here is with a wimpy sheriff and his ponytailed dep-u-ty," Big Nose George said with a growl. "They work for a witch named Judge June over in Muleshoe. We're fixin' to get rid of 'em. We got a plan."

"Does the sheriff ever come out here?" Tuff asked. "I don't like sheriffs."

"Nah. Nobody shows up," Big Nose

George answered. "The whole town thinks Stinkin' Springs is haunted. They're too scared to come out."

"Well, is it?" Tuff said.

"I hope not," Big Nose George said. "If it is I'll leave. I'm only afraid of one thing: ghosts."

"Me, too," Tuff fibbed.

"Yeah?" Big Nose George said. "Me and you are a lot alike."

No we're not, thought Tuff.

"Hey, get up you lazy knuckleheads." Big Nose George walked over and kicked the two sleeping teenagers on the floor. "We've got company."

Little Nose George and Tiny Nose Peggy hopped up.

"This here's a famous outlaw from California by the name of Skeeter Finch," Big Nose George said. "He's lookin' to hire us to come out to his territory. He needs help totin' all his gold and silver around.

He's got more than he can carry."

Tiny Nose Peggy stared at Tuff.

"What did you say yore name is?" she asked suspiciously. "You look awful familiar to me."

"My name's Skeeter Finch. I rob trains out in California. I'm known as the 'King of the Train Robbers'," Tuff said.

"That's funny," said Tiny Nose Peggy with a sneer. "'Cause you look just like Sheriff Tuff Brunson. He's our arch enemy. We're about to snuff him out. Him and his snotty dep-u-ty." She held up her doll. "This is my Dep-u-ty Sadie doll. I stick a needle in her every day."

"Don't insult me," Tuff said with a growl in his voice. "Those are fighting words, saying I look like a sheriff."

"Now, now," said Big Nose George. "There's no way this here outlaw is Sheriff Brunson. Take a whiff of him."

"Eww," cried Tiny Nose Peggy.

"Eww," hollered Little Nose George. "He stinks."

"I think I smell pretty good," Tuff said.

"See," laughed Big Nose George. "That wimpy sheriff wouldn't be caught dead smellin' so bad."

"Come over and join me, Skeeter," Big Nose George said. "Have some supper. We're eatin' roast razorback hog followed by wildcat puddin'. Dee-lish."

Tuff felt an icy blast as Little Nose George threw open the wooden shutters covering a window.

"What are you doin' George?" Big Nose George yelled at his little brother who stood at the window with two handfuls of jagged rocks.

"Just havin' fun. I'm gonna throw these rocks at a coupla Indians down there by a tipi," answered Little Nose George. Tuff was horrified.

"Stop it George," laughed Big Nose

George. "You know there's no target practice at mealtime."

Little Nose George lowered his hands. "OK, big brother," he said with an evil grin. He shut the window.

CHAPTER SEVEN

TUFF DISCOVERS THE PARROTS' PLAN

"So Big Nose George," Tuff said as they ate supper. "What about coming out to California? Big money for you."

"I'd like to," Big Nose George said, "but first we got somethin' to do here. I got to get rid of the sheriff and his dep-u-ty. They're crampin' my style."

"Yeah. They're crampin' our style," squeaked Tiny Nose Peggy. "I want that snotty nose Dep-u-ty Sadie all to myself. I don't like her one bit."

"Hang on, Peg," said Big Nose George. "We have to follow the plan."

"What's the plan again, big bro?" asked Little Nose George.

"Man, you're as dumb as that sheriff says you are," Big Nose George said to his little brother. "I'm tellin' you for the last time 'cause we're doin' this tomorrow mornin'."

"OK," whimpered Little Nose George.

"Before dawn tomorrow," said Big Nose George, "we saddle up our horses and ride into Muleshoe. Sheriff Brunson and Deputy Sadie will be asleep in their jailhouse. We dig a hole under the jailhouse and bury that box of explosives in the hole. Then 'BOOM!' We got enough dynamite in the box to blow them from here to China."

"Sounds like that should get 'em," Tuff said. "What about the other box – I could use it in California."

"Nope," said Big Nose George. "I got a special place for that box. It's goin' under

Judge June's hut. I've had enough of her too."

"Ha, ha, ha," laughed Little Nose George and Tiny Nose Peggy.

"Let's get some sleep, gang," Big Nose George said. "Big day tomorrow."

Oh dear, Tuff thought as he lay down and closed his eyes. *I can't say anything to Hooter or Sadie. Even Judge June is in great danger. I have to save them. But how?*

Tuff woke to the sound of hungry wild turkeys gobbling among the cacti and cottonwoods. The sun was not yet up but the turkeys were.

Wait, what's that? he wondered.

"Hoot, hoot, hoot, hoot, hoot."

Then

"Chirp, chirp, chirp, chirp, chirp."

Then

"POP!"

Tuff sat up. He stared right into the eyes of a vicious, bubblegum-chewing outlaw.

"You can get up now, Sheriff Brunson,"

snarled Big Nose George. "Your little game is over."

"What the –?" Tuff said.

"My sister may act dumb," Big Nose George said. "But she's a pretty smart cookie. You're right about my little brother though. George is a stupid idiot."

"So how did you figure me out?" Tuff asked as he carefully reached under his outfit, searching for his bullwhip.

Big Nose George said, "The first clue you weren't who you said you were was your bird language. We figured that out right away. Whistle, hoot, chirp for Finch, owl, Bluebird. We're The Parrot Gang. Our song is 'caw'. Did you really think we wouldn't understand?"

Tuff got up and looked around the room. He noticed that Peggy and Little Nose George were gone.

"Careful, Sheriff. I'm watchin' you," Big Nose George continued. "My gang's got your friends tied up down there. Sadie looks like a Hopi, 'cept a lot uglier. Our second clue was your horse. I recognized Silver Heels."

"You're just lucky," Tuff said as his mind raced to make a plan.

Wait, he thought. *Silver Heels can help. I must get to him.*

"It wasn't luck and you can stop lookin' for these," Big Nose George said, as he showed Tuff his outlaw belt. On it hung Tuff's bullwhip and the two pretend Colts. "Tiny Nose Peggy found them when you fell asleep. Real outlaws don't carry fake guns."

"Now what?" Tuff asked.

"Yore about to find out." Big Nose George pointed at the trapdoor. "Get down the rope ladder."

CHAPTER EIGHT

THE HIDEAWAY IS DESTROYED

Tuff clambered down the ladder. When his feet hit the ground, he looked over at the tipi. Sadie and Hooter were tied up, guarded by Tiny Nose Peggy.

Next to them were the two boxes of explosives, guarded by Little Nose George.

"Look what we got here," Tiny Nose Peggy shrieked at Tuff. "Yore pore wittle dep-u-ty is all tied up. I'm gonna chop those ponytails off!"

Tiny Nose Peggy got out her long, sharp hunting knife.

"Put the knife away," ordered Big Nose George. "I've got a better plan for the dep-u-ty. We're gonna hang her by her pony-tails over the edge of Buffalo Cliff. These Deputies are gonna be in serious trouble when they're standin' at the edge of that cliff."

"Yeah," Tiny Nose Peggy squealed. "Let's go."

Tuff looked at Silver Heels, Jenny and Speedy. They were still tied to Big Tree, which held up the tree house. Silver Heels stared back at him, then at the tree. *Hmmm...* Tuff was sure his plan would work. *Silver Heels can do it.*

"So you're taking us to Buffalo Cliff, are you?" Tuff asked calmly.

"That's right, Sheriff," said Big Nose George. "We'll drop you off there. Ha, ha, ha."

"Ha, ha, ha," laughed Tiny Nose Peggy, Little Nose George and all The Parrot Gang.

"Ha, ha, ha," neighed their naughty horses.

"Will you grant me one last request?" Tuff asked.

"OK, Sheriff, but I'm watchin' you," said Big Nose George.

"Little Nose George, could you please hand me Sadie's saddlebags?" Tuff asked politely.

"Sure, Sheriff, here ya go," Little Nose George said with a smile as he tossed the saddlebags to Tuff.

"Wait, no! Don't give him the saddlebags. It's a trick you idiot," shouted Big Nose George to his dim-witted little brother.

Too late for the outlaws, Tuff grabbed Sadie's spare bullwhip. "CRACK!"

"Look out you dirty outlaws," he cried. "Here comes Sheriff Tuff Brunson!"

The whip wrapped tightly around Big Nose George and Tuff's own bullwhip, which coiled back to his own hands. *Thank you Judge June*, Tuff thought. He never knew how he could make a whip do that.

Big Nose George was wrapped up tightly. Short Arm Sam and Borin' Bob took off, running into the trees.

"CRACK!" He lashed his own whip around Tiny Nose Peggy's legs and dropped her to the ground as Little Nose George stood watching with his mouth hanging open.

"Time for a neat trick from our horses," Tuff said. "Silver Heels, Jenny, Speedy. Back up from the tree now. Silver Heels lead the way!"

Led by Tuff's powerful stallion, the three horses dug their hooves into the ground and started backing up. The ropes that tied them to Big Tree grew tight. With a huge cracking and crashing sound, Big Tree started falling down. Silver Heels, Jenny, Speedy and the outlaw horses shook off their ropes and ran out from under the tumbling tree house.

"Look out," Big Nose George yelled. "Our Hideaway is crashing down."

"It's too late, outlaws," Tuff said. "You're trapped."

Tuff jumped over to Sadie and Hooter and untied them as The Parrot Hideaway smashed to the ground, smothering the three Parrots. A huge cloud of brown dust billowed in the air.

As the dust settled the only sound was the cold wind that rustled through the cottonwood trees. Big Nose George's two pet rattlesnakes had broken out of their cage and slithered away across the frozen ground.

"Whew. Nice work, Sheriff," said Hooter admiringly. "We were in a pretty tight spot."

"If you hadn't 'borrowed' that extra bullwhip, Sadie, I'm afraid we were toast," Tuff said. "Thanks, Deputy."

"I'm always glad to be helpful," Sadie said with a smile. "Let's grab our prisoners and take them in. I'm ready for a sarsaparilla with hot cream topping."

"Me, too," Tuff said. "Now that the Parrot nest is destroyed let's round up the gang. Listen, I think I hear Big Nose George asking for something."

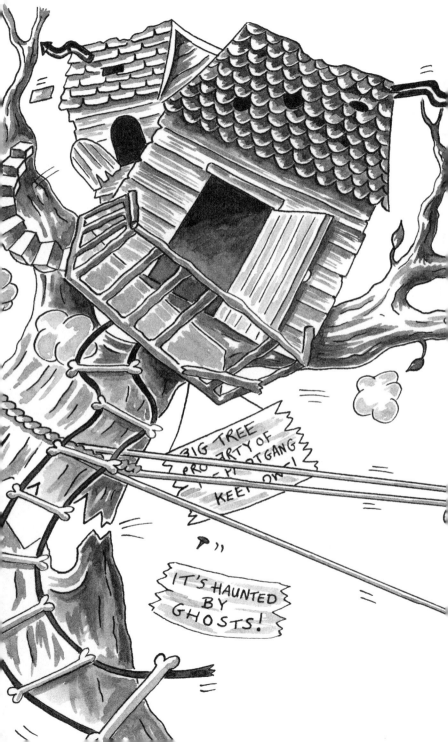

From under the rubble came Big Nose
George's weak voice, "Caw, caw, caw, caw,
caw."

"Let's all answer with Hooter's call!"
Tuff said.

"Hoot, hoot," they hollered, laughing.
"Woo, woo, woo, woo," sang
a menacing choir of voices
from behind them.

Tuff whirled around. Sadie and Hooter stepped right behind him.

Six milky white riders sat astride six milky white horses, staring down at them with angry bloodshot eyes.

"Oh dear," Tuff whispered. "What the –?"

"It seems our home has been destroyed," said the biggest rider with a snarl. "And you're the ones who did it."

CHAPTER NINE

PHANTOM OUTLAWS

The cold wind died down. The air stilled. The frozen breath of the riders appeared as smoke from their mouths. Frozen wheezes from the white horses reminded Tuff of old drawings of dragons.

The riders had no weapons. They stood still, as if they were statues covered in ice.

"Who are they, Tuff?" Sadie whispered. He could feel her shaking behind him. "They don't seem real."

"Only one way to find out," Tuff said. "Keep your fingers on your whip, Sadie."

"My fingers are frozen to my whip. Please get rid of them, Tuff."

Tuff held on to his bullwhip tightly. "Hello. My name is Sheriff Tuff Brunson. Behind me is Deputy Sadie Marcus and our friend Wise Hooting Owl," Tuff said as he moved carefully toward the riders. "We are on a peaceful job sent by Judge June Beak of Muleshoe. We came here to arrest the outlaw Parrot Gang. This tree house was their Hideaway."

The lead rider spurred his horse slowly toward Tuff. He leaned down and, in a voice like a hissing snake, said, "If you are a sheriff and she is a deputy where are your badges?"

Oh dear, Tuff thought.

"We don't have our badges because we are in disguise. We tricked the outlaws," Tuff said.

"In disguise?" the rider said as he turned and looked at the other riders. "So are we."

"We thought this tree house was the

Hideaway for The Parrot Gang. We didn't know it was your house," Tuff said.

"It wasn't just our house," said the rider. "It's where we kept our rifles."

Hooter stepped forward. "May I stroke your horse?" he asked the rider gently.

"No!" hissed the rider. "Don't come near me." The rider turned and walked his horse back to the others.

"Tuff," said Hooter, "he won't let me touch his horse because he knows I would put my claw right through it. They're ghosts."

"I knew it," Sadie said. "Let's get our prisoners and get out of here."

"Wait," Tuff said. "I think I know what they're after. When I was in the tree house I saw a stack of old rifles and ammunition. Big Nose George told me they weren't The Parrot Gang's. They must belong to the Wild West outlaws who used the Hideaway before them. These are Wild West outlaw ghosts on their ghost horses."

"Wild West ghosts looking for real rifles," Sadie said as she shivered. "That's very scary. We must keep them away from those rifles."

"Tuff," Hooter said. "I don't think they want to harm us. I'll keep them busy while you and Sadie round up Big Nose George and his brother and sister. When you're ready we'll say goodbye to the ghosts and calmly ride out of Stinking Springs."

"Then we'll ride like tornado winds to Muleshoe," Sadie said.

"What are you going to do to keep them busy?" Tuff asked.

"Leave it to me," Hooter answered, as he walked slowly toward the six phantom outlaws.

"Quick, Sadie, let's get this rubble moved so we can find the Parrots," Tuff said. He turned and ran back toward the wrecked tree house.

"I'm right behind you, Sheriff." Sadie joined him but couldn't help looking over her shoulder to make sure the ghosts weren't following.

First Tuff and Sadie gathered the gang's horses and tied them to Silver Heels, Jenny and Speedy. Then they found the three Parrots, who moaned, cried and whined like teeny babies who hadn't been fed.

"I can't move," whimpered Big Nose George. Tuff looked down at the outlaw. He didn't have a scratch on him.

"Sadie, listen," Tuff said, as the sound of a harmonica drifted over them. "What beautiful music."

The two Deputies looked in the direction the sound was coming from.

The six ghost riders had dismounted and sat on tree-trunk benches in a circle around a small campfire, listening. Their horses stood silently nuzzling each other.

The phantom outlaws straightened their hats. Lollipops hung out of their mouths as they relaxed. One of them took out knitting needles and wool and began to knit a cap. Another chewed bubblegum and

blew huge bubbles.

Hooter stood next to the fire in the center of the circle. He coddled the harmonica in his claws as he played old Wild West songs from years before.

"Amazing," Sadie whispered. "The music is so haunting and sad." A tear dropped from her eye.

The peaceful setting was interrupted.

"AWWWWWW!!!!" screamed Big Nose George. "HELP!!! GHOSTS!!!! RUN FOR YOUR LIVES!!!"

CHAPTER TEN

A NEST FOR THE PARROTS

Big Nose George, his brother and sister got to their feet and gaped in horror at the ghostly scene.

"I thought you were hurt too badly to stand up," Tuff said. "What's the matter? Scared of a few phantom outlaws?"

"Please get us out of here, Sheriff. Take us to your jail. Lock us up. Throw away the key," Big Nose George begged. "Just get us away from those ghosts."

"Let's tie 'em up, Sadie," Tuff said as he laughed. "Poor dinky bandits, afraid of the ghosts."

After they had the whimpering pandemonium of Parrots tied up and slung over their own horses, Tuff and Sadie walked over to Hooter.

"I think we can leave now, Hooter," Tuff said.

Hooter pocketed his harmonica. "Lovely to have a chance to play," he said. "I felt as though I had played for these ghosts once before."

The ghosts still sat silently around the campfire.

"There's something else I think we should do," Tuff said. "I know the ghosts seem harmless but they were outlaws after all. Please help me move these boxes of explosives over to the wrecked Hideaway. Let's blow it to bits."

They dumped the dynamite over the wreckage. After they had moved a safe distance away, Tuff prepared to light the fuse.

"Wait, the ghosts. They're still there," Sadie said.

"I wouldn't worry about them," Hooter said. "Watch."

Tuff lit the fuse.

"BOOM!"

The dynamite blew the Hideaway to smithereens sending a massive dust cloud into the air.

"Wow," Tuff whistled through his teeth as they watched the sight from Stinking Springs.

After the dust cleared, the phantom outlaws stood up, stretched their legs, put on their hats and mounted their horses. The lead rider turned and murmured "Adios, amigos" as they walked their horses away.

"Race you back to Muleshoe," Sadie hollered. "Last one there is a rotten cow's egg!"

"Cows don't lay eggs, silly," laughed Tuff.

"And ghosts don't exist," said Sadie, winking at Tuff.

The Deputies led the way into Muleshoe with The Parrot Gang bundled up behind them. Hooter guarded the prisoners from the rear.

"Look," said Jelly Roll Jim. "Sheriff Brunson and Deputy Sadie captured Big Nose George and his brother and sister. Come see, everybody."

Cheers from the children rang through Muleshoe as the parade of Deputies and outlaws rode into town.

"Look, there's the singing cowboy poet," Sadie said to Tuff as she pointed at the veranda of the Happy Days.

The little cowboy sat back in his rocking chair as he sang:

Big Nose George is caught
He's finished doing wrong
He's off to the jail
Where outlaws belong

Get the birdcage ready
For the bully gang
The next sound they hear
Is the jail door ringing "clang"

Judge June smiled as they trotted up to the jailhouse. "I can't think of a better way to start the New Year than to have these rascally rascals behind bars where they belong," she said as she walked around the prisoners. "Well, well. Looks like the chickens have come home to roost."

"We're not chickens," squeaked Tiny Nose Peggy.

"Yes we are," said Big Nose George. "We're finished as outlaws. I'm too scared to go back out to Stinkin' Springs."

"You're not going anywhere, Parrot," Judge June said with a scowl. "Tuff, you and Sadie will be happy to know that we have built a special jail for The Parrot Gang," she continued. "We have a big cell for Big Nose George, a little cell for Little Nose George, and a tiny cell for Tiny Nose Peggy. We even have a stables jail cell for their naughty horses. Lock 'em up, Deputy Dan."

Tuff's jailhouse assistant Deputy Dan left his massive lunch plate of tacos and burritos on the jailhouse veranda. "Right away Judge June," he said as he let out a bubbling belch.

"So I gather Hooter was able to assist you a wee bit?" Judge June said.

"He helped heaps," Tuff laughed. "What beautiful music he plays."

"Yes, musical talent runs in his family," Judge June said with a smile.

"Let's celebrate," Sadie said. "I'm dying for a sarsaparilla with hot cream and a piping hot plate of scrumptious s'mores."

"You shall have both," Judge June said as she led the crowd of smiling, singing children into the Happy Days. "Sadie, would you like to return Jelly Roll Jim's bullwhip now? I know you 'borrowed' it."

"Oh, yeah," Sadie said, handing the whip to Jelly Roll Jim. "Here it is. It came in handy."

"I'm glad it was useful, Sadie," said Jelly Roll Jim. "But would you please ask me next time you want to borrow something of mine?"

"Maybe," answered Sadie.

After a few plates of s'mores Judge June leaned over to Tuff and Sadie and said, "Now that you're home safely I'd like to ask you a question."

"Go ahead," said Tuff.

"Is it true? Are there really ghosts at Stinking Springs?" she asked.

Why would she ask that? Tuff wondered. *She's a witch.*

"You already know the answer," said Sadie with a grin. "That's why you sent Hooter to help us. He talks to the spirits just like you do."

"Oh dear," Judge June whispered. "I guess you know our secret. Don't tell anybody."

"We won't," Tuff and Sadie whispered back. "Your secret is safe with us."

THE END

Author's Note

The Hideout Kids series of books feature several of the same characters, animals, places and things. Here are some brief descriptions:

Charlie "Sir" Ringo: A cowboy detective.

Deputy Joe "Sawbones" Newton: Muleshoe's doctor, a deputy to Sheriff Tuff Brunson.

Deputy Sadie Marcus: Ten-year-old deputy of Muleshoe and Tuff's best friend.

Hooter: Judge June's familiar. An owl-shaped spirit who helps Judge June practice her magic.

Jack: Sawbones' horse.

Jelly Roll Jim, Toothless Tom, Deputy Dan Pigeon: Teenagers who grew up in Muleshoe and stayed on to help Judge June and the hideout kids.

Jenny: Sadie's Horse. A gift from Chief Ten Bears of the Comanche Tribe Indians.

Judge Junia "June" Beak: United States District Judge of the West. She is also a good and powerful witch.

Miss Hannah Humblebee: A Hopi Tribe Indian girl detective.

Mr. Zip: Tuff's pet. A beaver.

Muleshoe, Texas: Home of the hideout kids. Only children can find it and live there.

S'mores: Chocolate-covered marshmallows, served on sugar crackers. Dee-lish.

Sarsaparilla: The most popular soft drink of the Wild West. It's thought to have healing powers and is made from the root of the sarsaparilla vine. Yummy.

Sheriff Tuff Brunson: Ten-year-old sheriff of Muleshoe.

Silver Heels: Tuff's horse. Also a gift from Chief Ten Bears.

Spiky: A giant saguaro cactus that guards The Cave.

The Cave: A magical place where the kids can travel through time.

The Singing Cowboy Poet: A magical elf.

Wild Thing: Judge June's pet. A pink fairy armadillo.

Here are descriptions of a few animals, plants and things that you might not have seen before and which appear in this book:

Cottonwood trees: One of the few big trees able to grow near Muleshoe.

Diamondback rattlesnake: A dangerous snake, they usually eat small mammals such as mice. If they think they are in danger they use their rattle to warn that they are about to strike.

Mesquite trees: Typical tree of the Texas desert.

Pandemonium of parrots: A group of parrots.

Prairie wolves: Another name for a coyote.

Razorback hog: Wild hogs found in Texas. They have sharp tusks.

Tipi pronounced "tee-pee": A tall, circular tent most often used by Indian tribes in the Old West.

Tornado: A gigantic, circular, dangerous storm with very fast winds.

Turkey vulture: Also known as buzzards, they are commonly found in Texas.

Wildcat: Cats which live wild in the desert and mountains. Larger than a house cat.

BILLY THE KID & CROOKED JIM

Chapter One
A LIGHTNING STRIKE

Late one spring afternoon dark storm clouds gathered above the Wild West Texas town of Muleshoe. Gusts of wind threw old leaves and tiny dung beetles through the air.

Whirling clouds of dust, which the hideout kids called 'dust devils', danced around the town. Thunder rolled off the hills.

"We better duck for cover," Sheriff Tuff Brunson said as he walked up Main Street with his two deputies. "Here comes a nasty thunderstorm."

Tuff's deputies, Sadie Marcus and Joe "Sawbones" Newton, held on to their white hats and hurried into the Happy Days Saloon. "See you in a minute," Tuff shouted. "I'll make sure the jailhouse is secure."

Tuff ran to the wooden jailhouse. Locked up inside was The Parrot Gang, "Big Nose" George Parrot, the meanest outlaw in the West, his brother "Little Nose" George and sister "Tiny Nose" Peggy.

As the thunder boomed Big Nose George whimpered in a corner. Little Nose George was tucked under his arm, tears streaming down his cheeks.

"What's the matter, pretty Parrots?" Tuff laughed. "Scared of a little storm?"

"He's afraid of lightnin' and thunder, Sheriff," Little Nose George said. "Me too. Lightnin' might strike us. Even our horses are scared."

The jailhouse had a stables cell where Tuff locked up the outlaws' naughty horses.

"We're terrified," the horses whinnied.

"Your sister doesn't look scared," Tuff said. Tiny Nose Peggy stood by a window, grinning at the sky. Her arm stuck out between the metal bars.

Little Nose George stared at her. "Yeah, well, she's only thirteen. She don't know bad things can happen in a thunderstorm."

Tuff said, "Just relax. Your teenage brain is imagin –"

"BOOM! BOOM!"

A bright lightning flash set off a huge explosion of thunder.

Tuff was blinded. His ears rang and he fell to the floor. His head spun round and round...

"Tuff, Tuff, wake up," Sadie shouted. "C'mon Tuff, please wake up." She splashed his face with cold water.

Tuff sat up slowly, rubbing his eyes. He looked at Sadie. Sawbones stood next to her.

"What the –?" he gasped. "What happened to me?"

"Lightning struck the jailhouse," said Sawbones. "Sadie and I saw it from the doors of the saloon. Let me have a look at you." Sawbones was a doctor.

He examined Tuff carefully. "You should be OK. We need to keep one eye on you though."

"That won't be hard for you." Tuff giggled. Sawbones only had one eye. He lost his right eye in a fight.

"That's a good sign," said Sawbones. "You've still got your sense of humor."

Tuff looked over at the cells. "Big Nose George. The Parrot Gang. They're gone."

So far in the HIDEOUT KIDS series...

MIKE GLEASON

HIDEOUT KIDS

TUFF, SADIE
& THE WILD WEST

MIKE GLEASON

HIDEOUT KIDS

GENERAL MUSTER
& NO-TREES TOWN

MIKE GLEASON

HIDEOUT KIDS

GRIZZLY BEARS
& BEAVER PELTS

MIKE GLEASON

HIDEOUT KIDS

MACHO NACHO
& THE COWBOY BATTLE

MIKE GLEASON

HIDEOUT KIDS

THE PARROT GANG
& WILD WEST CHOSTS

MR. ZIP

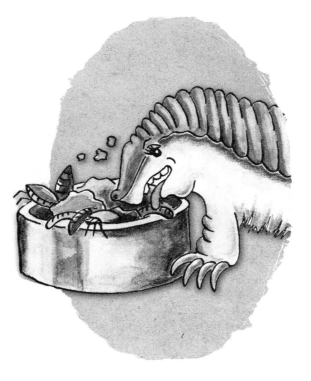

WILD THING

JUDGE JUNE

SPIKY

ABOUT THE AUTHOR

Hideout Kids author Mike Gleason comes from a small town in Texas. He grew up with cowboys, cowgirls and exciting stories of Wild West adventures. He was a wildcatter in the Texas oil fields and a board director at MGM in Hollywood. He created and produced an award-winning music television series at Abbey Road Studios. He lives and writes in London.

ABOUT THE ILLUSTRATOR

Hideout Kids illustrator Victoria Taylor comes from Cheltenham, England, and her love of art was inspired by her maternal grandmother. She trained at Plymouth University and worked for many years as a graphic designer. Having returned to her first love of painting and drawing, Victoria is now a freelance book illustrator. She lives in Gloucestershire with her husband and two children.

Printed in Great Britain
by Amazon

72476050R00075

GENERAL EDITOR: CHRISTOPHER RICKS

OVID IN ENGLISH

PUBLIUS OVIDIUS NASO was born in 43 BC at Sulmo (Sulmona) in central Italy. He was sent to Rome to attend the schools of famous rhetoricians but, realizing that his talent lay with poetry rather than politics, he began instead to cultivate the acquaintance of literary Romans and to enjoy the smart witty Roman society of which he soon became a leading member. His first published work was *Amores*, a collection of short love poems; then followed *Heroides*, verse-letters supposedly written by deserted ladies to their former lovers; *Ars Amatoria*, a handbook on love; *Remedia Amoris*; and *Metamorphoses*. Ovid was working on *Fasti*, a poem on the Roman calendar, when in AD 8 the emperor Augustus expelled him for some unknown offence to Tomis on the Black Sea. He continued to write, notably *Tristia* and *Epistulae ex Ponto*, and always spoke longingly of Rome. He died, still in exile, in AD 17 or 18.

CHRISTOPHER MARTIN received his doctorate from the University of Virginia, and he is currently Associate Professor of English at Boston University, where he has taught since 1987. His first book, *Policy in Love: Lyric and Public in Ovid, Petrarch and Shakespeare*, was published in 1994. His articles on Classical and Renaissance literature have appeared in journals such as *Illinois Classical Studies*, *English Literary Renaissance*, *Spenser Studies*, *Essays in Criticism* and *Shakespeare Quarterly*.

OVID IN ENGLISH

Edited by CHRISTOPHER MARTIN

PENGUIN BOOKS

PENGUIN BOOKS

Published by the Penguin Group
Penguin Books Ltd, 27 Wrights Lane, London w8 5TZ, England
Penguin Putnam Inc., 375 Hudson Street, New York, New York 10014, USA
Penguin Books Australia Ltd, Ringwood, Victoria, Australia
Penguin Books Canada Ltd, 10 Alcorn Avenue, Toronto, Ontario, Canada M4V 3B2
Penguin Books (NZ) Ltd, 182–190 Wairau Road, Auckland 10, New Zealand

Penguin Books Ltd, Registered Offices: Harmondsworth, Middlesex, England

First published 1998
10 9 8 7 6 5 4 3 2 1

Copyright © Christopher Martin, 1998
All rights reserved

The acknowledgements on pp. xi–xiii constitute an extension of this copyright page

The moral right of the editor has been asserted

Set in 10/12.5 pt Monotype Bembo
Typeset by Rowland Phototypesetting Ltd, Bury St Edmunds, Suffolk
Printed in England by Clays Ltd, St Ives plc

In memoriam
Tatiana Petrychenko
30 April 1937–26 November 1990

Tempora labuntur, tacitisque senescimus annis,
* et fugiunt freno non remorante dies.*
Fasti, 6.771–72

CONTENTS

ACKNOWLEDGEMENTS

For permission to reproduce copyright material in this book, the editor
and publishers gratefully acknowledge the following:

Carcanet Press Ltd: 'Ovid in Defeat' from *Poems 1914–1926* by Robert
Graves (Heinemann, 1928); *Metamorphoses* from *Collected Poems* by
C. H. Sisson (Methuen, 1968). By permission of the publisher.

Columbia University Press: 'Salmacis and Hermaphroditus' by Francis
Beaumont; *The Metamorphosis of Pigmalions Image* by John Marston;
Narcissus or the Self-Lover by James Shirley, from *Elizabethan Minor Epics*,
edited by Elizabeth Storey Donno. Copyright © Columbia University
Press, 1963. Reprinted by permission of the publisher.

Faber & Faber Ltd: 'Death of Orpheus' by Seamus Heaney; 'Creation/
Four Ages/Flood' by Ted Hughes; 'Deucalion and Pyrrha' by Chris-
topher Reid, from *After Ovid: New Metamorphoses* (1994), edited by
Michael Hoffmann and James Lasdun.

The Gallery Press: 'Ovid in Love' from *Selected Poems* by Derek Mahon
(1992). This collection copyright © Derek Mahon, 1991. By permission
of the author and publisher.

Harcourt Brace & Company: *Metamorphoses* from *The Metamorphoses
of Ovid: A New Verse Translation* by Allen Mandelbaum. Copyright
© Allen Mandelbaum, 1993. By permission of the publisher.

Houghton Mifflin Company: *The Book of the Duchess*, *The Former Age*
and *The Legend of Good Women – Thisbe* from *The Riverside Chaucer*,

edited by Larry D. Benson (Third Edition). Copyright © Houghton Mifflin Company, 1987. Reprinted by permission.

Indiana University Press: *Metamorphoses* from *Ovid: Metamorphoses*, translated by Rolfe Humphries. Copyright 1955 by the Indiana University Press; *Art of Love* and *The Remedies for Love* from *Ovid: The Art of Love*, translated by Rolfe Humphries. Copyright © Indiana University Press, 1957; *Roman Holidays* from *Ovid's Fasti: Roman Holidays*, translated by Betty Rose Nagle. Copyright © Betty Rose Nagle, 1995. By permission of the publisher.

The Johns Hopkins University Press: *Tristia* from *Ovid's Poetry of Exile* by David R. Slavitt (1990); *Metamorphoses* from *The Metamorphoses of Ovid* by David R. Slavitt (1994). By permission of the publisher.

John Murray (Publishers) Ltd: 'The Tibullus Elegy' from *Ovid's Amores*, translated by Guy Lee (Viking, 1968). By permission of John Murray Ltd.

Oxford University Press Ltd: *Metamorphoses* from *Ovid: Metamorphoses* by A. D. Melville (1986); *Amores* and *Cosmetics for Ladies* from *Ovid: The Love Poems* by A. D. Melville (1990). By permission of the publisher.

Penguin UK: *Amores* and *The Art of Love* from *Ovid: The Erotic Poems*, translated by Peter Green (1982); 'Ex Ponto' from *Ovid: The Poems of Exile*, translated by Peter Green (1994). Reproduced by permission of the publisher.

Penguin USA: *Metamorphoses* from *Ovid: The Metamorphoses*, translated by Horace Gregory. Translation copyright © The Viking Press, Inc., 1958, renewed 1986 by Patrick Bolton Gregory. Used by permission of Viking Penguin, a division of Penguin Books USA Inc.

Princeton University Press: *Heroides* from *Ovid's Toyshop of the Heart: Epistulae Heroidum* by Florence Verducci. Copyright © Princeton University Press, 1985. Reprinted by permission of the publisher.

Routledge Ltd: *The Art of Love* from *The Art of Love: Ovid's Ars Amatoria* by B. P. Moore (Blackie, 1935); 'In praise of Minerva' and 'In praise of Venus' from *The Mirror of Venus: Love Poems and Stories from Ovid's Amores etc.* by F. A. Wright (Routledge, 1925).

University of California Press: *Metamorphoses* from *Metamorphoses of Ovid* by A.E.Watts. Copyright 1954 by The Regents of the University of California. Reprinted by permission of the publisher.

University of Nebraska Press: 'Envy and Aglauros', 'Actaeon', 'Daedalus and Icarus', and 'Pygmalion' from *Ovid's Metamorphosis: Englished, Mythologized, and Represented in Figures* by George Sandys, edited by Karl K.Hulley and Stanley T.Vandersall. Copyright © University of Nebraska Press, 1970. Reprinted by permission of the publisher.

A. P. Watt Ltd: 'The assassination of Julius Caesar' from *The Fasti of Ovid* by Sir James Frazer (Macmillan, 1929). Reprinted by permission of A. P. Watt Ltd. on behalf of Trinity College, Cambridge.

Yale University Press: 'Medea to Jason' from *Ovid's Heroines: A Verse Translation of the Heroides* by Daryl Hine (1991); 'To Love' by John Wilmot from *The Complete Poems of John Wilmot, Earl of Rochester*, edited by David M.Vieth (1968). Reprinted by permission of the publisher.

Every effort has been made to obtain permission from all copyright holders whose material is included in this book, but in some cases this has not proved possible. The publishers therefore wish to thank all copyright holders who are included without acknowledgement. Penguin UK apologizes for any errors or omissions in the above list and would be grateful to be notified of any corrections that should be incorporated in the next edition of this volume.

PREFACE

Ovid first learned to speak English in the fourteenth century. He has, since that time, developed and maintained an impressive fluency. Even during those few historical patches when his reputation has ebbed, Ovid has excited the poetic strengths of an English readership eager to introduce his Latin to contemporary idioms.

The following anthology surveys Ovid's fortunes in our language through the lenses of these remarkably various translations. I have tried to represent the Ovidian canon broadly, drawing (wherever possible) complete elegies from the *Amores*, *Heroides* and the exile poems, and self-contained passages or episodes from the *Ars amatoria*, *Remedia amoris*, *Fasti* and *Metamorphoses*. Moreover, I have made my selections with an eye to those peculiar virtues each of our literary ages brings to the task of initiating Ovid into an English context. While such figures as Golding, Sandys and Dryden enjoy precedence, they share the light with less familiar names that have, in my view, done justice to their poet. In all cases, I hope that my inclusions contribute to an understanding of just how powerfully diverse an influence Ovid has exerted upon the imagination of his English audience over time.

In keeping with the goals of this series, I have given clear priority to close translations, or imitations that draw directly upon an Ovidian source text. The policy has necessitated several awkward omissions. Since some of our most profoundly 'Ovidian' authors offer little that qualifies in this fashion, Donne and Milton are conspicuously absent, while others like Shakespeare and Spenser are but thinly represented. *A Midsummer Night's Dream*, *The Faerie Queene*'s 'Mutability Cantos', Pope's *Eloisa to Abelard* or passages from Byron's *Don Juan* might well convey a better sense of Ovid's manner than some of the more literal renditions that I include. However, given the vast extent to which

Ovid pervades English poetry, the narrower editorial regulations governing my choices provide an essential – if at times arbitrary – means of keeping the project manageable.

I have retained the original spelling and punctuation featured in the early and scholarly editions used as copytexts. In the few instances where this practice might seriously obscure a passage, I have supplied corrective annotation. Throughout, explanatory notes are kept to a minimum. All citations of line numbers from Ovid's Latin texts listed in the individual headnotes refer to the Loeb Classical Library editions.

While compiling this anthology, I have enjoyed the kind of reinforcement that makes a pleasant task all the more rewarding. My wife Lydia provided even more than her usual support, in the form of a facsimile edition of Caxton's *Metamorphoses*: the gift was her most timely, though by no means greatest, contribution. I also acknowledge those institutions that helped fund my research. The Folger Shakespeare Library once again kindly gave me the opportunity to spend the summer in Washington DC, excavating both their own superb inventory of early editions and the Library of Congress's holdings of (at times even rarer) items from the 1800s. The Humanities Foundation at Boston University secured my privileges at Harvard's Widener and Houghton libraries; Boston University's own Mugar Library and the Boston Public Library also provided access to crucial primary texts. I am grateful to the staffs of all these collections for their help and guidance. Finally, I wish to thank Christopher Ricks for generously inviting me to undertake the project, and for all his encouragement.

C. M.

INTRODUCTION

In nova: Into the new. The *Metamorphoses'* opening words enfold, in good epic fashion, the poem's prevailing concern. Novelty itself becomes the subject of Ovid's greatest and most influential work, supplanting the heroic fare of Homer's Achillean wrath or Virgil's 'Arms and the man'. Appropriately, a sense of newness informs every register of Ovid's project. The *Metamorphoses* reinvents the traditional myths that it incorporates, just as its archly episodic style expands epic's constricted, culturally definitive focus. Perhaps most importantly, Ovid's sustained meditation upon the fluidity of human experience – how we endure through our adaptability to change – renovates the very concept of novelty, into an idea involved more with continuity than departure. In a paradoxical world of metamorphosis, where even the struggle to maintain integrity often involves the relinquishing of one's identifying features, something of the original form always inheres in what replaces it. Newness as process, as a continual transgression of boundaries, preoccupies the poet's imagination.

Ovidian metamorphosis has provided a convenient analogy for the complex process of literary translation, where an original text's essence must take up residence in an alien form. In a dedicatory poem to a 1640 version of the *Fasti*, one 'C. M.' praises the seventeenth-century translator John Gower in these terms:

> So here the Poet which is Sulmo's fame
> Keeps up in a strange dialect his name;
> Cloth'd in the Britain garb and modest fashion
> Looseth no vertue of the Latine nation,
> But Arethusa like, his purest strein
> Preserves, though passing through the English vein.

The image of translation as a mere re-outfitting of the source will not do, so the Arethusa allusion reaches for something grander; as another admirer of Gower more flatly declares, 'Ovid himself is Metamorphos'd here.' In its fuller implications, the comparison identifies the trauma that all parties involved in the enterprise inevitably hazard. In a 1983 essay entitled 'Metamorphosis as Translation', Charles Tomlinson cites Dryden on the 'Pithagorean Opinion', dear to so many poets, that the souls of past writers take new shape in the bodies of later authors. Tomlinson invokes the metaphor to elucidate the daunting prospect facing the translator: 'In translating poetry you are either "transfus'd" by the soul of your original or you are nowhere.'[1] The practice becomes a spiritually exacting one. The truly great translation, consequently, remains a rare thing indeed.

Ovid is no less formidable an author to translate than any of his classical peers. The exquisitely stylized surface of his poetry alone intimidates efforts to capture the flavour of Ovidian verse for the foreign tongue. At the same time, however, there is something about the spirit of irreverence commonly associated with his persona that makes him more approachable, and grants a certain latitude to those who would presume to transform his Latin. Throughout our literature, he has invited, encouraged, and even provoked his emulators to participate in his accomplishments, reassuring them that – with even the most basic measure of competence and respect – the spirit of his original work will not be lost, because it cannot be. This confidence in the face of all threatened alteration constitutes a distinctive legacy of the great poet of change.

Ovid's Life, Works and Reputation

Although no one has effectively disputed the boasts of immortality that punctuate Ovid's works, readers have often embraced him only with considerable reservation. The controversial nature of his life and writing colours a reputation more problematic than that of any other Roman

1 Charles Tomlinson, 'Metamorphosis as Translation', in *Poetry and Metamorphoses* (Cambridge: Cambridge University Press, 1983), p. 73.

poet. The trouble stems, in Richard A. Lanham's assessment, from the challenge that Ovid's playful eccentricity presents to the centralized ideals of a serious, Platonic philosophical tradition. Ovid's fundamentally subversive disposition (a textbook illustration of what W. R. Johnson terms the 'counter-classical sensibility') renders his poetry at once liberating and threatening.[2] Ovid's mystique rests upon this ambivalence. He emerges from the critical exchanges as a figure always at home in the classical literary canon, yet perennially in need of rehabilitation.

What we know of Ovid's life derives chiefly from his own testimony in the exile poems, particularly the great autobiographical sketch of *Tristia* 4.10. The elegy's frankness and quiet dignity overcome the bias that might otherwise qualify Ovid's self-perceptions. The picture that emerges is one of a man who, up to his fiftieth year, enjoyed a rather charmed existence. Comfortably born into a respectable, established family, Ovid displayed a precocious poetic talent that gained him early access to Rome's distinguished literary circles. Apart from the traditional disapproval that his artistic career won from his father, and the premature death of his beloved elder brother, the poet seems to have met with little adversity. The security of his experience left him free to cultivate his poetic persona, which he did with vigour and abandon.

Ovid's 'libertine' reputation is grounded in his earliest work, the *Amores*. This collection of erotic lyrics allegedly extended in its original form to five books, of which only an edited three-book version survives. The *Amores* marked Ovid's contribution to the vogue of erotic elegy established and maintained by his companions Gallus, Tibullus and Propertius. His polished verses recount a variety of sexual escapades with numerous Roman women, particularly the mistress he calls Corinna. From the remarkable opening account of his enforced induction into Love's service, to the final elegy's promise of greater accomplishments to come, Ovid sustains a spectacular performance that outstrips his peers in imaginative variety and sheer ambition. A subtly

---

2 Richard A. Lanham, *The Motives of Eloquence: Literary Rhetoric in the Renaissance* (New Haven: Yale University Press, 1976), pp. 36–64; W. R. Johnson, 'The Problem of the Counter-classical Sensibility and Its Critics', *California Studies in Classical Antiquity* 3 (1970), pp. 123–51.

incisive mockery of masculine self-flattery pervades the work. The critical strain adds depth to the exuberance of Ovid's urbane sexual predator, whose erotic pursuits come to seem a synecdoche for his grander infatuation with the glorious decadence of Rome itself.

The elder Seneca suggests that Ovid, who generally disdained formal argumentation, could in the days of his rhetorical training display a wry, adversarial passion when speaking on behalf of disadvantaged parties. The same inclination animates his next work, the equally successful *Heroides*. Though at times parodic in their excess, these elegiac epistles from mythic heroines to their men betray the poet's marked sympathy for his female speakers, largely the victims of their 'noble' paramours' self-serving games. Whether their indictments disclose crippling emotional dependency or rise to moral victory, Ovid's characters all reveal a powerful psychological complexity. Helen's reply to Paris, for instance, unfolds a seductiveness of which she herself seems only partially conscious. Medea (the subject of Ovid's celebrated but now lost tragedy) and Dido are equally fierce in their outrage, and Sappho is genuinely moving in her self-destructive despair. What could easily have lapsed into glib caricature of feminine folly is instead enriched by Ovid's anatomy of passion's debilitating force. By recasting these mythic romances from a female perspective, the *Heroides*' author implicitly takes to task the masculine presumption underlying epic traditions as eloquently as Virgil had in the *Aeneid*'s fourth book.

The most infamously antagonistic of all Ovid's works remains, however, the *Ars amatoria*, published around the turn of the Classical and Christian eras. Over the course of this elegiac manual's first two books, the *preceptor amoris*, or 'teacher of love', instructs his male audience in proper seduction techniques, all thoughtfully tested. '*Usus opus mouet hoc*', the poet declares: experience drives this work. In order to render the erotic contest more equitable and (consequently) more interesting, the final book offers similar counsels to women. In many regards, the *Ars* stands out as Ovid's most shimmering performance. The cynical comedy of sexual manners harbours a brilliant, barely muted satire on the absurdity of the moral reforms that Augustus had attempted to legislate. For Ovid, the propagandistic conceit of a new 'golden age' appeared bankrupt before the mercenary ethos of modern urban life:

> aurea sunt vere nunc saecula: plurimus auro
>   venit honos: auro conciliatur amor.   (*Ars* 2. 277–78)

> Today is truly the Golden
>   Age: gold buys honours, gold
> Procures love.   (Peter Green)

Ovid fittingly continued in this mock-didactic vein with the 'cures for love', *Remedia amoris*. Now, he plies his skills to reclaim those whom Love has snared: a futile enterprise, since the *preceptor* must ultimately confess his inability to cure himself of this malady. In the end, Love is only bemused by all efforts, political or poetic, to displace him.

Presumably with the exception of the lost play *Medea*, Ovid had so far composed all of his works in elegiac couplets. When he at last turned to his most ambitious – and, from the standpoint of public censure, least objectionable – project, a grand poetic digest of Graeco-Roman myth, he also took up the verse form of classical epic, dactylic hexameter. In typical Ovidian manner, however, the *Metamorphoses* strikes a more orthodox pose only to explode the narrative focus and subscription to a unified value system that has enabled epic as a genre. Fifteen books trace a steady course from the creation of the world down to Ovid's own time; but in stark contrast to the *Aeneid*'s historical vision, they collectively offer only a vista of persistent, restless and resistless change. In such a setting, where all is flux, systems of belief – particularly epic assertions of national destiny – are exposed as themselves grand fabrications, splendid monuments to the human drive for self-perpetuation.

Ovid's political observations seldom intrude into the foreground. What holds the poem together is not so much any deliberate advocacy of a 'counter-classical' disposition, as the emotional vitality of the legends he recounts. Many of the characters who undergo metamorphosis grow particularly eloquent in their suffering, and it is their moving final lamentations that we often best remember. Actaeon, transformed into a mute stag torn by his own faithful hounds in Book 3, seems particularly terrible against this backdrop: his very inability to articulate intensifies his agony. Survival, by contrast, involves a continued eagerness to speak, to parley, to tell stories. From Jove's angry condemnation of a debased humanity in Book 1, to the Pythagorean philosopher's lengthy speech near the end, the *Metamorphoses* becomes a tissue of monologues, wonderfully reinforced by the skill with multiple voices that Ovid had perfected in his amatory poems and *Heroides*.

The *Metamorphoses*' detachable narratives blend into one another with the same regularity that bodies transform into foreign shapes throughout the poem. Ovid sacrifices the coherent purposefulness of Virgilian epic; but his meandering storylines are, individually and collectively, no less consumed by a profound respect for human resilience. As his mythic characters respond to their circumstances, both comic and tragic, we infer a pervasive reassurance that fiction-building is itself a vital part of our capacity to endure. Phaeton's rash ambitions, Tereus's savagery, Myrrha's self-consuming passion, and the pious fidelity of Baucis and Philemon all cohere in the final book's Pythagorean sermon, where we learn that

> nec perit in toto quicquam, mihi credite, mundo,
> sed variat faciemque novat, nascique vocatur
> incipere esse aliud, quam quod fuit ante, morique
> desinere illud idem. cum sint huc forsitan illa,
> haec translata illuc, summa tamen omnia constant.   (*Met.* 15. 254–58)

> All things are alter'd, nothing is destroy'd,
> The shifted scene for some new show employ'd.
> Then, to be born, is to begin to be
> Some other thing we were not formerly:
> And what we call to die is not t' appear,
> Or be the thing, that formerly we were.
> Those very elements, which we partake
> Alive, when dead some other bodies make:
> Translated grow, have sense, or can discourse;
> But death on deathless substance has no force.
> (Dryden)

Arriving as it does at the end of Ovid's vast chronicle of change, however, even this last synthesis stands as only one more perspective amid a wide array of possibilities available to our ever-changing imaginations.

Ovid's interest in mythic narratives and their frameworks carried over to his poem on the Roman calendar, the *Fasti*, even though his dactylic hexameters did not. Composed to celebrate Caesar's *aras*, or altars, in contrast to the *arma* that others had treated, the *Fasti* would share the *Metamorphoses*' meditation on human ingenuity. In his tour of the year's religious and social festivities, Ovid uncovers multiple explanations for the various holidays and their corresponding rituals. These often conflicting justifications for why people honour the specific deities that they do may be construed as the poet's attempt to expose the arbitrariness of religious belief. On the other hand, his gathering of these disparate accounts may only serve (once again) to celebrate human creativity. Either way, Ovid's bemused affection for the fecundity of human wit warms the stories that comprise his poem, even in its fragmentary state.

Only six books of the *Fasti* have come down to us. The work had perhaps been abandoned earlier, or maybe fell victim to the grim circumstances that descended upon the poet in AD 8. The sensational, defining moment for Ovid's *Nachleben* arrived in his fifty-first year, when the emperor abruptly had him relegated to the remote village of Tomis, on the Black Sea. The ostensible motive for the banishment was the immorality of the *Ars amatoria*, published almost a decade earlier. Though most historians regard this charge as a political smokescreen, we are uncertain what actually did prompt Caesar's extreme reaction. As Peter Green has speculated, Ovid was likely implicated in the intrigue that infected the Augustan court's twilight.[3] In any case, the poet was condemned to leave Rome before the year's end. He would never see the city again. The continued efforts of his wife and friends to secure his pardon were to no avail, and he died in exile nine years later.

Ovid turned the literary energies of his last decade to two collections of elegiac poems, the *Tristia* in five books, and the *Epistolae Ex Ponto* in another four. Sent back to Rome over the course of his exile, the

---

3 Peter Green, 'Carmen et Error: The Enigma of Ovid's Exile', in *Classical Bearings: Interpreting Ancient History and Culture* (London: Thames and Hudson, 1989), pp. 210–39. John C. Thibault has compiled the (inconclusive) evidence in his *The Mystery of Ovid's Exile* (Berkeley: University of California Press, 1964).

poems poignantly chart the catastrophe with which he had to cope. They range from a harrowing account of his final night in Rome to ironic reflections on the bleakness of Tomis's frozen landscape; from endearing expressions of love for his distant wife to irritable, desperate recriminations that she is not doing enough on his behalf; from a moving encouragement of his stepdaughter's poetic efforts to the bitter indictment of false friends (a subject that would also prompt his only invective poem, the *Ibis*). It is painful to watch one who so relentlessly (though subtly) challenged authority reduced to the obsequious tone that often colours the two collections, but enough of Ovid's dignified sensibility survives, along with his sharp verbal wit, to reward our continued attention. Even if the poems' incessant pleas for some form of redemption occasion a certain degree of monotony, they remain impressively various performances, worthy of his previous accomplishments.

Ovid's political downfall deepened the critical ambiguity that began to collect around his works from the time of his death. The artistic self-indictment that burdens the exile poems stoked ungenerous suspicions that the poet genuinely merited official censure. The subject matter of his verse was *lascivus* ('frivolous') and its manner irresponsible. This harsher response gained particular authority in the pronouncements of two influential figures, the elder Seneca (55 BC – AD 37) and Quintilian (*c*. AD 30–100). Both regarded Ovid as a flawed genius, ruined by a self-indulgent refusal to curb his wit. Alison G. Elliott has traced the extent to which their condemnation of Ovid's rhetorical vices has shaped a critical tradition that extends to our own time.[4] Subsequent generations would have to read the poet against reiterated charges of his works' undisciplined style and superficiality.

Critical objections were of course unable to stem the tide of Ovid's popularity, which crested in the twelfth and thirteenth centuries – a period that scholars have come to designate the 'age of Ovid', *aetas Ovidiana*. Whatever moral protests the Christian audience had lodged against the poet were quelled by a wholesale allegorical appropriation

---

4 Alison G. Elliott, 'Ovid and the Critics: Senaca, Quintilian, and "Seriousness"', *Helios* 12 ns (1985), pp. 9–20.

of the works. 'Explicated' versions plumbed the poetry's alleged didactic purpose, unfolding assorted historical, moral and religious meanings. When Caxton came to translate the *Metamorphoses* into English in 1480, he consulted not the Latin original but the French prose *Métamorphoses moralisées* (c. 1460), itself redacted from a late fourteenth-century verse adaptation of Pierre Bersuire's Latin *Ovidius moralisatus* (c. 1330). Through this dense network of applied interpretation, the poet of pagan *amor* was welcomed into the religious fold as *Ovid Ethicus* and *Ovid Theologus*. The effort was both noble and essential, though not altogether successful in restoring Ovid's tarnished reputation. Writing upon the threshold of a new age he was to help initiate, Petrarch still found himself embarrassed to acknowledge the influence of one whom Dante had unhesitatingly placed in his sequence of the greatest classical authors.

The Renaissance would incorporate Ovid anew, recovering and engaging a less mediated image of the poet. The erotic poetry afforded a stimulating alternative to the Petrarchan vogue that dominated lyric practice. The *Metamorphoses*, taken up both for its handy compendium of pagan myth and for what Golding would refer to as its 'dark Philosophie', became, during the early modern period, the secular Bible. Its legends formed the basis for much of the greatest literature, painting and sculpture to emerge from this extraordinarily fertile cultural moment. No major secular poet of the era – and few religious ones – steered entirely free of Ovid's influence. Ironically, the Renaissance's spirited defences of Ovid perpetuated the compromised historical image that they strove to repair. Moreover, as the diffuseness of Renaissance culture contracted to the more disciplined manners of Enlightenment neoclassicism, the earlier impatience with Ovid's excitable poetic revived. His fortunes continued to decline throughout the nineteenth century, when Romanticism's Hellenistic preferences further discounted his achievement.

Ovid none the less survives intact. The twentieth century – a time when cultural and philosophical relativism has gained ascendency – has responded with fresh urgency to Ovid's trenchant images of mutability, dislocation, atrocity and hope. Two millennia after his birth in Sulmo, we are possibly better prepared to meet Ovid on his own field than at any previous moment. Despite his renewed claim on our attention, however, we continue to interrogate his 'profundity', his 'seriousness', and even his integrity. A certain tension will always probably strain his reception. Ovid remains for us a central figure who lingers wilfully on the margins. However, this is a position he might well have relished, given what we know of his desire to be at the heart of things, and his simultaneous critical discomfort with what he found there.

Ovid in English

Ovid's English exponents have over time contributed enthusiastically to the 'apologetic' promotion of their author. George Sandys, for instance, prefaces his 1626 translation of the *Metamorphoses* with a section entitled 'Ovid Defended', a series of testimonials to Ovid's artistic mastery gleaned (at times selectively) from a host of ancient and contemporary authorities. Sandys justified his own gesture with the observation that, 'Since divers, onely wittie in reproving, have profaned our Poet with their fastidious censures we, to vindicate his worth from detraction, and prevent prejudicacie, have here revived a few of those infinite testimonies, which the cleerest judgements of all Ages have given him.' Where Ben Jonson's *Poetaster* had, earlier in the century, cast Ovid as an inspired talent who falls victim to his outsized passions, Sir Aston Cokain's *The Tragedy of Ovid* (1662) imagines the exiled Ovid as a reformed figure, of whom one character observes

> I know the Noble Poet hath
> Subdued his Passions, and is now become
> As rigid in his behaviour, as the gravest
> Of all the ancient Philosophers.

It is a small step from such portrayals to the reconstruction of Ovid as romance hero: the kind of thing we find in '*Ovid to Julia*. A Letter', Aphra Behn's exercise in the *Heroides*' manner. The trend survives into our own century in such items as John Masefield's poem 'A Letter from Pontus', Robert Lowell's sonnet 'Ovid to Caesar's Daughter', and the novelist David Malouf's *An Imaginary Life*. But the best indicator of

Ovid's enduring vitality for his English audience remains the peculiarly rich tradition of translation that he has inspired.

'With Ovid ended the golden age of the Roman tongue,' Dryden observed in the Preface to his *Fables, Ancient and Modern* (1700); 'from Chaucer the purity of the English tongue began.' Fittingly, it is Chaucer who first provides Ovid with an English voice. Ovid served Chaucer as he served all medieval readers, as a repository of mythic and romance subject matter to be consulted, excerpted and appropriated. Chaucer's adaptation of Ovid to his narrative purposes can be at times ruthless: in the interests of his focus upon the heartbreak of lost love in *The Book of the Duchess*, his version of the Ceyx story will casually stop short of the climactic transformation scene. Formally, so far as Chaucer is concerned, Ovid is as well suited to the *Duchess*'s octosyllables as he is later to the decasyllabic couplets introduced in *The Legend of Good Women*. The temperamental kinship between the two poets that Dryden remarks goes far to ameliorate any such violations. What is lost in literal and technical accuracy is made up for by the Middle English's freshness and intimacy. Chaucer's tendency to compress his source ('to tellen shortly' is one of his favourite tags) concentrates the more tragic aspects of Ovid's various narratives. He delivers an Ovid who sounds fully acclimatized to his new English setting.

For all the liberties that he takes, Chaucer stands apart from more didactic medieval approaches to Ovid in his refusal to moralize explicitly the poet's storylines. In this he parts company with his fellow poet John Gower, whose *Confessio amantis* offers a fine counterpart to his colleague's Ovidian turns. Gower's version of the Ceyx myth, for instance, redirects Chaucer's stark emphasis on Ceyx's bitter loss towards a poignant unfolding of her reunion with Alcyone. Although Gower's 'Confessor' will gloss the story as a warning to take prophetic dreams seriously, the authorial commentary at no point subverts the romance's integrity. We must go to the latest 'medieval' English translation of the *Metamorphoses* to sample the most graphic religious appropriation of the pagan poem. Again, however, although the didactic inflections of William Caxton's mediating French source embellish his prose, these adjustments work curiously little damage to the literary effect. When Caxton proclaims that Procne resolved to murder her son Itys 'as the deuyl counceylled her', the moment's horrifying *frisson* is enhanced by Caxton's allusion to the larger spiritual forces he sees at work within Philomela's pathetic tale. Even in the often wooden prose of Caxton's translation, Ovid's narratives display a ready pliancy.

Caxton wrote in 1480, on the threshold of the modern age in England. A vast chasm separates his work from that quintessential Renaissance translation of Ovid, Arthur Golding's complete *Metamorphosis* (so titled) of 1567. Nothing that had intervened between the two undertakings presaged the unrestrained energy of Golding's text. An interest in Ovid's moral import endures for the Elizabethan audience, as Golding makes clear in his prefatory epistle:

> If Poets then with leesings and with fables shadowed so
> The certeine truth, what letteth us to plucke those visers fro
> Their doings, and too bring ageine the darkened truth too lyght,
> That all men may behold thereof the cleernesse shining bryght?
> The readers therefore earnestly admonisht are too bee
> Too seeke a further meening than the letter gives too see.

Such interpretative counsel is brushed to the margins, however, by the vigorous sweep of the translator's English. Golding's fourteener couplets at times channel the poem's key episodes into unintentionally comic rhythms, and almost always require him to pad out his lines – faults that inspire modern judgements that his translation is 'colourful, rumbustious, but quite un-Ovidian in its lack of stylistic polish'.[5] None the less, an unflagging confidence in the form's elasticity – enabled by his masterful use of enjambment – helped him to maintain the serious thrust of the Latin with impressive consistency. Golding provided his contemporaries with a delightfully readable version of Ovid that was also faithful to the original's sense and spirit. The complete rendition was sufficiently 'polished', in a distinctively Elizabethan manner, to inspire English poetic imaginations from Shakespeare (who may have drawn as much from Golding as he did from Ovid) down to Ezra Pound (whose notorious statement that Golding offers 'possibly the

---

5 Charles Martindale, 'Ovid, Horace, and Others', in Richard Jenkyns (ed.), *The Legacy of Rome: A New Appraisal* (Oxford: Oxford University Press, 1992), p. 184.

most beautiful book in our language' distinguishes him as the work's most ardent modern champion).

Golding inaugurated the first great phase of Ovid's translation into modern English. In the same year as his *Metamorphosis*, George Turbervile's *Heroycall Epistles* appeared, followed two years later by Thomas Underdown's *Ibis*. During the 1590s Christopher Marlowe's version of the *Amores* in crisp heroic couplets essentially reanimated the verse form that would prevail throughout the next two hundred years. By 1600 Thomas Heywood's *Art of Love* was probably in circulation, along with at least one anonymous rendition of the *Remedia*. The exile poetry, already undertaken in part by Thomas Churchyard in 1572, appeared over the course of the 1630s in the works of Wye Saltonstall, John Sherburne and Zachary Catlin. When in 1640 John Gower published his line-for-line translation of the *Fasti*, Ovid's complete *oeuvre* was available in English – many of the poems in multiple versions. Golding's own great work had been succeeded in 1626 by George Sandys's *Metamorphosis*, which the translator would go on to 'mythologize' in an elaborate, illustrated edition of 1632. The even-handed discipline of Sandys's pentameter couplets appealed to seventeenth-century tastes, for whom Golding had come to sound hopelessly antiquated. Much of the earlier translation's effusive energy is admittedly sacrificed on behalf of a more decorous tone: Sandys's verse is, as Gordon Braden puts it, 'deliberative and analytic where Golding's is thin and rapid'.[6] But Sandys's elegance and scholarship reconstituted Ovid as a philosophically sophisticated court wit, an impression vital to the poem's ongoing sense of immediacy for the period. His poetic achievement is, in this regard, every bit as important as Golding's literary watershed had been sixty years earlier.

The best evidence of Ovid's dominance over the period does not always take the form of literal translation. Although the English Renaissance's greatest authors – Spenser, Shakespeare, Donne and Milton – display a deep engagement with Ovid throughout their careers, they seldom pursued the kind of direct rendition discussed so far, opting

6 Gordon Braden, *The Classics and English Renaissance Poetry: Three Case Studies* (New Haven: Yale University Press, 1978), p. 50.

instead to emulate in their original works the Ovidian temperament they had so thoroughly internalized. Between their camp and that of the translators sprung up the unique English vogue for the 'epyllion', shorter verse narratives that derive their inspiration primarily from Ovidian myth and manners. At times, the epyllion relates only tangentially to a suggestion in the Ovidian source: Shakespeare's early poems *Venus and Adonis* and *The Rape of Lucrece*, like Marlowe's *Hero and Leander*, are exercises in this mode. Others adhere closely to the narrative base, but do so chiefly to secure an opportunity for exhibitions of original poetic fancy. (The epyllion writers represented in this anthology all belong to this group.) Francis Beaumont exemplifies the genre's impulse when, in his *Salmacis and Hermaphroditus*, he garnishes the *Metamorphoses*' description of Hermaphroditus as he enters the water:

> Then with his foote he toucht the silver streames,
> Whose drowzy waves made musicke in their dreames,
> And, for he was not wholy in, did weepe,
> Talking alowd and babbling in their sleepe . . .

None of this is in Ovid, though after reading Beaumont one feels that it should have been. In certain cases, the poet will play up the perceived ironies of Ovid's presentation to intensify the comedy, while at other times a more sinister mood infects the *levior* or 'trifling' subject matter. William Keach, one of the genre's best students, proposes that 'in going to Ovid's poetry with a new freedom and openness, the authors of epyllia were looking afresh at a poetic world which was as often dark and disturbing as it was light and entertaining.'[7] Though an isolated literary phenomenon, the epyllion enjoyed an extraordinary popularity, and would leave its imprint upon English poetry well into the Romantic period. Wherever Keats found his mythology for the erotic narrative *Endymion*, it was the epyllion tradition that stands squarely behind his ambition to 'make 4000 lines of one bare circumstance and fill them with Poetry'.

---

7 William Keach, *Elizabethan Erotic Narratives: Irony and Pathos in the Ovidian Poetry of Shakespeare, Marlowe, and Their Contemporaries* (New Brunswick: Rutgers University Press, 1977), p. 28.

Ovid's influence in England had reached its apogee during the fifty years that preceded the civil war and Commonwealth periods. The seventeenth century's dedicated interest in his works was, however, far from spent. The Restoration's chief poet after Milton's death, John Dryden, provided the impetus for the next great phase of translation. His prolific efforts established his reputation as Ovid's finest English interpreter, a distinction that endures to our own time. From the 1680 publication of *Ovid's Epistles* – to which he contributed a critical introduction and three of the twenty-one translations – on to the end of his life, Dryden worked to present Ovid in a polished manner that (he felt) his predecessors had sorely lacked. He imparted a new elegance to the couplets that Marlowe had reintroduced and Sandys had refined. In Dryden's hands, the form seems as natural to the colloquial snap of the love poems as it does to the mythic narratives' dreamy, majestic cast. Many of these translations first appeared, alongside the work of others inspired by his example, in the numerous poetry miscellanies released throughout the era. In one of these, the *Examen Poeticum* of 1693, Dryden declared and diagnosed his affinity for Ovid: he regarded his translations from the *Metamorphoses* 'the best of all my endeavours in this kind. Perhaps this poet is more easy to be translated than some others whom I have lately attempted; perhaps, too, he was more according to my genius. He is certainly more palatable to the reader than any of the Roman wits, tho' some of them are more lofty, some more instructive, and others more correct.' Coming from one of the language's most astute critics, Dryden's words went far to confirm Ovid's status anew for the refined neoclassical tastes of a self-styled 'Augustan' age.

Seventeen years after Dryden's death in 1700, his legacy would come to its fullest fruit in the composite translation edited by Samuel Garth, *Ovid's Metamorphoses in Fifteen Books*. Garth's text quickly went through multiple printings, displacing Sandys' as the chief English version of the poem for the coming centuries. Dryden's own translations comprise about one quarter of the volume; other contributors included such 'eminent hands' as Congreve, Addison, Pope, and Gay. The book affords as genuine a representation of eighteenth-century poetic manner as Golding's or Sandys's versions had of their respective times. Garth takes care in his introduction to articulate the Latin poet's virtues in a spirit consistent with Dryden's. 'The objection to *Ovid*, that he never knows when to give over, is too manifest. Tho' he frequently expatiates on the same thought, in different words; yet in his similes, that exuberance is avoided. There is in them all a simplicity, and a confinement to the present object; always a fecundity of fancy, but rarely an intemperance; nor do I remember that he has err'd above once by an ill-judg'd superfluity.' He goes on to praise 'how unforc'd his compliments, and how natural his transitions generally are', as well as the way in which 'Through the whole texture of his work, *Ovid* discovers the highest humanity, and a most exceeding good nature.'

Garth felt obliged to pose as Ovid's advocate, having watched the poet 'too much run down at present by the critical spirit of this nation'. His sense of the decline in Ovid's popularity was well grounded, for not even the great edition he compiled could effectively restore the poet to his previous place of honour. Ironically, the superlative efforts of Dryden and others to perfect Ovid's English had all but foreclosed further efforts at translation. As early as the 1690s, Matthew Prior mocked contemporary wits 'Not for abusing *Ovid*'s Verse, but *Sands*''. His contempt sounds quite a different note from that which had prevailed for over a century:

> Now, why should we poor *Ovid* yet pursue,
> And make his very Book an Exile too,
> In Words more barb'rous than the place he knew?

The burlesque tradition generated by Ovid's Restoration celebrity demonstrated considerable ingenuity, though its products commonly resorted to crude jests and scatology to effect their parodies. Pope, Swift and Fielding would all take Ovid up in the next century, but tastes had already shifted. As Horace's new preeminence displaced his younger rival's former authority, explicit traces of Ovid's presence became harder to discern. Still, the wry temperament that informed the age's satiric literature remained, at root, Ovidian. More expressly, the *Heroides* would help foster the renewed popularity of the verse epistle – a development that contributed so significantly to the novel's genesis. Ovid's influence was diffused, but not lost.

This situation obtained throughout the nineteenth century, when, as Norman Vance has observed, Ovid retired to the role of '*éminence grise*, a valuable imaginative asset with which no one was entirely at ease'.[8] Overtly, Ovid's reputation in England reached a nadir. His love poetry lacked the requisite sincerity to impress the Romantic poets, and his image as an 'immoral' poet alienated a potential Victorian readership. Moreover, just as Horace had upstaged him in the 1700s, the new century's turn towards Greece distanced Ovid even further from the literary establishment. Nor was the age formally comfortable with Ovidian technique. The Renaissance's generally misguided flirtation with quantitative metres had somehow passed Ovid by, with minor exceptions such as Abraham Fraunce's bizarre experiments in *The Countess of Pembroke's Ivychurch* (1591). Unfortunately, relegating Ovid to the couplets that had sustained most of the translation lost his elegies' trademark 'limp', occasioned by the sacrifice of one metrical foot from every other line. Purist attempts to recover Ovid's uneven quantities that surfaced in the 1800s failed to match their success to their earnestness. Coleridge could neatly mimic elegy's gait in 'The Ovidian Elegiac Metre, Described and Exemplified':

‒ ˘ ˘ / ‒ ˘ ˘ / ‒ ˘ ˘ /‒ ‒ / ‒ ˘ ˘ /‒ ‒

In the hexameter rises the fountain's silvery column;

‒ ˘ ˘ / ‒ ˘ ˘/‒ //‒ ˘ ˘ / ‒ ˘˘ /‒

In the pentameter aye falling in melody back.

Efforts to sustain this sort of accommodation, however, overwhelmed classicists as dedicated as Arthur Hugh Clough and Henry Wadsworth Longfellow. Less ambitious translators, who duteously stuck by the received English forms, too often straitened the verse into a mock-Miltonic formality that ends up sounding sterile or pompous, remote from Ovid's characteristic grace. (Emma Garland's modest renderings of the *Heroides*, and F. H. Hummel's and A. A. Brodribb's playful feints at the amatory verse stand out as notable exceptions to this trend.)

8 Norman Vance, 'Ovid and the nineteenth century,' in Charles Martindale (ed.), *Ovid Renewed: Ovidian Influences on Literature and Art From the Middle Ages to the Twentieth Century* (Cambridge: Cambridge University Press, 1988), p. 215.

Once again, however, Ovidian influence found more subtle avenues of expression. The impact of his mythology and poetic voice can be detected in works as disparate as Keats's *Endymion*, Tennyson's *Oenone*, and Browning's monologues. Even such a proponent of high seriousness as Matthew Arnold is capable of reinventing what he absorbed from the *Metamorphoses* into a brilliant lyrical passage of his *Empedocles on Etna*. The Latin poet had adapted well to the most adverse circumstances, accommodating the tastes of those who might otherwise prefer to see him ostracized.

However, Ovid would have to wait for a significant change in cultural climate before he could hope to recover his central role in the English literary scene. Amid the chaos of the twentieth century – as older political, philosophical and religious ideals felt the shocks of military and economic catastrophe, and scientific advances left humanity increasingly aware of its smallness in a sea of vast, ever-altering universes – Ovid was about to undergo another golden age of his own. He was (the title of L. P. Wilkinson's landmark 1955 study proposes) ready to be 'recalled', as a newly conditioned audience turned with fresh interest to the sceptical but humane complexities of his verse. Since the middle of the century, English translations have appeared with amazing regularity, making our own time the most prolific in this regard since the late 1600s. Metrically innovative translators like Rolfe Humphries and Peter Green have perfected English lines that approximate Ovidian elegy each in an unobtrusive and highly readable manner. The poet might well approve of the communal rivalry and the hunger for variety that continue to provoke these efforts. He would certainly revel in the superb creative re-formations that characterize the 1994 volume *After Ovid*, in which some of our best poets recast episodes from the *Metamorphoses*. The collection stands as a tribute at once to the powerful insight these modern writers bring to their source, and to Ovid's perennial capacity to address and inspire directly the imagination of such a diverse company.

On the eve of the next millennium, no classical poet is better positioned to sustain his popular appeal than Ovid. His own understanding of the profound cooperation between *translatio* (literally, a carrying across) and *transmissio*, or sending forth, has much to do with this endurance. If poets are to find the kind of reception that Ovid so coveted, they must be prepared to see their works adapt to the alien terrain through which they pass. Ovid's staying power derives, primarily, from his willingness to let go, to entrust his accomplishment to other capable hands. His many English respondents have done well by him, honouring his challenge to take up his works and make them their own. In this, Ovid has brought many of his emulators to a fuller realization of their potentiality, while they in turn have helped substantiate the *Metamorphoses*' closing promise: 'I shall live', *vivam*.

FURTHER READING

General Studies:

John Barsby. *Ovid*. Oxford: Clarendon Press, 1978.

Eduard Fränkel. *Ovid: A Poet Between Two Worlds*. Berkeley: University of California Press, 1945.

Sara Mack. *Ovid*. New Haven: Yale University Press, 1988.

L. P. Wilkinson. *Ovid Recalled*. Cambridge: Cambridge University Press, 1955. Abridged by Cambridge as *Ovid Surveyed* in 1962.

Studies of Individual Works:

Harry B. Evans. *Publica Carmina: Ovid's Books from Exile*. Lincoln: University of Nebraska Press, 1983.

G. Karl Galinsky. *Ovid's Metamorphoses: An Introduction to Its Basic Aspects*. Berkeley: University of California Press, 1975.

Geraldine Herbert-Brown. *Ovid and the Fasti: An Historical Study*. Oxford: Clarendon Press, 1994.

Howard Jacobson. *Ovid's Heroides*. Princeton: Princeton University Press, 1974.

Christopher Martin. *Policy in Love: Lyric and Public in Ovid, Petrarch and Shakespeare*. Pittsburgh: Duquesne University Press, 1994.

Molly Myerowitz. *Ovid's Games of Love*. Detroit: Wayne State University Press, 1985.

Brooks Otis. *Ovid as an Epic Poet*. 2nd ed. Cambridge: Cambridge University Press, 1970.

Florence Verducci. *Ovid's Toyshop of the Heart: Epistulae Heroidum*. Princeton: Princeton University Press, 1985.

Reception:

William S. Anderson, ed. *Ovid: The Classical Heritage*. New York: Garland, 1995.

E. K. Rand. *Ovid and His Influence*. New York: Cooper Square Publishers, 1963.

Charles Martindale, ed. *Ovid Renewed: Ovidian influences on literature and art from the Middle Ages to the twentieth century*. Cambridge: Cambridge University Press, 1994.

Lee T. Pearcy, *The Mediated Muse: English Translations of Ovid 1560–1700*. Hamden: Archon Books, 1984.

TABLE OF DATES

43 BC Publius Ovidius Naso born into established equestrian family at Sulmo, 75 miles east of Rome.

31 Octavian's victory at Actium concludes civil war. Ovid arrives in Rome to pursue his education, where he enters Messala's literary circle. Befriends Tibullus and Propertius.

27 Augustus becomes emperor. Ovid assumes *toga virilis*, the formal garb of manhood, making him eligible for senatorial rank. Contracts first marriage, which will end in divorce within two years.

25 Public readings of poems that will come to form the *Amores*.

c.24–22 Travels to Greece, Asia minor, and Sicily, in the company of the poet Macer. Upon return to Rome, completes his legal training and serves in lesser administrative posts until assuming quaestorship in 16 BC.

19 Deaths of Virgil and Tibullus.

18 Augustus's 'moral' legislation, the *Lex Iulia de adulteriis coercendis* and *Lex Iulia de maritandis ordinibus*, enacted.

c.16–14 Publication of first edition of *Amores*. Its apparent success confirms Ovid's decision to pursue an artistic rather than a senatorial career. Second marriage, also short-lived, produces a daughter.

c.14–2 Over this period, the release of the second, abbreviated edition of *Amores*, publication of *Heroides*, and the success of his (now lost) play *Medea* establish Ovid's literary fame in Rome.

c.6 Third marriage.

2 Augustus's daughter Julia banished, supposedly for violation of adultery laws.

1 BC–AD2 *Ars amatoria*, *Remedia amoris*, and *Medicamina faciei femineae* published. Father's death grants Ovid full inheritance.

AD 2–8 At work on *Fasti* and *Metamorphoses*.

8   Allegedly outraged by the immorality of the *Ars amatoria* and an 'error' on the poet's part, Augustus suddenly relegates Ovid to the Black Sea outpost of Tomis. The *Ars* is banned from the shelves of Rome's public libraries. Upon his departure, Ovid requests that copies of his unrevised (though substantially complete) *Metamorphoses* be destroyed. The *Fasti*, only half finished, is abandoned.

9–12   From exile, Ovid completes the *Tristia* and invective *Ibis*.

13   First three books of *Epistulae ex Ponto* completed.

14   Death of Augustus. Tiberius succeeds as emperor. Desultory revision of the *Fasti*'s first book.

16   Final book of *Epistulae ex Ponto*.

*c.*17 Ovid dies in Tomis.

GEOFFREY CHAUCER
(c. 1343–1400)

Chaucer's career as a diplomat exposed him first hand to the continental poetic influences evident in the following passages. Ovid first appears in English in *The Book of the Duchess*'s clipped octosyllables, but by the time of *The Legend of Good Women* – which draws conspicuously upon the *Heroides* throughout – Chaucer has graduated into the decasyllabic couplets of his greatest works. In both instances, he uniquely curtails the Ovidian narratives to his own purposes, suppressing the crucial moments of metamorphosis in order to achieve more pointedly tragic effects. While *The Former Age* takes Boethius as its most commonly acknowledged source, it also draws directly upon the *Metamorphoses*: Chaucer's dramatically juxtaposed accounts of the Golden and Iron Ages enhance the power of his lyric's social commentary.

The Book of the Duchess, 62–217 [Met. 11.410–748] *Ceyx and Alcyone*

This was the tale: There was a king
That highte Seys, and had a wif,
The beste that mighte bere lyf,
And this quene highte Alcyone.
So it befil thereafter soone
This king wol wenden over see.
To tellen shortly, whan that he
Was in the see thus in this wise,
Such a tempest gan to rise
10   That brak her mast and made it falle,
And clefte her ship, and dreinte hem alle,

---

2 *highte*: was called

That never was founde, as it telles,
Bord ne man, ne nothing elles.
Right thus this king Seys loste his lif.
   Now for to speke of Alcyone, his wif:
This lady, that was left at hom,
Hath wonder that the king ne com
Hom, for it was a longe terme.
Anon her herte began to erme;
20 And for that her thoughte evermo
It was not wele he dwelte so,
She longed so after the king
That certes it were a pitous thing
To telle her hertely sorowful lif
That she had, this noble wif,
For him, alas, she loved alderbest.
Anon she sent bothe eest and west
To seke him, but they founde nought.
'Alas!' quod she, 'that I was wrought!
30 And wher my lord, my love, be deed?
Certes, I nil never ete breed,
I make avow to my god here,
But I mowe of my lord here!'
Such sorowe this lady to her tok
That trewly I, that made this book,
Had such pittee and such rowthe
To rede hir sorwe that, by my trowthe,
I ferde the worse al the morwe
Aftir to thenken on hir sorwe.
40   So whan this lady koude here noo word
That no man myghte fynde hir lord,
Ful ofte she swouned, and sayed 'Alas!'
For sorwe ful nygh wood she was,
Ne she koude no reed but oon;
But doun on knees she sat anoon

---

19 *erme*: grieve   **30** *wher*: what if   **44** *koude no reed*: knew no counsel

And wepte that pittee was to here.
    'A, mercy, swete lady dere!'
Quod she to Juno, hir goddesse,
'Helpe me out of thys distresse,
50   And yeve me grace my lord to se
Soone or wite wher-so he be,
Or how he fareth, or in what wise,
And I shal make yow sacrifise,
And hooly youres become I shal
With good wille, body, herte, and al;
And but thow wolt this, lady swete,
Send me grace to slepe and mete
In my slep som certeyn sweven
Wherthourgh that I may knowen even
60   Whether my lord be quyk or ded.'
    With that word she heng doun the hed
And fel a-swowne as cold as ston.
Hyr women kaught hir up anoon
And broghten hir in bed al naked,
And she, forweped and forwaked,
Was wery; and thus the dede slep
Fil on hir or she tooke kep,
Throgh Juno, that had herd hir bone,
That made hir to slepe sone.
70   For as she prayede, ryght so was don
In dede; for Juno ryght anon
Called thus hir messager
To doo hir erande, and he com ner.
    Whan he was come, she bad hym thus:
'Go bet,' quod Juno, 'to Morpheus –
Thou knowest hym wel, the god of slep.
Now understond wel and tak kep!

---

51 *wite*: discover   58 *sweven*: dream   60 *quyk*: alive
67 *or she tooke kep*: before she knew it   68 *bone*: prayer   75 *Go bet*: Hurry

Sey thus on my half: that he
Go faste into the Grete Se,
80   And byd hym that, on alle thyng,
He take up Seys body the kyng,
That lyeth ful pale and nothyng rody.
Bid hym crepe into the body
And doo hit goon to Alcione
The quene, ther she lyeth allone,
And shewe hir shortly, hit ys no nay,
How hit was dreynt thys other day;
And do the body speke ryght soo,
Ryght as hyt was woned to doo
90   The whiles that hit was alyve.
Goo now faste, and hye the blyve!'
     This messager tok leve and wente
Upon hys wey, and never ne stente
Til he com to the derke valeye
That stant betwixe roches tweye
Ther never yet grew corn ne gras,
Ne tre, ne noght that ought was,
Beste, ne man, ne noght elles,
Save ther were a fewe welles
100 Came rennynge fro the clyves adoun,
That made a dedly slepynge soun,
And ronnen doun ryght by a cave
That was under a rokke ygrave
Amydde the valey, wonder depe.
There these goddes lay and slepe,
Morpheus and Eclympasteyr,
That was the god of slepes heyr,

---

91 *hye the blyve*: travel swiftly
106 *Eclympasteyr*: a god of dreams (spurious medieval conflation of 'Icelon' and 'Phobetora', both mentioned in line 640 of Ovid's original)

That slep and dide noon other werk.
This cave was also as derk
110   As helle-pit overal aboute.
They had good leyser for to route,
To envye who myghte slepe best.
Somme henge her chyn upon hir brest
And slept upryght, hir hed yhed,
And somme lay naked in her bed
And slepe whiles the dayes laste.
        This messager com fleynge faste
And cried, 'O how! Awake anoon!'
Hit was for noght; there herde hym non.
120   'Awake!' quod he, 'whoo ys lyth there?'
And blew his horn ryght in here eere,
And cried 'Awaketh!' wonder hyë.
This god of slep with hys oon yë
Cast up, and axed, 'Who clepeth ther?'
        'Hyt am I,' quod this messager.
'Juno bad thow shuldest goon' –
And tolde hym what he shulde doon
(As I have told yow here-to-fore;
Hyt ys no nede reherse hyt more)
130   And went hys wey whan he had sayd.
Anoon this god of slep abrayd
Out of hys slep, and gan to goon,
And dyde as he had bede hym doon:
Took up the dreynte body sone
And bar hyt forth to Alcione,
Hys wif the quene, ther as she lay
Ryght even a quarter before day,
And stood ryght at hyr beddes fet,
And called hir ryght as she het

---

124 *clepeth*: calls

140   By name, and sayde, 'My swete wyf,
      Awake! Let be your sorwful lyf,
      For in your sorwe there lyth no red;
      For, certes, swete, I am but ded.
      Ye shul me never on lyve yse.
      But, goode swete herte, that ye
      Bury my body, for such a tyde
      Ye mowe hyt fynde the see besyde;
      And farewel, swete, my worldes blysse!
      I praye God youre sorwe lysse.
150   To lytel while oure blysse lasteth!'
        With that hir eyen up she casteth
      And saw noght. 'Allas!' quod she for sorwe,
      And deyede within the thridde morwe.
      But what she sayede more in that swow
      I may not telle yow as now;
      Hyt were to longe for to dwelle.   (*c.* 1368–72)

The Former Age [Met. 1.89–112] *The Golden Age*

A blisful lyf, a paisible and a swete,
Ledden the peples in the former age.
They helde hem payed of the fruites that they ete,
Which that the feldes yave hem by usage;
They ne were nat forpampred with outrage.
Unknowen was the quern and ek the melle;
They eten mast, hawes, and swich pounage,
And dronken water of the colde welle.

---

144 *on lyve yse*: see me alive   **5** *forpampred with outrage*: spoiled with excess
6 *quern, melle*: different kinds of grist mills
7 *mast, hawes, and swich pounage*: nuts, fruits and such feed

Yit nas the ground nat wounded with the plough,
10   But corn up-sprong, unsowe of mannes hond,
The which they gnodded and eete nat half ynough.
No man yit knew the forwes of his lond,
No man the fyr out of the flint yit fond,
Unkorven and ungrobbed lay the vyne;
No man yit in the morter spyces grond
To clarre ne to sause of galantyne.

No mader, welde, or wood no litestere
Ne knew; the flees was of his former hewe;
No flesh ne wiste offence of egge or spere.
20   No coyn ne knew man which was fals or trewe,
No ship yit karf the wawes grene and blewe,
No marchaunt yit ne fette outlandish ware.
No trompes for the werres folk ne knewe,
Ne toures heye and walles rounde or square.

What sholde it han avayled to werreye?
Ther lay no profit, ther was no richesse;
But cursed was the tyme, I dare wel seye,
That men first dide hir swety bysinesse
To grobbe up metal, lurkinge in derknesse,
30   And in the riveres first gemmes soghte.
Allas, than sprong up al the cursednesse
Of coveytyse, that first our sorwe broghte.

Thise tyraunts putte hem gladly nat in pres
No wildnesse ne no busshes for to winne,
Ther poverte is, as seith Diogenes,
Ther as vitaile is ek so skars and thinne

---

14 *ungrobbed*: uncultivated
17 The dyer [did not yet know] the plants used for making tints.
19 *egge*: blade's edge   25 *werreye*: make war   36 *vitaile*: food

That noght but mast or apples is therinne;
But, ther as bagges ben and fat vitaile,
Ther wol they gon, and spare for no sinne
40   With al hir ost the cite for to asayle.

Yit was no paleis-chaumbres ne non halles;
In caves and wodes softe and swete
Slepten this blissed folk withoute walles
On gras or leves in parfit quiete.
Ne doun of fetheres ne no bleched shete
Was kid to hem, but in seurtee they slepte.
Hir hertes were al oon withoute galles;
Everich of hem his feith to other kepte.

Unforged was the hauberk and the plate;
50   The lambish peple, voyd of alle vyce,
Hadden no fantasye to debate,
But ech of hem wolde other wel cheryce.
No pryde, non envye, non avaryce,
No lord, no taylage by no tyrannye;
Humblesse and pees, good feith the emperice.

Yit was nat Jupiter the likerous,
That first was fader of delicacye,
Come in this world; ne Nembrot, desirous
To regne, had nat maad his toures hye.
60   Allas, allas, now may men wepe and crye!
For in our dayes nis but covetyse,
Doublenesse, and tresoun, and envye,
Poyson, manslawhtre, and mordre in sondry wyse. (c. 1380–87)

---

38 *bagges*: purses   47 *withoute galles*: unbroken   54 *taylage*: taxation
55 *emperice*: rule (The stanza lacks a line.)
56 *Jupiter*: deposer of his father Saturn, who presided over the Golden Age
58 *Nembrot*: Nimrod, mythic architect of the Tower of Babel

The Legend of Good Women, 706–923 [Met. 4.55–166] *The Legend of Thisbe*

At Babiloyne whylom fil it thus,
The whyche toun the queen Semyramus
Let dychen al aboute and walles make
Ful hye, of hard tiles wel ybake:
There were dwellyng in this noble toun
Two lordes, whiche that were of gret renoun,
And woneden so nygh, upon a grene,
That ther nas but a ston-wal hem betweene,
As oft in grete tounes is the wone.
10 And soth to seyne, that o man hadde a sone,
Of al that lond oon of the lustyeste.
That other hadde a doughter, the fayreste
That estward in the world was tho dwellynge.
The name of everych gan to other sprynge
By women that were neighebores aboute.
For in that contre yit, withouten doute,
Maydenes been ykept, for jelosye,
Ful streyte, lest they diden som folye.
This yonge man was called Piramus,
20 Tysbe hight the maide, Naso seyth thus;
And thus by report was hire name yshove
That, as they wex in age, wex here love.
And certeyn, as by resoun of hire age,
There myghte have ben bytwixe hem maryage,
But that here fadres nolde it nat assente;
And bothe in love ylyke sore they brente,
That non of alle hyre frendes myght it lette,
But pryvyly som tyme yit they mette

---

7 *woneden* : dwelt   **9** *wone*: custom   **21** *yshove*: broadcast
27 *lette*: think or be aware of

By sleyghte, and spoken som of here desyr;
30   As wry the glede and hotter is the fyr,
Forbede a love, and it is ten so wod.
   This wal, which that bitwixe hem bothe stod,
Was clove a-two, ryght from the cop adoun,
Of olde tyme of his fundacioun;
But yit this clyfte was so narw and lyte
It nas nat sene, deere ynogh a myte.
But what is that that love can nat espye?
Ye loveres two, if that I shal nat lye,
Ye founden first this litel narwe clifte;
40   And with a soun as softe as any shryfte,
They lete here wordes thourgh the clifte pace,
And tolden, whil that they stode in the place,
Al here compleynt of love and al here wo,
At every tyme whan they durste so.
Upon that o syde of the wal stod he,
And on that other side stod Thesbe,
The swote soun of other to receyve.
And thus here wardeyns wolde they deceyve,
And every day this wal they wolde threte,
50   And wisshe to God that it were doun ybete.
Thus wolde they seyn: 'Alas, thow wikkede wal!
Thorgh thyn envye thow us lettest al.
Why nylt thow cleve or fallen al a-two?
Or at the leste, but thou woldist so,
Yit woldest thow but ones lat us mete,
Or ones that we myghte kyssen swete,
Thanne were we covered of oure cares colde.
But, natheles, yit be we to thee holde,
In as muche as thow sufferest for to gon
60   Oure wordes thourgh thy lym and ek thy ston.

---

30 *wry the glede*: cover up the coal   **31** *ten so wod*: exacerbated tenfold
36 *deere ynogh a myte*: even slightly

Yit oughte we with the been wel apayd.'
And whan these ydele wordes weren sayd,
The colde wal they wolden kysse of ston,
And take here leve and forth they wolden gon.
And this was gladly in the eve-tyde,
Or wonder erly, lest men it espyde.
And longe tyme they wroughte in this manere,
Tyl on a day, whan Phebus gan to cleere –
Aurora with the stremes of hire hete
70 Hadde dreyed up the dew of herbes wete –
Unto this clyft, as it was wont to be,
Com Piramus, and after com Thysbe,
And plyghten trouthe fully in here fey
That ilke same nyght to stele awey,
And to begile here wardeyns everichon,
And forth out of the cite for to goon;
And, for the feldes ben so brode and wide,
For to mete in o place at o tyde,
They sette mark here metynge sholde be
80 There kyng Nynus was grave under a tre –
For olde payens that idoles heryed
Useden tho in feldes to ben beryed –
And faste by this grave was a welle.
And shortly of this tale for to telle,
This covenaunt was affermed wonder faste;
And longe hem thoughte that the sonne laste,
That it nere gon under the se adoun.
    This Tisbe hath so gret affeccioun
And so gret lykinge Piramus to se,
90 That whan she say hire tyme myghte be,
At nyght she stal awey ful pryvyly,
With hire face ywympled subtyly;

---

80 *Nynus*: fabled founder and ruler of Nineveh   81 *heryed*: worshipped

For alle hire frendes – for to save hire trouthe –
She hath forsake; allas, and that is routhe
That evere woman wolde ben so trewe
To truste man, but she the bet hym knewe.
And to the tre she goth a ful good pas,
For love made hire so hardy in this cas,
And by the welle adoun she gan hyre dresse.
100   Allas! Than cometh a wilde lyonesse
Out of the wode, withoute more arest,
With blody mouth, of strangelynge of a best,
To drynken of the welle there as she sat.
And whan that Tisbe hadde espyed that,
She rist hire up, with a ful drery herte,
And in a cave with dredful fot she sterte,
For by the mone she say it wel withalle.
And as she ran hire wympel let she falle
And tok non hed, so sore she was awhaped,
110   And ek so glad that that she was escaped;
And thus she sit and darketh wonder stylle.
Whan that this lyonesse hath dronke hire fille,
Aboute the welle gan she for to wynde,
And ryght anon the wympel gan she fynde,
And with hire blody mouth it al torente.
Whan this was don, no lengere she ne stente,
But to the wode hire weye thanne hath she nome.

      And at the laste this Piramus is come;
But al to longe, allas, at hom was he!
120   The mone shon, and he myghte wel yse,
And in his wey, as that he com ful faste.
His eyen to the ground adoun he caste,
And in the sond, as he byheld adoun,
He sey the steppes brode of a lyoun,

---

107 *say*: saw   **109** *awhaped*: terrified   **111** *darketh*: lay hidden

And in his herte he sodeynly agros,
And pale he wex; therwith his heer aros,
And ner he com, and fond the wimpel torn.
'Allas,' quod he, 'the day that I was born!
This o nyght wol us lovers bothe sle!
130 How shulde I axe mercy of Tisbe,
Whan I am he that have yow slayn, allas!
My biddyng hath yow slayn, as in this cas.
Allas, to bidde a woman gon by nyghte
In place there as peril falle myghte!
And I so slow! Allas, I ne hadde be
Here in this place a furlong wey or ye!
Now what lyoun that be in this forest,
My body mote he renten, or what best
That wilde is, gnawe mote he nowe myn herte!'
140 And with that word he to the wympel sterte,
And kiste it ofte, and wep on it ful sore,
And seyde, 'Wympel, allas! There is no more
But thow shalt feele as wel the blod of me
As thow hast felt the bledyng of Thisbe!'
And with that word he smot hym to the herte.
The blod out of the wounde as brode sterte
As water whan the condit broken is.
    Now Tisbe, which that wiste nat of this,
But sittynge in hire drede, she thoughte thus:
150 'If it so falle that my Piramus
Be comen hider, and may me not yfynde,
He may me holde fals and ek unkynde.'
And out she cometh and after hym gan espien,
Bothe with hire herte and with hire yen,
And thoughte, 'I wol hym tellen of my drede,
Bothe of the lyonesse and al my deede.'

---

125 *agros*: trembled

And at the laste hire love thanne hath she founde,
Betynge with his heles on the grounde,
Al blody, and therwithal a-bak she sterte,
160   And lik the wawes quappe gan hire herte,
And pale as box she was, and in a throwe
Avisede hire, and gan hym wel to knowe,
That it was Piramus, hire herte deere.
Who coude wryte which a dedly cheere
Hath Thisbe now, and how hire heer she rente,
And how she gan hireselve to turmente,
And how she lyth and swouneth on the grounde,
And how she wep of teres ful his wounde;
How medeleth she his blod with hire compleynte;
170   How with his blod hireselve gan she peynte;
How clyppeth she the deede cors, allas!
How doth this woful Tisbe in this cas!
How kysseth she his frosty mouth so cold!
'Who hath don this, and who hath been so bold
To sle my leef? O spek, my Piramus!
I am thy Tisbe, that the calleth thus.'
And therwithal she lifteth up his hed.
   This woful man, that was nat fully ded,
Whan that he herde the name of Tisbe cryen,
180   On hire he caste his hevy, dedly yen,
And doun agayn, and yeldeth up the gost.
Tysbe ryst up withouten noyse or bost,
And saw hire wympel and his empty shethe,
And ek his swerd that hym hath don to dethe.
Thanne spak she thus: 'My woful hand,' quod she,
'Is strong ynough in swich a werk to me;
For love shal yeve me strengthe and hardynesse
To make my wounde large ynough, I gesse.

---

160 *lik the wawes quappe*: to pound like the waves   **161** *box*: boxwood

I wol thee folwe ded, and I wol be
190 Felawe and cause ek of thy deth,' quod she.
'And thogh that nothing, save the deth only,
Mighte thee fro me departe trewely,
Thow shalt no more departe now fro me
Than fro the deth, for I wol go with thee.
And now, ye wrechede jelos fadres oure,
We that whilom were children youre,
We preyen yow, withouten more envye,
That in o grave yfere we moten lye,
Sith love hath brought us to this pitous ende.
200 And ryghtwis God to every lovere sende,
That loveth trewely, more prosperite
Than evere yit had Piramus and Tisbe!
And lat no gentil woman hyre assure
To putten hire in swich an aventure.
But God forbede but a woman can
Ben as trewe in lovynge as a man!
And for my part, I shal anon it kythe.'
And with that word his swerd she tok as swythe,
That warm was of hire loves blod, and hot,
210 And to the herte she hireselven smot.
And thus are Tisbe and Piramus ygo.
Of trewe men I fynde but fewe mo
In alle my bokes, save this Piramus,
And therfore have I spoken of hym thus.
For it is deynte to us men to fynde
A man that can in love been trewe and kynde.
Here may ye se, what lovere so he be,
A woman dar and can as wel as he.   (c. 1380–87)

---

207 *kythe*: demonstrate

JOHN GOWER (c. 1325–1408)

Like Chaucer, with whom he was well acquainted, John Gower served
the court of Richard II with his poetic talents, and survived his colleague
into the reign of Henry IV. Though the Latin poetry for which he was
celebrated in his own day is now forgotten, Gower's *Confessio amantis*
maintains its status as one of Middle English literature's greatest achievements. Ovid presides over the work, both as a principal source for the
poem's erotic tales and (in his more uniquely medieval guise) as moralist.
Compare Gower's fuller treatment of the Ceyx and Alcyone story with
Chaucer's, above.

Confessio amantis 4.2927–3123 [Met. 11.410–748]
The story of Ceyx and Alcyone

    This finde I write in Poesie:
Ceïx the king of Trocinie
Hadde Alceone to his wif,
Which as hire oghne hertes lif
Him loveth; and he hadde also
A brother, which was cleped tho
Dedalion, and he per case
Fro kinde of man forschape was
Into a Goshauk of liknesse;
10 Wherof the king gret hevynnesse
Hath take, and thoghte in his corage
To gon upon a pelrinage
Into a strange regioun,
Wher he hath his devocioun
To don his sacrifice and preie,
If that he mihte in eny weie

---

4 *oghne*: own

Toward the goddes finde grace
His brother hele to pourchace,
So that he mihte be reformed
20   Of that he hadde be transformed.
To this pourpos and to this ende
This king is redy forto wende,
As he which wolde go be Schipe;
And forto don him felaschipe
His wif unto the See him broghte,
With al hire herte and him besoghte,
That he the time hire wolde sein,
Whan that he thoghte come ayein:
'Withinne,' he seith, 'tuo Monthe day.'
30   And thus in al the haste he may
He tok his leve, and forth he seileth
Wepende, and sche hirself beweileth,
And torneth hom, ther sche cam fro.
Bot whan the Monthes were ago,
The whiche he sette of his comynge,
And that sche herde no tydinge,
Ther was no care forto seche:
Wherof the goddes to beseche
Tho sche began in many wise,
40   And to Juno hire sacrifise
Above alle othre most sche dede,
And for hir lord sche hath so bede
To wite and knowe hou that he ferde,
That Juno the goddesse hire herde,
Anon and upon this matiere
Sche bad Yris hir Messagere
To Slepes hous that sche schal wende,
And bidde him that he make an ende
Be swevene and schewen al the cas
50   Unto this ladi, hou it was.

---

49 *Be swevene*: By means of a dream

This Yris, fro the hihe stage
Which undertake hath the Message,
Hire reyny Cope dede upon,
The which was wonderli begon
With colours of diverse hewe,
An hundred mo than men it knewe;
The hevene lich unto a bowe
Sche bende, and so she cam doun lowe,
The god of Slep wher that sche fond.

60   And that was in a strange lond,
Which marcheth upon Chymerie:
For ther, as seith the Poesie,
The god of Slep hath mad his hous,
Which of entaille is merveilous.
Under an hell ther is a Cave,
Which of the Sonne mai noght have,
So that noman mai knowe ariht
The point betwen the dai and nyht:
Ther is no fyr, ther is no sparke,

70   Ther is no dore, which mai charke,
Wherof an yhe scholde unschette,
So that inward ther is no lette.
And forto speke of that withoute,
Ther stant no gret Tree nyh aboute
Wher on ther myhte crowe or pie
Alihte, forto clepe or crie:
Ther is no cok to crowe day,
Ne beste non which noise may
The hell, bot al aboute round

80   Ther is growende upon the ground
Popi, which berth the sed of slep,
With othre herbes suche an hep.

---

53 *Cope*: cloak   **61** *marcheth*: borders   **70** *charke*: creak
71 *yhe*: eye   **72** *lette*: tumult

A stille water for the nones
Rennende upon the smale stones,
Which hihte of Lethes the rivere,
Under that hell in such manere
Ther is, which yifth gret appetit
To slepe. And thus full of delit
Slep hath his hous; and of his couche
90 Withinne his chambre if I schal touche,
Of hebenus that slepi Tree
The bordes al aboute be,
And for he scholde slepe softe,
Upon a fethrebed alofte
He lith with many a pilwe of doun:
The chambre is strowed up and doun
With swevenes many thousendfold.
Thus cam Yris into this hold,
And to the bedd, which is al blak,
100 Sche goth, and ther with Slep sche spak,
And in the wise as sche was bede
The Message of Juno sche dede.
Fulofte hir wordes sche reherceth,
Er sche his slepi Eres perceth;
With mochel wo bot ate laste
His slombrende yhen he upcaste
And seide hir that it schal be do.
Wherof among a thousend tho,
Withinne his hous that slepi were,
110 In special he ches out there
Thre, whiche scholden do this dede:
The ferste of hem, so as I rede,
Was Morpheüs, the whos nature
Is forto take the figure

---

85 *hihte*: was called   **91** *hebenus*: ebony

Of what persone that him liketh,
Wherof that he fulofte entriketh
The lif which slepe schal be nyhte;
And Ithecus that other hihte,
Which hath the vois of every soun,
120   The chiere and the condicioun
Of every lif, what so it is:
The thridde suiende after this
Is Panthasas, which may transforme
Of every thing the rihte forme,
And change it in an other kinde.
Upon hem thre, so as I finde,
Of swevenes stant al thapparence,
Which otherwhile is evidence
And otherwhile bot a jape.
130   Bot natheles it is so schape,
That Morpheüs be nyht al one
Appiereth until Alceone
In liknesse of hir housebonde
Al naked ded upon the stronde,
And hou he dreynte in special
These othre tuo it schewen al.
The tempeste of the blake cloude,
The wode See, the wyndes loude,
Al this sche mette, and sih him dyen;
140   Wherof that sche began to crien,
Slepende abedde ther sche lay,
And with that noise of hire affray
Hir wommen sterten up aboute,
Whiche of here ladi were in doute,
And axen hire hou that sche ferde;
And sche, riht as sche syh and herde,

---

120 *chiere*: appearance

Hir swevene hath told hem everydel.
And thei it halsen alle wel
And sein it is a tokne of goode;
150   Bot til sche wiste hou that it stode,
Sche hath no confort in hire herte,
Upon the morwe and up sche sterte,
And to the See, wher that sche mette
The bodi lay, withoute lette
Sche drowh, and whan that sche cam nyh,
Stark ded, hise armes sprad, sche syh
Hire lord flietende upon the wawe.
Wherof hire wittes ben withdrawe,
And sche, which tok of deth no kepe,
160   Anon forth lepte into the depe
And wolde have cawht him in hire arm.

This infortune of double harm
The goddes fro the hevene above
Behielde, and for the trowthe of love,
Which in this worthi ladi stod,
Thei have upon the salte flod
Hire dreinte lord and hire also
Fro deth to lyve torned so,
That thei ben schapen into briddes
170   Swimmende upon the wawe amiddes.
And whan sche sih hire lord livende
In liknesse of a bridd swimmende,
And sche was of the same sort,
So as sche mihte do desport,
Upon the joie which sche hadde
Hire wynges bothe abrod sche spradde,
And him, so as sche mai suffise,
Beclipte and keste in such a wise,

---

148 *halsen*: interpret

As sche was whilom wont to do:
180 Hire wynges for hire armes tuo
Sche tok, and for hire lippes softe
Hire harde bile, and so fulofte
Sche fondeth in hire briddes forme,
If that sche mihte hirself conforme
To do the plesance of a wif,
As sche dede in that other lif:
For thogh sche hadde hir pouer lore,
Her will stod as it was tofore,
And serveth him so as sche mai.
190 Wherof into this ilke day
Togedre upon the See thei wone,
Wher many a dowhter and a Sone
Thei bringen forth of briddes kinde;
And for men scholden take in mynde
This Alceoun the trewe queene,
Hire briddes yit, as it is seene,
Of Alceoun the name bere.   (1390)

Confessio amantis 5.6807–6935 [Fas. 2.303–58]
The story of Hercules and Faunus

    The myhtieste of alle men
Whan Hercules with Eolen,
Which was the love of his corage,
Togedre upon a Pelrinage
Towardes Rome scholden go,
It fell hem be the weie so,

---

187 *hir pouer lore*: lost her human attributes
2 *Eolen*: Iole. Gower confuses Omphale, the Lydian queen to whom Ovid here refers (*Maeonis*, 'woman of Lydia'), with Hercules's later mistress.

That thei upon a dai a Cave
Withinne a roche founden have,
Which was real and glorious
10   And of Entaile curious,
Be name and Thophis it was hote.
The Sonne schon tho wonder hote,
As it was in the Somer tyde;
This Hercules, which be his syde
Hath Eolen his love there,
Whan thei at thilke cave were,
He seide it thoghte him for the beste
That sche hire for the hete reste
Al thilke day and thilke nyht;
20   And sche, that was a lusti wyht,
It liketh hire al that he seide:
And thus thei duelle there and pleide
The long dai. And so befell,
This Cave was under the hell
Of Tymolus, which was begrowe
With vines, and at thilke throwe
Faunus with Saba the goddesse,
Be whom the large wildernesse
In thilke time stod governed,
30   Weere in a place, as I am lerned,
Nyh by, which Bachus wode hihte.
This Faunus tok a gret insihte
Of Eolen, that was so nyh;
For whan that he hire beaute syh,
Out of his wit he was assoted,
And in his herte it hath so noted,
That he forsok the Nimphes alle,
And seide he wolde, hou so it falle,

---

10 *Entaile*: layout   11 *hote*: called   32 *insihte*: infatuation

Assaie an other forto winne;
40   So that his hertes thoght withinne
He sette and caste hou that he myhte
Of love pyke awey be nyhte
That he be daie in other wise
To stele mihte noght suffise:
And therupon his time he waiteth.
    Nou tak good hiede hou love afaiteth
Him which withal is overcome.
Faire Eolen, whan sche was come
With Hercules into the Cave,
50   Sche seide him that sche wolde have
Hise clothes of and hires bothe,
That ech of hem scholde other clothe.
And al was do riht as sche bad,
He hath hire in hise clothes clad
And caste on hire his gulion,
Which of the Skyn of a Leoun
Was mad, as he upon the weie
It slouh, and overthis to pleie
Sche tok his grete Mace also
60   And knet it at hir gerdil tho.
So was sche lich the man arraied,
And Hercules thanne hath assaied
To clothen him in hire array:
And thus thei jape forth the dai,
Til that her Souper redy were.
And whan thei hadden souped there,
Thei schopen hem to gon to reste;
And as it thoghte hem for the beste,
Thei bede, as for that ilke nyht,
70   Tuo sondri beddes to be dyht,

---

42 *pyke*: steal   **55** *gulion*: overgarment   **67** *schopen*: prepared

For thei togedre ligge nolde,
Be cause that thei offre wolde.
Upon the morwe here sacrifice.
The servantz deden here office
And sondri beddes made anon,
Wherin that thei to reste gon
Ech be himself in sondri place.
Faire Eole hath set the Mace
Beside hire beddes hed above,
80 And with the clothes of hire love
Sche helede al hire bed aboute;
And he, which hadde of nothing doute,
Hire wympel wond aboute his cheke,
Hire kertell and hire mantel eke
Abrod upon his bed he spredde.
And thus thei slepen bothe abedde;
And what of travail, what of wyn,
The servantz lich to drunke Swyn
Begunne forto route faste.
90   This Faunus, which his Stelthe cast,
Was thanne come to the Cave,
And fond thei weren alle save
Withoute noise, and in he wente.
The derke nyht his sihte blente,
And yit it happeth him to go
Where Eolen abedde tho
Was leid al one for to slepe;
Bot for he wolde take kepe
Whos bed it was, he made assai,
100 And of the Leoun, where it lay,
The Cote he fond, and ek he fieleth
The Mace, and thanne his herte kieleth,

---

71 *ligge nolde*: would not lie   **81** *helede*: overspread   **102** *kieleth*: cools

That there dorste he noght abyde,
Bot stalketh upon every side
And soghte aboute with his hond,
That other bedd til that he fond,
Wher lai bewympled a visage.
Tho was he glad in his corage,
For he hir kertell fond also
110 And ek hir mantell bothe tuo
Bespred upon the bed alofte.
He made him naked thanne, and softe
Into the bedd unwar he crepte,
Wher Hercules that time slepte,
And wende wel it were sche;
And thus in stede of Eole
Anon he profreth him to love.
But he, which felte a man above,
This Hercules, him threw to grounde
120 So sore, that thei have him founde
Liggende there upon the morwe;
And tho was noght a litel sorwe,
That Faunus of himselve made,
Bot elles thei were alle glade
And lowhen him to scorne aboute:
Saba with Nimphis al a route
Cam doun to loke hou that he ferde,
And whan that thei the sothe herde,
He was bejaped overal.   (1390)

---

124 *elles*: the others   125 *lowhen*: laughed   129 *bejaped*: made a mockery of

WILLIAM CAXTON (*c.* 1422–1491)

England's first printer, Caxton was also a prolific translator, chiefly from French sources. His massive prose rendering of the *Metamorphoses* itself drew upon a moralized French redaction (see the Introduction, pp. xxiv and xxvi). We have no evidence that his text ever saw publication. Until the early 1960s, only the portion of Caxton's manuscript covering Books 10–15 was known to exist; the complete work – of which a facsimile was published in 1968 – is now in the collection of Magdalene College, Cambridge.

The following excerpt from Book 6 offers a particularly strong moment from Caxton's prose. Tereus, king of Thrace, rapes and mutilates Philomela, sister to his wife Procne, and afterwards secretly holds her prisoner. From captivity, Philomela designs to reveal her plight to Procne, who thinks her dead. A tapestry depicting the rape, sent discreetly to the queen, reveals the crime and leads to the revenge plot.

the booke Intituled Ovyde of Methamorphoseos.
The vi. booke, c. xi–xii [Met. 6.571–674] *The reunion of Procne and Philomela and their revenge against Tereus*

How prone receyued the cortyne fro phylomena her suster, by which she knewe wher she was And how she delyueryd her.

Whan Phylomena had apperceyuyd that was don to her al her playsyr, whan she sawe her tyme, she wente & fette the curtyne that she hade tyssued & wrought And sythe cam to her maistresse that knew al her sygnes aswel as she hade spoken with her mouth, and made sygne to her that she shold sende this courtyne by her doughter and presentid to the quene of the cyte. She vnderstode it anone, and thought that she sholde haue therby som rewarde or gwerdon, and doubted nothynge, but charged her doughter

---

2 *curtyne*: tapestry   **6** *quene of the cyte*: Procne

therwith, And sayde, Doughter, bere this vnto the quene and
presente it to her, and that don retorne anon agayn.

Phylomena was tho moch recomforted whan she sawe the
courtyne borne forth & hoped therby to haue socour. The mayd
taryd not tyl she cam to the quene & presente to her the courtyne.
The quene behelde it ententyuely & knew wel the werke, but
she dyscouered not her thought ne wold not crye ne make noyse.
She comanded her that brought it that she goo home agayn, &
so she dyde. The quen folowed her aferre withoute losynge the
syghte of her in such wyse as the mayde apperceyued it not vnto
the tyme that she was entred in to the lytyl hows. Thenne the
quene as mad or out of her wytte, cam to the hows whyche was
fast shette and smote the dore with her foot withoute spekyng
of ony worde And the olde woman helde her stelle and spake
not. And Phylomena ran for to haue opend the dore, but the
vylayn that trembled for dredd reteyned her. And Prone smote
and knocked so hard that at laste she brake the dore open And
the olde woman that durst not abyde fledde and hydde her in a
chambre.

Thene came Prone in al araged cryenge, Phylomena, wher art
thou, be not aferde I am thy suster Prone. Thenne came Phylomena vnto her withoute taryenge. And Prone toke her in her
armes and kyssed her, why she almost for sorow went out of her
wytte. Suster sayde she come with me ye haue ben ouerlonge
here. In an vnhappy day was it whan the fel traytre wedded me,
whyche also hath you enforced defloured and in suche wyse
defowled that to me ye may not speke.

Thenne departed the damoyselles toward the Cyte without
holdyng waye or path, tyl Prone brought her suster in to a
chambre vnder erthe for more secretly to mak theyre sorowe.
Ther sayde Prone wepyng to her suster Phylomena, I am heuy
& sorowful that I may not auenge yow of the felon traytre that
so hath trespaced to yow, the goddes gyue hym hys deserte, with

---

22 *helde her stelle*: remained fixed

this wordes came Ytis her sone to her in an euyl aduenture as it
happed to hym.

Whan the moder sawe her sone, she sayde softly as the deuyl
counceylled her, Ha, a, sayd she thyng lyke vnto the felon traytre,
for the felonye and forfayt of thy fader, thou muste dye withoute
cause, ffor as moch only as I sawe neuer thyng resemble mor to
other, than thou dost to thy fader. The chylde that herde nothynge
herof ran to her and kyssed her. Wel ought Prone to absteyne
50   and put fro her this derke & mortal thought by very ryghts &
moderly pyte & loue and that she sholde not slee her sone. But
whan she remembred the traytre she sayd, that what so euer
happed she wold cut of hys heed and gyue it to hys fader for to
ete, and that so she wolde auenge her sorow & her susters, whom
the felon traytre hade so defowled & deshonnoured.

Thenne as the chylde halsed hys moder in chierte she cutte of
hys heed as the deuyl counceylled her And bytwene hem bothe
they appoynted & dyghted the flesshe of the Chylde, one parte
boyled in the pote, and another parte was rosted, and whan it
60   was tyme & oure of dyner and that the flesshe was soden and
rosted Prone for to fulfylle her wyll came to the kynge, and
prayde hym for the loue of the thynge that he most loued in the
worlde, that he wold come and dyne with her allone without
ony companeye sauynge they two, and she wolde serue hym of
al thyng.

The kynge graunte her with agood wylle, so that hys sone Ytis
sholde be also there. Veryly sayde Prone he shal be there, and so
we thre shal be there togydre, and by my wylle ther shal be no
moo, com whan it pleseth yow, ffor al thyng is now redy, and
70   we shal mak good chiere.

Thereus knewe not of what mete he shold ete. She broughte
hym forth & sette hyme moche playsantly to thende that the
dyner sholde better plese hym. The place was notably arayed
wher the kyng satte. She broughte hym an haunche of hys sone

---

56 *halsed . . . in chierte*: tenderly hugged

Ytys, and he began wel to ete therof And after demanded where
hys son Ytis was, and sayd Dame ye promysed me, that he shold
be here with vs. Syre sayde Prone haue ye no doubte, ffor ye
shal be anon fylled of hys syghte, he is not fer hens, he shal be
here anon. Then she wente & fette an other hanche And Thereus
80   what he ete & dyde, sayde agayne to Prone, Dame ye holde me
not couenant whan ye bryng not to me Ytys, it ouer moche
greueth me that he cometh not, and I wote not whome I may
sende for hym but yf I goo my selfe. I pray yow to goo & fecche
hym.

How prone and phylomena brought the heed of Ythys for to ete to his
fader, & how they wer transformed that on of them in to a swalowe, and
that other in to a nyghtyngale.

Prone might no lenger abyde ne hyde fro thereus her lorde of
what mete that he ete and wherof she hade seruyd hym, but
sayde to hym in grete anger, False & dysloyal traytre, thou hast
of hym that thou demandest for, parte in thy body, and part is
withoute. Wyth this wordes yssued out Philomena of a chambre
90   nygh by, where as she hade ben hyde, and brought in the heed
of the chylde and threwe it in the vysage of Thereus, in suche
wyse that it be bledde hym.

Thereus sawe thenne that he was betrayed. He was so abasshed
a whyle of angwysshe and of shame, that he meued not ne spak
one worde. Whan he knewe that it was the hede of hys chylde
And knewe for trouth that Prone hade gyuen hym to hym for
to ete, and that he saw Phylomena, he shoof the table from hym
and caste al doun and toke a swerde for tauenge the deth of hys
sone, whyche was hangyng on the walle, but the two susters tho
100   durst there no lenger abyde ffor he chaced them for to haue
slayn them. But thenne as it plesed the destynees befyll the grettest
meruayll of the worlde or that to fore hade ben herde, ffor Thereus
became a lapwynch, whych is a fowl byrde and a vylaynous for

---

98 *tauenge*: to avenge

the trayson that he hade don to the damoyselle Phylomena. Prone
becam a swalowe, and Phylomena became a nyghtyngale. Yet
her songe cryeth out vpon alle vntrew lovers, and sayth that they
shal be destroyed And for bycause she hateth them, she syngeth
the moost swetly that she can whan the prymtemps is comen in
the buscage, occy, occy, occy.   (1480)

SIR THOMAS CHALONER
(1520–1565)

Sir Thomas Chaloner's ambassadorial duties spanned the reigns of four
Tudor monarchs. An accomplished humanist, honoured in his own
lifetime for his talents as a poet and Latinist, Chaloner is best remembered
now as the first translator of Erasmus's *The Praise of Folly*. His foray into
Ovid's work went unpublished until the nineteenth century, but this
version of *Heroides* 17 marks the first effort to approximate Ovid's
elegiac metre in English. Despite the occasionally awkward rhyme and
forced syntax, Chaloner's 'inverted' poulter's measure (alternating lines
of seven and six stresses) displays an impressive stamina. In the original,
Helen's coy self-disclosure provides the opportunity for an Ovidian
tour de force, something the translator here nicely approximates. Compare
Heywood's version, below.

Helen to Paris [Her. 17]

Now that myn eyes, thy pistle red, already have suffred stayn,
Small prayse my pen shold wyn from answer to refrayn.
Thou shamest nought (a straunger here) all honest custom
    broke,
Agaynst her wedlocke vowe thyne hostes to provoke.

---

109 *occy*: Caxton's imitation of the bird's song

Was that the cause thy weried ship, long tost with wind and
        wether,
Of purpose (as thou saydest) her course dyrected hyther?
Or herefore did our palaice gates unfolded to the stand,
A gest unknowen to us, of unaquaynted land;
To th' end that for our gentlenes we shold be wronged so;
Whan thou didest entre wyth this mynd was thow our frend or
        foe?
It may be for my wryting thus, thow wilt me symple call,
As if I had no cause to playn for this at all.
Ye, symple let me still remayn, so not forgettyng shame,
As long as no new blot my wonted chastnes blame.
Thoughe in my face no fayned chere doth counterfeat the sad,
With frownyng browes to seem as if no myrth I had;
Yet hetherto for deed or thought my fame hath ben
        untouched,
Of none adulterer may my spouse-breache well be vouched.
I muse the more what confydens impelleth the hereto,
Or what sign geves the hope I newly shold mysdoo.
If Theseus dyd once afore by force of rape possesse me,
Woldest thow, therefore, of right the second tyme distresse
        me?
Myne wer the fault if willingly I had agreed therto;
But tane ageynst my will, what could I therwyth doo?
Yet gote he not for all his payn the frute of me he sought,
(The fear I had except) at hym I ayled nought.
A sory kisse or twayn, perhaps, wyth strugling he bereft me,
(Save that) a virgin pure so as he found he left me.
Wold Paris wyth no further gayn have ben content as he,
God sheld me from all such, he was not lyke to the.
A mayden to restore me home it lessened half his cryme,
Youth playd his part, but yet repentaunce cam in tyme.
Did Theseus repent hym than for Paris to succeede,
That in the peples mouthes my name agayn shold spreed? –
But thinke not I am angry now, for who wold not be loved,
In case the love thou shewest unfaynedly be moved.

Yet stand I halfe in doubt thereof, not for I nede to fear,
As yf I wyst not well what shap and face I bear:
But seyng our credulytie us ladyes doth undoo,
40   So hardely may your wordes wyth othes be trusted to.
Yet others synne and matrones chast ben rare thou sayst to see,
What lettes among those rare my name enrold to be?
For where thou thynkst my mothers dede myght serve me, as
     it were,
A president whereby what I shold do to lear:
Mystaking was her giltes excuse, where Jove (his godhed hid)
In lykenes of a swan, his pleasure on her dyd.
But if I synne, I can not say unwittingly to do it,
No errour in this case can serve for shadow to it.
Happy was she to synne so well, through th' autour of the
     same,
50   But where have I a Jove to honor for my shame?
Thou bostest eke thyne auncestry wyth royall names ysett.
As yf we dyd our house from baser titles fett:
All Pelops lyne, with Tyndarus and Jove to overpasse,
Thoughe to my husbandes syre gret graund father he was;
My mother geaves me names ynough, Jove's daughter that I
     am,
Who, under semblaunt fauls, transfourmed to her cam.
Now go, and boste thy Trojan stocke, of famous rote to
     growe,
With Priam take good heed, Laomedon thou show;
Whom I esteme but thus, thou seest, that Jove at fifth degree
60   Suche glory to thy blode, is but the first from me.
I graunt the sceptres of thy Troy ben great as thou dost say,
Yet do I not suppose these here for lesse than they.

---

42 *lettes*: prevents
43 *my mothers dede*: Leda was raped by Jupiter in the form of a swan.
44 *lear*: learn   **53** *to overpasse*: not to mention
58 *Laomedon*: Priam's father, Paris's grandfather

Nombre of goodes and men, perchaunce, thy land hath more
    than myne,
Yet may I say, it is not barbarous as thyn.
Soche promyses of presentes great thy golden lynes do make
    me,
As well through them myght move the goddesses to take the.
But sure and yf that any thing myght move me to relent,
Thyselfe sholdest be more cause t' enforse me to consent.
Eyther I will preserve my name unspotted as it stode,
70   Or rather shall I yeld to Paris, than his good?
Yet do I not contempn thy gyftes for gyfts ar had in store,
Suche as the gevers sake comendeth, twyse the more;
But more do I commend thy love, that am the same for
    whome
Thy travayled ship hath cut the trustles salt see fome:
And though I fayn to marke it nought, yet do I marke right
    well,
At table when we sit, thy countenaunce every deal.
Sometyme thyn eyes behold me fast, wyth long attractyve
    looke
Whose stedfast percyng rayes myn eyes can scarsly brooke.
Then doost thou sighe, or take the cup where I afore did sipp,
80   Forgetting nought whiche syde I turned to my lypp.
How often have I marked eke signes wyth thy fingers made,
How often with thy browes, whiche well nere speking had
So farfurth as I feared least my husband shuld help ye,
And blusshed at som things not handled covertly.
Not ones or twyse then wordes I sayd, wyth murmor long or
    low,
Is he no whit ashamd! wyche nowe I prove ryght so: –
I noted eke about the borde where my name set above,
Thy finger dipt in wyne, subscribed had – *I love!*
Whiche natheles, I beheld with eyes renouncyng it was so,
90   But now, alas! suche signes for wordes may serve I know:

Those dalyaunces, if ought could cause, shuld sonest cause my
    synne,
Those were the rediest traynes to make me fall therein.
Thy face therto, I do confesse, is rare, and suche as may
Move any womans wisshe wyth such a lord to play;
But rather let som others hap be happy, voyd of cryme,
Than I my wyfely trouth in straungers love to lyme.
Lerne then, by me, these beaulties fayr to can want and
    refrayn,
A vertu it is from weal desyred to abstain.
That thow dost wysh hath ben the wyshe of yongmen more
    then one,
100   What than, to judge aright hath Paris eies alone?
Nay, sure thou seest no more than they, but more thou rashly
    darest,
They know as moch as thou, but lesse for shame thou sparest.
Then, lo! I would wyth hasted ship thou hyther haddest ben
    brought,
When me, a mayden yet, a thousand woers sought;
A thousand if I had yet seen had gon wythout thy gayn,
My husband shall in this forgeve my judgement playn.
But now to com for pleasures past and joies enjoyed, I say
Thy hope was overslacke, and other hath got thy pray;
Nat so unleef, that I shold wysh to be thy Trojan wyfe,
110   Wyth Menelay I lead no such displeasant lyf.
Do way, therefore, wyth fawnyng wordes my tendre hart to
    presse;
And do not brew her hurt whose love thou dost professe.
But suffer me to broke at leest in worth my fortunes will,
To shamefull were thy spoyles, my shamefastnes to spill.
But Venus did behight it so, when in the vales of Ide
Three goddesses by the ther naked beaulties tryed:

---

109 *unleef*: improper

So where the first dyd profer state, the second knighthode
    gave,
The third, thou saiest, dyd plight that Heleyn thou sholdst
    have; –
It may well be, but sure I trow full hardly yet that they
120   From heavin down wold com thy judgement to obey:
That if they dyd the tother part is but thyn own devyse,
Where I of thyn award am sayd to be the pryse.
I do not thynke above the rest my beaultie so moche worthe,
As it for greatest gifte a goddes shuld set forth:
Sufficeth, that my sely fourme do mortall eyes detain,
But undre Venus prayse I fear som secret trayn.
Yet do I not refuse the same, for why shold I make coy,
With outward wordes to squaym my inward thursted joye?
Nor be thou wrath, wyth moch a doo, that scant I do beleve
    the,
130   A weighty case as is, requyres slacke fayth to preve the.
My fourme therefore I dobled hold, to Venus prayse referrd,
And likewyse, by thy choyse, for gretest gift preferred:
That neyther Pallas profers large, nor Juno's hests might move
Thy mode (my name ones hard) ther parties to approve.
For my sake then, dyd Paris leave both prowes, state, and
    havyour?
What adamant could chose so free an hart but favour.
I am not made of athamant, althoughe I ame not prone
To love hym that I scarse could thynke wold be myn own.
Why shold I seke to plow the sand whose print the flood
    replyeth,
140   Or geave myself suche hope as place itself denyeth?
I can not skill on Venus stelthes, and Jove my witnes be,
My husband never yet deceyved was by me.
Yea, wher I now to aunswer thyne, this pystle undretake,
Thinke how it is the first whiche ever I dyd make.

---

128 *squaym*: dissemble   **135** *havyour*: wealth

Happy be they that knowe the trade, but I, through practyse
  small,
Suppose the way right hard, to syn and scape wythall.
The fear it self is ill ynough, alredy I geave place,
As if a worldes eies stode poring in my face:
Nor yet in vayn mysgeves my mynd, I know what people say,
My damsel Ethra hard som backe tales yesterday.
So eyther thou must cloke thy love, or leave wyth love to
  mell,
But why shold love be left, which thou maist cloke so well?
Play, but beware, and thinke we have more libertie nat most,
That Menelay is nowe departed from this coast:
He, for affaiers which touch'd hym nere, good man, the seas
  hath past;
A great and laufull cause his sodeyn gate dyd hast:
And partely I, where doubting yet what best was to be done,
I bade hym go with spede to spede hym home as sone.
Glad for the lucke my wordes hym gave, he kyssed me, 'and
  see
Thou loke well to our hous, and chere our ghest,' – qd. he.
Skarse could I then my laughter kepe, wyth struglyng backe to
  call,
One word, I had not more, for answer, but – 'I shall;' –
And so his sayles, wyth wynd at will, to Creteward he
  unfolded:
But let not thy conceit be therfore to moche bolded.
His absence is not suche, but that his spials present ar,
The proverbe sayth (thou knowest) a kings hand stretcheth
  farr.
My fame also reputed fayr, shall now this combraunce do me,
The more I am belykid, to cause hym loke more to me:
So that the prayse which set me fourth is now my setter backe.
Me lever were mens eyes had found in me som lacke.

150 (marginal line number)
160 (marginal line number)
170 (marginal line number)

---

156 *gate*: journey   **165** *spials*: spies

Yet marvaill not, though parted hence with Paris he durst leave
    me;
My maners and good lyfe such credit maks hym geave me.
My face may cause hym stand in drede, my lyfe hym self will
    swear
Is such as well what doubt my beaultie moves, can clear.
But tyme, thou sayst, thus proferd us, we shold not lose alday
His symplenes to take for vauntage while we may: –
I wold, and yet I fear to will, my mynd I wot nor how,
Half geaven to consent, half doth it disalow.
My husband is from home I wot, and thou alone dost lye,
180   My beaultie perceth thyn, thyn perced hath myn eye;
These nyghtes ar long, and now in spech we joyn, and wo is
    me;
So fayr thy wordes ar sett, and both in one house be.
And never have I joye, unles all things provoke me to it,
But ay this elvish drede revokes me to undo it.
O that thou hadst the pour to force that ill thou dost perswade,
So, lo! a symple wight more skillfull shold be made:
An injury sometime doth turne unto theyr bote that byd it,
So were I happy, loo! to say – compeld I dyd it.
But rather let me leave this love ere further it encreseth;
190   A fyer but newly made with little water ceaseth.
S' unstedfast is this straungers love, it wandreth eft as they,
Whan moost we thinke it sure, it sonest flyeth away.
Hipsiphile and Ariadne can hereof witnes bear,
Both joynd to other beddes, by whom betrayed they were;
And thou lykewyse, unfaythfull man, art sayd to have forsaken,
Enone, eke that so long was for thy mastres taken;
Nor yet thy self denyest it, and thynke not but I know,
By depe enquyry made, how all thy doynges goo.

---

193 *Hipsiphile*: ruler of Lemnos, who bore Jason two sóns

But yf thou woldest be fyrme in love, how lyeth it in thy
        pour?
200   Thy maryners do loke for passage every hour:
Whyles we do treat, or whiles the night long hopt for, hard at
        hand,
A thankeles wynd shall blow directly for thy land:
Then, as thy ship doth ronne her course, thy new sought joyes
        and I
Here lefte behynd, our love into the wynd shall flye.
Or, shall I folow by thy reed, thy famous Troy to see,
There, nere unto the great Laomedon to be.
Nay, yet I do not set so light by brute of flyeng fame,
That she, the worldes cares shuld burden wyth my shame;
What will my toun of Spart than doo, what may hole
        Grekeland say?
210   Wyll Asye, or Troy itself, from blamyng of me stay?
Will Priam, or king Priam's wyf, excuse my dede herein,
Thy brethern, or ther wyves, with other of thy kyn?
Wilt thou thy selfe hereafter hope that faythfull I wold byde?
Nat rather to suspect thyn own example tryed?
What ever gest in foreyn ship Troy haven then dyd entre,
Shuld cause thy jelous hart to fear thyn own aventure.
Then, lo, at every lytle jarr, adultres! wilt thou say —
Forgetting of my cryme, thyn own to bere the brey;
And so shall he that made me synne condemp my synne also: —
220   Ere that day com, I wish my carcas laid full lowe.
But goodes, thou sayst, with richer wede obteyn I shall at
        Troy,
There gyfts in dede above thy promes to enjoye.
Such purple robes, soch cloth of gold, soch jewells, pyleng to
        the,
Wyth treasour pyld in hourdes, presented shall I be.
Thy presentes suer forgeave it me, I do not so allow,
To leave my natyve ground more leef I wot nere how.
How, if in Troy I suffer wrong, whose succour shall me steed?
Whence shall I claym my kynne, or brothers ayd, at nede?

Medea was constraynid at last from Esons hous to go,

230   How ever Jason false dyd promes her nat soo:

But where had she her father than, her mother, or her syster,

Dispysed so by him, for refuge to assist her.

Now, as I fear no soch myshap no more Medea dyd,

But often on good hope yll chaunces heve betid. –

A ship that is amyds the seas turmented to and fro,

At setting from the port myght fynd the waves full low.

The fyerbrand eke wyth Hecuba before thy byrth dyd seme

All bloddy to bryng fourth, moch make me to mysdeme:

And sore I drede the prophecy whyche commeth thus, they
    say,

240   That Ylion shall burne wyth Grekysh fyre one day:

And lyke as Venus is thy frend, bycause she wan and welded

Two tryumphes at one tyme, whiche thyn award her yelded;

So fear I, yf thy vaunt be true, the tothers just dysdayn,

Who, standing to thy dome, dyd not theyr cause obtayn.

And sure I ame that followyng the, warr foloweth next at
    hand,

To tryall of the sworde our love, alas! must stand.

For ravyshed Hippodame, the beastly Centaures pray,

Betwene her frendes and them how bloddy was the fray.

Will Tyndarus or Menelay, wyth both my brethern than,

250   Forgeave the, and not seke revengement all they can?

Now where thou doost thy manhood bost for warly feates
    achyeved,

That beaultie of thyn forbidds thy wordes to be belyved:

---

229 *Medea was constraynid . . . to go*: Jason's ambition to marry Glauce displaced
Medea from his father's (Aeson's) house.

237 *The fyerbrand*: While pregnant with Paris, Hecuba dreamed that she bore a
flaming brand that would one day consume Troy. Priam consequently exposed
the infant, who was adopted by a shepherd and eventually returned to the royal
household.

Those tendre lymmes, not made for Mars, in Venus' camp
    shuld play,
Let warryoures fight ther fill, thou, Paris, love all day.
Byd Hector, whom thou praysest so, fyght for the if he
    will,
An other maner fight pertayneth to thy skill.
Conclude that yf I had the wyt or spryte therto I shuld
Thyn ample profers take, as she, that wyse is, wold.
Or I perchaunce will take them to, my shamefast fear
    upcast,
260   And yeld me to the tyme that may me wyn at last:
Where thou desierst som secret place to treat betwen us two,
I know thy trayn, and how our treaty than shold goo.
But soft a whyle, what nedes this hast, thy corn ys yet but
    grene,
Thy tarying all this whyle, perchaunce thy frend hath bene.
Thus hetherto my pen that put my secret mynd in wryting,
Syns weried in my hand, shall cease now from endyting:
The rest hereof by Clemenee and Ethra thou shalt know,
My pryvy damsels both, and counsayloures also.

                              (unknown; pub. 1804)

---

267 *Clemenee and Ethra*: two of Helen's companions

ANONYMOUS

The fable of Ouid treting of Narcissus, 117–58
[Met. 3.442–73] *Narcissus's lament*

The sole distinction of this performance – once attributed to the poet Thomas Howell – is its status as the first English translation from the *Metamorphoses* to rely solely upon the original Latin text. (In this it predates Golding by five years.) A lengthy poetic 'moral' follows the tale. The author's poulter's measure declines significantly from what we find in Chaloner, although several moments in Narcissus's mournful self-discovery glimmer.

Hath euer loue, oh woodes delte crueller with man
you knowe that hyding place, hath bene to louers now and
    than
  Now can you call to mynde, you that suche worldes haue
    laste
that euer anye pyned so, by loue in ages paste.
  I see and lyke it well, but that I lyke and see
yet fynde I not suche errour loe, this loue doth bring to mee
  And to increase my grefe, no say nor yrkesome waye
no hylles nor valeys, with closyd gates, dothe saye our meting
    nay
  A lytle water here, dothe seuer vs in twayne,
10 he seketh I see, that I desyre, to be imbraced as fayne,
  For looke how ofte my lippes, I moue to kysse the lake
so oft he sheweth his mouthe, content, full well the same to
    take

---

7 *say*: sea

To touche thee, mighte full well, a man wolde thinke be
    dime
it is the leste of other thinges, that louers oughte to shine
    What so thou be come forthe, why doste thou me disseyue
why flyest thou hym, that the somuche, desyreth to receyue
    My bewtie and mine age, truely me thynkes I se
it is not that thou doste mislyke, for nimphes haue loued me
    Thou promyste to me a hope, I wotnot howe
with frendly cheare, and to mine armes the same thou dost
20   vnbowe
    Thou smylest when I laughe, and eke thy trekeling teares
when I doe weepe I ofte espy, with sines thy countenaunce
    steares
    By mouing of thy lyppes, and as I ges I lerne
thou speakest words, the sence whereof, myne eares can not
    deserne
    Euen this I am I se, my proper shape I knowe
wyth louing of my selfe, I borne I mone, & beare the gloue
    What shall I doe, and if I aske what shall I craue
aboundaunce brings me want, with me, it is that I would craue
    Oh wolde to God I myght, departe my body fro
30 in hym loues this that wyshe is strang, hys lyking to forgo
    But nowe my strength, throughe payne is fled, and my
        yeares
full sone or lyke to ende, thus dethe away my youth it beares
    Yet dethe that endeth my wooes, to me it is not so sure
He whom I loue ryght fayne, I wold myght lyue alenger houre
    Nowe to one quod he, together let vs dye
In euell estate and to his shape, returneth by and by

---

13 *dime*: misprint for 'done'? 14 *shine*: misprint for 'shone'?
26 *beare the gloue*: i.e., I am pledged
30 The line is garbled: possibly, 'however strange it is for a lover to wish separation
from the object of his love'.

And wyth his gusshynge tearys, so vp the water starte
hys shape that ther by darkened was, whiche when he sawe
    departe
Nowe whether doste thou go, abyde he cryed faste
40   forsake not hym so cruelly, hys loue that on the cast
    Thoughe thee I may not touche, my sorowes to asswage
yet maye I looke, relefe to geue vnto my wretched rage (1560)

ARTHUR GOLDING (1536–1606)

In the dedicated translator Arthur Golding, Ovid's *Metamorphoses* found
a sustained English voice. Golding deployed the 'fourteener' couplet
with a remarkable verve. Golding's delivery replicates Ovid's at its
artless best. The energy and lexical ingenuity he brings to the text lend
a colour and freshness that more than compensate for the metrical
quaintness that often (to the modern ear, at least) gives his narrative a
burlesque tone. His version would be displaced by Sandys's translation
in the next century, but not before leaving an indelible impression on
the period's greatest artists, Shakespeare chief among these.

   Golding published his rendition of the poem's first four books in
1565, followed two years later by the complete translation. The following passages – some of the poem's best-known moments – come from
the 1567 text.

The XV. Bookes of P. Ouidius Naso, entytuled Metamorphosis 1.545–700 [Met. 1.452–567]
Apollo and Daphne

Peneian Daphne was the first where *Phebus* set his love,
Which not blind chaunce but *Cupids* fierce and cruel wrath
   did move.

The *Delian* God but late before surprisde with passing pride
For killing of the monstrous worme, the God of love espide,
With bowe in hand alredy bent and letting arrowes go:
To whome he sayd, and what hast thou thou wanton baby so
With warlike weapons for to toy? It were a better sight,
Too see this kinde of furniture on my two shoulders bright:
Who when we list with stedfast hand both man and beast can
        wound,
Who tother day wyth arrowes keene, have nayled to the
10   ground
The serpent *Python* so forswolne, whose filthie wombe did
        hide
So many acres of the grounde in which he did abide.
Content thy selfe sonne, sorie loves to kindle with thy brand,
For these our prayses to attaine thou must not take in hand.
To him quoth *Venus* sonne againe: Well *Phebus* I agree
Thy bow to shoote at every beast, and so shall mine at thee.
And looke how far that under God eche beast is put by kinde,
So much thy glorie lesse than ours in shooting shalt thou finde.
This saide, with drift of fethered wings in broken ayre he flue,
20   And up the forkt and shadie top of Mount *Parnasus* drue.
There from hys quiver full of shafts two arrowes did he take
Of sundrie workes: tone causeth Love, the tother doth it slake.
That causeth love, is all of golde with point full sharpe and
        bright,
That chaseth love is blunt, whose steele with leaden head is
        dight.
The God this fired in the Nymph *Peneis* for the nones
The tother perst *Apollos* hart and overraft his bones.
Immediately in smoldring heate of Love the tone did swelt,
Againe the tother in hir heart no sparke nor motion felt.

---

4 *worme*: the serpent Python, an exploit recounted in the preceding passage
25 *Peneis*: Daphne, daughter of Peneus

In woods and forrests is hir joy, the savage beasts to chase,
30   And as the price of all hir paine too take the skinne and case.
Unwedded *Phebe* doth she haunt and follow as hir guide,
Unordred doe hir tresses wave scarce in a fillet tide.
Full many a wooer sought hir love: she lothing all the rout,
Impacient and without a man walkes all the woods about.
And as for *Hymen*, or for love, and wedlocke often sought,
She tooke no care, they were the furthest end of all hir
        thought.
Hir father many a time and oft would saye, my daughter deere
Thow owest me a sonneinlaw too bee thy lawfull feere.
Hir father many a time and oft would say, My daughter deere
Of Nephewes thou my debtour art, their Graundsires heart to
40   cheere.
She hating as a haynous crime the bond of bridely bed,
Demurely casting downe hir eyes, and blushing somwhat
        red,
Did folde about hir fathers necke with fauning armes: and
        sed,
Deere father, graunt me whyle I live my maidenhead for to
        have,
As too *Diana* heretofore hir father freely gave.
Thy father (*Daphne*) could consent to that thou doest require,
But that thy beautie and thy forme impugne thy chaste desire;
So that thy will and his consent are nothing in this case,
By reason of the beautie bright that shineth in thy face.
50   *Apollo* loves and longs to have this *Daphne* to his Feere,
And as he longs he hopes, but his foredoomes doe fayle him
        there.
And as light hame when corne is reapt, or hedges burne with
        brandes,
That passers by when day drawes neere throwe loosely fro
        their handes;

---

30 *case*: hide, pelt   **38** *feere*: mate   **40** *Nephewes*: grandsons
52 *hame*: straw

So intoo flames the God is gone and burneth in his brest,
And feedes his vaine and barraine love in hoping for the best.
Hir heare unkembd about hir necke downe flaring did he see
O Lord and were they trimd (quoth he) how seemely would
    shee bee?
He sees hir eyes as bright as fire the starres to represent,
He sees hir mouth which to have seene he holdes him not
    content.
60   Hir lillie armes mid part and more above the elbow bare,
Hir handes, hir fingers and hir wrystes, him thought of beautie
    rare.
And sure he thought such other partes as garments then did
    hyde,
Excelled greatly all the rest the which he had espyed.
But swifter than the whyrling winde shee flees and will not
    stay,
To give the hearing to these wordes the which he had to say.
    I pray thee Nymph *Penæis* stay, I chase not as a fo:
    Stay Nymph: the Lambes so flee the Wolves, the Stags the
      Lions so.
With flittring feathers sielie Doves so from the Gossehauke
    flie,
And every creature from his foe. Love is the cause that I
70   Do followe thee: alas alas how woulde it grieve my heart,
To see thee fall among the briers, and that the bloud should
    start
Out of thy tender legges, I wretch the causer of thy smart.
The place is rough to which thou runst, take leysure I thee
    pray,
Abate thy flight, and I my selfe my running pace will stay.
Yet would I wishe thee take advise, and wisely for to viewe
What one he is that for thy grace in humble wise doth sewe.
I am not one that dwelles among the hilles and stonie rockes,
I am no sheephearde with a Curre, attending on the flockes:

I am no Carle nor countrie Clowne, nor neathearde taking
    charge
80 Of cattle grazing here and there within this Forrest large.
Thou doest not know, poore simple soule, God wot thou dost
    not knowe,
From whome thou fleest. For if thou knew, thou wouldste not
    flee me so.
In *Delphos* is my chief abode, my Temples also stande
At *Glaros* and at *Patara* within the *Lycian* lande.
And in the Ile of *Tenedos* the people honour mee.
The king of Gods himself is knowne my father for to bee.
By me is knowne that was, that is, and that that shall ensue,
By mee men learne to sundrie tunes to frame sweete ditties
    true.
In shooting have I stedfast hand, but surer hand had hee
That made this wound within my heart that heretofore was
90 free.
Of Phisicke and of surgerie I found the Artes for neede
The powre of everie herbe and plant doth of my gift proceede.
Nowe wo is me that neare an herbe can heale the hurt of love
And that the Artes that others helpe their Lord doth helpelesse
    prove.
  As *Phœbus* would have spoken more, away *Penæis* stale
    With fearefull steppes, and left him in the midst of all his
    tale.
And as she ran the meeting windes hir garments backewarde
    blue,
So that hir naked skin apearde behinde hir as she flue,
Hir goodly yellowe golden haire that hanged loose and slacke,
100 With every puffe of ayre did wave and tosse behind hir backe.
Hir running made hir seeme more fayre, the youthfull God
    therefore
Coulde not abyde to waste his wordes in dalyance any more.

---

79 *Carle*: churl   **93** *neare*: never

But as his love advysed him he gan to mende his pace,
And with the better foote before the fleeing Nymph to chace.
And even as when the greedie Grewnde doth course the sielie
    Hare,
Amiddes the plaine and champion fielde without all covert
    bare,
Both twaine of them doe straine themselves and lay on
    footemanship,
Who may best runne with all his force the tother to outstrip,
The tone for safetie of his lyfe, the tother for his pray,
The Grewnde aye prest with open mouth to beare the Hare
110   away,
Thrusts forth his snoute, and gyrdeth out, and at hir loynes
    doth snatch,
As though he would at everie stride betweene his teeth hir
    latch:
Againe in doubt of being caught the Hare aye shrinking slips,
Upon the sodaine from his Jawes, and from betweene his lips:
So farde *Apollo* and the Mayde: hope made *Apollo* swift,
And feare did make the Mayden fleete devising how to shift.
Howbeit he that did pursue of both the swifter went,
As furthered by the feathred wings that *Cupid* had him lent:
So that he would not let hir rest, but preased at hir heele
So neere that through hir scattred haire she might his breathing
120   feele.
But when she sawe hir breath was gone and strength began to
    fayle,
The colour faded in hir cheekes, and ginning for to quayle,
Shee looked to *Penæus* streame and sayde, nowe Father dere,
And if yon streames have powre of Gods, then help your
    daughter here.

---

105 *Grewnde*: greyhound

O let the earth devour me quicke, on which I seeme too fayre,
Or else this shape which is my harme by chaunging straight
    appayre.
This piteous prayer scarsly sed: hir sinewes waxed starke,
And therewithall about hir breast did grow a tender barke.
Hir haire was turned into leaves, hir armes in boughes did
    growe,
Hir feete that were ere while so swift, now rooted were as
130   slowe.
Hir crowne became the toppe, and thus of that she earst had
    beene,
Remayned nothing in the worlde, but beautie fresh and
    greene.
Which when that *Phœbus* did beholde (affection so did move)
The tree to which his love was turnde he coulde no lesse but
    love.
And as he softly layde his hande upon the tender plant,
Within the barke newe overgrowne he felt hir heart yet pant.
And in his armes embracing fast hir boughes and braunches
    lythe,
He proferde kisses to the tree: the tree did from him writhe.
Well (quoth *Apollo*) though my Feere and spouse thou can not
    bee,
140 Assuredly from this time forth yet shalt thou be my tree.
Thou shalt adorne my golden lockes, and eke my pleasant
    Harpe,
Thou shalt adorne my Quyver full of shaftes and arrowes
    sharpe,
Thou shalt adorne the valiant knyghts and royall Emperours:
When for their noble feates of armes like mightie conquerours,
Triumphantly with stately pompe up to the Capitoll,
They shall ascende with solemne traine that doe their deedes
    extoll.

---

126 *appayre*: make less attractive

Before *Augustus* Pallace doore full duely shalt thou warde,

The Oke amid the Pallace yarde aye faythfully to garde,

And as my heade is never poulde nor never more without

A seemely bushe of youthfull haire that spreadeth rounde

150   about:

Even so this honour give I thee continually to have

Thy braunches clad from time to tyme with leaves both fresh
          and brave.

Now when that *Pean* of this talke had fully made an ende,

The Lawrell to his just request did seeme to condescende,

By bowing of hir newe made boughs and tender braunches
          downe,

And wagging of hir seemely toppe, as if it were hir crowne.

(1567)

The XV. Bookes of P. Ouidius Naso, entytuled Metamorphosis 8.913–1088 [Met. 8.728–878]
The story of Erysichthon and his daughter

There are O valiant knyght sum folke that had the powre to
          take

Straunge shape for once, and all their lyves continewed in the
          same,

And othersum to sundrie shapes have power themselves to
          frame,

As thou O *Protew* dwelling in the sea that cleepes the land.

For now a yoonker, now a boare, anon a Lyon, and

Streyght way thou didst become a Snake, and by and by a Bull,

That people were afrayd of thee too see thy horned skull.

---

149 *poulde*: bare   **153** *Pean*: Apollo
1 The river-god Achelous addresses the story to his guest, Theseus.
4 *cleepes*: clips, embraces   **5** *yoonker*: youth

And oftentymes thou seemde a stone, and now and then a tree,
And counterfetting water sheere thou seemedst oft to bee
10   A River: and another whyle contrarie thereunto
Thou wart a fyre. No lesser power than also thus too doo
Had *Erisicthons* daughter whom *Awtolychus* tooke to wyfe.
Her father was a person that despysed all his lyfe
The powre of Gods, and never did vouchsauf them sacrifyse.
He also is reported to have heawen in wicked wyse
The grove of *Ceres*, and to fell her holy woods which ay
Had undiminisht and unhackt continewed to that day.
There stood in it a warrie Oke which was a wood alone.
Uppon it round hung fillets, crownes, and tables, many one,
20   The vowes of such as had obteynd theyr hearts desyre. Full oft
The Woodnymphes underneath this tree did fetch theyr frisks
        aloft,
And oftentymes with hand in hand they daunced in a round
About the Trunk, whose bignesse was of timber good and
        sound
Full fifteene fadom. All the trees within the wood besyde,
Were untoo this, as weedes to them: so farre it did them hyde.
Yit could not this move *Triops* sonne his axe therefro too hold,
But bade his servants cut it downe. And when he did behold
Them stunting at his hest, he snatcht an axe with furious mood
From one of them, and wickedly sayd thus. Although thys
        wood
30   Not only were the derling of the Goddesse, but also
The Goddesse even herself: yet would I make it ere I go
Too kisse the clowers with her top that pranks with
        braunches so.
This spoken, as he sweakt his axe asyde to fetch his blow,
The manast Oke did quake and sygh, the Acornes that did
        grow

---

26 Triops *sonne*: Erysichthon   **32** *pranks*: preens   **33** *sweakt*: swung
34 *manast*: menaced

Thereon toogither with the leaves to wex full pale began,
And shrinking in for feare the boughes and braunches looked
    wan.
Assoone as that his cursed hand had wounded once the tree,
The blood came spinning from the carf, as freshly as yee see
It issue from a Bullocks necke whose throte is newly cut
40   Before the Altar, when his flesh to sacrifyse is put.
They were amazed everychone. And one among them all
Too let the wicked act, durst from the tree his hatchet call.
The lewd *Thessalian* facing him sayd: Take thou heere too thee
The guerdon of thy godlynesse: and turning from the tree,
He chopped of the fellowes head. Which done, he went agen
And heawed on the Oke. Streight from amid the tree as then
There issued such a sound as this, Within this tree dwell I
A Nymph too *Ceres* very deere, who now before I dye
In comfort of my death doo give thee warning thou shalt bye
50   Thy dooing deere within a whyle. He goeth wilfully
Still thorrough with his wickednesse, until at length the Oke
Pulld partly by the force of ropes, and cut with axes stroke,
Did fall, and with his weyght bare downe of under wood great
    store.
The Woodnymphes with the losses of the woods and theyrs
    ryght sore
Amazed, gathered on a knot, and all in mourning weede
Went sad too *Ceres*, praying her too wreake that wicked deede
Of *Erisichthons*. *Ceres* was content it should bee so.
And with the mooving of her head in nodding too and fro,
Shee shooke the feeldes which laden were with frutefull
    Harvest tho.
60   And therewithall a punishment most piteous shee proceedes
To put in practyse: were it not that his most heynous deedes,
No pitie did deserve to have at any bodies hand.
With helplesse hungar him to pyne, in purpose shee did stand.

---

42 *let*: prevent

And forasmuch as shee herself and famin myght not meete,
(For fate forbiddeth famin too abyde within the leete
Where plentie is) shee thus bespake a fayrie of the hill.
There lyeth in the utmost bounds of Tartarie the chill
A Dreerie place, a wretched soyle, a barreine plot: no grayne,
No frute, no tree, is growing there: but there dooth aye
    remayne
Unweeldsome cold, with trembling feare, and palenesse white
70   as clowt,
And foodlesse famin. Will thou her immediately withowt
Delay too shed herself intoo the stomacke of the wretch,
And let no plentie staunch her force but let her working
    stretch
Above the powre of mee. And least the longnesse of the way
May make thee wearie, take thou heere my charyot: take I say
My draggons for to beare thee through the aire. In saying so
She gave hir them. The Nymph mounts up: and flying thence
    as tho
Alyghts in *Scythy* land, and up the cragged top of hye
Mount *Caucasus* did cause hir Snakes with much a doo too
    stye.
Where seeking long for famin, shee the gaptoothd elfe did
80   spye
Amid a barreine stony feeld a ramping up the grasse
With ougly nayles, and chanking it. Her face pale colourd was.
Her heare was harsh and shirle, her eyes were sunken in her
    head.
Her lyppes were hore with filth, her teeth were furd and rusty
    red.
Her skinne was starched, and so sheere a man myght well
    espye

---

65 *leete*: court
70 *clowt*: a piece of undyed cloth (traditional expression in Golding's day)
82 *chanking*: munching   **83** *shirle*: rough   **84** *furd*: encrusted

The verie bowels in her bulk how every one did lye.
And eke above her coorbed loynes her withered hippes
    were seene.
In stead of belly was a space where belly should have beene.
Her breast did hang so sagging downe as that a man would
    weene
That scarcely to her ridgebone had hir ribbes beene fastned
90   well.
Her leannesse made her joynts bolne big, and kneepannes for
    too swell,
And with exceeding mighty knubs her heeles behynd boynd
    out.
Now when the Nymph behild this elfe a farre (she was in dout
To come too neere her:) shee declarde her Ladies message.
    And
In that same little whyle although the Nymph aloof did stand,
And though shee were but newly come, yit seemed shee too
    feele
The force of famin. Wheruppon shee turning backe her
    wheele
Did reyne her dragons up aloft: who streyght with courage
    free
Conveyd her into *Thessaly*. Although that famin bee
100   Ay contrarye too *Ceres* woork: yit did shee then agree
Too doo her will, and glyding through the Ayre supported by
The wynd, she found thappoynted house: and entring by and
    by
The caytifs chamber where he slept (it was in tyme of nyght)
Shee hugged him betweene her armes there snorting bolt
    upryght.
And breathing her into him, blew uppon his face and brest,
That hungar in his emptie veynes myght woorke as hee did
    rest.

---

87 *coorbed*: bent

And when she had accomplished her charge, shee then
    forsooke
The frutefull Clymates of the world, and home ageine betooke
Herself untoo her frutelesse feeldes and former dwelling place.
110 The gentle sleep did all this whyle with fethers soft embrace
The wretched *Erisicthons* corse. Who dreaming streight of
    meate
Did stirre his hungry jawes in vayne as though he had too eate:
And chanking tooth on tooth apace he gryndes them in his
    head,
And occupies his emptie throte with swallowing, and in stead
Of food devoures the lither ayre. But when that sleepe with
    nyght
Was shaken of, immediatly a furious appetite
Of feeding gan to rage in him, which in his greedy gummes
And in his meatlesse maw dooth reigne unstauncht. Anon
    there cummes
Before him whatsoever lives on sea, in aire or land:
120 And yit he crieth still for more. And though the platters stand
Before his face full furnished, yit dooth he still complayne
Of hungar, craving meate at meale. The food that would
    susteine
Whole householdes, Towneships, Shyres and Realmes suffyce
    not him alone:
The more his pampred paunch consumes the more it maketh
    mone.
And as the sea receyves the brookes of all the worldly Realmes,
And yit is never satisfyde for all the forreine streames:
And as the fell and ravening fyre refuseth never wood,
But burneth faggots numberlesse, and with a furious mood
The more it hath, the more it still desyreth evermore,
130 Encreacing in devouring through encreasement of the store:
So wicked *Erisicthons* mouth in swallowing of his meate
Was ever hungry more and more, and longed ay to eate.

Meate tolld in meate: and as he ate the place was empty still.
The hungar of his brinklesse Maw the gulf that nowght might
  fill
Had brought his fathers goods to nowght. But yit continewed
  ay
His cursed hungar unappeasd: and nothing could alay
The flaming of his starved throte. At length when all was
  spent,
And into his unfilled Maw bothe goods and lands were sent:
An only daughter did remayne unworthy too have had
140 So lewd a father. Hir he sold, so hard was he bestad.
But shee of gentle courage could no bondage well abyde.
And therefore stretching out her hands to seaward there
  besyde,
Now save mee quoth shee from the yoke of bondage I thee
  pray,
O thou that my virginitie enjoyest as a pray.
Neptunus had it: Who too this her prayer did consent.
And though her maister looking backe (for after him shee
  went)
Had newly seene her: yit he turnd hir shape and made hir
  man,
And gave her looke of fisherman. Her mayster looking than
Upon her, sayd. Good fellow thou that on the shore doost
  stand
150 With angling rod and bayted hooke and hanging lyne in hand,
I pray thee as thou doost desyre the Sea ay calme too thee,
And fishes for to byght thy bayt, and striken still to bee,
Tell where the frizzletopped wench in course and sluttish
  geere,
That stoode right now uppon this shore (for well I wote that
  heere

---

133 *Meate tolld in meate*: one meal immediately summoned another

I saw her standing) is become. For further than this place
No footstep is appering. Shee perceyving by the cace
That *Neptunes* gift made well with her, and beeing glad to see
Herself enquyrd for of herself, sayd thus: Who ere you bee
I pray you for to pardon mee. I turned not myne eye
160   A tonesyde ne a toother from this place, but did apply
My labor hard. And that you may the lesser stand in dowt,
So *Neptune* further still the Art and craft I go abowt,
As now a whyle no living Wyght uppon this levell sand
(Myself excepted) neyther man nor woman heere did stand.
Her maister did beleeve her words: and turning backward
        went
His way beguyld: and streight too her native shape was sent.
But when her father did perceyve his daughter for too have
A bodye so transformable, he oftentymes her gave
For monny, but the damzell still escaped, now a Mare ⎫
And now a Cow, and now a Bird, a Hart, a Hynd, or ⎬
170   Hare, ⎥
And ever fed her hungry Syre with undeserved fare. ⎭
But after that the maladie had wasted all the meates
As well of store as that which shee had purchast by hir feates:
Most cursed keytife as he was, with bighting hee did rend ⎫
His flesh, and by diminishing his bodye did intend ⎬
To feede his bodye, till that death did speed his fatall end. ⎭

(1567)

---

156 *cace*: event
160 *A tonesyde ne a toother*: neither to one side, nor to the other

The XV. Bookes of P. Ouidius Naso, entytuled
Metamorphosis 15.66–83, 158–532 [Met. 15.60–74,
143–478] *Pythagoras's sermon*

Heere dwelt a man of *Samos* Ile, who for the hate he had
    To Lordlynesse and Tyranny, though unconstreynd was glad
Too make himself a bannisht man. And though this persone
        werre
Farre distant from the Goddes by site of heaven: yit came he
        neere
To them in mynd. And he by syght of soule and reason
        cleere
Behild the things which nature dooth too fleshly eyes denye.
And when with care most vigilant he had assuredly
Imprinted all things in his hart, he set them openly
Abroade for other folk to lerne. He taught his silent sort
(Which woondred at the heavenly woordes theyr mayster did
10   report)
The first foundation of the world: the cause of every thing:
What nature was: and what was God: whence snow and
        lyghtning spring:
And whither *Jove* or else the wynds in breaking clowdes doo
        thunder:
What shakes the earth: what law the starres doo keepe theyr
        courses under:
And what soever other thing is hid from common sence.
He also is the first that did injoyne an abstinence
To feede of any lyving thing. He also first of all
Spake thus, although ryght lernedly, yit too effect but small:

★

My God *Apollos* temple I will set you open, and
Disclose the woondrous heavens themselves, and make you
20   understand
The Oracles and secrets of the Godly majestye.
Greate things, and such as wit of man could never yit espye,
And such as have beene hidden long, I purpose too descrye.
I mynd too leave the earth, and up among the starres too stye,
I mynd too leave this grosser place, and in the clowdes too
        flye,
And on stowt *Atlas* shoulders strong too rest my self on hye,
And looking downe from heaven on men that wander heere
        and there
In dreadfull feare of death as though they voyd of reason were,
To give them exhortation thus, and playnely too unwynd
30   The whole discourse of destinie as nature hath assignd.
O men amaazd with dread of death, why feare yee *Limbo Styx*,
And other names of vanitie, which are but *Poets* tricks?
And perrills of another world, all false surmysed geere?
For whither fyre or length of tyme consume the bodyes heere,
Yee well may thinke that further harmes they cannot suffer
        more.
For soules are free from death. Howbee't, they leaving
        evermore
Theyr former dwellings, are receyvd and live ageine in new.
For I myself (ryght well in mynd I bear it too be trew)
Was in the tyme of Trojan warre *Euphorbus*, *Panthewes* sonne,
Quyght through whoose hart the deathfull speare of *Menelay*
40   did ronne.
I late ago in *Junos* Church at *Argos* did behold
And knew the target which I in my left hand there did hold.

---

33 *geere*: rubbish   **42** *target*: shield

All things doo chaunge. But nothing sure dooth perrish.
  This same spright
Dooth fleete, and fisking heere and there dooth swiftly take
  his flyght
From one place to another place, and entreth every wyght
Removing out of man too beast, and out of beast too man.
But yit it never perrisheth nor ever perrish can.
And even as supple wax with ease recyveth fygures straunge,
And keepes not ay one shape, ne bydes assured ay from
  chaunge,
50   And yit continueth alwayes wax in substaunce: So I say
The soule is ay the selfsame thing it was, and yit astray
It fleeteth intoo sundry shapes. Therfore lest Godlynesse
Bee vanquisht by outragious lust of belly beastlynesse,
Forbeare (I speake by prophesie) your kinsfolkes ghostes to
  chace
By slaughter: neyther nourish blood with blood in any cace.
And sith on open sea the wynds doo blow my sayles apace,
In all the world there is not that that standeth at a stay.
Things eb and flow, and every shape is made too passe away.
The tyme itself continually is fleeting like a brooke.
For neyther brooke nor lyghtsomme tyme can tarrye still. But
60   looke
As every wave dryves other foorth, and that that commes
  behynd
Bothe thrusteth and is thrust itself: even so the tymes by kynd
Doo fly and follow bothe at once, and evermore renew.
For that that was before is left, and streyght there dooth ensew
Anoother that was never erst. Eche twincling of an eye
Dooth chaunge. Wee see that after day commes nyght and
  darks the sky,
And after nyght the lyghtsum Sunne succeedeth orderly.
Like colour is not in the heaven when all thinges weery lye

At midnyght sound a sleepe, as when the daystarre cleere
    and bryght
Commes foorth uppon his milkwhyght steed. Ageine in
70   other plyght
The morning, *Pallants* daughter fayre the messenger of lyght
Delivereth into *Phebus* handes the world of cleerer hew.
The circle also of the sonne what tyme it ryseth new
And when it setteth, looketh red, but when it mountes most
    hye,
Then lookes it whyght, bycause that there the nature of the
    skye
Is better, and from filthye drosse of earth dooth further flye.
The image also of the Moone, that shyneth ay by nyght,
Is never of one quantitie. For that that giveth lyght
To day, is better than the next that followeth, till the full.
80 And then contrarywyse eche day her lyght away dooth pull.
What? Seest thou not how that the yeere as representing
    playne
The age of man, departes itself in quarters fowre? First bayne
And tender in the spring it is, even like a sucking babe.
Then greene, and voyde of strength, and lush, and foggye is
    the blade,
And cheeres the husbandman with hope. Then all things
    florish gay.
The earth with flowres of sundry hew then seemeth for too
    play,
And vertue small or none to herbes there doth as yit belong.
The yeere from springtyde passing foorth too sommer, wexeth
    strong,
Becommeth lyke a lusty youth. For in our lyfe through out
90 There is no tyme more plentifull, more lusty whote and stout.
Then followeth Harvest when the heate of youth growes
    sumwhat cold,
Rype, meeld, disposed meane betwixt a yoongman and an old,
And sumwhat sprent with grayish heare. Then ugly winter last
Like age steales on with trembling steppes, all bald, or overcast

With shirle thinne heare as wyght as snowe. Our bodies also
    ay
Doo alter still from tyme to tyme, and never stand at stay.
Wee shall not bee the same wee were to day or yisterday.
The day hath beene, wee were but seede and only hope of
    men,
And in our moothers womb wee had our dwelling place as
    then,
Dame Nature put too conning hand and suffred not that
100   wee
Within our moothers streyned womb should ay distressed
    bee,
But brought us out too aire, and from our prison set us free.
The chyld newborne lyes voyd of strength. Within a season
    tho
He wexing fowerfooted lernes like savage beastes to go.
Then sumwhat foltring, and as yit not firme of foote, he
    standes
By getting sumwhat for to help his sinewes in his handes.
From that tyme growing strong and swift, he passeth foorth
    the space
Of youth, and also wearing out his middle age apace,
Through drooping ages steepye path he ronneth out his race.
This age dooth undermyne the strength of former yeeres, and
110   throwes
It downe: Which thing old *Milo* by example planely showes.
For when he sawe those armes of his (which heeretoofore had
    beene
As strong as ever *Hercules* in woorking deadly teene
Of biggest beastes) hang flapping downe, and nought but
    empty skin,
He wept. And *Helen* when shee saw her aged wrincles in

---

95 *shirle*: coarse   **113** *teene*: harm

A glasse, wept also: musing in herself what men had seene,
That by twoo noble princes sonnes shee twyce had ravisht
      beene.
Thou tyme, the eater up of things, and age of spyghtfull
      teene,
Destroy all things. And when that long continuance hath them
      bit,
120   You leysurely by lingring death consume them every whit.
And theis that wee call Elements doo never stand at stay.
The enterchaunging course of them I will before yee lay.
Give heede thertoo. This endlesse world conteynes therin I
      say
Fowre substances of which all things are gendred. Of theis
      fower
The Earth and Water for theyr masse and weyght are sunken
      lower.
The other cowple Aire and Fyre the purer of the twayne
Mount up, and nought can keepe them downe. And though
      there doo remayne
A space between eche one of them: yit every thing is made
Of themsame fowre, and into them at length ageine doo fade.
130   The earth resolving leysurely dooth melt too water sheere,
The water fyned turnes too aire. The aire eeke purged cleere
From grossenesse, spyreth up aloft, and there becommeth fyre.
From thence in order contrary they backe ageine retyre.
Fyre thickening passeth intoo Aire, and Ayer wexing grosse,
Returnes to water: Water eeke congealing intoo drosse,
Becommeth earth. No kind of thing keepes ay his shape and
      hew.
For nature loving ever chaunge repayres one shape a new
Uppon another, neyther dooth there perrish aught (trust
      mee)
In all the world, but altring takes new shape. For that which
      wee
140   Doo terme by name of being borne, is for too gin too bee

Another thing than that it was: And likewise for too dye,
Too cease too be the thing it was. And though that varyably
Things passe perchaunce from place too place: yit all from
        whence they came
Returning, doo unperrished continew still the same.
But as for in one shape, bee sure that nothing long can last.
Even so the ages of the world from gold too Iron past;
Even so have places oftentymes exchaunged theyr estate.
For I have seene it sea which was substanciall ground alate,
Ageine where sea was, I have seene the same become dry lond,
150   And shelles and scales of Seafish farre have lyen from any
        strond,
And in the toppes of mountaynes hygh old Anchors have
        beene found.
Deepe valleyes have by watershotte beene made of levell
        ground,
And hilles by force of gulling oft have intoo sea beene worne.
Hard gravell ground is sumtyme seene where marris was
        beforne,
And that that erst did suffer drowght, becommeth standing
        lakes.
Heere nature sendeth new springs out, and there the old in
        takes.
Full many rivers in the world through earthquakes heretoofore
Have eyther chaungd theyr former course, or dryde and ronne
        no more.
Soo *Lycus* beeing swallowed up by gaping of the ground,
160   A greatway of fro thence is in another channell found.
Even so the river *Erasine* among the feeldes of *Arge*
Sinkes onewhyle, and another whyle ronnes great ageine at
        large.
Caycus also of the land of *Mysia* (as men say)
Misliking of his former head, ronnes now another way.
In *Sicill* also *Amesene* ronnes sumtyme full and hye,
And sumtyme stopping up his spring, he makes his chanell
        drye.

Men drank the waters of the brooke *Anigrus* heretoofore,
Which now is such that men abhorre too towche them any
    more.
Which commes to passe (onlesse wee will discredit Poets
    quyght)
170 Bycause the *Centaures* vanquisshed by *Hercules* in fyght
Did wash theyr woundes in that same brooke. But dooth not
        Hypanis
That springeth in the Scythian hilles, which at his fountaine is
Ryght pleasant, afterward becomme of brackish bitter taste?
Antissa, and *Phenycian Tyre*, and *Pharos* in tyme past
Were compast all about with waves, but none of all theis three
Is now an Ile. Ageine the towne of *Lewcas* once was free
From sea, and in the auncient tyme was joyned too the land,
But now environd round about with water it dooth stand.
Men say that *Sicill* also hath beene joyned to *Italy*,
180 Untill the sea consumde the bounds beetweene, and did supply
The roome with water. If yee goo to seeke for *Helicee*
And *Burye*, which were Cities of *Achaia*, you shall see
Them hidden under water, and the shipmen yit doo showe
The walles and steeples of the townes drownd under as they
        rowe.
Not farre from *Pitthey Troyzen* is a certeine hygh ground found
All voyd of trees, which heeretoofore was playne and levell
        ground,
But now a mountayne: For the wyndes (a woondrous thing
        too say)
Inclosed in the hollow caves of ground, and seeking way
To passe therefro, in struggling long to get the open skye, ⎫
In vayne (bycause in all the cave there was no vent   ⎪
190   wherby   ⎬
Too issue out) did stretch the ground and make it swell on ⎪
        hye,   ⎭
As dooth a bladder that is blowen by mouth, or as the skinne
Of horned Goate in bottlewyse when wynd is gotten in.

The swelling of the foresayd place remaynes at this day
    still,
And by continuance waxing hard is growen a pretye hill.
Of many things that come to mynd by heersay, and by
    skill
Of good experience, I a fewe will utter to you mo.
What? dooth not water in his shapes chaunge straungely too
    and fro?
The well of horned *Hammon* is at noonetyde passing cold,
At morne and even it wexeth warme. At midnyght none can
200   hold
His hand therin for passing heate. The well of *Athamane*
Is sayd too kindle woode what tyme the moone is in the wane.
The *Cicons* have a certeine streame which beeing droonke
    dooth bring
Mennes bowwelles intoo Marble hard: and whatsoever thing
Is towcht therwith, it turnes to stone. And by your bounds
    behold
The rivers *Crathe* and *Sybaris* make yellow heare like gold
And Amber. There are also springs (which thing is farre more
    straunge)
Which not the bodye only, but the mynd doo also chaunge.
Whoo hath not hard of *Salmacis* that fowle and filthye sink?
210 Or of the lake of *Aethyop*, which if a man doo drink,
He eyther ronneth mad, or else with woondrous drowzinesse
Forgoeth quyght his memorie. Whoo ever dooth represse
His thirst with drawght of *Clitor* well, hates wyne, and dooth
    delyght
In only water: eyther for bycause there is a myght
Contrary untoo warming wyne by nature in the well,
Or else bycause (for so the folk of *Arcadye* doo tell)
Melampus Amythaons sonne (when he delivered had

---

203 *Cicons*: Thracian tribes

King *Prætus* daughters by his charmes and herbes from being
    mad),
Cast intoo that same water all the baggage wherewithall
220   He purdgd the madnesse of theyr mynds. And so it did befall
That lothsomnesse of wyne did in those waters ay remayne.
Ageine in *Lyncest* contrarie effect too this dooth reigne.
For whoo so drinkes too much therof, he reeleth here and
    there,
As if by quaffing wyne no whyt alayd he droonken were.
There is a Lake in *Arcadye* which *Pheney* men did name
In auncient tyme, whose dowtfulnesse deserveth justly
    blame.
A nyght tymes take thou heede of it, for if thou taste the
    same
A nyghttymes, it will hurt, but if thou drink it in the day
It hurteth not. Thus lakes and streames (as well perceyve yee
    may)
230   Have divers powers and diversly. Even so the tyme hath beene
That *Delos* which stands stedfast now, on waves was floting
    seene.
And Galyes have beene sore afrayd of frusshing by the Iles
Symplegads which toogither dasht upon the sea erewhyles,
But now doo stand unmovable ageinst bothe wynde and tyde.
Mount *Aetna* with his burning Oovens of brimstone shall not
    byde
Ay fyrye: neyther was it so for ever erst. For wither
The earth a living creature bee, and that to breathe out hither
And thither flame, great store of vents it have in sundry places,
And that it have the powre too shift those vents in divers caces,
Now damming theis, now opening those, in moving too and
240   fro;
Or that the whisking wynds restreynd within the earth bylowe,

---

232 *Galyes*: ships, galleys; *frusshing*: striking, running aground

Doo beate the stones ageinst the stones, and other kynd of
  stuffe
Of fyrye nature, which doo fall on fyre with every puffe;
Assoone as those same wynds doo cease, the caves shall streight
  bee cold.
Or if it bee a Rozen mowld that soone of fyre takes hold,
Or brimstone mixt with clayish soyle on fyre dooth lyghtly
  fall:
Undowtedly assoone as that same soyle consumed shall
No longer yeeld the fatty foode to feede the fyre withall,
And ravening nature shall forgo her woonted nourishment,
Then being able too abyde no longer famishment,
For want of sustenance it shall cease his burning. I doo fynd
By fame, that under *Charlsis* wayne in *Pallene* are a kynd
Of people which by dyving thryce three tymes in *Triton* lake
Becomme all fethred, and the shape of birdes upon them take.
The *Scythian* witches also are reported for to doo
The selfsame thing (but hardly I give credit therunto)
By smearing poyson over all theyr bodyes. But (and if
A man too matters tryde by proof may saufly give beleef),
Wee see how flesh by lying still a whyle and ketching heate
Dooth turne too little living beastes. And yit a further feate,
Go kill an Ox and burye him, (the thing by proof man sees)
And of his rotten flesh will breede the flower gathering Bees,
Which as theyr father did before, love feeldes exceedingly,
And unto woork in hope of gayne theyr busye limbes apply.
The Hornet is engendred of a lusty buryed Steede.
Go pull away the cleas from Crabbes that in the sea doo
  breede,
And burye all the rest in mowld, and of the same will spring
A Scorpion which with writhen tayle will threaten for too
  sting.
The Caterpillers of the feelde the which are woont too weave

250

260

---

266 *cleas*: claws

Hore filmes uppon the leaves of trees, theyr former nature
270   leave,
(Which thing is knowen too husbandmen) and turne to
        Butterflyes.
The mud hath in it certeine seede wherof greene frosshes ryse.
And first it brings them footlesse foorth. Then after, it dooth
        frame
Legges apt to swim: and furthermore of purpose that the same
May serve them for too leape afarre, theyr hinder part is mych
More longer than theyr forepart is. The Bearwhelp also which
The Beare hath newly littred, is no whelp immediately,   ⎫
But like an evill favored lump of flesh alyve dooth lye.   ⎬
The dam by licking shapeth out his members orderly   ⎭
280   Of such a syse, as such a peece is able to conceyve.
Or marke yee not the Bees, of whom our hony wee receyve,
How that theyr yoong ones which doo lye within the
        sixsquare wax
Are limblesse bodyes at the first, and after as they wex
In processe take bothe feete and wings. What man would think
        it trew
That Ladye *Venus* simple birdes the Dooves of silver hew,
Or *Junos* bird that in his tayle beares starres, or *Joves* stowt
        knyght
The Earne, and every other fowle of whatsoever flyght,
Could all be hatched out of egges, onlesse he did it knowe?
Sum folk doo hold opinion when the backebone which dooth
        growe
290   In man, is rotten in the grave, the pith becommes a snake.
Howbeete of other things all theis their fyrst beginning take.
One bird there is that dooth renew itself and as it were
Beget it self continually. The Syrians name it there
A *Phœnix*. Neyther corne nor herbes this *Phœnix* liveth by,
But by the jewce of frankincence and gum of *Amomye*.

And when that of his lyfe well full fyve hundred yeeres are
    past,
Upon a Holmetree or uppon a Date tree at the last
He makes him with his talants and his hardened bill a nest:
Which when that he with Casia sweete and Nardus soft
    hathe drest,
300 And strowed it with Cynnamom and Myrrha of the best,
He rucketh downe uppon the same, and in the spyces dyes.
Soone after, of the fathers corce men say there dooth aryse
Another little *Phœnix* which as many yeeres must live
As did his father. He (assoone as age dooth strength him give
Too beare the burthen) from the tree the weyghty nest dooth
    lift,
And godlyly his cradle thence and fathers herce dooth shift.
And flying through the suttle aire he gettes too *Phebus* towne,
And there before the temple doore dooth lay his burthen
    downe.
But if that any noveltye woorth woondring bee in theis,
310 Much rather may we woonder at the *Hyen* if we please.
To see how interchaungeably it one whyle dooth remayne
A female, and another whyle becommeth male againe.
The creature also which dooth live by only aire and
    wynd,
All colours that it leaneth to dooth counterfet by kynd.
The Grapegod *Bacchus*, when he had subdewd the land of
    Inde,
Did fynd a spotted beast cald *Lynx*, whoose urine (by report)
By towching of the open aire congealeth in such sort,
As that it dooth becomme a stone. So Corall (which as long
As water hydes it is a shrub and soft) becommeth strong

---

297 *Holmetree*: oak   **301** *rucketh*: nestles   **310** *Hyen*: hyena

And hard assoone as it dooth towch the ayre. The day
    would end,

320

And *Phebus* panting steedes should in the *Ocean* deepe
    descend,

Before all alterations I in woordes could comprehend.

So see wee all things chaungeable. One nation gathereth
    strength,

Another wexeth weake, and bothe doo make exchaunge at
    length.

So Troy which once was great and strong as well in welth as
    men,

And able tenne yeeres space too spare such store of blood as
    then,

Now beeing bace hath nothing left of all her welth too
    showe,

Save ruines of the auncient woorkes which grasse dooth
    overgrowe,

And tumbes wherin theyr auncetours lye buryed on a rowe.

330

Once *Sparta* was a famous towne: Great *Mycene* flourisht trim:

Bothe *Athens* and *Amphions* towres in honor once did swim.

A pelting plot is *Sparta* now: great Mycene lyes on ground.

Of *Theab* the towne of *Oedipus* what have we more than
    sound?

Of *Athens*, king *Pandions* towne what resteth more than name?

Now also of the race of *Troy* is rysing (so sayeth fame)

The Citie *Roome*, which at the bank of *Tyber* that dooth ronne

Downe from the hill of *Appennyne* already hath begonne

With great advysement for to lay foundation of her state.

This towne then chaungeth by increase the forme it had alate,

340

And of the universall world in tyme to comme shall hold

The sovereintye, so prophesies and lotts (men say) have told.

And as (I doo remember mee) what tyme that *Troy* decayd,

The prophet *Helen Priams* sonne theis woordes ensewing sayd

---

343 *Helen*: Helenus (cf. *Aeneid* 3.374–462)

Before *Aenæas* dowting of his lyfe in weeping plyght:

O Goddesse sonne, beleeve mee (if thou think I have foresyght

Of things too comme) *Troy* shalnot quyght decay whyle thou
    doost live.

Bothe fyre and swoord shall unto thee thy passage freely give.

Thou must from hence: and *Troy* with thee convey away in
    haste,

Untill that bothe thyself and *Troy* in forreine land bee plaast

350 More freendly than thy native soyle. Moreover I foresee,

A Citie by the offspring of the Trojans buylt shall bee,

So great as never in the world the lyke was seene before ⎤

Nor is this present, neyther shall be seene for evermore. ⎬

A number of most noble peeres for manye yeeres afore ⎦

Shall make it strong and puyssant: but hee that shall it make

The sovereine Ladye of the world, by ryght descent shall take

His first beginning from thy sonne the little *Iule*. And when

The earth hathe had her tyme of him, the sky and welkin then

Shall have him up for evermore, and heaven shall bee his end.

360 Thus farre (I well remember mee) did *Helens* woordes extend

To good *Aenæas*. And it is a pleasure untoo mee

The Citie of my countrymen increasing thus to see,

And that the Grecians victorie becommes the Trojans weale.

But least forgetting quyght themselves our horses happe to
    steale

Beyond the mark: the heaven and all that under heaven is
    found,

Dooth alter shape. So dooth the ground and all that is in
    ground.

And wee that of the world are part (considring how wee bee

Not only flesh, but also sowles, which may with passage free

Remove them into every kynd of beast both tame and wyld)

370 Let live in saufty honestly with slaughter undefyld,

The bodyes which perchaunce may have the spirits of our
    brothers,

Our sisters, or our parents, or the spirits of sum others

Alyed too us eyther by sum freendshippe or sum kin,
Or at the least the soules of men abyding them within.
And let us not *Thyestes*lyke thus furnish up our boordes
With bloodye bowells. Oh how leawd example he avoordes?
How wickedly prepareth he himself too murther man
That with a cruell knyfe dooth cut the throte of Calf, and
    can
Unmovably give heering to the lowing of the dam,
380 Or sticke the kid that wayleth lyke the little babe, or eate
The fowle that he himself before had often fed with meate?
What wants of utter wickednesse in woorking such a feate?
What may he after passe too doo? well eyther let your steeres
Weare out themselves with woork, or else impute theyr death
    to yeeres.
Ageinst the wynd and weather cold let Wethers yeeld yee
    cotes,
And udders full of batling milk receyve yee of the Goates.
Away with sprindges, snares, and ginnes, away with Risp and
    net,
Away with guyleful feates: for fowles no lymetwiggs see yee
    set.
No feared fethers pitche yee up to keepe the Reddeere in,
390 Ne with deceytfull bayted hooke seeke fishes for to win.
If awght doo harme, destroy it, but destroyt and doo no more.
Forbeare the flesh, and feede your mouthes with fitter foode
    therfore.

(1567)

---

375 *boordes*: tables   **376** *avoordes*: affords   **386** *batling*: nourishing
387 *Risp*: lime twig

The XV. Bookes of P. Ouidius Naso, entytuled
Metamorphosis 15.984–95 [Met. 15.869–78] *Epilogue*

Now have I brought a woork to end which neither *Joves*
   feerce wrath,
Nor swoord, nor fyre, nor freating age with all the force it
   hath
Are able too abolish quyght. Let comme that fatall howre
Which (saving of this brittle flesh) hath over mee no powre,
And at his pleasure make an end of myne uncerteyne tyme.
Yit shall the better part of mee assured bee to clyme
Aloft above the starry skye. And all the world shall never
Be able for to quench my name. For looke how farre so ever
The Romane Empyre by the ryght of conquest shall extend,
So farre shall all folke reade this woork. And tyme without all
10   end
(If Poets as by prophesie about the truth may ame)
My lyfe shall everlastingly bee lengthened still by fame.   (1567)

GEORGE TURBERVILE
(*c.* 1540–1610)

Turbervile's office as secretary to Elizabeth's ambassador Thomas Ran-
dolph took him as far afield as Russia. At home, his scholarly and literary
accomplishments won considerable respect. His chief volume of original
verse, the *Epitaphs, Epigrams, Songs and Sonnets*, was released in 1567,
the same year as his complete translation of the *Heroides*. Although
Turbervile's metrical achievement in the translations is uneven, his
mastery of a homely, colloquial diction often imparts a quiet but firm
dignity to the rhetoric, true to Ovid's original. In his version of Oenone's
bitter address to her faithless lover Paris, Turbervile turns in his consist-
ently strongest performance. In his 'Notes on Elizabethan Classicists',

Ezra Pound remarked of the translation that 'The pastoral note is at least not unpleasing, and the story more real than in the mouths of the later poets'.

The Heroycall Epistles of the Learned Poet Publius Ovidius Naso, The Fift Epistle: Oenone to Parris [Her. 5]

To Paris that was once her owne, though now it be not so,
From Ida, Oenon greeting sendes as these her Letters show.
May not thy novell wyfe endure that thou my Pistle reade?
That they with Grecian fist were wrought thou needst not
    stand in dread.
Pegasian Nymph renound in Troy Oenone hight by name,
Of thee, (that art mine owne) complaine if thou permit the
    same.
What froward God doth seeke to barre Oenone to be thine?
Or by what guilt have I deservde that Parris should decline?
Take paciently deserved woe and never grutch at all:
10   But undeserved wronges wyll greeve, a woman at the gall.
Scarce were thou of so noble fame, as flatly doth appeare:
When I (the offspring of a floud) did choose thee for my
    Feere.
And thou who now art Priams sonne: (all reverence layd apart)
Were tho a Hiard to behold when first thou wanst my hart.
How oft have we in shaddow layne, whilst hungry flocks have
    fed?
How oft have we of grasse and groaves, prepard a homely bed?
How oft on simple stacks of straw and bennet did we rest?
How oft the dew and foggie mist our lodging hath opprest?

---

14 *Hiard*: haynyarde, a low-born wretch. At the time of their meeting, Paris was a mere shepherd, not yet aware of his royal patrimony.

Who first discoverd thee the holtes and Lawndes of lurcking
    game?
Who first displaid thee where the whelps lay sucking of their
20   Dame?
I sundry times have holpe to pitch thy toyles for want of ayde
And forst thy houndes to climbe the hils that gladly would
    have stayd.
The boysteous Beech Oenons name in outward barke doth
    beare:
And with thy carving knife is cut Oenon every where.
And as the trees in time doo waxe so doth increase my name:
Go to, grow on, erect your selves, helpe to advaunce my fame.
There growes (I mind it very well) upon a bancke, a tree
Whereon there doth a fresh recorde and will remaine of mee.
Live long thou happy tree, I say, that on the brinck dost
    stande:
30 And hast ingraved in thy barcke these words, with Paris hand.
When pastor Paris shall revolt and Oenons love forgoe:
Then Xanthus waters shall recoyle, and to their fountains floe.
Now River backward bend thy course, let Xanthus streame
    retier:
For Paris hath renownst the Nymph and proovde himself a
    lier.
That cursed day bred all my dole, the winter of my joy,
With clowdes of froward fortune fraught, procurde me this
    annoy:
When cankred crafty Juno came with Venus, (Nurce of love)
And Pallas eke, that warlike wench, their beauties pride to
    proove.
No sooner heard I of that hap which thou thy selfe didst tell
But streight through all my quivering bones a trembling feare
40   there fell.
And plunged all in doubtfull dreade, of aged folkes I sought
What might this gastly matter meane: some haynous thing they
    thought.

Then with a trice the trees were cut, the timber went to
    wracke:
And tallowed Keeles did forrow seas and made the cables
    cracke.
At parture saltish teares were shed thou canst but say the same:
In fayth this latter love of thine deserves the greater shame.
Then showres of brackish brine began of eyther side to rayne:
And both repleate with greefe alike at parture gan to plaine.
Not Bacchus braunches so imbrace, ne limber limmes of vine
50   Environ that whereof it growes as thou this necke of mine.
How often were thou wroth with windes when windes did
    serve thee well?
Thy journey mates began to smyle when they thy sleights did
    smell.
How oft didst thou me sweetely kisse and then unkisse again?
How did thy (last adue) procure thy foltring tongue to payne?
With wished wind thy sayles were stuft that hung upon thy
    Mast:
The waters waxt as greene as grasse the Oares went on so fast.
With sight as long as sight would serve thy Barcke I did
    pursue,
And when mine eye might see no more, my hart began to rue.
To greene Neriedes I did sue that thou mightst soone retire:
60   And I (to further this my wo) thy gainecome did desire.
Whose comming is to others use procured by my sute:
(Alas) of all my travayling toyle a harlot hath the fruite.
A huge and haughty hill there is that gapes into the flodde,
Repelling all the waltring waves, that beate his bancke a good.
From thence I tooke my prime prospect and knew full well
    thy ship:
A sodaine joy well nigh hath made me from the Mount to
    skyp.

---

59 *Neriedes*: sea goddesses   **60** *gainecome*: return

But whilst I stayde I sawe in toppe a purple banner shine:
Which colours made me sore adradde, I knew they were not
    thine.
The ship that slacked not to sayle came by and by to shore,
70   With quaking heart I sawe a Lasse I never knewe before.
Ne yet could that perdie suffice, (but wherefore made I stay)
The hatefull harlot out of hand her manners did display.
Then mourning gan I rent my Robes, than beate I on my
    brest:
And with unfreendly fist my face in waylfull wyse was drest.
My yelling clamors Ida heard, and witnest all my woe:
I carred thither to my Cotte my teares that fell as snow.
So graunt ye Gods that Helen rue and spoyled of her Make,
Of these my greefes procurd by her, the greatest share may
    take.
Now hast thou brought them home by Seas, and over wandred
    waves:
That have their loyall husbands fledde, and left as loathsome
80   slaves.
But when thou were in vile estate and led a Hiards life:
Poore Paris had but Oenon tho to his approoved wife.
I am not she that wayes thy wealth thy Pallace mooves me
    nought:
Ne to be Priam's daughter I by earnest sute have sought.
Yet needelesse is that Priam should of such a daughter shame:
What should procure olde Hecuba, to blush to be my Dame?
I well deservde, and very faine a Princes spouse would be:
A Scepter would beseeme my hande and passing well agree.
Though I with thee in open holte amid the sedge were seene:
90   Disdaine me not, a purple bed were fitter for a Queene.
In fine my love is voyde of dread thou needst not warre at all:
Revenger ships are not in sight to sacke the Trojan wall.

---

71 *perdie*: indeed

But hatefull Helen is requird with wreakfull warre againe:
This is a dainty dowre indeed where bloodshed is the gaine.
Aske Hectors counsell in this case where thou shouldst her
    restore:
Deiphobus, Polydamus, with other Trojans more.
Let sage Antenors tale be heard, let Priam give advise:
For they by long expence of yeeres have gotten to be wise.
It is a shamefull thing indeede, a strumpet to prefarre:
The goodnesse of thy cause appeares, the Greekes doo justly
100   warre.
Mayst thou assure her to be true or ought in her affie,
Whom thou so quickly wanst with words and made her
    countrie flie?
As young Atrides doth lament and sorrow this his fate,
And takes in greefe a straunger shoulde enjoy his wedded
    Mate.
So Paris shall in processe proove, and sweare that gaged faith
Once falsed, may not be restord till life doe end by death.
Put case she loves thee (Paris) well, so did shee love the
    Greeke:
But now the silly man is sole, his Helen is to seeke.
Thrise happy was sir Hectors wife, her luck was passing good;
Thou shouldst have followde Hectors trade and to thy bargaine
110   stoode.
More light art thou then partched leaves when suck and sap is
    lost,
That with the wind for want of weight from place to place are
    tost.
In thee lesse surety to be found, then weight in bearde of
    Wheate,
That is surprizde with sunnie rayes and Phœbus fervent heate.

---

101 *affie*: trust

I call to mind thy sisters sawes which tho I tooke as vaine:

The Prophetesse pronownst in proofe that now is passing
plaine.

What madnes makes thee thus inragde to sowe thy seede in
sand?

O Nimph (she said) with bootles plough thou breakst a
barraine land.

A Greekish Hayfer comes to Troy, that both thy Country
soyle

And thee, thy house, (which Gods forefend) wyll bring to utter
120   foyle.

With speede goe sinck that shameful shippe let drowne the
beastly Barcke

That fraughted is with Phrygian blood repleate with Trojan
carcke.

No sooner had this Sibyll sayd, her Vassels thought her wood:

But with quacking feare was rapt, my hayre erected stoode.

Thy words (Cassandra) were of weight thou art a Sibyll true:

The hayfer leaps within my leaze that makes my heart to rue.

Surpassing though her beauty be dishonest is her life,

That leaves her Country Gods, and is, become a straungers
wyfe.

Once was she earst away convayde, from Greece by Theseus
theft:

130   I wote not by what Theseus, but by Theseus was she reft.

Might she with Maydenheade make retyre from such a wanton
guest?

No, no, I know the trade of love as well as doth the best.

Well, pose it to be rape and stealth, so cloake the crime with
name,

Yet she that was so often wrongde assented to the same.

---

115 *sisters sawes*: Cassandra's prophecies   **119** *Hayfer*: heifer, i.e. Helen

Oenon never swarvde her hest though Paris were unjust:
Of right thou shouldst have beene beguilde, in whom was
    slender trust.
Sage, swift, and seemely Satyrs woulde, with me beene
    coupled faine,
Whom they in leavie woods have sought, with great and
    grieffull paine.
The fonded Faunus oft in Ide my freendshyp did request:
Whose head with hurtlesse hornes, and bowes of Pine was
140   bravely drest.
The faythfull Phœbus (Trojans trust and rampire) lovde me
    well:
Untill such time my daintie fruit unto sir Phœbus fell,
And that by force: in proofe wherof, I rent his golden heare,
And scratcht his face with froward fist, the signes as yet
    appeare.
No jewels I, ne Gemmes receivde for filthy lurkers hyre:
T'is beastly so t'ingage the corps for greedie mucks desire.
He deemde it recompence enough, hys Phisicke to bestow:
My skillesse hand and barraine skull he taught his Art to
    knowe.
What hearbe soever were of powre or vertue to recure,
150 To learne his force and lurcking might I could my selfe assure.
Aye me, the most unhappy wenche, unluckiest under Sunne:
Though I in Phisick have good sight by love my skill is
    wunne.
Apollo Physick that devisde Admetus flocke did feede:
And had his godly brest incent with Oenons partching gleede.
But Paris wotst thou what? the health that neither hearbes may
    lende
Ne Gods may graunt, thy friendly fist at once to me may send.

---

141 *rampire*: rampart, defender   **145** *lurkers*: secret mistress, 'kept' woman
146 *mucks*: money, profit
153 In Turbervile's embellishment, it was during his imposed servitude to Admetus
– a punishment from Jupiter – that Apollo encountered and raped Oenone.
154 *gleede*: fire

Thou canst and I have well deservde, take mercy of a Mayde:
I come not like a Greekish foe, Atrides powre to ayde.
But thine I am and from thy youth thy lover have I beene:
And wilt (whilst lunges shall lende mee breath) thy faithful
160   friend be seene.
                                        (1567)

THOMAS UNDERDOWNE
(*fl.* 1566–1587)

Thomas Underdowne's reputation as one of his age's great translators
rests mainly upon his version of Heliodorus's Greek prose romance,
the *Aethiopica*, published in 1569. That same year, Underdown also
translated *Ibis*, the invective Ovid penned from his exile in the 'frosen
Zone' of Tomis. (In antiquity, the ibis was considered to be a particularly
vile bird; the Greek poet Callimachus had used the insult in one of
his invectives, and Ovid follows his lead.) This minor poem's dense
allusiveness appealed to Underdown's antiquarian interests, and his text
is broken throughout by lengthy prose explications. Underdowne
manages his fourteeners with exemplary restraint, to achieve the first
line-for-line English rendition of Ovid's Latin.

Ouid his inuectiue against Ibis, 1–14, 95–132, 147–64, 639–44 [Ibis 1–14, 95–134, 145–62, 639–44]

Whole fifty years be gone & past since I a lyue haue been:
Yet of my Muse ere now there hath no armed verse be seen.
Among so many thousand works, yet extant to be had:
No bloody letter can be red, that euer *Naso* made.

---

157 *canst and*: know if
158 *Atrides*: Helen's husband Menelaus and (by extension) the Greek host
4 *Naso*: Ovid

Nor yet no man (set me a side) my bookes haue caus'd to
    smart:
Syth I my selfe am cast away, by my inuented arte.
One man there is that wyll not let, (this is a greuous payne)
The tytle of my curteyse verse, for euer to remaine.
What so he be, as yet his name, shall not by me be wrayde:
Who me constraynes to take in hand, No weapens erst assayde.
He will not let me scent almost, vnto the frosen *Zone*:
In banishment take restles ease, and there to ly vnknowne.
That cruel man doth vexe my wounds, that seeke for needefull
    rest:
And sclanderous wordes doth vtter oft, Where great resort is
    prest.

★

I him do curse, who knoweth well, what meaneth *Ibis* name:
Whose conscience knoweth wel that he deserued hath the
    same.
Without delay I redy prest, my cawses wyl pursue:
Who so art at my sacrifice, doe it with silence vew.
Who so art at this sacrifice, doe dolefully lament:
And goe to *Ibis*, all thy cheekes, with moisty teares besprent.
With all yll lucke that may befall, with lefte feete meete him
    sone:
Let vestures blacke your bodyes hide, as is of mourners done.
And thou why dost thou doute to take thy deathlike bandes of
    force?
Now standes the Altar (as thou seest) prepared for thy corse.
Let no delayes my banning stay, pompe is prepard for thee:
A cursed sacrifice thy throte vnto my kniues apply.
Let th'earth deny thee fruit, and stream his waters holde from
    thee:
Let euery winde deny fitte blastes, for thy commoditie.

---

25 *banning*: cursing

Let not the Sun shine bright on thee, nor glistering Moone by
    night:
30 And of thy eyes let glimsing starres, forsake the wished sight.
Let not the fire graunt thee his heate, nor Ayre humiditie:
Let neither earth nor yet the Sea, free passage graunt to thee.
That banyshed and poore thou mayst, straunge houses seeke in
    vayne:
That crauing to, with trembling voyce small almes mayst
    obtayne.
That neither sownd of body, nor thy mynde in perfect plight:
This night be worse then passed day, and next day than this
    night.
That thou mayst still be pitifull, but pited of none:
And that no man nor woman may, for thy mischaunces mone.
And that thy teares may hatred moue, thou iudged worthy to:
On whom (though many mischiefes light) yet worthy many
40   mo.
And that, that seldome comes to passe, I wishe thy whole
    estate:
All wonted fauour for to want, and be replete with hate.
And that thou want no cause of death, but mayst be voyde of
    powre:
And that thy lyfe be forste to flye, of death the wished houre.
And that thy soule with troubles tost, constrayned styl to stay:
May leaue thy wery limmes at length, tormanted with delay.
It shal be so, and *Phebus* to, that this in force should stande:
Did geue a signe, a dolfull byrde, did fly on my left hande.
And sure I thinke that what I wish, the Gods on high shal
    moue:
I will (O wretch) be fedde with Hope, till death thee hence
50   remoue.
Hereof shal that day make an ende, that shal thee take from
    me:
Hereof shall that day make an ende, that comes to late to me.

★

Whether I by yeares consumed long, (which I would not) shall
dye:

Or else shal be by force of hand, resolued by and by.

Or whether tost amyd the Seas, shall suffer wrack with
greefe:

And Fyshes strange vpon my corse, shall seeke to fynde
releefe.

Or whether that the Rauens shall, make of my fleshe theire
foode:

Or greedy Wolues shal haue their lyps embrewed with my
blood.

Or whether some may wel vouchsafe, me vnder ground to
laye:

60 Or cast me into flaming fyre, When lyfe is gone away.

What so I bee, I mynde to come from Hell, that vgly place:

And then with colde (reuenging) hands, will scratch thee by
the face.

Thou waking shalt me see, with gostes, my selfe Ile secret
keepe:

Then wyll I seeme t'appeare too thee, to wake thee from thy
sleepe.

And last what so thou dost, before thy face and eyes, Ile
flee:

And wyll complaine so that no where, in quiet thou shalt
bee.

The cruell strokes wherewith I wyll thee smyte, shal sownd
againe:

And hellish brandes before thee styll, shall smoke vnto thy
payne.

Alyue the furyes shall thee vexe, and after Death also:

70 So that thy lyfe shall shorter be, then either payne or wo.

★

These things in soddain mode thus pend to thee directed be:
That thou neede not complayne that I vnmindefull am of
    thee.
They are but few, I graunt, but God can geue my prayers
    more,
And with his fauour my requestes can multiply with store.
Hereafter thou much more shalt reade wherein shal be thy
    name:
And in such verse as men are wont such cruell warres to
    frame.

(1569)

THOMAS CHURCHYARD
(c. 1520–1604)

The prestige and popularity enjoyed by the fourteener couplet throughout the 1560s had by the beginning of the next decade decidedly
run their course. The minor poet and translator Thomas Churchyard
presents us with what is perhaps the final breath of an exhausted form.
A hanger-on at court, Churchyard has often been reviled as a sycophant,
and some speculate that his temperament was naturally drawn to what
many regard (unfairly) as the distastefully obsequious cast of Ovid's
exile poetry. He was, in any case, the first to take on the *Tristia*. Despite
the grim syntactical contortions to which he is prone, Churchyard
reaches out to the sombre earnestness of Ovid's retrospective counsel.
In this, he at least matches the efforts of those who will take on these
verses in the next century. The translation first appeared in 1572; the
following text comes from the 1578 edition.

The Three first Bookes of Ouid de Tristibus [Trist.
3.4] *To his frend, that he should eschew the companie of great men*

O Deare in deede alwayes to mee, but in this time distrest,
Now trusty tryde since myne estate, so sore hath lyed opprest,
If ought thou doe thy frend beleue, wel taught by practise
    proofe,
Lyue to thy selfe, from haughtie names, of might, flye thou
    aloofe.
Liue to thy selfe, and for thy power, great noblenesse eschew,
Right noble is the Castle whence, this cruel lightning flewe.
For though in handes of mightie men, to helpe alone it lyes,
They do not helpe, but rather hurt, in worsest wicked wyse.
The ship whose sayle is stricken lowe, escapes the stormy blast.
10   But slackye sayle and broad extent, more feare then lesser cast.
Thou seest how Corke with little waight, on top of water
    fleetes,
When heauy loade through paise, it selfe, and nets in bottom
    weetes.
If I my selfe these warninges with, had warned bene or this,
The towne where right doth wil me dwel, perhaps I should
    not mis.
Whilst yet with thee I dwelt, and whilst the pypeling wynde
    be put,
This boate of myne, through calmy seas, her quiet way she cut.
Who falleth on euen ground (as scant, the same doth euer
    chaunce,)
So falles as when to earth it comes, may vp agayne aduaunce.

---

12 The sense is that, under their own weight, the heavy nets sink to the bottom.
15 *the pypeling wynde be put*: the shrill wind was still

But that poore soule *Elpenor* fel, a downe from height of Hall,
20   Whose mourneful spyrite his king vnto, appeared after fall.
What ment it then that *Dedalus*, his winges could slicker safe?
And *Icarus* to largie seas, his name assyned gafe.
Forsooth because aloft this one: that other flew below,
For both of them did others winges, their sides vpon bestow.
Beleeue me this who hidden wel: hath lurkt he lyueth wel,
And eche man ought within his lot, to him appoynted dwel.
Eumenides should not, bene Childles, if his foolish sonne,
Had not so much desired on, *Achilles* horse to runne.
And *Merops* if to *Phaeton,* he Father stil had bene,
His Sonne in fyre, his Daughters, and in trees should not haue
30   seene.
So thou likewise for euer feare, to lofty matters hye,
And draw together I the pray, the sayles of purpose nye.
For thou wel worthy art foorthwith vnspurned foote to runne,
Thy course of lyfe: and haue thy fate, more fauouablye spunne.
With gentle loue that I should pray, for thee thou doest
        deserue,
And faythful fayth that will from mee, at no time euer swerue.
With countnaunce like my carefull case, I saw thee to lament,
As wel it may beleeued bee, my face did represent.
I saw thy teares with trickling fall, vpon my visage sad,
Which all at once were poured foorth, with trusty wordes thou
40   had.
Now thou also thy Freend remoude, with diligence defendes,
And ils which scant may eased bee, with mitigating mendes.
All voyde of Enuie see thou liue, without renowne dispatch,
Thy yeares in quiet and thy selfe, with equall Frendship match.
And loue the name of *Naso* thine, which thing is yet alone,
Vnbanished remaynes, the rest, in *Scythia* seas be gone.

---

20 For Elpenor's story, cf. *Odyssey* 10.552−60 and 11.51−80.
30 For the story of Dolon, Eumedes's son, cf. *Iliad* 10; for Phaeton, cf. *Met.*
2.1−400.

In land which neerest ioynes to starre, of *Erymanthus* beare,
I byde where Frost congealed hard, the ground with cold do
    teare.
The *Bospher* streame and *Tanais*, with other lakes there bee,
50 In *Scythia* sea and names a few, of place skant knowne to mee.
And eke there is nothing saue cold, which none can saufely
    byde,
Alas how neare the furthest land, approacheth to my syde.
But far away my country is, and far my dearest wyfe,
And what thing els besydes these two, was pleasaunt in my life?
Euen so these thinges be absent as, the same I cannot get,
In body: but in minde they may, be all beholded yet.
Before myne eyes my house and towne, and forme of places
    show,
And euery place together wyth, their deedes I shortly know.
Before myne eyes like as my wife, in present shape appeares,
60 My state she greuous presseth downe, and vp againe she reares.
She absent greeues, but lighter makes, that lasting loue she
    lends,
And heauy charge vppon her laid, she constantly defends.
So you (O frends) full firmely sticke, within my fixed hart,
Whom I desyre to speake vnto, by each mans name apart.
But fainting feare that is beware, my duty due doth let,
And you I thincke vnwilling would, within my verse be set.
Afore you would and did regard, it as thy loue most kind,
That in my verse the Reader might, your names so placed find,
Which thing because is doubtful now, in secret brest eche one,
70 I shall talke with and will because, of quaking feare to none.
Nor in my verse my hidden frends, betraying forth I will,
Expresse: if any priuely, haue loued loue he still.
Know this although in Region farre, is now my resting place,
Wyth all my hart you inwardly, I euermore embrace.
And by such meanes as ech man may, releeue my ils I pray,
Your faithful hand to frend outcast, in grief do not denay.
So prosper fortune unto you, and happy still remayne,
As neuer in like lot the same, to aske ye may be fayne.   (1578)

EDMUND SPENSER (1552–1599)

No writer comes closer to the Ovidian temperament of the *Metamorphoses* than the chief non-dramatic poet of the Elizabethan era, Edmund Spenser. Virtually every movement of *The Faerie Queene*, culminating in the magnificent 'Cantos of Mutability', betrays Ovid's influence, even though Spenser at no point in the poem undertakes expressly to translate his master. His beautiful account of the Garden of Adonis from Book 3, one of the romance-epic's most famous passages, distils the *Metamorphoses*' governing notion in its description of Adonis as one 'eterne in mutabilitie'. In his delightful shorter work, *Muiopotmos*, Spenser follows his Ovidian source more immediately, though even here the poet freely bends the Arachne story to his own poetic purpose.

The Faerie Queene 3.6.44–48 [Met. 10.519–793]
The Garden of Adonis

And in the thickest couert of that shade,
There was a pleasant arbour, not by art,
But of the trees owne inclination made,
Which knitting their rancke braunches part to part,
With wanton yuie twyne entrayld athwart,
And Eglantine, and Caprifole emong,
Fashiond aboue within their inmost part,
That nether *Phœbus* beams could through them throng,
Nor *Aeolus* sharp blast could worke them any wrong.

10   And all about grew euery sort of flowre,
To which sad louers were transformd of yore;
Fresh *Hyacinthus*, *Phœbus* paramoure,
And dearest loue,

---

4 *rancke*: dense

Foolish *Narcisse*, that likes the watry shore,
Sad *Amaranthus*, made a flowre but late,
Sad *Amaranthus*, in whose purple gore
Me seemes I see *Amintas* wretched fate,
To whom sweet Poets verse hath giuen endlesse date.

There wont faire *Venus* often to enioy
20   Her deare *Adonis* ioyous company,
And reape sweet pleasure of the wanton boy;
There yet, some say, in secret he does ly,
Lapped in flowres and pretious spycery,
By her hid from the world, and from the skill
Of *Stygian* Gods, which doe her loue enuy;
But she her selfe, when euer that she will,
Possesseth him, and of his sweetnesse takes her fill.

And sooth it seemes they say: for he may not
For euer die, and euer buried bee
30   In balefull night, where all things are forgot;
All be he subiect to mortalitie,
Yet is eterne in mutabilitie,
And by succession made perpetuall,
Transformed oft, and changed diuerslie:
For him the Father of all formes they call;
Therefore needs mote he liue, that liuing giues to all.

There now he liueth in eternal blis,
Ioying his goddesse, and of her enioyd:
Ne feareth he henceforth that foe of his,
40   Which with his cruell tuske him deadly cloyd:
For that wilde Bore, the which him once annoyd,
She firmely hath emprisoned for ay,
That her sweet loue his malice mote auoyd,
In a strong rocky Caue, which is they say,
Hewen vnderneath that Mount, that none him losen may.

(1590)

Muiopotmos, Or The Fate of the Butterflie, 257–
352 [Met. 6.1–145] *Arachne's competition with Athena*

The cause why he this Flie so maliced,
Was (as in stories it is written found)
For that his mother which him bore and bred,
The most fine-fingred workwoman on ground,
Arachne, by his meanes was vanquished
Of *Pallas*, and in her owne skill confound,
When she with her for excellence contended,
That wrought her shame, and sorrow neuer ended.

For the *Tritonian* Goddesse hauing hard
10 Her blazed fame, which all the world had fil'd,
Came downe to proue the truth, and due reward
For her prais-worthie workmanship to yeild
But the presumptuous Damzel rashly dar'd
The Goddesse selfe to chalenge to the field,
And to compare with her in curious skill
Of workes with loome, with needle, and with quill.

Minerua did the chalenge not refuse,
But deign'd with her the paragon to make:
So to their worke they sit, and each doth chuse
20 What storie she will for her tapet take.
Arachne figur'd how *Ioue* did abuse
Europa like a Bull, and on his backe
Her through the sea did beare; so liuely seene,
That it true Sea, and true Bull ye would weene.

---

9 Tritonian *Goddesse*: Athena   **20** *tapet*: tapestry

She seem'd still backe vnto the land to looke,
And her play-fellowes aide to call, and feare
The dashing of the waues, that vp she tooke
Her daintie feete, and garmants gathered neare:
But (Lord) how she in euerie member shooke,
30   When as the land she saw no more appeare,
But a wilde wildernes of waters deepe:
Then gan she greatly to lament and weepe.

Before the Bull she pictur'd winged Loue,
With his yong brother Sport, light fluttering
Vpon the waues, as each had been a Doue;
The one his bowe and shafts, the other Spring
A burning Teade about his head did moue,
As in their Syres new loue both triumphing:
And manie Nymphes about them flocking round,
40   And manie *Tritons*, which their hornes did sound.

And round about, her worke she did empale
With a faire border wrought of sundrie flowres,
Enwouen with an Yuie winding trayle:
A goodly worke, full fit for Kingly bowres,
Such as Dame *Pallas*, such as Enuie pale,
That al good things with venemous tooth deuowres,
Could not accuse. Then gan the Goddesse bright
Her selfe likewise vnto her worke to dight.

She made the storie of the olde debate,
50   Which she with *Neptune* did for *Athens* trie:
Twelue Gods doo sit around in royall state,
And *Ioue* in midst with awfull Maiestie,
To iudge the strife betweene them stirred late:

---

37 *Teade*: torch

Each of the Gods by his like visnomie
Eathe to be knowen; but *Ioue* aboue them all,
By his great lookes and power Imperiall.

Before them stands the God of Seas in place,
Clayming that sea-coast Citie as his right,
And strikes the rockes with his three-forked mace;
60   Whenceforth issues a warlike steed in sight,
The signe by which he chalengeth the place,
That all the Gods, which saw his wondrous might
Did surely deeme the victorie his due:
But seldome seene, foreiudgement proueth true.

Then to her selfe she giues her *Aegide* shield,
And steelhed speare, and morion on her hedd,
Such as she oft is seene in warlicke field:
Then sets she forth, how with her weapon dredd
She smote the ground, the which streight foorth did yield
70   A fruitfull Olyue tree, with berries spredd,
That all the Gods admir'd; then all the storie
She compast with a wreathe of Olyues hoarie.

Emongst those leaues she made a Butterflie,
With excellent deuice and wondrous slight,
Fluttring among the Oliues wantonly,
That seem'd to liue, so like it was in sight:
The veluet nap which on his wings doth lie,
The silken downe with which his backe is dight,
His broad outstretched hornes, his hayrie thies,
80   His glorious colours, and his glistering eies.

---

54 *visnomie*: visage

Which when *Arachne* saw, as ouerlaid,
And mastered with workmanship so rare,
She stood astonied long, ne ought gainesaid,
And with fast fixed eyes on her did stare,
And by her silence, signe of one dismaid,
The victorie did yeeld her as her share:
Yet did she inly fret, and felly burne,
And all her blood to poysonous rancor turne.

That shortly from the shape of womanhed
90   Such as she was, when *Pallas* she attempted,
She grew to hideous shape of dryrihed,
Pined with griefe of follie late repented:
Eftsoones her white streight legs were altered
To crooked crawling shankes, of marrowe empted,
And her faire face to fowle and loathsome hewe,
And her fine corpes to a bag of venim grewe.   (1590)

ABRAHAM FRAUNCE
(*fl.* 1587–1633)

Abraham Fraunce's keen ear for fine poetry sparked his intimacy with
some of the leading literary talents of his day. His own poetic efforts
offer a fascinating glimpse of the mannered extremes to which the
period's literary experimentation could be taken. The following passage
exemplifies the effort to force English verse into classical poetry's
quantitative metre. The oddities of Fraunce's 'hexameter' lines combine

---

86 In pronouncing Arachne the decided loser of the competition, Spenser departs
significantly from Ovid's account, which stresses Athena's fury at her own inferior
craftsmanship: '*Non illud Pallas, non illud carpere Livor / possit opus*' (*Met.* 6.129–
30: Neither Pallas nor Envy could find fault with [Arachne's] work).

with his startling reiterations and dialect passages to fashion a weirdly attractive version of Ovid's tale.

The Third part of the Countesse of Pembrokes Yuychurch: Entituled, *Amintas Dale* [Met. 2.679–707] *Mercury and Battus*

Once in an eu'ning-tide, whilst *Phœbus* lay in a valley,
And with rurall pipe bestowd himself on a loues-lay,
His sheepe (sheepe indeede, that leant no eare to a loues-lay)
Through *Pylian* pastures chaunst heere and there to be straying.
    Mercury, Ioues prety Page, fine-filcher *Mercury*, saw them,
Caught and brought them away, and kept them close in a
      thicket.
Phœbus knew nothing; for no-bodie saw, but an ould churle,
One ould canckred churle, which there kept *Mares* by the
      mountains,
Called bald *Battus:* whome *Mercury* friendly saluted,
Tooke him apart by the hand, and best perswasion vsed,
Gaue him a lambe for a bribe, and prayd him so to be silent.
Feare not, alas, faire sir, qd *Battus:* it is but a trifle,
Tis but a trick of youth, some stragling sheepe to be taking:
Kings may spare, and lend to the poore: And this very senceles
Stone (and points to a stone) of this fact shalbe reporter
As soone, as *Battus: Ioues Nuntio* gladly retired,
Yet, for a further proofe, both face and fashion altred,
And, as a countrey clowne, to a countrey lowt he returned.
    Gaffer, I misse viue sgore vatt wedders: zawst any vilching
Harlot, roague this way of late? canst tell any tydings?
Ichill geue the an eawe, with a vayre vatt lamb for a guerdon.
Battus perceauing his former bribe to be doobled,

10

20

---

19 *Gaffer . . . wedders*: Master, I've lost five score fat rams
21 *Ichill . . . guerdon*: I'll give you a ewe and a fair fat lamb as a prize

Turnd his tale with a trice, and theaft to the theefe he reuealed.
Vnder yonsame hill they were, yeare while, by the thicket,
And 'cham zure th'are there. Iste true, qd *Mercury* smiling,
Ist tr'ue, thou false knaue, and wilt thou needes be betraying
Mee to myself? and then false *Battus* turnd to a Tutch stone,
Tutch stone, yet true stone; which each thing truely bewraieth,
And no-man thenceforth for no bribe falsely betrayeth.   (1592)

JOHN MARSTON *(c.* 1575–1634)

Throughout his career as dramatist, John Marston would collaborate
with such prominent contemporaries as Jonson, Chapman and Webster.
Earlier on, he contributed to the vogue for Ovidian erotic narrative or
'epyllion' with the following poem, a recasting of the Pygmalion
story. Marston embellishes freely with comic personal asides and satiric
digressions (here largely omitted). His gestures are often playful, even
glib; but the form's success is mostly measured by the panache that an
author brings to the task, and Marston never lacks for this. He adopts
the stanzaic form featured in Spenser's *Shepheardes Calender* (1579), and
popularized by Shakespeare's *Venus and Adonis* of 1593.

The Metamorphosis of Pigmalions Image, 1–18, 73–90, 127–86, 223–34 [Met. 10.243–97]

1

Pigmalion, whose hie love-hating minde
Disdain'd to yeeld servile affection,
Or amorous sute to any woman-kinde,
Knowing their wants, and mens perfection.
    Yet Love at length forc'd him to know his fate,
    And love the shade, whose substance he did hate.

2

For having wrought in purest Ivorie,
So faire an Image of a Womans feature,
That never yet proudest mortalitie
10   Could show so rare and beautious a creature.
    (Unlesse my Mistres all-excelling face,
      Which gives to beautie, beauties onely grace.)

3

Hee was amazed at the wondrous rarenesse
Of his owne workmanships perfection.
He thought that Nature nere produc'd such fairenes
In which all beauties have their mantion.
    And thus admiring, was enamored
      On that fayre Image himselfe portraied.

★

13

And fondly doting, oft he kist her lip.
20   Oft would he dally with her Ivory breasts.
No wanton love-trick would he over-slip,
But still observ'd all amorous beheasts.
    Whereby he thought he might procure the love
      Of his dull Image, which no plaints coulde move.

14

Looke how the peevish Papists crouch, and kneele
To some dum Idoll with their offering,
As if a senceles carved stone could feele
The ardor of his bootles chattering,
    So fond he was, and earnest in his sute
30   To his remorsles Image, dum and mute.

---

16 *mantion*: dwelling

15

He oft doth wish his soule might part in sunder
So that one halfe in her had residence:
Oft he exclaimes, o beauties onely wonder,
Sweet modell of delight, faire excellence,
    Be gracious unto him that formed thee,
    Compassionate his true-loves ardencie.

★

22

With that he takes her in his loving armes,
And downe within a Downe-bed softly layd her.
Then on his knees he all his sences charmes,
To invocate sweet Venus for to raise her
    To wished life, and to infuse some breath,
    To that which dead, yet gave a life to death.

23

Thou sacred Queene of sportive dallying,
(Thus he begins,) Loves only Emperesse,
Whose kingdome rests in wanton revelling,
Let me beseech thee show thy powerfulnesse
    In changing stone to flesh, make her relent,
    And kindly yeeld to thy sweet blandishment.

24

O gracious Gods, take compassion.
Instill into her some celestiall fire,
That she may equalize affection,
And have a mutuall love, and loves desire.
    Thou know'st the force of love, then pitty me,
    Compassionate my true loves ardencie.

25

Thus having said, he riseth from the floore,
As if his soule divined him good fortune,
Hoping his prayers to pitty mov'd some power.
For all his thoughts did all good luck importune.
    And therefore straight he strips him naked quite,
60   That in the bedde he might have more delight.

26

Then thus, Sweet sheetes he sayes, which now doe cover,
The Idol of my soule, the fairest one
That ever lov'd, or had an amorous lover.
Earths onely modell of perfection,
    Sweet happy sheetes, daine for to take me in,
    That I my hopes and longing thoughts may win.

27

With that his nimble limbs doe kisse the sheetes,
And now he bowes him for to lay him downe,
And now each part, with her faire parts doe meet,
70 Now doth he hope for to enjoy loves crowne:
    Now doe they dally, kisse, embrace together,
    Like Leda's Twins at sight of fairest weather.

28

Yet all's conceit. But shadow of that blisse
Which now my Muse strives sweetly to display
In this my wondrous metamorphosis.
Daine to beleeve me, now I sadly say:
    The stonie substance of his Image feature,
    Was straight transform'd into a living creature.

---

72 *Leda's Twins*: Castor and Pollux, patrons of sailors during storms at sea

29

For when his hands her faire form'd limbs had felt,
And that his armes her naked wast imbraced,
Each part like Waxe before the sunne did melt,
And now, oh now, he finds how he is graced
　　By his owne worke. Tut, women will relent
　　When as they find such moving blandishment.

30

Doe but conceive a Mothers passing gladnes,
(After that death her onely sonne hath seazed
And overwhelm'd her soule with endlesse sadnes)
When that she sees him gin for to be raised
　　From out his deadly swoune to life againe:
　　Such joy Pigmalion feeles in every vaine.

31

And yet he feares he doth but dreaming find
So rich content, and such celestiall blisse.
Yet when he proves & finds her wondrous kind,
Yeelding soft touch for touch, sweet kisse, for kisse,
　　He's well assur'd no faire imagery
　　Could yeeld such pleasing, loves felicity.

★

38

Who knowes not what ensues? O pardon me
Yee gaping eares that swallow up my lines.
Expect no more. Peace idle Poesie,
Be not obsceane though wanton in thy rimes.
　　And chaster thoughts, pardon if I doe trip,
　　Or if some loose lines from my pen doe slip.

39
Let this suffice, that that same happy night
So gracious were the Gods of marriage
Mid'st all there pleasing and long wish'd delight
Paphus was got: of whom in after age
    Cyprus was Paphos call'd, and evermore
    Those Ilandars do Venus name adore.   (1598)

CHRISTOPHER MARLOWE
(1564–1593)

However various were the sources of his great plays, the bulk of
Marlowe's non-dramatic verse takes its inspiration from Ovid. His *Hero
and Leander* stands out as perhaps the finest of the Ovidian epyllia, while
his complete translation of the *Amores* offered Ovid's shorter poems to
the English audience for the first time. Once regarded as hackwork –
the product of Marlowe's student days at Cambridge – these lyrics have
since found their champions, who detect in their pentameter couplets a
vitality and skill unsurpassed by any subsequent translation. A pirated
selection from Marlowe's *Elegies* was published posthumously, sometime before 1599 (the year it was officially suppressed). Two complete
editions were released in Holland, perhaps as early as the following year.

All Ovids Elegies: Liber Primus, Elegia 1 [Am. 1.1]

We which were *Ovids* five bookes now are three,
For these before the rest preferreth he.
If reading five thou plainst of tediousnesse,
Two tane away, thy labour will be lesse.

---

4 Marlowe builds these four lines, separated as a preliminary epigram in modern
editions, into the text of the opening elegy. Ovid alludes here to an earlier
five-book edition of the *Amores*, no longer extant.

With Muse upreard I meant to sing of Armes,
Choosing a subject fit for fierce alarmes.
Both verses were a like till love (men say)
Began to smile and tooke one foote away.
Rash boy, who gave thee power to change a line?
We are the Muses Prophets, none of thine.
What if thy mother take *Dianas* bowe?
Shall *Dian* fanne, when loue begins to glowe.
In wooddie groves ist meete that *Ceres* raigne?
And quiver-bearing *Dian* till the plaine.
Who'le set the faire trest sunne in battell ray
While *Mars* doth take the *Aonian* Harpe to play.
Great are thy kingdomes, over strong and large,
Ambitious impe, why seekst thou further charge?
Are all things thine? the Muses *Tempe* thine?
Then scarse can *Phoebus* say, this Harpe is mine.
When in this workes first verse I trod aloft,
Love slackt my Muse, and made my numbers soft.
I have no mistresse, nor no favorit,
Being fittest matter for a wanton wit.
Thus I complain'd, but love unlockt his quiver,
Tooke out the shaft ordain'de my hart to shiver:
And bent his sinewie bowe upon his knee,
Saying Poet heere's a worke beseeming thee.
Oh woe is mee, hee never shootes but hits,
I burne, love in my idle bosome sits.
Let my first verse be sixe, my last five feete,
Fare-well sterne warre, for blunter Poets meete.
Elegian Muse, that warblest amorous laies,
Girt my shine browe with Sea-banke Mirtle praise.   (c. 1600)

10

20

30

7–8 The poet's intention to write in epic hexameters is thwarted by Cupid, who reduces his couplets to elegy by removing one metrical foot from the second line.   16 Aonian *Harpe*: property of the Muses

All Ovids Elegies: Liber Primus, Elegia 5 [Am. 1.5]

In summers heate and mid-time of the day
To rest my limbes upon a bed I lay,
One window shut, the other open stood,
Which gave such light, as twincles in a wood,
Like twilight glimps at setting of the Sunne,
Or night being past, and yet not day begunne.
Such light to shamefast maidens must be showne,
Where they may sport, and seeme to be unknowne.
Then came *Corinna* in a long loose gowne,
10   Her white neck hid with tresses hanging downe:
Resembling fayre *Semiramis* going to bed
Or *Layis* of a thousand wooers sped,
I snatcht her gowne: being thin, the harme was small,
Yet striv'd she to be covered there withall.
And striving thus as one that would be cast,
Betray'd her selfe, and yeelded at the last.
Starke naked as she stood before mine eye,
Not one wen in her body could I spie.
What arms and shoulders did I touch and see,
20   How apt her breasts were to be prest by me.
How smooth a belly under her wast saw I?
How large a legge, and what a lustie thigh?
To leave the rest all lik'd me passing well,
I cling'd her naked body, downe she fell,
Judge you the rest, being tirde she bade me kisse;
Jove send me more such after-noones as this.   (*c.* 1600)

---

9 *Corinna*: name of the principal love interest in the *Amores*
11–12 *Semiramis, Layis*: queen and courtesan famed for their beauty
18 *wen*: blemish

All Ovids Elegies: Liber Secundus, Elegia 4 [Am. 2.4]

I meane not to defend the scapes of any,
Or justifie my vices being many.
For I confesse, if that might merite favour,
Heere I display my lewd and loose behaviour.
I loathe, yet after that I loathe, I runne,
Oh how the burthen irkes, that we should shunne.
I cannot rule my selfe, but where love please,
Am driven like a ship upon rough seas.
No one face likes me best, all faces move,
10   A hundred reasons make me ever love.
If any eye me with a modest looke,
I blush, and by that blushfull glance am tooke.
And she thats coy I like for being no clowne,
Me thinkes she would be nimble when shees downe.
Though her sowre lookes a *Sabines* browe resemble,
I thinke sheele do, but deepely can dissemble.
If she be learn'd, then for her skill I crave her,
If not, because shees simple I would have her.
Before *Callimachus* one preferres me farre,
20   Seeing she likes my bookes why should we jarre?
An other railes at me and that I write
Yet would I lie with her if that I might.
Trips she, it likes me well, plods she, what than?
Shee would be nimbler, lying with a man.
And when one sweetely sings, then straight I long
To quaver on her lips even in her song.
Or if one touch the Lute with arte and cunning
Who wold not love those hands for their swift running?

---

1 *scapes*: transgressions   **15** Sabines *browe*: figure of sombre chastity

And her I like that with a majesty
30 Folds up her armes and makes lowe curtesy.
To leave my selfe, that am in love with all
Some one of these might make the chastest fall.
If she be tall, shees like an *Amazon*,
And therefore filles the bed she lies upon.
If short, she lies the rounder to say troth
Both short and long please me, for I love both.
I thinke what one undeckt would be, being drest
Is she attired, then shew her graces best.
A white wench thralles me, so doth golden yellowe
40 And nut-browne girles in doing have no fellowe.
If her white necke be shadoed with blacke haire
Why so was *Ledas*, yet was *Leda* faire.
Amber trest is she, then on the morne thinke I
My love alludes to every history:
A yong wench pleaseth, and an old is good
This for her lookes that for her woman-hood.
Nay what is she that any *Roman* loves
But my ambitious ranging minde approves.   (*c.* 1600)

All Ovids Elegies: Liber Secundus, Elegia 18 [Am. 2.18]

To tragick verse while thou *Achilles* trainst,
And new sworne souldiours maiden armes retainst,
Wee *Macer* sit in *Venus* slothfull shade,
And tender love hath great things hatefull made.
Often at length, my wench depart, I bid,
Shee in my lap sits still as earst she did.

---

3 *Macer*: poet-companion of Ovid, addressed here as an advocate of more 'serious' heroic verse from which the speaker excuses himself (a convention known formally as *recusatio*)

I sayd it irkes me, halfe to weping framed,
Aye me she cries, to love, why art a shamed?
Then wreathes about my necke her winding armes,
10   And thousand kisses gives, that worke my harmes:
I yeeld, and back my wit from battells bring,
Domesticke acts, and mine owne warres to sing.
Yet tragedies, and scepters fild my lines,
But though I apt were for such high deseignes,
Love laughed at my cloak, and buskines painted,
And rule so soone with private hands acquainted.
My Mistris deity also drewe me fro it,
And love triumpheth ore his buskind Poet.
What lawfull is, or we professe loves art,
20   (Alas my precepts turne my selfe to smart)
We write, or what *Penelope* sends *Ulysses*,
Or *Phillis* teares, that her *Demophoon* misses,
What thanklesse *Jason*, *Macareus*, and *Paris*,
Phedra, and *Hipolite* may read, my care is,
And what poore *Dido* with her drawne sword sharpe,
Doth say, with her that lov'd the *Aonian* harpe.
As soone as from strange lands *Sabinus* came,
And writings did from diverse places frame,
White-cheekt *Penelope* knewe *Ulisses* signe
30   The stepdame read *Hyppolitus* lustlesse line.
Eneas to *Elisa* answere gives,
And *Phillis* hath to reade, if now she lives.
Jasons sad letter doth *Hipsipile* greete,
Sappho her vowed harpe laies at *Phoebus* feete.
Nor of thee *Macer* that resoundst forth armes,
Is golden love hid in *Mars* mid-alarmes.

---

15 *cloak . . . buskines*: the garment and boots associated with tragic poetry
21ff. These lines allude to the *Heroides*, and the poetic 'responses' (now lost)
allegedly written by Ovid's fellow poet Sabinus.

There *Paris* is, and *Helens* crymes record,
With *Laodameia* mate to her dead Lord.
Unlesse I erre to these thou more incline,
40   Then warres, and from thy tents wilt come to mine.   (*c.* 1600)

All Ovids Elegies: Liber tertius, Elegia 2 [Am. 3.2]

I sit not here the noble horse to see,
Yet whom thou favourst, pray may conquerer be.
To sit, and talke with thee I hether came,
That thou maiest know with love thou mak'st me flame.
Thou views the course, I thee: let either heed,
What please them, and their eyes let either feede.
What horse-driver thou favourst most is best,
Because on him thy care doth hap to rest.
Such chaunce let me have: I would bravely runne,
10   On swift steedes mounted till the race were done.
Now would I slacke the reines, now lash their hide,
With wheeles bent inward now the ring-turne ride.
If running if I see thee, I shall stay,
And from my hands the reines will slip away.
Ah *Pelops* from his coach was almost feld,
Hippodameias lookes while he beheld.
Yet he attain'd by her support to have her,
Let us all conquer by our mistris favour.
In vaine why flyest backe? force conjoynes us now:
20   The places lawes this benefit allowe.
But spare my wench thou at her right hand seated,
By thy sides touching ill she is entreated.
And sit thou rounder, that behind us see,
For shame presse not her backe with thy hard knee.
But on the ground thy cloathes too loosely lie,

20ff. What follows is an enactment of the counsels codified at *Ars* 1.135–62.

Gather them up, or lift them loe will I.
Envious garments so good legges to hide,
The more thou look'st, the more the gowne envide.
Swift *Atalantas* flying legges like these,
30 Wish in his hands graspt did *Hippomenes*.
Coate-tuckt *Dianas* legges are painted like them,
When strong wilde beasts, she stronger hunts to strike them.
Ere these were seene, I burnt: what will these do?
Flames into flame, flouds thou powrest seas into.
By these I judge, delight me may the rest,
Which lie hid under her thinne veile supprest.
Yet in the meane time wilt small windes bestowe,
That from thy fanne, mov'd by my hand may blow?
Or is my heate, of minde, not of the skie?
40 Ist womens love my captive brest doth frie?
While thus I speake, blacke dust her white robes ray:
Foule dust, from her faire body, go away.
Now comes the pompe; themselves let all men cheere:
The shout is nigh; the golden pompe comes heere.
First victory is brought with large spred wing,
Goddesse come here, make my love conquering.
Applaud you *Neptune*, that dare trust his wave,
The sea I use not: me my earth must have.
Souldiour applaud thy *Mars*: no warres we move,
50 Peace pleaseth me, and in mid peace is love.
With a*ugures Phoebus, Phoebe* with hunters standes,
To thee *Minerva* turne the craftes-mens hands.
Ceres and *Bacchus* Country-men adore,
Champions pleace *Pollux, Castor* loves horsemen more.
Thee gentle *Venus*, and the boy that flies,
We praise: great goddesse ayde my enterprize.
Let my new mistris graunt to be beloved,
She beckt, and prosperous signes gave as she moved.
What Venus promisd, promise thou we pray,
60 Greater then her, by her leave th'art, Ile say.
The Gods, and their rich pompe witnesse with me,

For evermore thou shalt my mistris be.
Thy legges hang downe: thou maiest, if that be best,
Or while thy tiptoes on the foote-stool rest.
Now greater spectacles the *Praetor* sends,
Fower chariot-horses from the lists even ends.
I see whom thou affectest: he shall subdue,
The horses seeme, as thy desire they knewe.
Alas he runnes too farre about the ring,
70   What doest? thy wagon in lesse compasse bring.
What doest unhappy? her good wishes fade,
Let with strong hand the reine to bend be made.
One slowe we favour, *Romans* him revoke:
And each give signes by casting up his cloake.
They call him backe; least their gownes tosse thy haire,
To hide thee in my bosome straight repaire.
But now againe the barriers open lye;
And forthe the gay troupes on swift horses flie.
At least now conquer, and out-runne the rest:
80   My mistris wish confirme with my request
My mistris hath her wish, my wish remaine:
He holdes the palme: my palme is yet to gaine.
She smilde, and with quicke eyes behight some grace:
Pay it not heere, but in an other place.   (*c.* 1600)

All Ovids Elegies: Liber tertius, Elegia 6 [Am. 3.7]

Either she was foule, or her attire was bad,
Or she was not the wench I wisht t'have had.
Idly I lay with her, as if I lov'd not,
And like a burthen griev'd the bed that mov'd not.
Though both of us perform'd our true intent,

---

74 *casting up his cloake*: a signal of protest, indicating that the race is to be run over again

Yet could I not cast anckor where I meant.
She on my necke her Ivory armes did throwe.
Her armes far whiter then the *Sythian* snow.
And eagerly she kist me with her tongue,
10 And under mine her wanton thigh she flung.
Yea, and she soothd me up, and calld me sir,
And usde all speech that might provoke, and stirre.
Yet like as if cold Hemlock I had drunke,
It mocked me, hung downe the head, and sunke.
Like a dull Cipher, or rude block I lay,
Or shade, or body was I who can say?
What will my age do? age I cannot shunne,
When in my prime my force is spent and done.
I blush, that being youthfull, hot, and lustie,
20 I prove neither youth nor man, but old and rustie.
Pure rose she, like a Nunne to sacrifice,
Or one that with her tender brother lyes.
Yet boorded I the golden *Chie* twise,
And *Libas*, and the white cheekt *Pitho* thrice.
Corinna crav'd it in a summers night,
And nine sweete bowts we had before day-light.
What wast my limbs through some *Thessalian* charmes?
May spells, and drugges do silly soules such harmes?
With virgin waxe hath some imbast my joynts?
30 And pierc'd my liver with sharpe needles points?
Charmes change corne to grasse and make it die.
By charmes are running springs and fountaines dry.
By charmes mast drops from oakes, from vines grapes fal
And fruite from trees when ther's no winde at all.
Why might not then my sinewes be inchaunted?
And I grow faint as with some spirit haunted.

23-5 *Chie, Libas, Pitho, Corinna*: names of the speaker's various lovers

To this adde shame: shame to performe it quailde me
And was the second cause why vigour failde me.
My idle thoughts delighted her no more,

40 Then did the robe or garment which she wore.
Yet might her touch make youthful *Pylius* fire
And *Tithon* livelier then his yeares require.
Even her I had, and she had me in vaine,
What might I crave more, if I aske againe?
I thinke the great gods griev'd they had bestow'd,
The benefit: which lewdly I for-slow'd.
I wish to be receiv'd in, in I get me,
To kisse, I kisse; to lie with her she let me.
Why was I blest? why made King to refuse it?

50 Chuffe-like had I not gold and could not use it?
So in a spring thrives he that told so much,
And lookes upon the fruits he cannot touch.
Hath any rose so from a fresh yong maide,
As she might straight have gone to church and praide?
Well I beleeve, she kist not as she should,
Nor us'd the sleight and cunning which she could,
Huge oakes, hard adamants might she have moved,
And with sweet words cause deafe rocks to have loved.
Worthy she was to move both gods and men,

60 But neither was I man nor lived then.
Can deafe eares take delight when *Phemius* sings?
Or *Thamiras* in curious painted things.
What sweete thought is there but I had the same?
And one gave place still as another came.
Yet not-withstanding like one dead it lay,
Drouping more then a rose puld yester-day.

41f. *Pylius . . . Tithon*: Nestor and Tithonus, figures of extreme old age
50 *Chuffe-like*: like a miser   **61** *Phemius*: singer in the *Odyssey*
62 *Thamiras*: blind musician in the *Iliad*

Now when he should not jette, he boults upright,
And craves his taske, and seekes to be at fight.
Lie downe with shame, and see thou stirre no more,
70   Seeing thou wouldst deceive me as before.
Thou cousenest me: by thee surpriz'd am I,
And bide sore losse with endlesse infamy.
Nay more the wench did not disdaine a whit,
To take it in her hand, and play with it.
But when she sawe it would be no meanes stand,
But still droupt downe, regarding not her hand.
Why mockst thou me she cryed? or being ill
Who bad thee lie downe heere against thy will?
Either th'art witcht with bloud of frogs newe dead
80   Or jaded camst thou from some others bed.
With that her loose gowne on, from me she cast her,
In skipping out her naked feete much grac'd her.
And least her maide should know of this disgrace,
To cover it, spilt water on the place.   (c. 1600)

THOMAS HEYWOOD (c. 1573–1641)

Over the course of his prolific and eclectic literary career, Thomas
Heywood translated a substantial portion of Ovid's work. The anonymous version of the complete *Ars amatoria* that appeared sometime
during the first quarter of the seventeenth century is now confidently
ascribed to him; his renditions from the *Heroides* found a place in his
pseudo-historical *Troia Britanica*; and he freely borrowed subject matter
from the *Metamorphoses* for several brief dramatic works. A bit rough

---

71 *cousenest*: cheat
84 *spilt water*. She hides from her servant the embarrassing fact that nothing has
happened by acting as if she had cleansed herself with water after sex (supposedly
a common contraceptive practice in antiquity).

in his presentation, Heywood is capable of a fine subtlety when he attends his source: compare the splendid gradations of Helen's turn in his version of *Heroides* 17 with Chaloner's diligent but less kinetic performance, above.

Publii Ouidii Nasonis De Arte Amandi or, The Art of Love 1.1–48 [Ars 1.1–34] *The Proheme and Introduction*

If there be any in this multitude,
That in the Art of love is dull and rude,
Me let him read, and these my lines rehearse,
He shall be made a Doctor by my Verse.
By art of sailes and oares Seas are divided,
By art the Chariot runs, by art Love's guided.
By art the bridle's rein'd in, or let slip;
Typhis by art did guide the *Hemonian* ship.
And me hath *Venus* her Arts master made,
10   To teach her Science, and set up her trade;
And time succeeding shall call me alone,
Loves expert *Typhis* and *Antomedon.*
Love in himselfe is apish and untoward,
Yet being a child, I'le whip him when he's froward.
Achylles in his youth was taught to run
On the string'd Lute a sweete division.
Art on his rude and sterne aspect did cease,
Instructing him in old *Philerides*:
He that so oft his friends, so oft his foes
20   Made quake and tremble, when he would disclose.

---

8 Typhis . . . Hemonian ship: pilot of Jason's craft, the Argo
12 *Antomedon*: typographical slip for Automedon, Achilles's charioteer
18 *Philerides*: Chiron, son of Philyra

His furious rage, was *knowne* to be a Suitor,
And with submission *kneele* unto his Tutor.
Æneides by *Chiron* was instructed,
And by my Art is Love himselfe conducted,
Both goddesse sonnes, *Venus* and *Thetis* joyes,
Both shrewd, both waggish, and unhappy boyes:
Yet the stiffe Bulls *necke* by the *yoake* is worne,
The proud Steed chews the bit which he doth scorn.
And though *Loves* darts my owne heart cleaves asunder,
30   Yet by my Art the wag shall be kept under:
And the more deepe my flaming heart is found,
The more I will revenge me of my wound.
Sacred *Apollo*, witnesse of my flame,
Behold thy Arts, I doe not falsly clame,
Of *Clios* sisters, loe I take to keepe,
That in the vale of *Asca* feed their sheepe.
Proud *skill* I teach of what I have been taster,
Love bids me *speake*, I'le be your *skilfull Master*.
And what I *speake*, is true, thus I begin,
40   Be present at my labours, *Loves* faire Queene.

Keepe hence you modest maids, and come not neare,
That vse to blush, and shame-fac't garments weare;
That have scant ruffes and keepe your haire unseene:
Whose feete with your white aprons cover'd beene.
From Vesta's virgins here no place is left,
My Muse sings Venus spoiles, and Loves sweet theft,
What kind affections Lovers thoughts doe pierce,
And there shall be no foult in this my verse.   (*c.* 1600–1625)

---

23 *Æneides*: Achilles, grandson of Aeacus
35f. contrasting the divine inspiration that Hesiod had claimed in his *Theogony*

Troia Britanica canto 10.199–280 [Her. 17.115–62]
Hellen to Paris

But see how soone poore Women are deluded,
Venus her selfe this couenant hath concluded,
For in the *Idæan* Valleyes you espy
Three Goddesses, stript naked to your eie,
And when the first had promist you a Crowne,
The second Fortitude and warres renowne,
The third bespake you thus: Crowne, nor Wars pride
Will I bequeath, but *Hellen* to thy Bride,
I scarce belieue those high immortall Creatures,
Would to your eye expose their naked features,
Or say the first part of your Tale be pure,
And meet with truth: The second's false I am sure,
In which poore I was thought the greatest meede,
In such a hie cause by the Goddes decreed.
I haue not of my beauty such opinion
T'imagine it preferd before Dominion,
Or fortitude: nor can your words persuade me
The greatest gift of al, the Goddesse made me.
It is enough to me, men praise my face,
But from the Goddes, I merit no such grace,
Nor doth the praise you charge me with offend me,
If *Venus* doe not enuiously commend me.
But loe I graunt you, and imagine true,
Your free report, claiming your praise as due,
Who would in pleasing things call *Fame* a liar,
But giue that credit, which we most desire.
  That we haue mou'd these doubts be not you grieued,
The greatest wonders are the least beleeued,

10

20

Know then I first am pleasde that *Venus* ought me

30   Such vndeserued grace: Next, that you thought me
The greatest meede: Nor Scepter, nor Warres Fame,
Did you preferre before poore *Hellens* name.
(Hard-hart tis time thou shouldst at last come downe)
Therefore I am your valour, I your Crowne,
Your kindnesse conquers me do what I can,
I were hard-harted, not to loue this man;
Obdurate I was neuer, and yet coy,
To fauour him whom I can ner'e enioy.
What profits it the barren sandes to plow

40   And in the furrowes our affections sow,
In the sweete theft of *Venus* I am rude,
And know not how my Husband to delude;
Now I these Loue-lines write, my pen I vow
Is a new office taught, not knowne till now,
Happy are they that in this Trade haue skill,
(Alasse I am a Foole) and shall be still,
And hauing till this houre not stept astray,
Feare in these sports least I should mis my way
The feare (no doubt) is greater then the blame

50   I stand confounded and amaz'd with shame.
And with the very thought of what you seeke,
Thinke euery eie fixt on my guilty cheeke,
Nor are these suppositions meerely vaine,
The murmuring people whisperingly complaine,
And my maid *Æthra* hath by listning slily,
Brought me such newes, as toucht mine honor hily:
Wherefore (deere Lord) dissemble, or desist,
Being ouer-eyde, we cannot as we list,
Fashion our sports, our Loues pure haruest gather:

60   But why should you desist? dissemble rather:

---

29 *ought*: paid

Sport, (but in secret) sport where none may see,
The greater, but not greatest liberty
Is limitted to our Lasciuious play,
That *Menalaus* is farre hence away,
My Husband about great affaires is poasted,
Leauing his royall guest securely hoasted,
His businesse was important and materiall,
Being employd about a Crowne Imperiall:
And as he now is mounted on his Steed,
70   Ready on his long iourney to proceede,
Euen as he questions to depart or stay,
Sweet hart (quoth I) oh be not long away,
With that he reacht me a sweet parting kisse,
(How loath he was to leaue me, ghesse by this.)
Farewell fayre Wife (saith he) bend all thy cares
To my domesticke businesse, home affayres,
But as the thing that I affection best,
Sweet Wife, looke well vnto my *Troian* guest.
It was no sooner out, but with much paine,
80   My itching spleene from laughter I restraine,
Which striuing to keepe in and bridle still,
At length I wrung forth these few words (*I wil.*)   (1609)

Pleasant Dialogues and Dramma's, 5744–5906 [Met. 1.669–723] *Mercury's Tale of Pan and Syrinx, and the death of Argus*

Enter Argus *leading* Io *in an halter.*
Argus. How dost thou like thyne usage, madam *Cow?*
    Your lodging and your dyet? How dost thinke

---

s.d. After raping Io, Jupiter transforms her into a white cow in order to hide her from Juno's jealous inquiries. Undeceived, Juno demands the cow as a gift, and entrusts her to the hundred-eyed guardian Argus. Jupiter in turn charges Mercury to plot Io's escape.

This hempen chaine becomes thee? Will you see
Your sweet face in the riuer once againe?
Or how doth your faire beastship feele your selfe?
Wouldst thou not haue some Bulchin from the herd
To physicke thee of this venereall itch?
If not, I'le see what Nettles muddy streams,
Couch-grasse and weeds, thornes, briers, & flints can do.
10   These failing, here's a goad to prick your sides.
If all these medicines will not tame your lust,
I'le muster new inventions. Nay, I know
You looke for pitty, but it lives not here.
In this high watch-tower stand I sentinel,
To spy who comes and goes. I am made thy gardian,
Ile gard thee both from danger and from rest;
'Twas in thy hearing, *Iuno's* late behest.
            Enter Mercury *like a yong formal Shepheard*.
Merc. This shape may prove suspectlesse, and the fittest
To cloud a godhead in; my plumed hat
20   And fether'd sandals, by the which I am knowne,
I have left at foot of this descending hill:
My snaky Rod I have to this sheephooke turn'd.
Accommodated thus, to *Argus* now,
Aristors sonne: behooves him keepe good watch,
Whom *Mercury* (*Ioves* son) intends to catch.
But Many-eyes have spy'de me.
Arg. How now shepheard,
There's none who in that simpl shape or name
Needs treason feare: Should any come prepar'd
30   For mischiefe, I have lights about me shine
Sufficient to prevent it: but thou seem'st
None of such ranke. Come sit by me and talke.
Merc. The servant to the great *Saturnia*
Doth me no common grace.

---

6 *Bulchin*: young bull   **33** *Saturnia*: Juno (daughter of Saturn)

Arg. Thou know'st me then?

Merc. What shepheard but not only knowes your name,
But feares your strength?

Arg. Nay sit (by me th'art safe)
And tell some pretty tales to make me laugh:
40   I have not long been merry.

Merc. First resolve me;
Is that faire heifer of some neighbour herd,
You drag thus in an halter?

Arg. Shee's my charge,
A witty Brute, a most ingenious beast,
A very apprehensive *Animal*,
That can do tricks: she hath been taught, I tell thee,
To write and reade.

Merc. Argus, not possible.

50   *Arg.* 'Tis as I said before: but having her,
Some pretty tale, I prethee.

Merc. But what if
Some goddesse should live in this shape disguis'd,
To whom you are so churlish. I could tell you
A story to that end.

Arg. Such toyes I love.

Merc. Thus the *Pierides* report: The Gyants
Assembled and made war against the gods,
Heapt Ossa upon Pelion, Caucasus
60   Vpon Pernassus, Pindus above them;
Hill upon mountain, mountain vpon hill,
Till they had made a scale that reacht to heaven.
The conflict then began: the monstrous *Typhon*
Was Captain of the Gyants: Of the gods
Great *Iove*, Archduke. The Generals met and fought.
In briefe (to cut off circumstance) the earth
Prevaild 'gainst heauen. The gods are forc't to fly:

---

57 *Pierides*: the Muses

Iove, chac'd by *Typhon* into Egypt, chang'd
Himselfe into a Ram: *Apollo*, frighted,
70   Turnes to a Crow, *Bacchus* into a Goat,
Iuno a Cow, *Diana* to a Cat;
Venus into a Fish, and tooke the sea;
Mars to a Pigmy, lest he should be knowne:
And *Mercury*, syrnam'd the crafty god,
Into a Fox.
Arg. A Fox? But I would meet
That craft which would beguile *Argus* bright eyes.
Proceed, proceed, good shepheard.
Merc. Why may not then
80   Some goddesse be included in this shape?
Arg. A goddesse, saist thou? thinke me equall then
With one of these huge Gyants, if not greater,
That have the power and potencie to leade
A god-head in a string. But ha, what musick   (*Musicke.*
Was that strooke vp? 'Twas sweet and delicat,
Nor have I heard the like.
Merc. My fellow shepheards
Behinde that rocke (from whence an echo growes)
For the more grace have chus'd that place as fittest,
90   Prest to bestow their cunning vpon you,
Whom they have heard, much tyr'd with watching long.
Arg. And shall we have some merry Madrigall
To passe away the time with?
Merc. What you please.
Arg. I faine would know how first these Pipes came up,
That make this dainty musicke?
Merc. First from *Pan*
The god of Shepheards. In the memory
Of the Nymph *Syrinx*, Musicke strike and tell,
100   How in th' Arcadian plaines it once befell.

      Mercuries Song.

      Sirinx, one of Dian's *traine,*
      Hunting with her on the plaine,
      Arm'd alike with shafts and bow;
      Each from other would you know?
      Which from which could not be told,
      Saue ones was horne, the others gold.

Arg. Hey ho; very fine musicke I promise you.

Merc. Now it begins to worke.

      Pan he sees himselfe makes fine,
110   *In his cap he pricks a Pine:*
      Now growes carelesse of his heard,
      Sits by brookes to prune his beard,
      Meets her, and hath minde to wooe,
      Much he speakes, and lore would doe.

Arg. 'Tis pleasing, but it makes me melancholy,
    And drowsie too withall.

Merc. 'Twill do anon.   (*Aside.*

      Still he profers, she denies;
      He pursues (for Syrinx flies.)
120   *Past her knees her coats up flew,*
      He would faine see something new:
      By the leg and thigh he guest
      (It seemes) the virtue of the rest.

Arg. Were it not for my charge I'de take a nap.

Merc. This addes wings vnto his pace,
      The goale for which he is in chace.
      She addes feathers to her speed;
      Now it was no more than need.
      Almost caught, Alas she cries,
130   *Some chaste god my shape disguise.*

Arg. The rest may sleepe secure, so I can keepe
    But two eyes waking.

Merc. Here's a charme for them.

      Lædon heares, And girts her round,
      Spies a reed that makes sweet sound:

> *Such is* Syrinx. *Wondring* Pan
> *Puts it to his mouth anon:*
> *Yet* Syrinx *thou art myne he said,*
> *And so of her his first pipe made.*

140   My charm hath tooke effect; with these thyne eyes
         Take thy last sleepe, thou hast not one to see;
         My taske is done, and *Jo* thou now free.

                                    (*Cuts off his head. Exit.*

                        Enter Iuno.

Iuno. The dying groans of *Argus* call'd me down,
         To know what of his lustre is become.
         What, all extinct? and is no memorie
         Extant of their known brightnesse? hath one night
         (Whose nature should be to be proud of stars)
         Shut at one time an hundred? nay at once?
         Should euery piece of time depriue so many,
150   How shortly would these lights innumerable
         Be vanisht into nothing? But deare *Argus*,
         That all may know thou hadst a louing mistresse,
         Grieuing thou shouldst thus perish for her sake;
         And that these eies (now blinde) in after-times
         May giue a light to perpetuitie,
         And memorize thy name, thy faith and fall,
         Thy hundred eyes (who was for *Iuno* slain)
         I will transport into my Peacocks traine;
         Whilst such a bird hath breeding, and can bee,
160   Her painted feathers shall remember thee.   (1637)

F. L.

The first booke of Ouidius Naso, *intituled The Remedie of Loue*, 61–82, 99–114 [Rem. 41–54, 69–78] *Introduction*

This anonymous rendering of the *Remedia amoris* indicates the enduring popularity of Shakespeare's *Venus and Adonis* stanza, and how easily Ovidian 'instruction' (as well as narrative) fits into this mould.

11
Come then sick youth vnto my sacred skill,
Whose loue hath fallen crosse vnto your minde:
Learne how to remedie that pleasing ill,
Of him that taught you your owne harmes to finde.
    For in that selfesame hand your helpe is found,
    Whence first ye did receiue your careful wound.

12
So th'earth which yeelds vs herbs of souerain grace
Doth nourish weeds, of vertue pestilent;
The burning nettle chuseth oft her place,
10 Next to the Rose, that yeelds so sweete a sent.
    Achilles Speare, that wounded his sterne foe,
    Restord him health, & curde the greeuous blow.

11f. Telephus, healed with rust taken from the same spear with which Achilles had originally wounded him

13
Now what prescriptions we do giue to men,
Maides thinke them spoken vnto you likewise:
To both parts we giue weapons, vse them then
With secret Art, and with discretion wise.
    Of which if ought you finde that seemes not fit,
    Know in examples many things are writ.

14
And profitable is our Argument,
20 To quench that secret and consuming flame:
To free thy minde from sin and ill intent,
To loose those bands that drew thee into shame.

                            ★

[17]
Ile teach you to asswage the greedy bent
Of burning lust, and make the weather faire:
    Ile steare your Ship aright in seas of loue,
    And from each rock I will you safely moue.

18
Ouid was to be read with studious care,
When first your loue began with fruite to growe,
Ouid is to be read, in your ill fare,
30 When first your loue with deep disdain shal flowe.
    I do professe to gain your libertie,
    Then follow me, reuenge your miserie.

19
Be present o thou Prophet, Poets praise,
Phisicks first finder out, and nurse alone,
Crowne me professing both, with lasting bayes,

33f. Apollo, god of prophecy, poetry and healing

For both are vnder thy protection.
  Raine siluer showers of skill into my brest,
  That I may shewe each wretch the way to rest.   (1600)

BEN JONSON (1573–1637)

Jonson was as demanding a critic as he was a poet and playwright; he had doubtless scrutinized Marlowe's *Amores* translations as soon as they began to circulate. The following version, intended as an adjustment or 'improvement', appeared alongside Marlowe's original in the published text. Jonson thought well enough of his own effort to incorporate the poem subsequently into his *Poetaster*. Set in Augustan Rome, the play takes Ovid's downfall and banishment from court as one of its key subplots. Ovid himself recites the elegy, which serves as a virtual roll call of the most revered classical poets, among whom the speaker ranks himself.

Poetaster 1.1.43–84 [Am. 1.15]

Enuie, why twist thou me, my time's spent ill?
And call'st my verse, fruits of an idle quill?
Or that (vnlike the line from whence I sprung)
Wars dustie honours I pursue not young?
Or that I studie not the tedious lawes;
And prostitute my voyce in euerie cause?
Thy scope is mortall; mine, eternall fame:
Which through the world shall euer chaunt my name.
HOMER will liue, whil'st TENEDOS stands, and IDE,
Or, to the sea, fleet SIMOIS doth slide:
And so shall HESIOD too, while vines doe beare,
Or crooked sickles crop the ripened eare.
CALLIMACHVS, though in inuention lowe,
Shall still be sung: since he in art doth flowe.

No losse shall come to SOPHOCLES proud vaine.
With sunne, and moone, ARATUS shall remaine.
Whil'st slaues be false, fathers hard, and bawdes be whorish,
Whil'st harlots flatter, shall MENANDER flourish.
ENNIVS, though rude, and ACCIVS high-reard straine,
20   A fresh applause in euerie age shall gaine.
Of VARRO'S name, what eare shall not be told?
Of IASONS ARGO? and the fleece of gold?
Then shall LVCRETIVS loftie numbers die,
When earth, and seas in fire and flames shall frie.
TYTIRVS, Tillage, ÆNEE shall be read,
Whil'st ROME of all the conquer'd world is head.
Till CVPIDS fires be out, and his bowe broken,
Thy verses (neate TIBVLLVS) shall be spoken.
Our GALLVS shall be knowne from east to west:
30   So shall LYCORIS, whom he now loues best.
The suffering plough-share, or the flint may weare:
But heauenly *poesie* no death can feare.
Kings shall giue place to it, and kingly showes,
The bankes ore which gold-bearing *Tagus* flowes.
Kneel hindes to trash: me let bright PHŒBVS swell,
With cups full flowing from the MVSES well.
Frost-fearing myrtle shall impale my head,
And of sad louers Ile be often read.
'Enuie the liuing, not the dead, doth bite:
40   'For after death all men receiue their right.'
Then, when this bodie fals in funerall fire,
My name shall liue, and my best part aspire.   (1601)

39f. Marked off by Jonson in the text as a *sententia*, or 'choice' statement.

FRANCIS BEAUMONT (1584–1616)

Like many of the epyllion writers, Francis Beaumont is better known
for his dramatic works, particularly those he co-authored with John
Fletcher. Written when he was an 18-year-old resident of the Inner
Temple, Beaumont's *Salmacis and Hermaphroditus* displays a sheer delight
in the lush description that came to seem prerequisite to the genre,
along with a style that is, in William Keach's words, 'inventive, subtle,
and deftly controlled'. In the narrative's culmination, the water nymph
Salmacis finds herself unable to curb her infatuation with Hermaphroditus (son of Mercury and Venus), who has so far resisted her advances.

Salmacis and Hermaphroditus, 817–920 [Met. 4.334–388]

But then the boy did struggle to be gone,
Vowing to leave her and that place alone.
But then bright Salmacis began to feare,
And sayd: Fayre stranger, I wil leave thee here
Amid these pleasant places all alone.
So turning back, she fayned to be gone;
But from his sight she had no power to passe;
Therefore she turn'd, and hid her in the grasse,
When to the ground, bending her snow-white knee,
10   The glad earth gave new coates to every tree.
    He then supposing he was all alone,
(Like a young boy that is espy'd of none)
Runnes here, and there, then on the bankes doth looke,
Then on the cristall current of the brooke,
Then with his foote he toucht the silver streames,
Whose drowzy waves made musicke in their dreames,
And, for he was not wholy in, did weepe,
Talking alowd and babbling in their sleepe:

Whose pleasant coolenesse when the boy did feele,
20 He thrust his foote downe lower to the heele:
O'recome with whose sweet noyse, he did begin
To strip his soft clothes from his tender skin,
When strait the scorching Sun wept teares of brine,
Because he durst not touch him with his shine,
For feare of spoyling that same Iv'ry skin,
Whose whitenesse he so much delighted in;
And then the Moone, mother of mortall ease,
Would fayne have come from the Antipodes,
To have beheld him, naked as he stood
30 Ready to leape into the silver flood;
But might not: for the lawes of heaven deny,
To shew mens secrets to a womans eye:
And therefore was her sad and gloomy light
Confin'd unto the secret-keeping night.

     When beauteous Salmacis awhile had gaz'd
Upon his naked corps, she stood amaz'd,
And both her sparkling eyes burnt in her face,
Like the bright Sunne reflected in a glasse:
Scarce can she stay from running to the boy,
40 Scarce can she now deferre her hoped joy;
So fast her youthfull bloud playes in her vaynes,
That almost mad, she scarce her selfe contaynes.
When young Hermaphroditus as he stands,
Clapping his white side with his hollow hands,
Leapt lively from the land, whereon he stood,
Into the mayne part of the cristall flood.
Like Iv'ry then his snowy body was,
Or a white Lilly in a cristall glasse.

     Then rose the water-Nymph from where she lay,
50 As having wonne the glory of the day,
And her light garments cast from off her skin.
Hee's mine, she cry'd; and so leapt spritely in.
The flattering Ivy who did ever see
Inclaspe the huge trunke of an aged tree,

Let him behold the young boy as he stands,
Inclasp in wanton Salmacis's hands,
Betwixt those Iv'ry armes she lockt him fast,
Striving to get away, till at the last:
Fondling, she sayd, why striv'st thou to be gone?
Why shouldst thou so desire to be alone?
Thy cheeke is never fayre, when none is by:
For what is red and white, but to the eye?
And for that cause the heavens are darke at night,
Because all creatures close their weary sight;
For there's no mortall can so earely rise,
But still the morning waytes upon his eyes.
The earely-rising and soone-singing Larke
Can never chaunt her sweete notes in the darke;
For sleepe she ne're so little or so long,
Yet still the morning will attend her song,
All creatures that beneath bright Cinthia be,
Have appetite unto society;
The overflowing waves would have a bound
Within the confines of the spacious ground,
And all their shady currents would be plaste
In hollow of the solitary vaste,
But that they loathe to let their soft streames sing,
Where none can hear their gentle murmuring.
Yet still the boy, regardlesse what she sayd,
Struggled apace to overswimme the mayd.
Which when the Nymph perceiv'd, she 'gan to say:
Struggle thou mayst, but never get away.
So graunt, just gods, that never day may see
The separation twixt this boy and mee.
    The gods did heare her pray'r and feele her woe;
And in one body they began to grow.
She felt his youthfull bloud in every vaine;
And he felt hers warme his cold brest againe.
And ever since was womens love so blest,
That it will draw bloud from the strongest brest.

Nor man nor mayd now could they be esteem'd:
Neither, and either, might they well be deem'd,
When the young boy Hermaphroditus sayd,
With the set voice of neither man nor mayd:
Swift Mercury, thou author of my life,
And thou my mother, Vulcans lovely wife,
Let your poore offsprings latest breath be blest,
In but obtayning this his last request,
Grant that who e're heated by Phoebus beames,

100   Shall come to coole him in these silver streames,
May nevermore a manly shape retaine,
But halfe a virgine may returne againe.
    His parents hark'ned to his last request,
And with that great power they the fountaine blest.
And since that time who in that fountaine swimmes,
A mayden smoothnesse seyzeth halfe his limmes.   (1602)

SIR THOMAS OVERBURY
(1581–1614)

Sir Thomas Overbury's death by poison in the Tower stands out as
one of the more lurid episodes in the history of Jacobean court intrigue.
His sensational end eclipses a slight literary career, from which survives
this abbreviated imitation of the *Remedia amoris*. Overbury's compression of Ovid's counsels generally loses the relaxed charm of Ovid's
presentation, but he can at points rise splendidly to the moment. Given
what we know of Overbury's experience at court, we can easily speculate
that a grain of personal sentiment seasons the following passage.

The First and Second part of The Remedy of Loue
I.89−124 [Rem. 169−224] *Rural distractions*

If these faile, to the Country then repaire,
For any care extinguisheth this care:
There maist thou see the Oxe, the yoke obey,
And though the earth, ploughs eating throgh their way:
To whom thou maist set corne to vse, and see
For every corne, spring vp a little Tree.
The Sunne being Midwife, thou shalt oft finde there,
Trees bearing far more fruite then they can beare.
And how the siluer Brookes are riding post,
10   Till in some riuer they themselues haue lost.
There maist thou see Goates skale the highest Hill,
That they their bellies and their dugges may fill.
And harmelesse sheepe, to whom was no defence,
By nature euer giuen, but innocence.
There maist thou learne to graffe, and then note how,
The old tree nurseth the adopted bough;
And of his sap doth him allowance rate,
Though his fruite from him do degenerate.
There maist thou see the Hare tred many a ring,
20   The Hounds into a laborinth to bring:
Vntill he (hauing long his death delaide)
By his owne steps be to the dogs betraide,
Of Fishing vse, so thou the fish shalt see,
Punish'd to death for their credulity.
Do this, that thou maist weary be at night,
So sleepe in spight of thoughts shall close thy sight.
Let not thy memory things past repeate,
'Tis easier oft to learne then to forget.
Therefore keepe distance, and thy loue forsake,
30   This to effect some iourney vndertake:
I know thou wilt wish raine, and faine delay,
And oft thy doubtfull foote stand at a stay:

But how much more it greiues thee to be gone,
So much the more remember to go on.
Name not the miles nor once look backwards home,
The *Parthian* by flight doth ouercome.   (1620)

WILLIAM SHAKESPEARE
(1564–1616)

If we discount the broad parody of the Pyramus and Thisbe story in *A Midsummer Night's Dream*, Prospero's farewell to his magic in *The Tempest* constitutes our only discernible instance of Shakespeare's translation of Ovid. Scholars continue to debate whether the passage owes much more to Golding's version – which it clearly echoes – than to the Latin. Whatever the case, the speech's subtle reminiscence of Medea's address to the terrible powers at her disposal offers a brilliantly poignant contrast to the magician's resignation.

The Tempest 5.1.33–57 [Met. 7.192–206]

Ye Elues of hils, brooks, standing lakes & groues,
And ye, that on the sands with printlesse foote
Doe chase the ebbing-*Neptune*, and doe flie him
When he comes backe: you demy-Puppets, that
By Moone-shine doe the greene sowre Ringlets make,
Whereof the Ewe not bites: and you, whose pastime
Is to make midnight-Mushrumps, that reioyce
To heare the solemne Curfewe, by whose ayde
(Weake Masters though ye be) I haue bedymn'd

---

36 *Parthian*: excellent archers and horsemen, famed for their ability to shoot backwards from their mounts
4 *demy-Puppets*: a reference to the diminutive, doll-like size of the elves invoked

10   The Noone-tide Sun, call'd forth the mutenous windes,
And twixt the greene Sea, and the azur'd vault
Set roaring warre: To the dread ratling Thunder
Haue I giuen fire, and rifted *Ioues* stowt Oke
With his owne Bolt: The strong bass'd promomtorie
Haue I made shake, and by the spurs pluckt vp
The Pyne, and Cedar. Graues at my command
Haue wak'd their sleepers, op'd, and let 'em forth
By my so potent Art. But this rough Magicke
I heere abiure: and when I haue requir'd

20   Some heauenly Musicke (which euen now I do)
To worke mine end vpon their Sences, that
This Ayrie-charme is for, I'le breake my staffe,
Bury it certaine fadomes in the earth,
And deeper then did euer Plummet sound
Ile drowne my booke.

                                                      (1623)

GEORGE SANDYS (1578–1644)

George Sandys had travelled extensively before his appointment as treasurer to the Virginia Company in 1621. Over the course of his tenure in America he found time to translate Ovid's great work, publishing a version in 1626. By 1632 a third edition had appeared, augmented by a 'moralized' commentary (from which an excerpt is here provided). His faithful rendition tempers the energy of Golding into more refined pentameter couplets. Dryden, whose regard for Sandys's translation would vary over time, studied it carefully as a backdrop to his own superlative treatments of the *Metamorphoses'* narratives later in the century.

Ovid's Metamorphosis 2.835–918 [Met. 2.760–832]
Envy and Aglauros

Forth-with to *Envie's* cave her course she bent,
Furr'd with black filth, within a deepe descent
Betweene two hills; where *Phoebus* never showes
His chearfull face; where no winde ever blowes:
Repleat with sadnesse, and unactive cold;
Devoid of fire, yet still in smoak enrol'd.
Whether when as the fear'd in battell came,
Shee staid before the house (that hatefull frame
Shee might not enter) and the darke doore stroke
10 With her bright lance; which straight in sunder broke.
There saw she *Envie* lapping Vipers blood;
And feeding on their flesh, her vices food:
And, having seene her, turn'd-away her eyes.
The Caitiffe slowly from the ground doth rise
(Her halfe-devoured Serpents laid-aside)
And forward creepeth with a lazie stride.
Viewing her forme so faire; her armes, so bright;
Shee groan'd, and sigh't at such a chearfull sight.
Her body more than meager; pale her hew;
20 Her teeth all rustie; still shee looks askew;
Her breast with gall, her tongue with poyson sweld:
Shee only laught, when she sad sights beheld.
Her ever-waking cares exil'd soft sleepe:
Who lookes on good successe, with eyes that weepe;
Repining, pines: who, wounding others, bleeds:
And on her selfe revengeth her misdeeds.

---

1 *her course*: Minerva, bearing an earlier grudge against Cecrops's daughter Aglauros
and outraged by her attempt to extort bribes from Mercury when the god
attempted to seduce her sister, journeys to Envy's cave to seal the girl's doom.

Although *Tritonia* did the Hag detest;
Yet briefly thus her pleasure she exprest:
Aglauros, one of the *Cecropides*,
30   Doe thou infest with thy accurst disease.
This said; the hastie Goddesse doth advance
Her body, with her earth-repelling lance.
Envie cast after her a wicked eye,
Mutters, and could for very sorrow die
That such her power: a snaggy staffe then tooke
Wreathed with thornes; and her darke Cave forsooke.
Wrapt in black clouds, which way so ere she turnes,
The Corne she lodges, flowrie pastures burnes,
Crops what grows high; Townes, Nations, with her breath
40   Pollutes; and Vertue persecutes to death.
When shee the faire *Athenian* towres beheld,
Which so in wealth, in learned Arts exceld,
And feastfull Peace; to crie she scarce forbeares,
In that she saw no argument for teares.
When shee *Aglauros* lodging entred had,
Shee gladly executes what *Pallas* bade:
Her cankred hand upon her brest she lai'd,
And crooked thornes into her heart convay'd,
And breath'd in bainfull poyson; which she sheads
50   Into her bones, and through her spirits spreads.
And that her envy might not want a cause;
The God in his divinest forme shee drawes:
And with it, sets before her wounded eyes
Her happy sister, and their nuptiall joyes:
Augmenting all. These secret woes excite,
And gnaw her soule. Shee sighs all day, all night;
And with a slow infection melts away,
Like Ice before the Sunnes uncertaine ray.

---

27 *Tritonia*: Minerva   **29** *Cecropides*: daughters of Cecrops

Faire *Herse's* happy state such heart-burne breeds
60   In her black bosome, as when spiny weeds
Are set on fire: which without flame consume,
And seeme (so small their heat) to burne with fume.
Oft shee resolves to die, such sights to shun:
Oft, by disclosing, to have both undone.
Now sits she on the threshold, to prevent
The Gods accesse; who with lost blandishment,
And his best Art, perswades. Quoth shee; forbeare,
I cannot be remov'd, if you stay here.
I to this bargaine, he reply'd, will stand;
70   The figured doore then forces with his wand.
Striving to rise, to second her debate,
Her hips could not remove, prest with dull waight.
Againe shee struggl'd to have stood on end:
But, those unsupple sinewes would not bend.
Incroaching cold now enters at her nayles:
And lack of blood her veines blew branches pale's.
And as a Canker, slighting helplesse Arts,
Creeps from th' infected to the sounder parts:
So by degrees the winter of wan Death
80   Congeales the path of life, and stops her breath:
Nor strove she: had she strove to make her mone,
Voice had no way; her neck and face now stone.
There shee a bloodlesse Statue sate, all freckt:
Her spotted minde the Marble did infect.   (1632)

Ovid's Metamorphosis 3.155–268 [Met. 3.138–252]
Actaeon

In this thy every way so prosperous state,
Thy first misse-hap sprung from thy Nephew's fate:
Whose browes unnaturall branches ill adorne;
By his ungratefull doggs in peeces torne.
Yet fortune did offend in him; not he:
For, what offence may in an error be?
With purple blood, slaine Deare the Hills imbrew:
And now high Noone the shades of things withdrew;
While East and West the equall Sunne partake:

10 Thus, then, *Hyantius* to his Partners spake,
That trod the Mazes of the pathlesse Wood:
My Friends our nets and javelins reake with blood:
Enough hath beene the fortune of this day:
To morrow, when *Aurora* shall display
Her rosie cheeks, we may our sports renew.
Now, *Phoebus*, with inflaming eye doth view
The crannied Earth: Here let our labour end:
Take up your toyles. They gladly condescend.
A Vale there was with Pines and Cypresse crown'd,

20 *Gargaphie* call'd; for *Diana's* love renown'd.
A shadie Cave possest the inward part,
Not wrought by hands; there Nature witty Art
Did counterfeit: a native Arch she drew,
With Pumice and light Tofusses, that grew.
A bubbling Spring, with streames as cleere as glasse,
Ran chiding by, inclos'd with matted grasse,

---

2 *Thy first misse-hap*: The declining fortunes of Cadmus, Thebes's founder, begin with the plight of his grandson Actaeon.
10 *Hyantius*: Actaeon; also called Autonoëius at line 61, below
24 *Tofusses*: i.e. tufa, porous stones

The weary Huntresse usually here laves
Her Virgin lims, more pure than those pure waves.
And now her Bowe, her Jav'ling, and her Quiver;
30   Doth to a Nymph, one of her Squires, deliver:
Her light impoverisht Robes another held:
Her buskins two untie. The better skild
Ismenian Crocale, her long haire wound
In pleited-wreathes: yet was her owne unbound.
Neat *Hayle, Niphe, Rhanis, Psecas* (still
Imploy'd) and *Phiale* the Lavers fill.
While here *Titania* bath'd (as was her guise)
Lo *Cadmus* Nephew, tyr'd with exercise,
And wandring through the Woods, approacht this Grove
40   With fatall steps: so Destiny him drove!
Entring the Cave with skipping Springs bedeaw'd:
The Nymphs, all naked, when a man they view'd,
Clapt their resounding breasts, and fild the Wood
With sudden shreekes: like Ivory pales they stood
About their Goddesse: but shee, far more tall,
By head and shoulders over-tops them all.
Such as that colour, which the Clowds adorns,
Shot by the Sunne-beam's; or the rosie Morn's:
Such flusht in *Dians* cheeks, being naked tane.
50   And though inviron'd by her Virgin trayne,
Shee side-long turnes, looks back, and wisht her bow:
Yet, what she had, she in his face did throwe.
With vengefull Waters sprinkled; to her rage
These words shee addes, which future Fate presage:
Now, tell how thou hast seene me disarray'd;
Tell if thou canst: I give thee leave. This said,
She to his neck and eares new length imparts;
T' his Browe the antlers of long-living Harts:

---

31 *impoverisht*: stripped off   **32** *buskins*: boots   **37** *Titania*: Diana   **44** *pales*: stakes

His leggs and feet with armes and hands supply'd;
60 And cloth'd his body in a spotted hide.
To this, feare added. *Autonoëius* flyes,
And wonders at the swiftnesse of his thighes.
But, when his looks he in the River view'd,
He would have cry'd, Woe's me! No words insew'd:
His words were grones. He frets, with galling teares,
Cheeks not his owne; yet his owne mind he beares.
What should he doe? Goe home? or in the Wood
For ever lurke? Feare, this; shame that withstood.
While thus he doubts, his Doggs their Master view:
70 *Black-foot* and *Tracer*, opening first, persew:
Sure *Tracer*, *Gnossus*; *Black-foot Sparta* bare.
Then all fell in, more swift then forced Ayre:
Spie, *Ravener*, *Clime-cliffe*; these *Arcadia* bred:
Strong *Fawn-bane*, *Whirlewinde*, eager *Follow-dread*;
Hunter; for sent; for speede, *Flight* went before;
Fierce *Salvage*, lately gaunched by a Bore;
Greedy, with her two whelps; grim Wolf-got *Ranger*;
Stout *Shepherd*, late preserving flocks from danger;
Gaunt *Catch*, whose race from *Sicyonia* came;
80 *Patch*, *Courser*, *Blab*, rash *Tyger* never tame;
Blanch, *Mourner*, *Royster*, *Wolfe* surpassing strong;
And *Tempest*, able to continue long:
Swift, with his brother *Churle*, a *Cyprian* hound;
Bold *Snatch*; whose sable brows a white star cround;
Cole, shag-hair'd *Rug*, and *Light-foot* wondrous fleet,
Bred of a *Spartan* Bitch, his Sire of *Creet*:
White-tooth, and *Ring-wood* (others not to expresse.)
O're Rocks, o're Crags, o're Cliffs that want accesse,

69ff. The ensuing catalogue of Actaeon's dogs is a supreme instance of Ovid's poetic exhibitionism. As Sandys notes, 'The transposition of these names in divers places to sute with the numbers [i.e. the metre] have caused some to taxe there interpretations.'

Through streightned wayes, and where there was no way,
90   The well-mouth'd hounds pursue the princely prey.
Where oft he wont to follow, now he flyes;
Flyes from his family! in thought he cryes,
I am *Actaeon*, servants, knowe your Lord!
Thoughts wanted words. High skyes the noyse record.
First, *Collier* pincht him by the haunch: in flung
Fierce *Kill-deare*; *Hill-bred* on his shoulder hung.
These came forth last; but crost a nearer way
A-thwart the hills. While thus their Lord they stay,
In rush the rest; who gripe him with their phangs.
100   Now is no roome for wounds. Grones speake his pangs,
Though not with humane voyce, unlike a Hart:
In whose laments the knowne Rocks beare a part.
Pitcht on his knees, like one who pitty craves,
His silent looks, instead of Armes, he waves.
With usuall showts their Dogs the Hunters cheare;
And seeke, and call *Actaeon*. He (too neare!)
Made answer by mute motions, blam'd of all
For being absent at his present fall.
Present he was, that absent would have beene;
110   Nor would his cruell hounds have felt, but seene.
Their snowts they in his body bathe; and teare
Their Master in the figure of a Deare:
Nor, till a thousand wounds had life disseis'd,
Could quiver-bearing *Dian* be appeas'd.   (1632)

Ovid's Metamorphosis 8.209–266 [Met. 8.183–235]
Daedalus and Icarus

The Sea-impris'ned *Daedalus*, meane-while,
Weary of *Creet*, and of his long exile;
Toucht with his countries love, and place of birth;
Thus said: Though *Minos* bar both sea and earth;
Yet heaven is free. That course attempt I dare:
Held he the world, he could not hold the ayre.
This said; to arts unknowne he bends his wits,
And alters nature. Quils in order knits,
Beginning with the least: the longer still
10   The short succeeds; much like a rising hill.
Their rurall pipes, the shepheards, long agoe,
(Fram'd of unequall reeds) contrived so.
With threds the midst, with wax he joynes the ends:
And these, as naturall wings, a little bends.
Young *Icarus* stood by, who little thought
That with his death he playd; and smiling, caught
The feathers tossed by the wand'ring ayre:
Now chafes the yellow waxe with busie care,
And interrupts his Sire. When his last hand
20   Had made all perfect: with new wings he fand
The ayre that bare him. Then instructs his sonne:
Be sure that in the middle course thou run.
Dank seas will clog the wings that lowly fly:
The Sun will burne them if thou soar'st too high.
'Twixt either keepe. Nor on *Boötes* gaze,
Nor *Helicé*, nor sterne *Orions* rayes:
But follow me. At once, he doth advise;
And unknowne feathers to his shoulders tyes.

---

3 *place of birth*: Athens

Amid his worke and words the salt teares brake
30   From his dim eyes; with feare his fingers shake.
Then kist him, never to be kissed more:
And rais'd on lightsome feathers flies before;
His feare behind: as birds through boundlesse sky
From ayrie nests produce their young to fly;
Exhorts to follow: taught his banefull skill;
Waves his owne wings, his sonnes observing still.
These, while some Angler, fishing with a Cane;
Or Shepheard, leaning on his staffe; or Swaine;
With wonder viewes: he thinkes them Gods that glide
40   Through ayrie regions. Now on his left side
Leaves *Juno's Samos*, *Delos*, *Paros* white,
Lebynthos, and *Calydna* on the right,
Flowing with hony. When the boy, much tooke
With pleasure of his wings, his Guide forsooke:
And ravisht with desire of heaven, aloft
Ascends. The odor-yeelding wax more soft
By the swift Sunnes vicinitie then grew:
Which late his feathers did together glew.
That thaw'd; he shakes his armes, which now were bare,
50   And wanted where withall to gather ayre.
Then falling, Helpe o father, cries: the blew
Seas stopt his breath; from whom their name they drew.
His father, now no father, left alone,
Cry'd *Icarus!* whaer art thou? which way flowne?
What region, *Icarus*, doth thee containe.
Then spies the feathers floating on the Maine.
He curst his arts; interres the corpse, that gave
The land a name, which gave his sonne a grave.   (1632)

Ovid's Metamorphosis 10.259–328 [Met. 10.238–94] *Pygmalion*

Yet durst th' obscene *Propoetides* deny,
O *Venus*, thy all-ruling Deity.
The first that ever gave themselves for hire
To prostitution; urged by thy ire.
Their lookes imboldened, modestie now gone,
Convert at length to little-differing Stone.
    Pygmalion seeing these to spend their times
So beast-like; frighted with the many crimes
That rule in women; chose a single life:
10 And long forbore the pleasure of a wife.
Meanwhile, in ivory with happy art
A Statue carves; so gracefull in each part,
As women never equall'd it: and stands
Affected to the fabrick of his hands.
It seem'd a virgin, full of living flame;
That would have mov'd, if not with held by shame.
Such Art his art conceal'd: which he admires;
And from it drawes imaginary fires:
Then often feeles it with his hands, to try
20 If 'twere a body, or cold ivory.
Nor could resolve. Who kissing, thought it kist:
Oft courts, imbraces, wrings it by the wrist;
The flesh impressing (his conceit was such)
And feares to hurt it with too rude a touch.
Now flatters her; now sparkling stones presents,
And orient pearle (loves witching instruments)
Soft-singing birds, each severall colour'd flowre,
First Lillys, painted balls, and teares that powre
From weeping trees. Rich Robes her person deck;
30 Her fingers, rings; reflecting gems her neck;
Pendants her eares; a glittering zone her brest.
In all, shew'd well; but shew'd, when naked, best.

Now layes he her upon a gorgeous bed:
With carpets of *Sidonian* purple spred.
Now calls her wife. Her head a pillow prest,
Of plumy downe, as if with sense possest.
Now came the Day of *Venus* Festivall:
Through wealthy *Cyprus* solemniz'd by all.
White heifers, deckt with golden hornes, by strokes
40   Of axes fall: ascending incense smokes.
He, with his gift, before the Altar stands:
You Gods, if all we crave be in your hands,
Give me the wife I wish: one like, he said,
But durst not say, give me my ivory Maid.
The golden *Venus*, present at her feast,
Conceives his wish; and friendly signes exprest:
The fire thrice blazing, thrice in flames aspires.
To his admired Image he retires:
Lyes downe besides her, rais'd her with his arme;
50   Then kist her tempting lips, and found them warme.
That lesson oft repeates; her bosome oft
With amorous touches feeles, and felt it soft.
The ivory dimpled with his fingers, lacks
Accustom'd hardnesse: as *Hymettian* waxe
Relents with heat, which chafing thumbs reduce
To pliant formes, by handling fram'd for use.
Amaz'd with doubtfull joy, and hope that reeles;
Againe the Lover, what he wishes, feeles.
The veines beneath his thumbs impression beat:
60   A perfect Virgin full of juyce and heat.
The *Cyprian* Prince with joy expressing words,
To pleasure-giving *Venus* thanks affords.
His lips to hers he joynes, which seeme to melt:
The blushing Virgin now his kisses felt;

---

34 Sidonian *purple*: exotic, expensive dye
54 *Hymettian*: from the Greek mountain Hymettus, known for its bees

And fearfully erecting her faier eyes,
Together with the light, her Lover spies.
Venus the marriage blest which she had made.
And when nine Crescents had at full displayde
Their joyning hornes, repleat with borrowed flame,
70   She *Phaphus* bore: who gave that Ile a name.

Pygmalion . . . deterred by the beastly life of the *Propoetides*, and the many vices which raigned in women, resolved to live a single life: who carving the image of a Virgin in Ivory, surpassing the perfection of Nature, fell in love with his owne workmanship. Nor is it extraordinary for excellent artizans to admire their owne skill, which addes to industry, as industry to perfection. And perhaps the life which was given it by the Goddesse, was no other then the grace and beauty of the figure; which *Apelles*, in his pictures, called the *Venus*; which made it live in the estimation of those times, and admiration of Posterity: as his sonne by her might be taken for the honour acquired by his admirable art; the *Grecian* and the *Roman* statues, after so many hundred of yeares, affording as long a life to the fame of the Artificer. But taken historically, this statue may be some Virgin on whom *Pygmalion* was enamoured, who long as obdurate as the matter whereof she was made, was mollified at length by his obsequiousnesse: the Ivory expressing the beauty of her body, and her blushes the modesty of her mind . . . Blushing is a resort of the blood to the face; which, in the passion of shame, labours most in that part, and is seene in the brest as it ascendeth: but most apparent in those that are young; in regard of their greater heat, and tender complexions. Which proceeds not from an infirmity of the mind, but the novelty of the thing; nor can bee either put on or restrained. The ensigne of native Modesty, & the colour of virtue. A beautifull and modest wife is therefore here said to be given him by the Goddesse, in reward of his devotion, as the greatest temporall happinesse. Neither may *Pigmalions* being in love with an image be altogether fictitious: since both *Pliny* and *Lucian* make mention of a Youth of no ignoble family (his name supressed for the foulenesse of the fact) who grew so desperately enamored on that celebrated Statue of naked *Venus*, carved in *Parian* marble by *Praxitiles*, and inshrined in her Temple at *Gnidos*; that all the day long he would gaze thereon, moving his lips as if hee sued for acceptance, sigh, change colour, and expressing all the distemperatures of a lover; offering at her Altar whatsoever his meanes would afford. And so farre his fury increased, that hiding himselfe one evening in the Temple, and being lockt in by the Sexton, he ran to the Statue, imbraced it strictly in his armes, warming the cold marble with his burning kisses, and so contaminated it with his lust, that the staines ever after remained, as a monument of his impiety. Who either struck with the horror of the deed, or that it was not in Nature to satisfie his desires; threwe himselfe from a rocke and so perished. Beautiful women, though metamorphized into stone, would not want their lovers.   (1632)

WYE SALTONSTALL (*fl.* 1630–1640)

The finesse that George Sandys brought to the pentameter couplet is less evident in the relentlessly end-stopped lines of Wye Saltonstall's *Tristia*. None the less, Saltonstall managed to do for the work what Turbervile had done for the *Heroides* in the previous century: his evident respect for Ovid's emotional fervour in these poems compelled his audience to take seriously what had generally been dismissed as exercises in obsequiousness and self-pity. At its best, the translator's choppy manner mirrors the brokenness of Ovid's lamentations. Though the indefatigable Saltonstall's later endeavours – a version of the *Heroides* appeared in 1636, and a banal *de Ponto* three years later – sadly falter, his *Tristia* does not find a worthy replacement until our own century.

Tristium. Lib. I Elegie III [Trist. 1.3]

When I remember that same fatall night,
The last that I injoy'd the Cities sight;
Wherein I left each thing to me most deare,
Then from mine eyes there slideth downe a teare,

For when the morning once drew neare that I,
By Cæsars sentence must leave *Italie*;
I had no minde to thinke upon the way,
My heavy heart did seeke out all delay.
Servants, nor yet companions did I chuse,
10   Nor coine, nor cloathes which banisht man might use.
I stood amaz'd like one by thunder strooke,
Who lives, yet thinkes that life hath him forsooke.
But when this cloud of sorrow was oreblowne,
And all my senses were more able growne;
I bad farewell to each sad friend by name,
For now of many there did few remaine,
My wife wept, and me weeping did imbrace,
A shower of teares still raining on her face;
My daughter now was in the *Aphrick* land,
20   Nor of my sad fate could she understand.
Through all my house deepe grones and sighes I heare;
As if some funerall solemniz'd were.
My wife, my children, and my selfe were mourners,
And private griefe did vent it self in corners.
If humble sorrowes great examples brooke,
Such was the face of things when *Troy* was tooke.
It was the deepest silence of the night,
And *Luna* in her chariot shined bright:
When looking on the Cappitols high frame,
30   Which joyned was unto our house in vaine:
You gods (quoth I) whom these faire seats enfold,
And temples which I ne're shall more behold:
And all yee gods of Rome whom I must leave,
These my last tenderd prayers to you receive;
Though wounded I the buckler use too late,
Let exile ease me of the peoples hate.

---

19 Aphrick *land*: i.e. Libya

Tell *Cæsar* though I sinn'd by ignorance,
There was no wickednesse in my offence.
And as you know so let him know the same,
40 . That so his wrath may be appeas'd againe.
With larger prayers my wife did then beseech
The gods, untill that sobs cut off her speech.
Then falling downe with flowing haire long spred,
Shee kist the harth whereon the fire lay dead;
And to our Penates pourd forth many a word,
Which for her husband now no helpe afford,
Now growing night did haste delay againe,
And *Arctos* now had turnd about her Waine,
And loath was I to leave my countrey sight,
50 Yet this for exile was my sentenc'd night.
If any urged my haste I would reply,
Alasse consider whither, whence I fly.
And then my selfe with flattery would beguile:
And thinke no houre did limit my exile.
Thrice went I forth, and thrice returning finde,
Slow paces were indulgent to my minde;
Oft having bid farewell, I spake againe,
And many parting kisses gave in vaine.
Then looking backe upon my children deare,
60 The same repeated charge I gave them there.
Why make we hast? tis just to seeke delay,
Since I am sent from *Rome* to *Scythia*.
For I must leave my children, house and wife,
Who while I live must leade a widdowes life.
And you my loving friends that present be,
And were like *Theseus* faithful unto me:

---

45 *Penates*: household gods
48 *Arctos*: constellation of the greater and lesser bears, ushering in the morning of exile
66 *Theseus*: Ovid's attribution of 'faithfulness' to Theseus is intentionally dubious: cf. *Her.* 4.59, where he is termed *perfidus*, 'faithless'.

Let us imbrace, and use times little store,
Perhaps I never shall imbrace you more.
And then my words to action did give place,
70   While I each friend did lovingly imbrace.
But while I speake and teares bedew'd my eyes,
The fatall morning starre began to rise.
My heart was so divided therewithall,
As if my limbes would from my body fall.
So *Priam* griev'd when he too late did finde,
The *Grecian* horse with armed men was linde.
Then sorrow was in one lowde cry esprest:
And every one began to knocke his breast;
And now my wife her armes about me cast,
80   And while I wept she spoke these words at last.
Thou shalt not goe alone, for I will be
Thy wife in banishment and follow thee:
In the same ship with thee Ile goe aboard,
And one land shall to us one life afford.
Thee unto exile *Cæsars* wrath commandes,
Me love, which love to me for *Cæsars* stands.
This shee repeats which shee had spoke before,
And could not be perswaded to give ore.
Till at the last when I my haire had rent,
90   Forth like some living funerall I went:
And after (as I heard) when night grew on,
Being mad with griefe, shee threw her selfe along
Vpon the ground, while as her haire now lies,
Soild in the dust: and when that shee did rise,
Shee did bewaile her Gods, herselfe and all,
And on her husbands name did often call,
Greeving as much for this my late exile,
As if she saw me on the funerall pile;
Shee wishes death her sorrowes would releeve:
100   Yet then againe, for my sake she would live,
And may she live while I obey my fate;
And live to helpe me in this wretched state.

But now the keeper of the Beare was washt,
With waves which even to the heavens flasht,
While we the *Ionian* seas now ploughing were,
Feare made us bold even in the midst of feare.
Alasse, the windes the seas in blacke adorne,
And with the beating waves the sand grew warme,
When straight a sea ore poope and sterne too came;
110   Washing those Gods were painted on the same.
And now the planckes did grone, the ropes did cracke,
As if the ship lamented her owne wrack.
Our masters palenesse did confesse his feare,
And knowing not what to doe, gives ore to steare:
And as a man unable to restraine,
A headstrong horse doth slacke the bridle raine,
So he let loose the sailes unto the seas,
Leaving the ship to drive on where it please.
And had not *Ælous* other winds straight sent,
120   We had been droven backe from whence we went,
Illiria being on our starboard hand,
We came in sight of the *Italian* land.
Cease then you windes to drive us on that shoare,
Tis Cæsars will we should goe backe no more.
Thus fearing that which I did much desire,
The leaping waves did to the decks aspire:
Spare me you Gods of seas, some mercy show,
Let it suffice that *Cæsar* is my foe,
And let not death my weary soule invade,
130   If one already ruind may be sav'd.   (1633)

Tristium. Lib. III. Elegie VIII [Trist. 3.7]

Goe thou my letter being writ so fast,
And to salute *Perhilla* make thou hast:
To sit hard by her mother shee still uses,
Or else to be amongst her bookes and Muses:
What ere shee does, when shee knowes thou art come,
Sheele aske thee how I do that am undone?
Tell her I live, but wish I did not so,
Since length of time can never ease my woe.
Yet to my Muse I now returned am,
10   Making my words in verse to flow againe:
And aske her why shee doth her minde apply,
To common studdies not sweet Poesy.
Since nature first did make thee chaste and faire,
Giving thee wit with other things most rare.
I first to thee the Muses spring did show,
Least that sweet water should at waste stil flow.
For in thy virgin yeares thy wit I spy'd,
And was as 'twere thy father and thy guide.
Then if those fires still in thy brest doe dwell,
20   There's none but *Lesbia* that can thee excell:
But I doe feare that since I am orethrowne,
That now thy brest is dull and heavy growne:
For while we might we both did reade our lines,
I was thy judge and master oftentimes.
And to thy verse I an eare would lend,
And make thee blush, when thou didst make an end.
And yet perhaps it may be thou dost shunne,
All bookes because my ruine thence did come:
Feare not, *Perhilla*, but all feare remove,

---

2 *Perhilla*: Ovid's stepdaughter (by his third wife), whom he tutored in poetry
20 *Lesbia*: Sappho

30   So that thy writings doe not teach to love:
        Then learned maide no cause of sloath still frame,
        But to thy sacred art returne againe.
        That comely face will soone be spoild with yeares,
        While aged wrinckles in thy brow appeares.
        Old age will lay hold on thy outward grace,
        Which commeth on still with a silent pace.
        To have been faire it will a griefe then be,
        And thou wilt thinke thy glasse doth flatter thee.
        Thy wealth is small, though thou deservest more,
40   But yet suppose thou hadst of wealth great store:
        Yet fortune when shee lists doth give and take,
        And of rich *Cræsus* she can *Irus* make.
        All things are subject to mortality,
        Except the minde and ingenuity.
        For though I want my countrey, friends, and home,
        And all things tooke from me that could be gon:
        Yet still my Muses doe with me remaine,
        And *Cæsar* cannot take away my vaine:
        Who though he should me of my life deprive,
50   Yet shall my fame when I am dead survive.
        While Rome on seven hills doth stand in sight,
        My workes shall still be read with much delight:
        Then of thy studdie make this happie use,
        To shunne the power of death even by thy muse.   (1633)

JOHN SHERBURNE (*fl.* 1639)

John Sherburne claims that he set out to translate the *Heroides* with an eye to 'rectifying the wrongs our Author hath sustained through the rude attempts of a too-too busie pen', presumably Saltonstall's. He goes

---

42 *Cræsus*, *Irus*: caricatures of the wealthy lord and the beggar

on to say of his own work, by contrast, that one 'may herein meet with a strictness (such as is requisite) in the words, and a respective care towards the meaning of our Author; a sweetnesse too, as much as could conveniently be attained, having throughout observed a verse for verse traduction'. However little Sherburne's discipline may have sweetened the poetry, it does rein in certain elegies (such as Phaedra's passionate letter to her stepson Hippolytus) in ways that enhance Ovid's dramatic effect. Also in 1639, Sherburne released a translation of *Ex Ponto*, dedicated to John Suckling.

Ovids Heroical Epistles [Her. 4] *Phædra to Hippolytus*

The health she wants, except the same thou lend
Phædra to th'*Amazonian* youth doth send.
Pray read my letter, how can it annoy?
Perhaps ther's in it, that may cause thee joy.
By these are secrets borne through seas and land,
And one foe reads what comes from th'others hand.
Thrice did I strive to speake, thrice my weake tongue
Faild me; and in my mouth my words still hung.
Oft I with shame did mixe my love, too light:
10 But what I blusht to speake, love bad me write.
What love commands, wee ought not to despise,
Who rules and awes the powerfull Deities.
He first to me in doubt to write, did say,
Phædra, write on, thy love he shall obey.
Ayd me great *Love*, and as thou rul'st in mee,
So cause in him a mutuall sympathie.
By no base sin I'le break my marriage vowes,
My fame, shouldst thou enquire, no stain yet knows.
Love comes more heavie through its sloath: I hide
20 Within me flames, my breast doth wounds abide.
As the first yoake the tender Heifer paines,
As new backt Colt the curbing bit disdaines:
So rude, so rawly love's by me indur'd,

Nor is my minde to the new load inur'd.
Full hard in giddy youth we learn loves Art,
But in our riper yeares, with pain and smart.
My fames first sacrifice shall be to thee,
And both of us alike will guiltie bee.
'Tis something from fraught boughs ripe fruit to cull,
30   And budding rose with nimble hand to pull.
Yet though my life hath hitherto been chast,
Nor by impurer spots, or taints defac't;
I grieve not, since I noble love embrace,
As foule adulterer makes his sin more base.
Should *Iuno* yeeld to me her thunderer,
I before *Iove* would *Hippolite* preferre.
    Nay, trust me, I doe now delight in new
And unknowne sports, wilde beasts in chase pursue.
No goddesse now but *Delia* pleaseth mee,
40   Grac'd with her Bow, I love, I like, as thee.
Darke groves I visit, Deere to toyles constraine,
And cheer my full-mouth'd hounds o're empty plain.
The tremulous dart, with arme advanc'd, I shake,
Or on the grassie ground, repose doe take.
And oft in winged chariots while I ride,
With curbing raines the swift-heeld coursers guide.
Now like th'*Eleides* whom fury fils,
Or those who Tymbrels ring on *Ida's* hils.
Or like to them whom the strange uncouth sight
50   Of *Driad's*, or the horned Fawnes affright,
I madly run: for when my fury's ceast,
They tell me all: close fires do scortch my breast.
    Perhaps by Fate we thus to love are bent,
And *Venus* tribute seekes from th'whole descent.

---

39 *Delia*: Diana, who as goddess of the hunt would be especially reverenced by Hippolytus   **47** *Eleides*: the Maenads, Bacchus's female retinue

First *Iove* of faire *Europa* made a rape,
(From thence we spring) through Buls assumed shape:
My mother doting too on such a beast,
Foully her burthen and her crime encreast.
Faithless *Aegides* by a clew of thread,
60   And through my sisters ayd, his prison fled.
And loe! lest I should seeme degenerate,
Alike I yeeld unto my kindreds fate.
It is ordain'd our love thus crosse should prove,
I thee, thy father did my sister love.
By thee, and *Theseus*, are two sisters wonne,
Erect two Trophies of our house alone.
    What time that I unto *Eleusis* went,
Would *Gnossian* land had kept me from th'intent.
Oh! then it was (though thou before didst please)
70   Fierce love my quiet members did disease.
White were thy garments, chaplets crown'd thy head,
And modest rednesse did thy cheekes o're-spread.
That visage which to others harsh did seeme,
I for a stout and valiant looke did deeme.
I hate your youths in womanish attires,
A manly feature little dresse requires.
Thee that thy sternnesse, haires so loosly plac'd,
And dust-soyld cheekes became, and sweetly grac'd.
When thou with rains dost cause thy Courser bound,
80   I'dmire to see thee nimbly ride the round.
Or when with able arme thou throwst the dart,
Mine eyes are fixed on thy agile art.
Or when thy hunting Pole thou tak'st, with bright
Steel tipt: whats'ere thou dost doth please my sight.

---

57 *My mother*: Pasiphae, who lusted after a bull. The product of this union was
the Minotaur.
59 *Aegides*: Theseus, preserved from the labyrinth by Ariadne's help
68 Gnossian *land*: Crete

Thy harshnesse to the riged woods bequeath:
Nor is it fit for thee I suffer death.

    Why so in *Cynthia's* sports dost so delight,
And take from *Venus* all her due, her right?
What wants successive rest, can ne're endure:
90 This cheeres the limbes, and doth new stength procure.
Marke thou thy *Delia's* armes, her shafts, and Bow;
Which should it still stand bent, would limber grow.
Famous was *Cephalus* in woods: much game
Fell by his hands inevitable aime.
Yet hee *Aurora* lov'd: who oft would come
To sport with him in aged *Tythons* roome.
Adonis oft, and *Cytherea* faire,
Under some Okes large shade, the grasse did beare.
Oenides did *Atalanta* love;
100 And by his spoyles did his affection prove.
Let us at length be numbred then with these;
Take love away, and th'woods must needs displease.
I'le thy companion be, and follow o're
Darke rockie groves, nor feare the tusked Bore.

    Two Seas their waves doe against *Isthmos* reare:
And the small earth doth both their battries heare.
There in *Trœzena* wee'l together raigne,
I now for this my native soyle disdaine.
Theseus is hence, long may he keepe away,
110 The young *Perithous* him forsooth doth stay.
Whom (except we 'gainst truth opposers bee)
He before *Phœdra* doth preferre, or thee.
Nor have I felt his injuries alone,
But both of us his wrongs have largely knowne.

---

87 Cynthia's *sports*: the hunt
93ff. Phaedra proceeds with a catalogue of great hunters who managed (she asserts) to find time for love. **97** *Cytherea*: Venus **99** *Oenides*: Meleager
110 *Perithous*: King of the Lapithae; Theseus's friendship with him was legendary.

My brothers bones, with his three knotted Mace,
He broke; and left my sister in distresse.
The chiefest 'mongst the Axe-arm'd mayds brought forth
Thee to the world, a parent full of worth.
Yet her the cruell *Theseus* slew; nor was
120   So great a son's brave mother safe, alas!
And that 'fore marriage, lest thou mightst perchance
Obtaine his kingdome as inheritance.
Brothers thou hadst by me too: which not I,
I doe protest, but he inforc'd to dye.
And may she oh! thou fairest, that doth minde
To hinder thee, death in her labour finde.
    Why now doest reverence thy fathers bed,
Which he himselfe disclaimes, and thence is fled?
Let not vaine names affright thy manly minde,
130   'Cause I thy step dame am to thee so kinde.
That needlesse pietie was in *Saturnes* time
Esteem'd: but future yeares shall call't a crime.
Saturne's now gone; with him his lawes decay:
And *Jove* the world now rules; then *Iove* obay.
Who hath ordain'd that just, which doth delight,
And brothers may with sisters joyne as right.
That kindreds chain's the surer link'd, whose bands
Venus herselfe ties with conjugall hands.
Nor need we cloke our love, we'l thrive from thence,
140   Our kindreds name shall smother our offence.
If our embraces should be seene, each shall
Commend, and me a courteous stepdame call.
Nor need'st thou in the darke to ope my gate,
Or gull my Porter in thy coming late.

115ff. Phaedra alludes to Theseus's transgressions: his killing of her half-brother
the Minotaur, his abandonment of her sister Ariadne, and his alleged responsibility
for the death of Hippolytus's mother Hippolyta, queen of the Amazons (the
'Axe-arm'd mayds').

Wee in one house did, in one house will live,
Thou gav'st knowne kisses, shalt knowne kisses give.
With me thou shalt be safe, and freely seene
Layd in my bed, nay prais'd for this thy sinne.
Oh! then delay not, but let's straightway joyne.
150 So may love spare thy breast which scorcheth mine.
Thou seest I scorne not humbly to intreat:
Where's now my pride become, my speeches great!
I once resolv'd not for to yeeld at all,
(If in our loves we ought resolv'd may call)
Yet lo! my princely armes are rais'd to thee,
'Las! lovers know not what things fitting be!
Foyld shame hath fled his colours: oh! thou faire,
Grant my just suit, and to be coy forbeare.
What though my father rule a far-stretcht sea,
160 And thunder-darting *Iove* great Grand-sire be?
What though my Grand-sire's front's empall'd with rayes:
Who in his purple chariot guides the dayes?
Nobilitie submits to love: encline
To pitty then; if not for me, for mine.
    I for my dowre possesse *Creet, Ioves* lov'd land:
There my whole Court shall be at thy command.
My mother mov'd a Savage Bull: wilt thou
Then fierce and stubborne beasts, more cruell grow?
For *Venus* sake, thy *Phædra* not disdaine:
170 So mayst thou love, and still be lov'd againe.
So may *Diana* ayd thee at thy will;
So may the woods yeeld store of game to kill.
So love the Satyrs, and each rurall Pane,
So may the Boare fall by thy Iaveline slaine.
So may the Nymphs, though thou to maids art curst
Bring thee cool streams to quench thy burning thirst.
To these I adde my teares, doe thou surmise
(And read) to see them falling from my eyes.   (1639)

ZACHARY CATLIN (*fl.* 1633–1639)

Zachary Catlin, otherwise known only as a 'Master of Arts, *Suffolke*', who composed several sermons, had the ill fortune to bring out his version of the *Tristia* in Saltonstall's wake. As he self-effacingly acknowledges in his preface, 'The truth is, I had half done my worke before I came to see the other, but after that, (though I was sorry I should *Actum agere*) yet I thought better to perfit what I had begun than to desist and give over in the midst.' Though inferior, Catlin's publication demonstrates the kind of attention that Ovid's exile poetry continued to enjoy on the eve of the Civil War.

De Tristibus: or Mournefull Elegies, Lib. 5. Elegie 13 [Trist. 5.12]

He answers here his friend, that wisht him write,
Verses in's Exile for a small delite.

Thou writ'st that I should passe my mournfull time
With study, lest my minde with rust decline.
Tis hard my friend to doe, for Verses aske,
A quiet mind, being a cheerefull taske.
But my hard Fortune's driven with adverse wind,
Ai that a worse can hardly be assign'd.
Thou bidst King *Priam* at's sons funerals sport,
And childlesse *Niobe* keepe a dancing Court.
What, seeme I fit for study, or for mone,
10   Who to the utmost *Getes* am sent alone?
Had I a mind with matchlesse strength sustain'd,
Like *Socrates* whom *Anytus* defam'd,

---

8 *childlesse* Niobe: as related in *Met.* 6.165–312, Niobe's maternal vanity outrages Latona, who strikes down all of her offspring
12 *Anytus*: one of Socrates's accusers at his trial

Yet such a weight would sinke my wits at length
Ioves anger farre exceedeth humane strength.
That aged man whom *Phœbus* styled wise,
Could not have wrote in such a wofull guise.
For say I could forget my home and fall,
And have no feeling of my grief at all,
Yet feare it selfe this quiet taske would let,
20   Who am with sundry cruell foes beset.
Adde that my wit is dull'd, or rusted o're,
And growne much weaker then it was before.
The fertile field, ift be not duely tild,
Will nought but grasse, with thornes and thistles yeeld:
The resty Horse, runs slowly, and arrives,
Hindmost of those, which for the mastry strive.
The Boate that long stands dry, it is no wonder,
If it in time grow seare, and cleave in sunder.
Well then may I despaire (though weake before)
30   To reach that straine of verse I had of yore.
Continuall troubles make my *Genius* fade,
Much of my former vigour is decayde.

    Yet oft my Table bookes I take in hand,
Wooing my words in lawfull feete to stand:
Yet can no verses make, or such as these
Which sute the Authours time, and states disease.
Lastly tis glory which the minde doth raise,
And eloquent straines doe flow from love of praise:
With fames bright lustre was I mov'd of yore,
40   So long as prosperous winds my sayles outbore.
Now tis not so with me, to seeke for glory.
I rather wish that none should know my story.

    Because my verse at first had good successe
Wouldst have me still my former labours presse?
Ye sisters nine (Ile speak it with your leave)
Twas you that did of *Italy* me bereave.

And as in's Bull the Authour first did smart,
So am I justly punisht for my Art.
Twere meete, that I should verses quite forbeare,
50 And after shipwracke the rough Ocean feare.
But say I would resume my harmefull Muse,
Here are no tooles to serve a Poets use.
Here's not a booke, nor one to lend an eare
Or that can understand me when they heare.
Each place is full of rude and bruitish noyse,
Each place is full of *Geticke* fearefull voyce,
And I the Latine tongue have much forgot,
So fall to speake the rude *Sarmaticke* note.
     And yet (to say the truth) cannot refraine.
60 But now and then my Muse a verse will frame,
I write, and what I write with fire consume,
And all my study ends in flame and fume.
Nor can I make a verse, nor doe desire,
And therefore cast my labours in the fire.
So that to you, none of my fancies came,
But what by chance or stealth escap't the flame.
     Even so, I wish my Art it selfe had burn'd,
     Which to such sorrow hath her Authour turn'd.   (1639)

---

47 *the Authour*: To ingratiate himself with the cruel tyrant Phaleris, the inventor Perillus designed a bronze bull wherein victims were roasted alive. As a reward, Phaleris condemned Perillus to be executed in his own device.
58 *rude* Sarmaticke: the languages of 'Sarmatia', the region of his exile, barbaric to Ovid   **67** *my Art*: the *Ars amatoria*, an alleged cause of his exile

JOHN GOWER (*fl.* 1640)

By the mid seventeenth century, the *Fasti* alone of all Ovid's work remained to be translated. John Gower – unknown apart from his sole published work, *Ovids Festivalls* – completed the roster. From the brief descriptive passages to the longer mythic narratives comprising Ovid's fragmentary calendar poem, Gower's line-for-line translation maintains an ease and dignity that accommodate both the poem's comic and noble registers. His would remain the only version for another century; as a poetic rendition, it is still unsurpassed. The excerpt from *Tristia* 4 appeared in Gower's introductory essay.

Ovids Festivalls 1.71−88 [Fas. 1.71−88] *Janus*

A good day comes; let tongues from hearts salute:
Good words and greetings this good day do suit.
Let idle wranglings not molest the eare:
Ye brawling people now your suits deferre.
See how the heavens with spicy fires do shine,
And spikenard crackles on the hearths divine.
Transplendent flames do lash the temples gold,
A twinkling lustre to the roof extoll'd.
White robes now walk to our Tarpeian wall:
10   The people's deckt in gaytie festivall.
New purple shines: new rods now stalk in state:
The ivory'd benches bear another weight.
The fair fat ox, whose neck ne're felt the yoke,
Now yields it to the sacrificing stroke.

---

9 *Tarpeian wall*: located at the top of the Capitoline Hill, the procession's destination

Jove when he views the world from towring skies
Hath nought but Romane to imploy his eyes.
Hail holy-day; come alwayes fortunate:
Deserving worship of a world-great state.   (1640)

Ovids Festivalls 1.295–310 [Fas. 1.295–310]
Encomium of astronomers

What lets to sing the starres ascent and set?
This is a piece on which our Muse must treat.
Blest souls who first did this rare science love,
And striv'd to climb those crystall courts above!
From worldly vices and all baser toyes
They (doubtlesse) their diviner thoughts did raise.
Nor wine, nor love, nor warres, nor court-affairs
Did break those lofty-towring minds of theirs:
Nor varnish't glory, nor ambition light,
10   Nor thirst of riches did distract their spright.
They drew the starres familiar to our eyes,
And to their knowledge did submit the skies.
So heaven is scal'd, not as *Olympus* yerst
Did *Ossa* bear, the clouds with *Pelion* pierc'd.
We by those guides will meet those heavenly lines,
And point each day to his associate signes.   (1640)

Ovids Festivalls 2.1–18 [Fas. 2.1–18] *February invocation*

Janus is done: Our yeare with rhythmes doth run;
And with the Month another book's begun.
Now Elegies your sails you 'gin display:
Me thoughts you were but little flags to day.

13f. an allusion to the abortive revolt of the Giants, who piled up these mountains in an effort to scale the gods' realm

You were my nimble pages in my love,
When first our Muse in youthfull sports did rove:
Now Calendary Holy dayes you sing:
How should this new from that old subject spring?
This is my chivalry: these arms I wear:
10   Our hands not void of all imployments are.
What though our arm no javelins flight doth force,
Nor check the chidings of a foming horse,
Nor girt with sword, nor with a helmet fens'd?
(None but may vaunt in those habiliments)
We studiously, brave Cesar, search thy names,
And trace the Titles thy desert proclaims:
Accept this service with a calmed brow;
If freed a while from curbing of the foe.   (1640)

Ovids Festivalls 3.167–232 [Fas. 3.167–232]
Sabine matrons

    If Poets may (as fame abroad doth give)
Some private notions from the Gods receive;
Mars, tell me why thy feasts observed are
By Wives, when thou art all for manly warre?
As thus I spake, *Mars* laid aside his shield;
But in his right hand still a javelin held:
Lo I, the God of Warre, to Peace's gown,
Now first invited, march to tents unknown.
Nor think I much some time here to bestow,
10   Lest *Pallas* think she only this can do.
Thou studious Prophet of the *Romane* yeare,
Learn thy desire, and these my sayings heare.
Rome's elements were at the first but small:
Yet had that small great hopes of this great wall.
Those walls for Founders were too large a room;
But yet too strait for Citizens to come.

Ask you, wher stood my Nephews Court of old?
That thatch there, made of straw and reed, behold.
On locks of hay he laid his sleeping head:
20   Yet heaven he mounted from that strawy bed.
And now the *Romanes* name was spread and gone
Beyond his place: nor had he wife or sonne.
The fruitfull neighbors my poore race did flout;
And I ill author of a stock was thought.
In dwelling in plain stalls, in tilling ground,
And feeding sheep more hurt then good was found.
Both birds and beasts do couple with their make;
Engendring fellows hath the basest snake.
In other lands each man enjoys his woman:
30   But none there be to marry with the *Romane.*
I griev'd; and with my spirit endu'd my sonne:
Cease pray'rs (said I:) *it must with arms be done.*
Keep Consus *feast: that day, in which his feast*
You solemnize, he will suggest the rest.
The *Curets* and the rest rose up in storms:
Then first the father 'gainst the sonne took arms.
Now were the ravish'd almost mothers made:
The kindred-battel still is long delaid.
The wives assembled all to *Juno's* Fane:
40   To whom my daughter boldly thus began;
My ravish'd Mates, 't is all our case: behold,
We can no longer piously be cold.
The battel's pitch'd: Now choose for whom ye'll pray:
That side our fathers, this our husbands fray.
We now must widows or else orphans live.
To you I'll good and noble counsel give.

---

17 *Nephews*: i.e. his son, Romulus   **23** *neighbors*: the Sabines
33f. For the rape of the Sabines, cf. *Ars* 1.101–30. Following this event, the
women's relatives threatened Romulus with war, leading up to the incident that
Ovid presently narrates.   **39** *Fane*: temple
40 *my daughter*: i.e. Romulus's unnamed Sabine mate

They took her counsel; and their hairs let down,
And mournfull bodies clad in mourning gown.
Now stood the bands, resolv'd for arms and harms,
50   Expecting signalls of the trump's alarms:
The wives came running, with their babies dear
Cull'd in their arms, amid the armies there.
So soon as e're they came amid the field,
With locks all torn and scatter'd, down they kneel'd.
The babes (as sensible) with moving cries
Held out their little arms to grandsires eyes.
All those that could cri'd, *Ave*, presently:
Those that could not their mothers forc'd to crie.
Down fell their arms and anger; and, their swords
60   Put up, they all shook hands in kind accords.
Each hugg'd his daughter, and his grandchild held
Upon his shield: the sweetest use of shield.
Thence *Sabine* wives no small advantage challenge
To keep a day to me on my first Calends:
Because on naked swords they venturing
Themselves, our warres to friendly peace did bring . . .   (1640)

Ovids Festivalls 4.417–620 [Fas. 4.417–620]
Proserpine's rape

This place invites the Virgins rape to shew.
Heare many things comprized in a few.
A land with three rocks crouds into the sea,
From its *Triangle* call'd *Trinacria*:
Belov'd of *Ceres*; plentifully town'd:
There stands fair *Enna* on a fertil ground.
Cold *Arethuse* the Dames of heaven invites:
The corn-crown'd Goddesse comes to those delights.

---

4 *Trinacria*: Sicily

Her Daughter, tended with her usuall train,
10   Walk'd barefoot up and down her flow'ry plain.
Hard by a grovy vale a flat doth lie,
Well water'd with a sources fall from high.
The gaudy mead her pride much vary'd, clad
With all the colours Lady *Nature* had.
Which soon as spi'd, *Come Playfellows*, cries she,
And fill your aprons full of flow'rs with me.
Young Maidens minds delight in trifling spoil;
And fond desire calls off the sense of toil.
This fills her basket of fine osiers made;
20   This stores her apron; she her coats doth lade.
This Marigolds; she plies the Violet-beds:
Her dainty finger crops the Poppy-heads.
On Hyacynth and Amaranth some dote:
Some Thyme, some Crowfoot, some love Melilote
And other flow'rs: The Rose doth much delight:
She plucks the Saffron and the Lily white.
Her busie mind stil further off doth bear her;
And (as it chanc'd) none of her mates were near her:
Her Uncle spies her, and on sooty steeds
30   Rapes her away, and to his kingdome speeds.
She cries, and calls out, Io *my mother dear,*
I'm forc'd away; and off her clothes doth tear.
Forthwith the vault of *Pluto* doth display:
His light-auk steeds could not abide the day.
Her Maids, their baskets fill'd with flowery treasures,
Cried *Ho* Persephone, *come see thy pleasures.*
When nought was heard, with cries they fill the dale,
And smite their hands against their bosomes pale.
Ceres amaz'd at this to *Enna* flies;
40   And straight, *Ah woful!! Where's my Girl?* she cries.

---

19 *osiers*: willow branches   **29** *Her Uncle*: Pluto, god of the underworld

About she hurries in a dead distraction,
Like shrews of *Bacchus* in their frantick action:
Or as a Cow, rob'd of her late-calv'd Love,
Runs sadly lowing all about the grove;
So she could neither sighs nor flight refrain,
But runs, and first begins at *Enna's* plain.
There first her daughter's footsteps she doth note:
The ground betrays the passage of her foot.
Perchance she then had search'd the furthest ground,
50 Had not some swine disturb'd the tract she found.
The *Leontini*, and *Anisus* mazes
She search'd, with all the meadow-grounds of *Acis:*
Then *Cyane*, and mild *Anapus* fount,
And over *Gela's* dangerous gulf doth mount:
Then o're *Ortygia* and *Pantagia* goeth,
And *Megara*; then o're *Simethus* mouth:
Next to the *Cyclops* sooty forge she hy'th;
Thence to that place nam'd from the crooked *Sithe*.
Then *Himere, Didym, Agrigentum*, and
60 *Tauromenus*; thence to *Mela's* Holy-Ox-land.
Next *Camarine* with Swanny *Tempe* fair,
And *Thapsos*; *Eryx* free to Western air:
Then search'd she *Pachyne, Pelore, Lilybe,*
Her Countrey's horn-like promontories three.
Each nook she fills with monefull Elegies,
As when the Lapwing to his *Itys* cries.
Sometimes, *Persephone*; sometimes she cry'd,
My Daughter; and by course both names imply'd:
But no *Persephone* could *Ceres* heare;
70 Nor *Daughter*, Mother: Vain both titles were.
When she a Shepherd or a Plowman spi'd,
Saw you no Damsel passe this way? she cri'd.

---

66 alluding to the myth of Tereus, transformed into a lapwing, mourning his
murdered son Itys (cf. *Met.* 6.424–674)

Nights cole-black colour now alone possess'd
All things: now watchfull tongues of dogs did rest.
Where *Ætna* high *Typhœus* vast bulk tires,
Whose ground is scorch'd with ever-spuing fires;
Here for her torch two Pines she doth inflame:
Hence in her rites the Torches custome came.
There is a cave of rugged pumice made,
80   Which neither man nor beast could e're invade:
Here when she came, her bridled snakes she tyes
T'her coach, and dry-foot o're the water flies.
Next raught the *Syrts*, and to *Charybdis* pass'd,
And those naufragious Dogs of *Scylla* vast;
The spacious *Adriack*, and *Corinthum* bound
Within two seas; hence reach'd the *Attick* ground.
Sad, on a stone here rests she first of all,
Which stone th' *Athenians* hence from *Sadnesse* call.
There many dayes in th' air she did remain
90   Unstirr'd, and patient both of cold and rain.
No place but hath its fate. Now *Cereall*
Eleusis then was *Celeus* farm but small.
He home was trudging with a trusse of wood,
With mast and berries from the hedge, for food.
His daughter with two goats from field did come:
His young sonne lay in cradle sick at home.
The Wench said, *Mother* (Her that name did move)
What d'ye alone here in this desert grove?
Th'old man too stands there (though his load were sore)
100   And pray'd her enter to his Cottage poore.
She now an old wife in a mitre drest,
In these sad words denyes his urg'd request,
Go safe, blest Parent, my poore Daughter's gone:
Ah, sweet condition farre above mine own!

---

84 *naufragious*: causing shipwreck
91f. *Cereall Eleusis*: i.e. Eleusis, town sacred to Ceres

She wip'd her eyes; a pearly drop came from her
Much like a tear: for tears did not become her.
Th' old man and maid, both tender-hearted, make
A part in tears. The down-right Sage then spake,
God keep, God keep thy daughter safe from harm:
110 *Come, pray, arise; reject not our poore farm.*
Replies the Dame, *Thy argument is strong.*
So rising up she follows him along.
As on they walk'd, he this to her exprest,
His Sonne was sick and could by no means rest.
She, as she went into his little mound,
Sleep-poring poppy gathers on the ground.
The-whiles she pluck'd she tasted it ('t is said)
And unawares her long-long fasting stay'd.
The which because she in the Evening did,
120 Her supper is not till the sunne is hid.
Being entred in, great mourning she beheld:
No hope of life was in the senselesse child.
Th' old wife saluted (called *Menaline*)
She daigns the boy's mouth to her own to joyn.
His strength and colour instantly renew'd:
Such vigour her celestiall kisse ensu'd.
The whole house joy'd; to wit, the parents dear,
And little maid: these three the whole house were.
Forthwith they set the boord; curds, apples, plumbs,
130 And golden hony in the hony-combs.
But *Ceres* fasted, and in milk lukewarm
Gives poppy to the boy, his sleep to charm.
Sleeps midnight-Silence did all things enwrap;
Triptolemus she takes into her lap:
Thrice stroak'd him with her hand: three charms she sung,
Not to be utter'd by a mortall tongue:

---

108 *down-right*: plain-spoken

Then rak'd up in hot embers him doth lay,
That fire might purge his humane drosse away.
Up starts the fool-kind Mother, and stark wild
140 Cries out, *what mean you?* and snatch'd up her child.
She said, *Th' art evil in not being so:*
By thy fond fear my gifts are frustrate now.
Now he is Mortall: But he first shall till
The earth, whose plenty shall his garners fill.
Thus forth she goes, and with a cloud attended,
Her winged-Dragon-mounted coach ascended.
Exposed *Sunion* and retir'd *Piræum*
And right-hand-ports she search'd, and passes by'um:
Thence from th' *Aegean* all the *Cyclads* eye'd;
150 Hence pass'd th' *Icarian* and *Ionian* wide.
And through all *Asia's* towns the *Hellespont*
She raught, and over severall climes doth mount.
For spic'd *Arabians* she beholds awhile;
Then *Ind, Libs, Meroe,* and the thirsty soil:
Then pass'd *Hesperia, Po,* the *Rhene,* and *Rhode,*
And *Tyber,* since a pow'rfull River's God.
O hold! our pen in counting all would tire:
No place on Earth was left unransack'd by her.
Yea, Heaven she search'd: and ask'd the signes that roll
160 (Expell'd from th' Ocean) next the frozen Pole;
Ye Northern Stars, (ye sure all actions know,
Because ye never dive the seas below:)
Tell what's become of my Persephone.
To her demand thus answers *Helice,*
The Night's not conscious of her: ask the Sunne,
Who sees what-ever in the Day is done.
Sol asked, answered, *Toil no more in vain:*
Thy Daughter's marryed to the Tertian *reigne.*

---

168 *Tertian* reigne: Hades

Long having mourn'd to *Jove* she pleads her case;
170   Deep characters of sorrow in her face:
Had you remembred who my Proserpine
Begat, your care of her had equall'd mine.
The whole world's search affords me nought but this,
To know my wrong. The Pirate hath his prize.
This forced match my child deserved not;
Nor I, to have a Sonne-in-law thus got.
What heavier thrall could Gyges conquest bring
Then now sh' endures the while her Father's King?
Shall he go scot-free? we revengelesse mourn?
180   *Make him repent his crime, and her return.*
Jove pacifies: *Let Love excuse,* saith he;
Nor be asham'd of his affinity.
He is our Equall. Heaven's my throne: One Brother
Reigns in the Ocean; and in Styx *the other.*
But if no reason can thy will perswade,
But thou wilt break a match already made;
We'll try this means: Sh' is thine, if meat sh' abstein:
If not, she must th' Infernall Bride remain.
Caduceus sails to *Styx* on nimble wings,
190   And quick as thought eye-witness'd tidings brings;
She hath her stomach staid with kernels three
Of th' apple pluck'd from the pomegranate-tree.
She mourns as much as if herself had now
Been forc'd away, and scarce could grief out-grow:
And thus she cries, *Your Heaven to me is hatefull:*
Let me go live in Tartary *more gratefull.*
This had she done too, but that *Jove* did swear,
In heaven her Daughter should be half the yeare.
With this was *Ceres* chear'd and comforted,
200   And put a corn-ear'd garland on her head.

---

177 *Gyges*: one of the Giants who rebelled against the gods
189 *Caduceus*: Mercury

The rested fields gave huge encrease of grain,
Whose crouded treasures barns could scarce contein.
White pleases *Ceres*; in her *Cereals* wear
White vestures: black is out of date with her.   (1640)

Ovids Festivalls 6.349–94 [Fas. 6.349–94] *Jove Pistor*

    Jove Pistor's altar here must I relate
In his high tower, more fam'd for name then state.
The cruell *Gauls Romes Capitol* beset,
Whose lasting siege had caus'd a famine great.
Jove calls the Gods before his royall throne:
By whose appointment *Mars* first makes his mone;
And is our sad calamity still hid?
Is this souls wound now to be uttered?
Yet if I must speak out our shamefull wo,
10   *In brief,* Rome's *thralled by the* Alpine *foe.*
Jove, *this is she whose power should once extend*
Beyond all limits, and the World transcend.
Her hopes in progresse were; she had controll'd
Her neighbours: now her walls she cannot hold.
Her purple Fathers, old triumphers, I
Saw in their brazen courts drop down and die.
I saw Queen Vesta *from her temple flee.*
What? do they think that any Gods there be?
But should they know that You possesse those Towers
20   *And Fanes girt in by their presumptuous powers,*
Would they not say, No hopes for them remain
In all their Gods: their incense is in vain?
Give them but room enough to pitch the field;
And, if they cannot conquer, let them yield.

---

1 Jove Pistor: Jove the Baker   **20** Fanes: temples

But now they poorely die: base dearth them galls,
While stern Barbarians overcrop their walls.
Then Venus and Quirinus in his gown,
And Vesta pleaded stiffly for their Town.
Great Jove replies, Our care in generall
30   Is for that place. The Gaul shall pay for all.
Thou onely, Vesta, help thy people poore;
And make the foe believe th' abound in store.
That corn they have let them but grind, and kneed
The liquour'd meal, and bake it into bread.
To Joves prescription Vesta gave consent.
'T was midnight now, and all the Captains, spent
With care and travel, to their rest were laid:
Jove chides, and tells them an ambiguous aid;
Arise, says he, and throw down to your foe
40   That help which you are all most loth to do.
They rous'd, and mus'd on this dark mysterie,
What help that most dislik'd them that should be.
At last their corn it seem'd: Which down they threw;
The rattling loaves 'mong shields and helmets flew.
The foe quite out of hopes, their siege remove:
For this an Altar's raised to Pistor Jove.   (1640)

Ovid to Posteritie [Trist. 4.10.1—34, 37—132]

That after-times may know of me each thing;
I was the man who tender Love did sing.
My country, Sulmo, fed with fresh springs all;
Miles ninety distant from the Romane wall.
Here was I born: The very yeare to tell;
'T was when by one fate two Consuls fell.

---

27 Quirinus: Romulus, now a god
6 two Consuls: Hirtius and Pansa, killed in battle in 43 BC

May that avail, I was a Knight by bloud,
Not onely raised by my Fortunes good.
I was no first-born child: for one sonne more
My father had, born just a yeare before.
Both he and I were born upon one day,
And at one time our natall gifts did pay.
It was the first day of the bloudy lists
Presented at the great *Quinquatrian* feasts.
Our Parents then, to have us train'd up well,
Put us to such as did in Arts excell.
My brother from his youth did bend his mind
To Rhetorick, and to the Law inclin'd.
But I a child the *Thespian* sweets did favour,
And more and more did winne the Muses favour.
Leave, leave these fruitlesse Studies, Sonne, oft cry'd
My father: Homer *but a poore man dy'd.*
Mov'd at his words I left the dear delight
Of *Helicon*, and 'gan in prose to write.
Lo, verses of their own accord came fit:
It was a verse whate'r I spake or writ.
Years growing on, my brother dear and I
Together took a Gown of *Liberty*.
Rich purple Robes with badges broad we wore,
Those studies follow'd which we us'd before.
My brother now had pass'd his twenti'th yeare:
He dies in whom I lost my souls best share.
In youth to some preferment rais'd was I,
And took the office of *Triumviri*.

★

---

14 Quinquatrian *feasts*: held 19–23 March
28 *Gown of* Liberty: i.e. the *toga virilis*, or garment of manhood, assumed in the sixteenth year   **34** *Triumviri*: a lesser judicial office

Both mind and bodie were unapt for labour,
And vex'd ambition I could never savour.
And still the Muses did intice me still
To their calm sweets, which e'r had my good will.
I dearly lov'd the Poets of the time:
40   Each Poet was a God in my esteem.
Oft did I heare sage *Macer* reade his Birds,
And Serpents, and the help each Herb affords.
And oft *Propertius* my companion dear
With amorous raptures did present my ear.
Heroick *Ponticus*, Iambick *Battus*
With pleasing strains did often recreate us.
And tunefull *Horace* oft my ear delighted
With curious ditties on his harp recited.
Virgil I onely saw: and hastie Fate
50   *Tibullus* friendship did anticipate.
He followed *Gallus*; and *Propertius*, him:
I was the third man in the rank of time.
As I my Elders, so my Juniours me
Ador'd: my Muse grew famous suddenly.
Thrice and no more had I shav'n off my beard
When first my youthfull strains the people heard.
My Mistresse, in *Corinna* mask'd, did move
My wits: each village now could chaunt our love.
Much did I write: but what I faulty knew
60   Into the fault-correcting fires I threw.
And at my exile cast I into flame,
Vex'd with my Muses, many a work of fame.
My tender heart oft pierced through with Love
Each light occasion instantly did move.
But when I was from *Cupids* passions free,
My Muse was mute and wrote no Elegie.
A worthlesse, lovelesse Wife to me but young
Was match'd: with whom I led my life not long.
My second wife, though free from any crime,
70   Yet she continued but a little time.

My last, with whom most of my dayes I spent,
Endur'd the blemish of my banishment.
One Daughter have I, which once and again
Made me a Grandsire, but by husbands twain.
And now my Father full of silver-hairs
His dayes concluded just at ninetie years.
As he'd have mourn'd for me, so did I mourn
For him. Next Sorrow was my Mothers urn.
Both happie sure and in good houres did die,
80 Whose death did come before my miserie.
And happie I, in that they both being dead
No tears at all for my affliction shed.
Yet if, ye Dead, have ought beside a name;
If your light Ghosts escape the fatall flame:
Parentall Souls, if you have heard of me
In *Styx*; if there my crimes related be:
Be you assur'd, with whom I cannot lie,
My crime was Errour not Dishonestie.
Enough for them. To you now I retire,
90 My friends, who th' actions of my life enquire.
The Summer-tropick of my years now gone,
Declining Age with hoarie hairs came on.
Now since my birth ten times the Horse-courser
That won the race *Pisæan* wreaths did wear:
When ah, offended *Cæsar* doth command
My dolefull exile to the *Tomites* land!
The cause of this, too much to most reveal'd,
Must be for ever by my self conceal'd.
Nor friends, nor servants wrongs will I here vent:
100 I've suffered crosses next to banishment.
To which my mind did scorn to yield; and still
By its own strength did stand invincible.

***

93f. i.e. the space of ten Olympiads, or 50 years total

And sans regard of self or calm life led,
With artlesse arm the warres I followed.
As many troubles have surcharg'd this soul
As there be starres 'twixt North and Southern Pole.
Long being toss'd about, at length I met
The surly *Sarmat* and the bow-arm'd *Get.*
Here, though I'm startled with the noise of arms,
110   My Muse with her best skill my sorrows charms.
And though no eare can relish here one rhythme,
Yet so I passe and so delude the time.
For life therefore, and power against my toils,
For passing of the tedious houres somewhiles,
Thanks, Muse, to thee: Thou art my sole relief,
My ease, my physick in my wasting grief.
Thou me, my Guide and dear Companion,
Dost raise from *Ister* into *Helicon.*
Thou giv'st me, while I live, a name sublime,
120   The rarest gift that scorns both Tombe and Time.
No black Detraction to this day hath bit
With fangs of envie any work I writ.
And though our age so many Poets high
Hath bred, my fansie Fame did ne'r envy.
I others honour'd: others honoured
Me with the best; and through the world I'm read.
If then we Poets can the truth divine;
Come death whenever, Dust, I am not thine.
Whether by favour or desert I be
130   Thus fam'd; kind Reader, thanks I give to thee.   (1640)

---

108 *The surly* Sarmat ... *Get*: barbarian tribes of the region, feared for their
warlike natures and skill in archery

JAMES SHIRLEY (1596–1666)

By the time the poet and dramatist James Shirley brought forward his belated contribution to the epyllion vogue, the genre seemed as outworn as the Narcissus myth itself. Unexpectedly, Shirley revitalizes both. His free retelling of the story begins (following Ovid's original) with Echo's ill-fated passion before moving on to Narcissus's withdrawal to the wooded *locus* and sudden moment of fatal self-discovery in the pool, where the present selection picks up.

Narcissus or the Self-Lover, 535–624, 643–726 [Met. 3.339–510]

90
No portion of a Birds forsaken nest,
Fell from the Bowes to interrupt the calme,
No wither'd leafe did in his fall molest
The stilnesse of it, smoothe as setled balme,
   But Crystall lesse transparent. Such a mirrour,
   So form'd could onely shew disdaine his errour.

91
And now Narcissus humbled on the grasse,
And leaning with his breast upon the brinke,
Looks into th'water, where he spies a face,
10 And as he did incline his head to drinke;
   As faire a countenance seem'd to meet with his,
   Off'ring to entertaine him with a kisse.

92
Giving a little backe, he doth admire
The beauty of the face presented to him,
Thinking at first some water-Nymph was there,

And rising from her silver Couch to woe him:
    Yet Court she cannot whom she did surprise,
    Never from water did such flames arise.

93
His heart glowes in him. Punishment fulfills:
20 Love leaps into full age, at the first houre,
New wonders like the waves, with rouling hills
Follow his gazes: all that lov'd before,
    Have flung their gather'd flames into his breast,
    Fit him for Love, a Sacrifice and Priest.

94
But strucken with his owne, his burning eyes
Are onely thirsty now; he drinks apace
Into his soule the shadow that he sees,
And dotes on every wonder of the face.
    He stoops to kisse it, when the lips halfe way
30   Meet, he retreats, and th'other steales away.

95
He, mov'd at the unkindnesse which he took
By his owne teaching, bowes himself againe,
The other meets him in the silent brook,
They spie agen, but he cannot refraine
    To Court whom he desires, and at his talke,
    The lips within the water seem to walke.

96
And every smile doth send his owne agen.
This cheeres him, but he cannot heare a sound
Break from the watrie prison, and he then
40 Complains a fresh, that his unhappy wound
    Admits no cure, and as he beats his breast,
    The Conflict under water is exprest.

97

What e'er thou art, come forth, and meet me here
He cries; why dost deceive me with a look?
What meanes that imitation? come neare,
Leape from the depth of thy imprisoning brook.
    Fold not thy armes like mine, or smile on me,
    Unlesse I may enjoy thy company.

98

But whether is my wiser reason fled?
It is the shadow of my selfe, I see,
And I am curst to be enamoured.
Where did I lose my soule? or where am I?
    What god shall pardon me this sin, if here,
    I must become my owne Idolater?

99

Thou fatall Looking-glasse, that dost present
My selfe to me, (my owne incendiarie.)
Oh let my eyes in love with their lament,
Weep themselves out, and prove a part of thee:
    This I shall gaine, either my shade may fleet,
    Or if it stay, I may want eyes to see't.

100

Under this burthen of my love I faint,
And finde I am with too much plenty poore:
Wealthy I am in nothing but my want;
I have, and yet (O gods) want nothing more:
    Mysteriously divided thus I stand,
    Halfe in the water, halfe upon the land.

101

But sure it cannot be my selfe I love;
How with my selfe despaire I to agree?
By one example both must gentle prove,

70   If I Narcissus love, can he hate me?
It is no shade then doth my phansie flatter,
But something that's divine doth blesse the water.

102
Essence of all that's faire, ascend to me;
To thy acceptance I present my heart:
Let not these elements our prisons be,
I in a fire, and thou in water art;
O let a friendly kisse as we two meet,
From thy coole water rise t'allay my heat.

103
This said, Narcissus doth his hold secure,
80   And with intention to receive a kisse,
His lip descends to meet the other there,
But hence his expectation cousned is;
For touching but the superficies,
Hee did too soon the frightned Image lesse.

104
Th'offended water into Circles ran,
And with their motion so disturb'd the place,
The Lover could not see himselfe againe:
Then doth he call aloud unto this face;
Thou bright-beam'd star, oh wither art thou gone?
90   But newly shewne thy head, and set so soon?

★

108
In thy smooth bosom once more let me pray
A sight of that sweet figure I adore,
Unlesse to heaven return'd some other way;
And if it be, 'tis not so farre before;
But I can dye, and off this flesh Robe hurl'd,
Ile overtake it in the other world.

109

Now doth each swelling Circle gently haste
To be dissolv'd, and spread themselves to aire;
No polish'd Marble seem'd more smooth, and fast;
The Boy takes this a fruit of his owne prayer,
 Yet e'er he thank'd the gods, he thought it fit,
 To see his love, and seen, forgot them quite.

110

Fearing to be depriv'd agen, he woes,
As every sillable had bled a life,
A sigh, at every clamorous period goes,
With greater noise then it, but no reliefe.
 His aire of tongue, and breast, thus spent, a look
 Presents their stories, doubled in the brook.

111

But all in vaine, the face, he saw before,
Is in the same ill-shewing silence drest,
Chang'd to more sad, but not one accent more,
Deafe as the streame, and now he beats his breast,
 Condemn'd agen to his more haplesse thought,
 He had but all this while his shadow sought.

112

This multiplies his grief into despaire,
Since his owne Image doth procure the fire,
And nothing left in nature to repaire
His vext affections, that now grow higher;
 That face, his owne, or whose so e're, was that
 Which took him first, to unlove is too late.

113

He beckens to the figure, that replies,
Taught by his posture how to call him thither;
To lift him from the water then he tries,

But when their white hands should have met together,
   A new distraction fell upon the streame,
   And his (because alone) thence weeping came.

114

When he to bear that company, lets fall
More teares than would have made another spring
Till griefe had not another drop to call,
Though to have cur'd his eyes, but will this bring
   The loved shade agen? No; every teare
   Was both his owne, and t'others murderer.

115

But more then this must be (Narcissus) borne,
As a revenge for many Nimphes that lov'd,
And dy'd upon the torture of thy scorne;
And see his eyes that once so charming mov'd
   Do loose their beames, and hasten to be dead
   In their owne hollowes, borne and buried.

116

See what a dotage on himselfe hath sent,
That brow that challeng'd late the snow, for white;
Veines that were made to shame the Firmament,
The cheek that so much wonder drew to it,
   The voice, when tun'd to love, might gods entice
   To change for earth their immortalities.

117

All, all is vanish'd, Nemesis have yet
Some pitty, let him live; he faints, he dies,
'Twere safer for the Boy himselfe to hate,
Then if he love, to pay so deare a price.
   He did but love himselfe, and if he die
   That loves, propose the haters destinie.

118

But Nemesis irrevocable doom,
Must be obey'd, though Eccho late repent,
Who with a murmuring pace unseen was come
To mourne for his, and her owne punishment.
    His groanes had thrild her soule, and at his death
    She comes to catch his fare-well taking breath.

119

And as a glimmering Taper almost spent,
Gasping for moisture to maintaine its fire,
After some darke contentions, doth present
A short-liv'd blaze, and presently expires:
    So he, collecting ebbing Nature, cryes,
    Oh youth, belov'd in vaine, farewell! and dyes.

120

Farewell, poore Eccho did repeat; and fled
With what wings sorrow lent, t'embalme the boy;
But looking carefully to finde the dead,
She miss'd the shadow of her livelesse joy:
    His body, vanish'd; by what mysterie
    Convey'd, not found by her inquiring eye.

121

But in the place where he did disappeare,
Out of the ground a lovely flower betrayes
His whiter leaves, and visibly did reare
His tufted head, with Saffron-colour'd rayes:
    Upon a smooth stemme all this beauty growes;
    This change to heaven the lost Narcissus owes.   (1646)

ROBERT HERRICK (1591–1674)

Herrick occupies a unique position as our poetry's best epigrammatist or, more precisely, imitator of the verses wrongly ascribed to the Greek poet Anacreon. He digested Ovid thoroughly, and his 1648 volume *Hesperides* offers numerous brilliant glimpses of the Latin poet's influence. All of the following poems from this collection are based on, incorporate lines from, or provide 'sententious' translations of passages from Ovid.

No Loathsomenesse in love [Am. 2.4]

What I fancy, I approve,
No Dislike there is in love:
Be my Mistresse short or tall,
And distorted there-withall:
Be she likewise one of those,
That an *Acre* hath of Nose:
Be her forehead, and her eyes
Full of incongruities:
Be her cheeks so shallow too,
10   As to shew her *Tongue* wag through:
Be her lips ill hung, or set,
And her grinders black as jet;
Ha's she thinne hair, hath she none,
She's to me a *Paragon*.

Love kill'd by Lack [Rem. 135–68]

Let me be warme; let me be fully fed:
Luxurious Love by Wealth is nourished.
Let me be leane, and cold, and once grown poore,
I shall dislike, what once I lov'd before.

Orpheus [Met. 10.1–77]

Orpheus he went (as Poets tell)
To fetch *Euridice* from Hell;
And had her; but it was upon
This short but strict condition:
Backward he should not looke while he
Led her through Hells obscuritie:
But ah! it hapned as he made
His passage through that dreadfull shade:
Revolve he did his loving eye;
(For gentle feare, or jelousie)
And looking back, that look did sever
Him and *Euridice* for ever.

10

The present time best pleaseth [Ars 3.121–22]

Praise they that will Times past, I joy to see
My selfe now live: *this age best pleaseth me.*

The end of his worke [Ars 1.771–72]

Part of the worke remaines; one part is past:
And here my ship rides having Anchor cast.

To Crowne it [Rem. 811–12]

My wearied Barke, O Let it now be Crown'd!
The Haven reacht to which I first was bound.

[Postscript] [Trist. 2.354]

To his Book's end this last line he'd have plac't,
Jocund his Muse was; but his Life was chast.   (1648)

HENRY VAUGHAN (1622–1695)

Henry Vaughan is best remembered for the secular and devotional lyrics
that comprise his 1650 collection *Silex Scintillans*. His four translations
from Ovid's exile poems are featured in the volume *Olor Iscanus*,
gathered amid the trauma of civil war in 1647, but not published until
1651. The wrenched poetic sensibilities that characterize this phase of
Vaughan's career are particularly well matched both to the nostalgic,
celebratory moment in the *Tristia* when Ovid recalls Roman Bacchic
festivities, and to the moral outrage of *Ex Ponto* 4.3.

Tristium Lib. 5. Eleg. 3a To his fellow-Poets at *Rome*, upon the birth-day of *Bacchus* [Trist. 5.3]

This is the day (blith god of *Sack*) which wee
If I mistake not, Consecrate to thee,
When the soft *Rose* wee marry to the *Bayes*,
And warm'd with thy own wine reherse thy praise,
'Mongst whom (while to thy *Poet* fate gave way)
I have been held no small part of the day,
But now, dull'd with the Cold *Bears* frozen seat,
Sarmatia holds me, and the warlike *Gete*.
My former life, unlike to this my last,
10   With *Romes* best wits of thy full Cup did tast,

---

8 Sarmatia *holds* . . . gete: See p. 180, n. 108.

Who since have seen the savage *Pontick* band,
And all the *Choler* of the Sea and Land:
Whether sad Chance, or heav'n hath this design'd,
And at my birth some fatall Planet shin'd,
Of right thou shouldst the *Sisters* knots undoe,
And free thy *Votarie* and *Poet* too.
Or are you Gods (like us) in such a state
As cannot alter the decrees of fate?
I know with much adoe thou didst obtain
20   Thy *Jovial godhead*, and on earth thy pain
Was no whit lesse, for wandring thou didst run
To the *Getes* too, and Snow-weeping *Strymon*,
With *Persia*, *Ganges*, and what ever streams
The thirsty *Moore* drinks in the mid-day beames.
But thou wert twice-born, and the Fates to thee
(To make all sure) doubled thy miserie,
My suffrings too are many: if it be
Held safe for me to boast adversitie,
Nor was't a Common blow, but from above
30   Like his, that died for Imitating *Jove*,
Which when thou heardst, a ruine so divine
And *Mother*-like, should make thee pitty mine.
And on this day, which *Poets* unto thee
Crown with full bowles, ask, *What's become of me?*

   Help bucksome God then! so may thy lov'd *Vine*
Swarm with the num'rous grape, and *big* with Wine
Load the kind *Elm*, and so thy *Orgyes* be
With priests lowd showtes, and *Satyrs* kept to thee!
So may in death *Lycurgus* ne'r be blest,
40   Nor *Pentheus* wandring ghost find any rest!

---

15 *Sisters*: the Fates
25 *twice-born*: At Semele's death Jupiter preserved the infant Bacchus by sewing him up in his thigh.
30 Capaneus, one of the Seven against Thebes, struck down for ignoring Jupiter's will

And so for ever bright (thy *Chiefe* desires,)
May thy *Wifes Crown* outshine the lesser fires!
If but now, mindfull of my love to thee,
Thou wilt, in what thou canst, my helper be.
You *Gods* have Commerce with your selves, try then
If *Cæsar* will restore me *Rome* agen.
    And you my trusty friends (the Jollie Crew
Of careless *Poets*!) when, without me, you
Perform this dayes glad Myst'ries, let it be
50 Your first Appeal unto his Deitie,
And let one of you (touch'd with my sad name)
Mixing his wine with tears, lay down the same,
And (sighing) to the rest this thought Commend,
O! Where is Ovid *now our banish'd friend?*
This doe, if in your brests I e'r deserv'd
So large a share, nor spitefully reserv'd,
Nor basely sold applause, or with a brow
Condemning others, did my selfe allow.
And may your happier wits grow lowd with fame
60 As you (my best of friends!) preserve my name.   (1651)

De Ponto, Lib. 4. Eleg. 3a. To his Inconstant friend, translated for the use of all the *Judases* of this touch–stone–Age [Pont. 4.3]

Shall I complain, or not? Or shall I mask
Thy hatefull name, and in this bitter task
Master my just Impatience, and write down
Thy crime alone, and leave the rest unknown?
Or wilt thou the succeeding years should see
And teach thy person to posteritie?
No, hope it not; for know, most wretched man,
'Tis not thy base and weak detraction can
Buy thee a *Poem*, nor move me to give
10 Thy name the honour in my Verse to live.

Whilst yet my *Ship* did with no stormes dispute
And temp'rate winds *fed* with a calme salute
My prosp'rous sailes, thou wert the only man
That with me then an equall fortune ran,
But now since angry heav'n with Clouds and night
Stifled those *Sun*-beams, thou hast ta'ne thy flight,
Thou knows't I want thee, and art meerly gone
To shun that rescue, I rely'd upon;
Nay, thou dissemblest too, and doest disclaime
20   Not only my *Acquaintance*, but my name;
Yet know (though deafe to this) that I am he
Whose *years* and *love* had the same *Infancie*
With thine, Thy *deep familiar*, that did share
Soules with thee, and partake thy *Joyes* or *Care*,
Whom the same *Roofe* lodg'd, and my *Muse* those nights
So solemnly endear'd to her delights;
But now, perfidious traitour, I am grown
The *Abject* of thy brest, not to be known
In that *false Closet* more; Nay, thou wilt not
30   So much as let me know, I am forgot.
If thou wilt say, thou didst not love me, then
Thou didst dissemble: or, if love agen,
Why now Inconstant? came the Crime from me
That wrought this Change? Sure, if no Justice be
Of my side, thine must have it. Why dost hide
Thy reasons then? for me, I did so guide
My selfe and actions, that I cannot see
What could offend thee, but my miserie.
'Las! if thou wouldst not from thy store allow
40   Some rescue to my wants, at least I know
Thou couldst have writ, and with a line or two
Reliev'd my *famish'd Eye*, and eas'd me so.
I know not what to think! and yet I hear,
Not pleas'd with this, th'art *Witty*, and dost Jeare;
Bad man! thou hast in this those tears kept back
I could have shed for thee, shoulds't thou but lack.

Know'st not that *Fortune* on a *Globe* doth stand,
Whose *upper* slipprie part without command
Turns *lowest* still? the sportive leafes and wind
50   Are but dull *Emblems* of her fickle mind,
In the whole world there's nothing I can see
Will throughly parallel her wayes, but thee.
All that we hold, hangs on a slender twine
And our best states by sudden chance decline;
Who hath not heard of *Cræsus* proverb'd gold
Yet knowes his foe did him a pris'ner hold?
He that once aw'd *Sicilia's* proud Extent
By a poor art could famine scarse prevent;
And mighty *Pompey* e'r he made an end
60   Was glad to beg his slave to be his friend;
Nay, he that had so oft *Romes* Consull bin,
And forc'd *Jugurtha*, and the *Cimbrians* in,
Great *Marius*! with much want, and more disgrace
In a foul Marsh was glad to hide his face.
A divine hand swayes all mankind, and wee
Of one short houre have not the certaintie;
Hadst thou one day told me, the time should be
When the *Getes* bowes, and th'*Euxine* I should see,
I should have check'd thy madness, and have thought
70   Th' hadst need of all *Anticira* in a draught;
And yet 'tis come to passe! nor though I might
Some things foresee, could I procure a sight
Of my whole destinie, and free my state
From those eternall, higher *tyes* of fate.
Leave then thy pride, and though now *brave* and *high*,
Think thou mayst be as *poore* and *low* as *I*.   (1651)

---

57 Dionysus II, brought down from a tyrant's heights to the humble office of a
schoolteacher
63 *Marius*: the consul who reputedly took shelter in the marshlands when driven
from Rome by Sulla
70 *Anticira*: Phocian town known for its hellebore, which was thought to restore
one's senses

JOHN DRYDEN (1631–1700)

After Milton's death in 1674, Dryden stepped forward as the preeminent English man of letters. His poetic reputation stands not least upon his striking capabilities as a translator of the classics. His versions of Ovid's works – from which he translated widely – are among his greatest achievements.

Most of Dryden's Ovid first appeared in collections and miscellanies published during the last twenty years of his life. Dido's letter to Aeneas comes from *Ovids Epistles* (1680); *Amores* 2.19 appeared alongside versions of Theocritus's third idyll and Virgil's fourth and ninth eclogues in the first *Miscellany Poems* published by Jacob Tonson in 1684. The *Metamorphoses*' opening book, along with episodes from Books 9 and 13, appeared in the third miscellany, *Examen Poeticum* (1693). Other passages followed in his last work, *Fables Ancient and Modern* (1700). All of Dryden's *Metamorphoses* translations were incorporated into Samuel Garth's composite 1717 edition of Ovid's poem. His first book of the *Ars amatoria* was finally released in 1709, along with work by Congreve and Tate. Dryden regarded this last work, in progress at the time of his death, as 'very incorrect', but also had enough honest self-awareness to recognize that 'none could do it better'.

Dido to Æneas [Her. 7]

So, on *Mæander*'s banks, when death is nigh,
The mournful *Swan* sings her own Elegie.
Not that I hope, (for oh, that hope were vain!)
By words your lost affection to regain;
But having lost what ere was worth my care,
Why shou'd I fear to lose a dying pray'r?
'Tis then resolv'd poor *Dido* must be left,
Of Life, of Honour, and of Love bereft!

While you, with loosen'd Sails and Vows, prepare
10   To seek a Land that flies the Searchers care.
Nor can my rising Tow'rs your flight restrain,
Nor my new Empire, offer'd you in vain.
Built Walls you shun, unbuilt you seek; that Land
Is yet to Conquer; but you this Command.
Suppose you Landed where your wish design'd,
Think what Reception Forreiners would find.
What People is so void of common sence,
To Vote Succession from a Native Prince?
Yet there new Scepters and new Loves you seek;
20   New Vows to plight, and plighted Vows to break.
When will your Tow'rs the height of *Carthage* know?
Or when, your eyes discern such crowds below?
If such a Town and Subjects you cou'd see,
Still would you want a Wife that lov'd like me.
For, oh, I burn, like fires with incense bright;
Not holy Tapers flame with purer light:
Æneas is my thoughts perpetual Theme:
Their daily longing, and their nightly dream.
Yet be ungrateful and obdurate still:
30   Fool that I am to place my heart so ill!
My self I cannot to my self restore:
Still I complain, and still I love him more.
Have pity, *Cupid*, on my bleeding heart;
And pierce thy Brothers with an equal dart.
I rave: nor canst thou *Venus'* offspring be,
Love's mother cou'd not bear a Son like Thee.
From harden'd Oak, or from a Rocks cold womb,
At least thou art from some fierce *Tygress* come,
Or, on rough Seas, from their foundation torn,
40   Got by the winds, and in a Tempest born:

---

34 *Brothers*: Cupid and Aeneas were both sons of Venus

Like that which now thy trembling Sailors fear:
Like that, whose rage should still detain thee here.
   Behold how high the Foamy Billows ride!
The winds and waves are on the juster side.
To Winter weather and a stormy Sea,
I'll owe what rather I wou'd owe to thee.
Death thou deserv'st from Heav'ns avenging Laws;
But I'm unwilling to become the cause.
To shun my Love, if thou wilt seek thy Fate,
50   'Tis a dear purchase, and a costly hate.
Stay but a little, till the Tempest cease;
And the loud winds are lull'd into a peace.
May all thy rage, like theirs, unconstant prove!
And so it will, if there be pow'r in Love.
Know'st thou not yet what dangers Ships sustain,
So often wrack'd, how darst thou tempt the Main?
Which, were it smooth; were every wave asleep,
Ten thousand forms of death are in the deep.
In that abyss the gods their vengeance store,
60   For broken Vows of those who falsely swore.
There winged storms on Sea-born *Venus* wait,
To vindicate the Justice of her State.
Thus, I to Thee the means of safety show:
And lost my self, would still preserve my Foe.
False as thou art, I not thy death design:
O rather live to be the cause of mine!
Shou'd some avenging storm thy Vessel tear,
(But Heav'n forbid my words shou'd Omen bear,)
Then, in thy face thy perjur'd Vows would fly;
70   And my wrong'd Ghost be present to thy eye.
With threat'ning looks, think thou beholdst me stare,
Gasping my mouth, and clotted all my hair.
Then, shou'd fork'd Lightning and red Thunder fall,
What coud'st thou say, but I deserv'd 'em all?
Lest this shou'd happen, make not hast away:
To shun the danger will be worth thy stay.

Have pity on thy Son, if not on me:
My death alone is guilt enough for thee.
What has his Youth, what have thy gods deserv'd,
80   To sink in Seas, who were from fires preserv'd?
But neither Gods nor Parent didst thou bear,
(Smooth stories all, to please a Womans ear.)
    False was the tale of thy Romantick life;
Nor yet am I thy first deluded wife.
Left to pursuing Foes *Creüsa* stai'd,
By thee, base man, forsaken and betray'd.
This, when thou told'st me, struck my tender heart,
That such requital follow'd such desert.
Nor doubt I but the Gods, for crimes like these,
90   Sev'n Winters kept thee wand'ring on the Seas.
Thy starv'd Companions, cast a Shore, I fed,
Thy self admitted to my Crown and Bed.
To harbour Strangers, succor the distrest,
Was kind enough; but oh too kind the rest!
Curst be the Cave which first my ruin brought:
Where, from the storm, we common shelter sought!
A dreadful howling eccho'd round the place,
The Mountain Nymphs, thought I, my Nuptials grace.
I thought so then, but now too late I know
100   The Furies yell'd my Funerals from below.
O Chastity and violated Fame,
Exact your dues to my dead Husbands name!
By Death redeem my reputation lost;
And to his Arms restore my guilty Ghost!
Close by my Palace, in a Gloomy Grove,
Is rais'd a Chappel to my murder'd Love.

---

77 *thy Son*: Ascanius
85 *Creüsa*: In *Aeneid* 2 Aeneas's wife Creusa disappears in the chaos of Troy's fall, despite Aeneas's efforts to rescue her.
95 *the Cave*: where, with Venus's prompting, their affair is consummated at *Aeneid* 4.160–72
102 *dead Husbands name*: Sychaeus, murdered by Dido's brother

There, wreath'd with boughs and wool his Statue stands,
The pious Monument of Artful hands:
Last night, methought, he call'd me from the dome,
110   And thrice with hollow voice, cry'd, *Dido*, come.
She comes: thy Wife thy lawful summons hears:
But comes more slowly, clogg'd with conscious fears.
Forgive the wrong I offer'd to thy bed,
Strong were his charms, who my weak faith misled.
His Goddess Mother, and his aged Sire,
Born on his back, did to my Fall conspire.
O such he was, and is, that were he true,
Without a blush I might his Love pursue.
But cruel Stars my birth day did attend:
120   And as my Fortune open'd, it must end.
My plighted Lord was at the Altar slain,
Whose wealth was made my bloody Brothers gain:
Friendless, and follow'd by the Murd'rers hate,
To forein Countrey's I remov'd my Fate;
And here, a suppliant, from the Natives hands,
I bought the ground on which my City stands,
With all the Coast that stretches to the Sea;
Ev'n to the friendly Port that shelter'd Thee:
Then rais'd these Walls, which mount into the Air,
130   At once my Neighbors wonder, and their fear.
For now they Arm; and round me Leagues are made
My scarce Establisht Empire to invade.
To Man my new built Walls I must prepare,
An helpless Woman and unskill'd in War.
Yet thousand Rivals to my Love pretend;
And for my Person, would my Crown Defend:
Whose jarring Votes in one complaint agree,
That each unjustly is disdain'd for Thee.
To proud *Hyarbas* give me up a prey;
140   (For that must follow, if thou go'st away.)

---

139 *Hyarbas*: barbarian ruler of an African kingdom neighbouring Dido's

Or to my Husbands Murd'rer leave my life;
That to the Husband he may add the Wife.
Go then; since no complaints can move thy mind:
Go perjur'd man, but leave thy Gods behind.
Touch not those Gods by whom thou art forsworn;
Who will in impious hands no more be born.
Thy Sacrilegious worship they disdain,
And rather wou'd the *Grecian* fires sustain.
Perhaps my greatest shame is still to come;
150   And part of thee lies hid within my womb.
The Babe unborn must perish by thy hate,
And perish guiltless in his Mothers Fate.
Some God, thou say'st, thy Voyage does command:
Wou'd the same God had barr'd thee from my Land.
The same, I doubt not, thy departure Steers,
Who kept thee out at Sea so many years.
Where thy long labours were a price so great,
As thou to purchase *Troy* wouldst not repeat.
But *Tyber* now thou seek'st; to be at best
160   When there arriv'd, a poor precarious Ghest.
Yet it deludes thy search: perhaps it will
To thy Old Age lie undiscover'd still.

A ready Crown and Wealth in Dow'r I bring;
And without Conqu'ring here thou art a King.
Here thou to *Carthage* may'st transfer thy *Troy*;
Here young *Ascanius* may his Arms employ:
And, while we live secure in soft repose,
Bring many Laurells home from Conquer'd Foes.
By *Cupids* Arrows, I adjure thee, stay;
170   By all the Gods, Companions of thy way.
So may thy *Trojans*, who are yet alive,
Live still, and with no future Fortune strive:
So may thy Youthful Son old age attain,
And thy dead Fathers Bones in peace remain,
As thou hast pity on unhappy me,
Who know no Crime but too much Love of thee.

I am not born from fierce *Achilles'* Line:
Nor did my Parents against *Troy* combine.
To be thy Wife, if I unworthy prove,
180 By some inferiour name admit my Love.
To be secur'd of still possessing thee,
What wou'd I do, and what wou'd I not be!
Our *Libyan* Coasts their certain seasons know,
When free from Tempests Passangers may go.
But now with Northern Blasts the Billows roar,
And drive the floating Sea-weed to the Shore.
Leave to my care the time to Sail away;
When safe, I will not suffer thee to stay.
Thy weary Men wou'd be with ease content;
190 Their Sails are tatter'd, and their Masts are spent:
If by no merit I thy mind can move,
What thou deny'st my merit, give my Love.
Stay, till I learn my loss to undergo;
And give me time to struggle with my woe.
If not; know this, I will not suffer long;
My life's too loathsome, and my love too strong.
Death holds my pen, and dictates what I say,
While cross my lap thy *Trojan* Sword I lay.
My tears flow down; the sharp edge cuts their flood,
200 And drinks my sorrows, that must drink my blood.
How well thy gift does with my Fate agree!
My Funeral pomp is cheaply made by thee.
To no new wounds my bosom I display:
The Sword but enters where Love made the way.
But thou, dear Sister, and yet dearer friend,
Shalt my cold Ashes to their Urn attend.
Sichæus Wife let not the Marble boast,
I lost that Title when my Fame I lost.
This short Inscription only let it bear,
210 'Unhappy *Dido* lies in quiet here.
'The cause of death, and Sword by which she dy'd,
'*Æneas* gave: the rest her arm supply'd.'

(1680)

Several of Ovid's Elegies, Book II. Elegy the Nineteenth [Am. 2.19] *To a cuckold*

If for thy self thou wilt not watch thy Whore,
Watch her for me that I may love her more;
What comes with ease we nauseously receive,
Who but a Sot wou'd scorn to love with leave?
With hopes and fears my Flames are blown up higher,
Make me despair, and then I can desire.
Give me a Jilt to tease my Jealous mind,
Deceits are Vertues in the Female kind.
Corinna my Fantastick humour knew,
Play'd trick for trick, and kept her self still new:
She, that next night I might the sharper come,
Fell out with me, and sent me fasting home;
Or some pretence to lye alone wou'd take,
When e'er she pleas'd her head and teeth wou'd ake:
Till having won me to the highest strain,
She took occasion to be sweet again.
With what a Gust, ye Gods, we then imbrac'd!
How every kiss was dearer than the last!
    Thou whom I now adore be edify'd,
Take care that I may often be deny'd.
Forget the promis'd hour, or feign some fright,
Make me lye rough on Bulks each other Night.
These are the Arts that best secure thy reign,
And this the Food that must my Fires maintain.
Gross easie Love does like gross diet, pall,
In squeasie stomachs Honey turns to Gall.
Had *Danae* not been kept in brazen Tow'rs,
Jove had not thought her worth his Golden Show'rs.

10

20

---

22 *Bulks*: doorsteps

When *Juno* to a cow turn'd *Io*'s Shape,
30   The Watchman helpt her to a second Leap.
Let him who loves an easie Whetstone Whore,
Pluck leaves from Trees, and drink the Common Shore.
The Jilting Harlot strikes the surest blow,
A truth which I by sad Experience know.
The kind poor constant Creature we despise,
Man but pursues the Quarry while it flies.

But thou dull Husband of a Wife too fair,
Stand on thy Guard, and watch the pretious Ware;
If creaking Doors, or barking Dogs thou hear,
40   Or Windows scratcht, suspect a Rival there;
An Orange-wench wou'd tempt thy Wife abroad,
Kick her, for she's a Letter-bearing Bawd:
In short be Jealous as the Devil in hell;
And set my Wit on work to cheat thee well.
The sneaking City Cuckold is my Foe,
I scorn to strike, but when he Wards the blow.
Look to thy hits, and leave off thy Conniving,
I'll be no Drudge to any Wittall living;
I have been patient and forborn thee long,
50   In hope thou wou'dst not pocket up thy wrong:
If no Affront can rouse thee, understand
I'll take no more Indulgence at thy hand.
What, ne'er to be forbid thy House and Wife!
Damn him who loves to lead so dull a life.
Now I can neither sigh, nor whine, nor pray,
All those occasions thou hast ta'ne away.
Why art thou so incorrigibly Civil?
Doe somewhat I may wish thee at the Devil.

---

30 *a second Leap*: Dryden's free rendering. Ovid suggests that Juno's efforts to ostracize Io only made her more alluring.
31 *Whetstone*: alluding to Whetstones–park, a well-known centre of prostitution
48 *Wittall*: a man who is indifferent to his status as cuckold

For shame be no Accomplice in my Treason,
60   A Pimping Husband is too much in reason.
     Once more wear horns before I quite forsake her,
     In hopes whereof I rest they Cuckold-maker.   (1684)

The First Book of *Ovid*'s Metamorphoses, 1–112
[Met. 1.1–88] *Creation*

Of Bodies chang'd to various Forms I sing:
Ye Gods, from whom these Miracles did spring,
Inspire my Numbers with Cœlestial heat;
Till I, my long laborous Work compleat:
And add perpetual Tenour to my Rhimes,
Deduc'd from Nature's Birth, to *Cæsar*'s Times.
     Before the Seas, and this Terrestrial Ball,
And Heav'n's high Canopy, that covers all,
One was the Face of Nature; if a Face,
10   Rather a rude and indigested Mass:
A lifeless Lump, unfashion'd, and unfram'd;
Of jarring Seeds; and justly Chaos nam'd.
No Sun was lighted up, the World to view;
No Moon did yet her blunted Horns renew:
Nor yet was Earth suspended in the Skye;
Nor pois'd, did on her own Foundations lye:
Nor Seas about the Shoars their Arms had thrown;
But Earth and Air and Water were in one.
Thus Air was void of light, and Earth unstable,
20   And Waters dark Abyss unnavigable.
No certain Form, on any was imprest;
All were confus'd, and each disturb'd the rest.
For hot and cold, were in one Body fixt;
And soft with hard, and light with heavy mixt.
     But God or Nature, while they thus contend,
To these intestine Discords put an end:
Then Earth from Air, and Seas from Earth were driv'n,

And grosser Air, sunk from Ætherial Heav'n.
Thus disembroil'd, they take their proper place;
30   The next of kin, contiguously embrace;
And Foes are sunder'd, by a larger space.
The force of Fire ascended first on high,
And took its dwelling in the vaulted skie:
Then Air succeeds, in lightness next to Fire;
Whose Atoms from unactive Earth retire.
Earth sinks beneath, and draws a numerous throng
Of pondrous, thick, unweildy Seeds along.
About her Coasts, unruly Waters roar;
And, rising on a ridge, insult the Shoar.
40   Thus when the God, what ever God was he,
Had form'd the whole, and made the parts agree,
That no unequal portions might be found,
He moulded Earth into a spacious round:
Then with a breath, he gave the Winds to blow;
And bad the congregated Waters flow.
He adds the running Springs, and standing Lakes;
And bounding Banks for winding Rivers makes.
Some part, in Earth are swallow'd up; the most
In ample Oceans, disembogu'd, are lost.
50   He shades the Woods, the Vallies he restrains
With Rocky Mountains, and extends the Plains.
      And as five Zones th' Ætherial regions bind,
Five Correspondent, are to Earth assign'd:
The Sun with Rays, directly darting down,
Fires all beneath, and fries the middle Zone:
The two beneath the distant Poles, complain
Of endless Winter, and perpetual Rain.
Betwixt th' extreams, two happier Climates, hold
The Temper that partakes of Hot and Cold.
60   The Feilds of liquid Air, inclosing all,
Surround the Compass of this Earthly Ball:
The lighter parts, lye next the Fires above;
The grosser near the watry Surface move:

Thick Clouds are spread, and Storms engender there, ⎫
And Thunders voice, which wretched Mortals fear,   ⎬
And Winds that on their Wings, cold Winter bear.   ⎭
Nor were those blustring brethren left at large,
On Seas, and Shoars, their fury to discharge:
Bound as they are, and circumscrib'd in place,
70   They rend the World, resistless, where they pass;
And mighty marks of mischief leave behind;
Such is the Rage of their tempestuous kind.
First *Eurus* to the rising Morn is sent,
(The Regions of the balmy Continent;)
And *Eastern* Realms, where early *Persians* run,
To greet the blest appearance of the Sun.
Westward, the wanton *Zephyr* wings his flight;
Pleas'd with the remnants of departing light:
Fierce *Boreas*, with his Off-spring, Issues forth
80   T' invade the frozen Waggon of the *North*.
While frowning *Auster*, seeks the *Southern* Sphere;
And rots with endless Rain, th' unwholsom year.

High o'er the Clouds and empty Realms of wind,
The God a clearer space for Heav'n design'd;
Where Fields of Light, and liquid Æther flow;
Purg'd from the pondrous dregs of Earth below.

Scarce had the Pow'r distinguish'd these, when streight
The Stars, no longer overlaid with weight,
Exert their Heads, from underneath the Mass;   ⎫
90   And upward shoot, and kindle as they pass, ⎬
And with diffusive Light, adorn their Heav'nly place. ⎭
Then, every void of Nature to supply,
With Forms of Gods he fills the vacant Skie:
New Herds of Beasts he sends, the plains to share: ⎫
New Colonies of Birds, to people Air: ⎬
And to their Oozy Beds, the finny Fish repair.   ⎭
A creature of a more Exalted Kind
Was wanting yet, and then was Man design'd:

Conscious of Thought, of more capacious Breast,
100 For Empire form'd, and fit to rule the rest:
Whether with particles of Heav'nly Fire
The God of Nature did his Soul Inspire,
Or Earth, but new divided from the Skie,
And, pliant, still, retain'd the Ætherial Energy:
Which Wise *Prometheus* temper'd into paste,
And mixt with living Streams, the Godlike Image cast.
Thus, while the mute Creation downward bend
Their Sight, and to their Earthy Mother tend,
Man looks aloft; and with erected Eyes
110 Beholds his own Hereditary Skies.
From such rude Principles our Form began;
And Earth was Metamorphos'd into Man.

(1693)

The Speeches of Ajax and Ulysses. From Ovid's Metamorphoses Book XIII, 205–56, 317–74, 435–59, 553–92 [Met. 13.128–58, 196–237, 280–95, 363–83] *Ulysses's reply to Ajax*

If Heav'n, my Lords, had heard our common Pray'r,
These Arms had caus'd no Quarrel for an Heir;
Still great *Achilles* had his own possess'd,
And we with great *Achilles* had been bless'd;
But since hard Fate, and Heav'n's severe Decree
Have ravish'd him away from you and me,
(At this he sigh'd, and wip'd his Eyes, and drew
Or seem'd to draw some Drops of kindly Dew)

---

1 After Achilles's death, the Greek camp at Troy is left to decide who will inherit the fallen hero's arms, Ajax or Ulysses. Ajax speaks first in the debate, denigrating Ulysses as a rhetorician rather than a warrior (cf. Robert Forbes's eighteenth-century dialect rendition of this portion of the exchange, below). Ulysses's eloquent reply predictably wins the day.

Who better can succeed *Achilles* lost,
10   Than he who gave *Achilles* to your Hoast?
This only I request, that neither He
May gain, by being what he seems to be,
A stupid Thing, nor may I lose the Prize,
By having Sense, which Heav'n to him denies:
Since, great or small, the Talent I enjoy'd
Was ever in the common Cause employ'd:
Nor let my Wit, and wonted Eloquence
Which often has been us'd in your Defence
And in my own, this only time be brought
20   To bear against my self, and deem'd a Fault.
Make not a Crime, where Nature made it none;
For ev'ry Man may freely use his own.
The Deeds of long descended Ancestors
Are but by grace of Imputation ours,
Theirs in effect; but since he draws his Line
From *Jove*, and seems to plead a Right Divine,
From *Jove*, like him, I claim my Pedigree;
And am descended in the same degree:
My Sire *Laertes* was *Arcesius* Heir,
30   *Arcesius* was the son of *Jupiter*.
No Paricide, no banish'd Man is known
In all my Line: Let him excuse his own.
Hermes ennobles too, my Mother's Side,
By both my Parents to the Gods ally'd.
But not because that on the Female Part
My Blood is better, dare I claim Desert,
Or that my Sire from Paricide is free;
But judge by Merit betwixt Him and Me:

---

10 When, at his mother's prompting, Achilles sought to avoid accompanying the
Greek expedition against Troy, Ulysses exposed his ruse and effectively enlisted
his help.

The Prize be to the best; provided yet,
40   That *Ajax* for a while his Kin forget,
And his great Sire, and greater Uncles, Name,
To fortifie by them his feeble Claim:
Be Kindred and Relation laid aside,
And Honours Cause by Laws of Honour try'd:
For if he plead Proximity of Blood;
That empty Title is with Ease withstood.
Peleus, the Hero's Sire, more nigh than he,
And *Pyrrhus*, his undoubted Progeny,
Inherit first these Trophies of the Field;
50   To *Scyros*, or to *Phthya*, send the Shield:
And *Teucer* has an Uncle's Right; yet he
Waves his Pretensions, nor contends with me.

*

Arriv'd at *Troy*, your choice was fix'd on me
A fearless Envoy, fit for a bold Embassy:
Secure, I enter'd through the hostile Court,
Glitt'ring with Steel, and crowded with Resort:
There, in the midst of Arms, I plead our Cause,
Urge the foul Rape, and violated Laws;
Accuse the Foes, as authors of the Strife,
60   Reproach the Ravisher, demand the Wife.
Priam, *Antenor*, and the wiser few,
I mov'd; but *Paris* and his lawless Crew
Scarce held their Hands, and lifted Swords: But stood
In Act to quence their impious Thirst of Blood:
This *Menelaus* knows; expos'd to share
With me the rough Preludium of the War.
Endless it were to tell what I have done,
In Arms, or Council, since the Siege begun:
The first Encounters past, the Foe repell'd,
70   They skulk'd within the Town, we kept the Field.
War seem'd asleep for nine long Years; at length
Both Sides resolv'd to push, we try'd our Strength

Now what did *Ajax* while our Arms took Breath,
Vers'd only in the gross mechanick Trade of Death?
If you require my Deeds, with ambush'd Arms
I trap'd the Foe, or tir'd with false Alarms;
Secur'd the Ships, drew Lines along the Plain,
The Fainting chear'd, chastis'd the Rebel-train,
Provided Forage, our spent Arms renew'd;
Employ'd at home, or sent abroad, the common Cause
80   pursu'd.
    The king, deluded in a Dream by *Jove*,
Despair'd to take the Town, and order'd to remove.
What subject durst arraign the Pow'r supreme,
Producing *Jove* to justifie his Dream?
Ajax might wish the Soldiers to retain
From shameful Flight, but Wishes were in vain:
As wanting of effect had been his Words,
Such as of course his thundring Tongue affords.
But did this Boaster threaten, did he pray, ⎫
90   Or by his own Example urge their stay?   ⎬
None, none of these, but ran himself away.   ⎭
I saw him run, and was asham'd to see;
Who ply'd his Feet so fast to get aboard as He?
Then speeding through the Place, I made a stand, ⎫
And loudly cry'd, O base degenerate Band,   ⎬
To leave a Town already in your Hand!   ⎭
After so long expence of Blood, for Fame,
To bring home nothing, but perpetual Shame!
These Words, or what I have forgotten since
100   (For Grief inspir'd me then with Eloquence)
Reduc'd their Minds; they leave the crowded Port,
And to their late forsaken Camp resort:
Dismay'd the Council met: This Man was there,
But mute, and not recover'd of his Fear.

81ff. Cf. *Iliad* 2.110–41.

Thersites tax'd the King, and loudly rail'd,
But his wide opening Mouth with Blows I seal'd.
Then rising I excite their Souls to Fame,
And kindle sleeping Virtue into Flame.
From thence, whatever he perform'd in Fight
110   Is justly mine, who drew him back from Flight.

★

Why am I forc'd to name that fatal Day,
That snatch'd the Prop and Pride of *Greece* away?
I saw *Pelides* sink, with pious Grief,
And ran in vain, alas, to his Relief;
For the brave Soul was fled: Full of my Friend
I rush'd amid the War his Relicks to defend:
Nor ceas'd my Toil 'till I redeem'd the Prey,
And, loaded with *Achilles*, march'd away:
Those Arms, which on these Shoulders then I bore,
120   'Tis just you to these Shoulders should restore.
You see I want not Nerves, who cou'd sustain
The pond'rous Ruins of so great a Man:
Or if in others equal Force you find,
None is endu'd with a more grateful Mind.
Did *Thetis* then, ambitious in her Care,   ⎫
These Arms thus labour'd for her Son prepare;   ⎬
That *Ajax* after him the heav'nly Gift shou'd wear. ⎭
For that dull Soul to stare with stupid Eyes,
On the learn'd unintelligible Prize!
130   What are to him the Sculptures of the Shield,
Heav'n's Planets, Earth, and Oceans watry Field?

---

129 *Prize*: Forged by Vulcan, Achilles's shield was a masterpiece of divine art; cf.
the description at *Iliad* 18.468–616.

The *Pleiads*, *Hyads*; less, and greater Bear,
Undipp'd in Seas; *Orion's* angry Star;
Two diff'ring Cities, grav'd on either Hand;
Would he wear Arms he cannot understand?

★

Brawn without Brain is thine: my prudent Care
Foresees, provides, administers the War:
Thy Province is to Fight; but when shall be
The time to Fight, the King consults with me:
140   No dram of Judgment with thy Force is join'd,
Thy Body is of Profit, and my Mind.
By how much more the Ship her Safety owes
To him who steers, than him that only rows,
By how much more the Captain merits Praise
Than he who Fights, and Fighting but obeys;
By so much greater is my Worth than thine,
Who can'st but execute what I design.
What gain'st thou brutal Man, if I confess
Thy Strength superiour when thy Wit is less?
150   Mind is the Man: I claim my whole Desert,
From the Mind's Vigour, and th' immortal part.
    But you, O *Grecian* Chiefs, reward my Care,
Be grateful to your Watchman of the War:
For all my Labours in so long a space,
Sure I may plead a Title to your Grace:
Enter the Town; I then unbarr'd the Gates,
When I remov'd their tutelary Fates.
By all our common hopes, if hopes they be
Which I have now reduc'd to Certainty;

---

157 *tutelary Fates*: With Diomedes, Ulysses stole from Troy the Palladium (the 'fatal Statue' of l. 171, below) without which Troy was, according to prophecy, unable to stand.

160   By falling *Troy*, by yonder tott'ring Tow'rs,
    And by their taken Gods, which now are ours;
    Or if there yet a farther Task remains,
    To be perform'd by Prudence or by Pains;
    If yet some desperate Action rests behind
    That asks high Conduct, and a dauntless Mind;
    If ought be wanting to the *Trojan* Doom
    Which none but I can manage and o'ercome,
    Award, those Arms I ask, by your Decree:
    Or give to this what you refuse to me.
170   He ceas'd: And ceasing with Respect he bow'd,
    And with his Hand at once the fatal Statue show'd.
    Heav'n, Air and Ocean rung, with loud Applause,
    And by the gen'ral Vote he gain'd his Cause.
    Thus conduct won the Prize, when Courage fail'd,
    And Eloquence o'er brutal Force prevail'd.

                                                 (1700)

Cinyras and Myrrha, Out of the Tenth Book of Ovid's Metamorphoses, 238–389 [Met. 10.431–524]
Cinyras and Myrrha

    The Solemn Feast of *Ceres* now was near,
When long white Linen Stoles the Matrons wear;
Rank'd in Procession walk the pious Train,
Off'ring First-fruits, and Spikes of yellow Grain:
For nine long Nights the Nuptial-Bed they shun,
And sanctifying Harvest, lie alone.
    Mix'd with the Crowd, the Queen forsook her Lord,
And *Ceres'* Pow'r with secret Rites ador'd:

---

175 Dryden's verdict mutes the ambiguity of the original *fortisque uiri tulit arma disertus*, 'and the arms of the brave man were awarded to the skilful speaker'.
1 Ovid has told of how Myrrha develops an incestuous lust for her father Cinyras. She discovers the passion to her nursemaid, who arranges a plot to realize her mistress's desires.

The Royal Couch, now vacant for a time,
The crafty Crone, officious in her Crime,
The cirst Occasion took: The King she found
Easie with Wine, and deep in Pleasures drown'd,
Prepar'd for Love: The Beldame blew the Flame,
Confess'd the Passion, but conceal'd the Name.
Her Form she prais'd; the Monarch ask'd her Years,
And she reply'd, The same thy *Myrrha* bears.
Wine and commended Beauty fir'd his Thought;
Impatient, he commands her to be brought.
Pleas'd with her Charge perform'd, she hies her home,
And gratulates the Nymph, the Task was overcome.
Myrrha was joy'd the welcom News to hear;
But clogg'd with Guilt, the Joy was unsincere:
So various, so discordant is the Mind,
That in our Will, a diff'rent Will we find.
Ill she presag'd, and yet pursu'd her Lust;
For guilty Pleasures give a double Gust.
'Twas Depth of Night: *Arctophylax* had driv'n
His lazy Wain half round the Northern Heav'n;
When *Myrrha* hasten'd to the Crime desir'd,
The Moon beheld her first, and first retir'd:
The Stars amaz'd, ran backward from the Sight,
And (shrunk within their Sockets) lost their Light.
Icarius first withdraws his holy Flame:
The Virgin Sign, in Heav'n the second Name,
Slides down the Belt, and from her Station flies,
And Night with Sable Clouds involves the Skies.
Bold *Myrrha* still pursues her black Intent;⎫
She stumbl'd thrice, (an Omen of th' Event;)⎬
Thrice shriek'd the Fun'ral Owl, yet on she went,⎭
Secure of Shame, because secure of Sight;
Ev'n bashful Sins are impudent by Night.
Link'd Hand in Hand, th' Accomplice, and the Dame,
Their Way exploring, to the Chamber came:

The Door was ope they blindly grope their Way,
Where dark in Bed th' expecting Monarch lay:
Thus far her Courage held, but here forsakes;
Her faint Knees knock at ev'ry Step she makes.
The nearer to her Crime, the more within
She feels Remorse, and Horrour of her Sin;
50 Repents too late her criminal Desire,
And wishes, that unknown she cou'd retire.
Her, lingring thus, the Nurse (who fear'd Delay
The fatal Secret might at length betray)
Pull'd forward, to compleat the Work begun,
And said to *Cinyras*, Receive thy own:
Thus saying, she deliver'd Kind to Kind,
Accurs'd, and their devoted Bodies join'd.
The sire, unknowing of the Crime, admits
His Bowels, and profanes the hallow'd Sheets;
60 He found she trembled, but believ'd she strove
With Maiden–Modesty against her Love,
And sought with flatt'ring Words vain Fancies to remove. }
Perhaps he said, My Daughter, cease thy Fears
(Because the Title suited with her Years;)
And Father, she might whisper him agen,
That Names might not be wanting to the Sin.
Full of her Sire, she left th' incestuous Bed,
And carry'd in her Womb the Crime she bred:
Another, and another Night she came;
70 For frequent Sin had left no Sense of Shame:
Till *Cinyras* desir'd to see her Face,
Whose Body he had held in close Embrace,
And brought a Taper; the Revealer, Light
Expos'd both Crime, and Criminal to Sight:
Grief, Rage, Amazement, cou'd no Speech afford,
But from the Sheath he drew th' avenging Sword;
The Guilty fled: The Benefit of Night,
That favour'd first the Sin, secur'd the Flight.

Long wand'ring through the spacious Fields, she bent
80   Her Voyage to th' *Arabian* Continent;
Then pass'd the Region which *Panchæa* join'd,
And flying left the Palmy Plains behind.
Nine times the Moon had mew'd her Horns; at length
With Travel weary, unsupply'd with Strength,
And with the Burden of her Womb oppress'd,
Sabæan Fields afford her needful Rest:
There, loathing Life, and yet of Death afraid,
In anguish of her Spirit, thus she pray'd.
Ye Pow'rs, if any so propitious are
90   T' accept my Penitence, and hear my Pray'r;
Your Judgments, I confess, are justly sent;
Great Sins deserve as great a Punishment:
Yet since my Life the Living will profane,
And since my Death the happy Dead will stain,
A middle State your Mercy may bestow,
Betwixt the Realms above, and those below:
Some other Form to wretched *Myrrha* give,
Nor let her wholly die, nor wholly live.
The Pray'rs of Penitents are never vain;
100   At least, she did her last Request obtain:
For while she spoke, the Ground began to rise,
And gather'd round her Feet, her Leggs, and Thighs;
Her Toes in Roots descend, and spreading wide,
A firm Foundation for the Trunk provide:
Her solid Bones convert to solid Wood,
To Pith her Marrow, and to Sap her Blood:
Her Arms are Boughs, her Fingers change their Kind,
Her tender Skin is harden'd into Rind.
And now the rising Tree her Womb invests,
110   Now, shooting upwards still, invades her Breasts,
And shades the Neck; when weary with Delay,
She sunk her Head within, and met it half the Way.
And though with outward Shape she lost her Sense,
With bitter Tears she wept her last Offence;

And still she weeps, nor sheds her Tears in vain;
For still the precious Drops her Name retain.
Mean time the mis-begotten Infant grows,
And, ripe for Birth, distends with deadly Throws
The swelling Rind, with unavailing Strife,
To leave the wooden Womb, and pushes into Life.
The Mother-Tree, as if oppress'd with Pain,
Writhes here and there, to break the Bark, in vain;
And, like a Lab'ring Woman, wou'd have pray'd,
But wants a Voice to call *Lucina's* Aid:
The bending Bole sends out a hollow Sound,
And trickling Tears fall thicker on the Ground.
The mild *Lucina* came uncall'd, and stood
Beside the struggling Boughs, and heard the groaning Wood:
Then reach'd her Midwife-Hand to speed the Throws,
And spoke the pow'rful Spells that Babes to Birth disclose.
The bark divides, the living Load to free,
And safe delivers the Convulsive Tree.
The ready Nymphs receive the crying Child,
And wash him in the Tears the Parent-Plant distill'd.
They swath'd him with their Scarfs; beneath him spread
The Ground with Herbs; with Roses rais'd his Head.
The lovely Babe was born with ev'ry Grace,
Ev'n Envy must have prais'd so fair a Face:
Such was his Form, as Painters when they show
Their utmost Art, on naked Loves bestow:
And that their Arms no Diff'rence might betray,
Give him a Bow, or his from *Cupid* take away.
Time glides along, with undiscover'd haste,
The Future but a Length behind the past;
So swift are Years: The Babe whom just before
His Grandsire got, and whom his Sister bore;

120
130
140

124 *Lucina*: goddess of childbirth **125** *Bole*: trunk

The Drop, the Thing, which late the Tree inclos'd,
And late the yawning Bark to Life expos'd;
A Babe, a Boy, a beauteous Youth appears,
150 And lovelier than himself at riper Years.
Now to the Queen of Love he gave Desires,
And, with her Pains, reveng'd his Mother's Fires.   (1700)

Ovid's Art of Love. Book I. 498–553 [Ars 1.437–86] *Writing*

By Letters, not by Words, thy Love begin;
And Foord the dangerous Passage with thy Pen.
If to her Heart thou aim'st to find the way,
Extreamly Flatter, and extreamly Pray.
Priam by Pray'rs did *Hector*'s Body gain;
Nor is an Angry God invok'd in vain.
With promis'd Gifts her easy Mind bewitch;
For ev'n the Poor in promise may be Rich.
Vain Hopes a while her Appetite will stay;
10 'Tis a deceitful, but commodious way.
Who gives is Mad; but make her still believe
'Twill come, and that's the cheapest way to give.
Ev'n barren Lands fair promises afford;
But the lean Harvest cheats the starving Lord.
Buy not thy first Enjoyment; lest it prove
Of bad example to thy future Love:
But get it *gratis*; and she'll give thee more,
For fear of losing what she gave before.
The losing Gamester shakes the Box in vain,
20 And Bleeds, and loses on, in hopes to gain.
    Write then, and in thy Letter, as I said,
Let her with mighty Promises be fed.

---

149 *A Babe*: Adonis, whose story follows in the *Metamorphoses*

Cydippe by a letter was betray'd,
Writ on an Apple to th' unwary Maid.
She read her self into a Marriage Vow;
(And ev'ry Cheat in Love the Gods allow.)
Learn Eloquence, ye noble Youth of *Rome*;
It will not only at the Bar o'ercome:
Sweet words, the People and the Senate move;
30   But the chief end of Eloquence, is Love.
But in thy Letter hide thy moving Arts;
Affect not to be thought a Man of Parts.
None but vain Fools to simple Women Preach;
A learned Letter oft has made a Breach.
In a familiar Style your Thoughts convey;
And Write such things, as Present you wou'd say;
Such words as from the Heart may seem to move:
'Tis Wit enough, to make her think you Love.
If Seal'd she sends it back, and will not read;
40   Yet hope, in time, the business may succeed.
In time the Steer will to the Yoke submit;
In time the restiff Horse will bear the Bit.
Ev'n the hard Plough-share, use will wear away;
And stubborn Steel in length of time decay.
Water is soft, and Marble hard; and yet
We see, soft water through hard Marble Eat.
Though late, yet *Troy* at length in Flames expir'd;
And ten years more, *Penelope* had tir'd.
Perhaps, thy Lines unanswer'd she retain'd;
50   No Matter; there's a Point already gain'd:
For she who Reads, in time will Answer too;
Things must be left, by just degrees to grow.

---

23 *Cydippe*: Acontius had inscribed an apple with a marriage vow and rolled this into the temple where Cydippe was worshipping. When she read the inscription aloud before the altar, she was bound by the promise she had unintentionally spoken.

Perhaps she Writes, but Answers with disdain;
And sharply bids you not to Write again:
What she requires, she fears you shou'd accord;
The Jilt wou'd not be taken at her word.   (1709)

JOHN OLDHAM (1653–1683)

The satirist and poet John Oldham had, by the time of his premature
death, formed close friendships with some of the leading literary figures
of his day. He is now well remembered from Dryden's elegy in his
honour. Along with a version of the *Metamorphoses*' Byblis story, Oldham
translated *Amores* 2.5 and the following poem.

Some Elegies out of Ovid's Amours, Imitated, Book II. Elegy IV: That he loves Women of all sorts and sizes. [Am. 2.4]

Not I, I never vainly durst pretend
My Follies and my Frailties to defend:
I own my Faults, if it avail to own,
While like a graceless wretch I still go on:
I hate my self, but yet in spite of Fate
Am fain to be that loathed thing I hate:
In vain I would shake off this load of Love,
Too hard to bear, yet harder to remove:
I want the strength my fierce Desires to stem,
Hurried away by the impetuous stream.
'Tis not one Face alone subdues my Heart,
But each wears Charms, and every Eye a Dart:
And wheresoe're I cast my Looks abroad,
In every place I find Temptations strow'd.
The modest kills me with her down-cast Eyes,
And Love his ambush lays in that disguise.

The Brisk allures me with her gaity,
And shews how Active she in Bed will be:
If Coy, like cloyster'd Virgins, she appears,
20   She but dissembles, what she most desires:
If she be vers'd in Arts, and deeply read,
I long to get a learned Maidenhead:
Or if Untaught and Ignorant she be,
She takes me then with her simplicity:
One likes my Verses, and commends each Line,
And swears that *Cowley*'s are but dull to mine:
Her in mere Gratitude I must approve,
For who, but would his kind Applauder love?
Another damns my Poetry, and me,
30   And plays the Critick most judiciously:
And she too fires my Heart, and she too charms,
And I'm agog to have her in my arms.
One with her soft and wanton Trip does please,
And prints in every step, she sets, a Grace:
Another walks with stiff ungainly tread;
But she may learn more pliantness abed.
This sweetly sings; her Voice does Love inspire,
And every Breath kindles and blows the fire:
Who can forbear to kiss those Lips, whose sound
40   The ravish'd Ears does with such softness wound?
That sweetly plays: and while her Fingers move,   ⎫
While o'er the bounding Strings their touches rove, ⎬
My Heart leaps too, and every Pulse beats Love: ⎭
What Reason is so pow'rful to withstand
The magick force of that resistless Hand?
Another Dances to a Miracle,
And moves her numerous Limbs with graceful skill:
And she, or else the Devil's in't, must charm,
A touch of her would bed-rid Hermits warm.

---

26 *Cowley's*: Oldham's contemporary substitution for Ovid's *Callimachus*

50   If tall; I guess what plenteous Game she'l yield,
        Where Pleasure ranges o'er so wide a Field:
        If low; she's pretty: both alike invite,
        The Dwarf, and Giant both my wishes fit.
        Undress'd; I think how killing she'd appear,
        If arm'd with all Advantages she were:
        Richly attir'd; she's the gay Bait of Love,
        And knows with Art to set her Beauties off.
        I like the Fair, I like the Red-hair'd one,
        And I can find attractions in the Brown:
60   If curling Jet adorn her snowy Neck,
        The beauteous *Leda* is reported Black:
        If curling Gold; *Aurora*'s painted so:
        All sorts of Histories my Love does know.
        I like the Young with all her blooming Charms,
        And Age it self is welcom to my Arms:
        There uncropt Beauty in its flow'r assails,
        Experience here, and riper sense prevails.
        In fine, whatever of the Sex are known
        To stock this spacious and well-furnish'd Town;
70   Whatever any single man can find
        Agreeable of all the num'rous kind:
        At all alike my haggard Love does fly,
        And each is Game, and each a Miss for me.   (1683)

THOMAS CREECH (1659–1700)

A lifelong dedication to classical literature upholds Thomas Creech's translations of a broad range of authors, including Lucretius, Horace and Theocritus. His handling of Ovid in the light elegy on the death of Corinna's parrot, and his sombre compression of the *Fasti*'s Lucretia narrative, reveal a subtle facility with and respect for Ovid's various moods. Both appeared in the *Miscellany Poems* of 1684.

Several of Ovid's Elegies, Book II. Elegy the Sixth [Am. 2.6]

Alas, poor *Poll*, my *Indian* talker, dyes!
Go Birds, and celebrate his *Obsequies*.
Go Birds, and beat your Breasts, your Faces tear,
And pluck your gaudy plumes, instead of hair.
Let dolefull Tunes the frighted Forests wound,
And your sad Notes supply the Trumpets sound.
Why *Philomel* dost mourn, the *Thracian* rage?
It is enough, thy Grief at last assuage; }
His Crimson faults are now grown white with Age.
Now mourn this Bird, the Cause of all thy woe
Was great 'tis true, but it was long ago.
Mourn all ye wing'd Inhabitants of Air,
But you, my *Turtle*, take the greatest share!
You two liv'd constant Friends, and free from strife,
Your Kindness was intire, and long as life.
What *Pylades* to his *Orestes* vow'd,
To thee, poor *Poll*, thy friendly *Turtle* show'd }
And kept his Love as long as Fate allow'd.

10

---

13 *Turtle*: turtledove, i.e. Corinna

But ah, what did thy Faith, thy Plumes and Tail,
20 And what thy pretty Speaking-art avail?
And what that thou wert given, and pleas'd my Miss,
Since now the Birds unhappy Glory dyes?
A lovely *verdant* Green grac't every Quill,
The deepest *vivid* Red did paint thy Bill:
In speaking thou didst every Bird excell,
None prattled, and none lisp'd the words so well.
'Twas envy only sent this fierce Disease, ⎫
Thou wert averse to War, and liv'dst in peace, ⎬
A talking harmless thing, and lov'dst thy Ease. ⎭
30 The fighting Quails still live midst all their strife,
And even that, perhaps, prolongs their Life.
Thy meat was little, and thy pratling tongue
Would ne'er permit to make thy Dinner long:
Plain Fountain-water all thy drink allow'd,
And Nut, and Poppy-Seed were all thy Food.
The preying *Vultures*, and the *Kites* remain,
And the unlucky *Crow* still caws for Rain.
The *Chough* still lives, midst fierce *Minerva*'s hate,
And scarce nine hundred years conclude her Fate.
40 But my poor *Poll* now hangs his sickly head,
My *Poll*, my present from the East, is dead.
Best things are soonest snatcht by cov'tous Fate,
To worse she freely gives a longer date.
Thersites brave *Achilles* Fate surviv'd;
And *Hector* fell, whilst all his Brothers liv'd.
Why should I tell, what Vows *Corinna* made?
How oft she beg'd thy Life, how oft she pray'd?
The Seventh-day came, and now the Fates begin,
To end the thread, they had no more to Spin.

---

44 *Thersites*: deformed and cowardly buffoon among the Greeks at Troy

50   Yet still he talkt, and when death nearer drew,
       His last breath said, *Corinna*, now Adieu.
       There is a shady Cypress Grove below,
       And thither (if such doubtfull things we know)   ⎫
       The Ghosts of pious Birds departed go.   ⎭
       'Tis water'd well, and verdant all the year,
       And Birds obscene do never enter there:
       There harmless *Swans* securely take their rest,
       And there the single *Phœnix* builds her nest.
       Proud *Peacocks* there display their gaudy Train,
60   And billing *Turtles* Coo o'er all the Plain.
       To these dark Shades my *Parrot*'s soul shall go,
       And with his Talk divert the Birds below.
       Whilst here his bones enjoy a Noble Grave,
       A little Marble, and an Epitaph:

        In talking I did every Bird excell,
        And my Tomb proves my Mistress lov'd me well.   (1684)

The Story of *Lucretia* out of Ovid *de Fastis*. Book II [Fas. 2.685–852]

Now *Tarquin* the last King did govern *Rome*,
Valiant abroad 'tis true, tho fierce at home;
Some Towns he won, some he did fairly beat,
And took the *Gabii* by a mean deceit;
For of his Three brave Youths his youngest Son,
His Nature fierce, his Manners like his own,
His Father's Child Outright pretends a flight,
And came amidst the Enemies by Night;
They drew their Swords, Come kill me now he said,
10   My Father will rejoyce to see me dead:
     See how his Rods my tender Entrails tore,
     (To prove this true he had been whipt before)

The men grow mild, they sheath their threatning swords
And view his wounds, and those confirm his words:
Then each man weeps, and each his wrongs resents
And begs to side with them, and he consents.
Thus gull'd, the crafty Youth, and once in Trust,
The first occasion sought to be unjust,
And the unthinking *Gabii*'s Town betray,
20   Consults his Father for the surest way.
There was a Garden crown'd with fragrant Flowers, ⎫
A little Spring ran through the pleasant Bowers, ⎬
The soft retreat of *Tarquin*'s thinking hours. ⎭
There when the message came he chanc't to stand,
And lopt the tallest Lilies with his wand:
With that the Messenger return'd, and said,
I saw your Father crop the lofty head
Of each tall Flower, but not one word to you;
Well, says the Son, I know what I must doe,
30   And streight the Nobles kill'd; When those were gone
He soon betray'd the poor defenceless Town.
When lo (a wond'rous sight) a Serpent came,
And snatcht the Entrails from the dying Flame;
Phoebus advis'd, and thus the Answer ran ⎫
He that shall kiss (for so the Fates ordain) ⎬
His Mother first shall be the greatest man. ⎭
Then streight with eager haste th'unthinking Crowd
Their Mothers kiss't, nor understood the God.
But wiser *Brutus*, who did act the Fool,
40   Lest *Tarquin* should suspect his rising Soul,
Fell down, as if't had been a Casual fall,
And kiss't his Mother Earth before them all.
Now *Ardea* was besieg'd, the Town was strong,
The men resolv'd, and so the Leaguer long:

---

44 *Leaguer:* siege

And whilst the Enemy did the War delay, }
Dissolv'd in Ease the careless Souldiers lay, }
And spent the vacant time in sport and play. }
Young *Tarquin* doth adorn his Noble Feasts,
The Captains treats, and thus bespeaks his Guests;
50 Whilst we lye lingring in a tedious War,
And far from Conquest tired out with Care,
How do our Women lead their Lives at *Rome*?
And are we thought on by our Wives at home?
Each speaks for his, each says I'll swear for mine,
And thus a while they talkt, grown flusht with Wine;
At last young *Collatine* starts up and cryes,
What need of words, come let's believe our Eyes;
Away to *Rome*, for that's the safest Course,
They all agree, so each man mounts his Horse.
60 First to the Court, and there they found no Guard,
No Watchmen there, and all the Gates unbar'd;
Young *Tarquin*'s Wife, her hair disorder'd lay
And loose, was sitting there at Wine and play.
Thence to *Lucretia*'s, She a lovely Soul
Her Basket lay before her, and her Wooll,
Sate midst her Maids, and as they wrought she said,
Make haste, 'tis for my Lord as soon as made;
Yet what d'ye hear? (for you perchance may hear)
How long is't e'er they hope to end the War?
70 Yet let them but return; But ah, my Lord
Is rash, and meets all dangers with his Sword:
Ah when I fansie that I see him fight,
I swoon and almost perish with the fright.
Then wept, and leaving her unfinisht thread
Upon her bosome lean'd her lovely head.

---

56 *Collatine*: Lucretia's husband

All this became, gracefull her grief appears,
And she, chast Soul, lookt beauteous in her tears.
Her Face lookt well, by Natures art design'd,
All charming fair, and fit for such a mind.

80   I come, says *Collatine*, discard thy Fear,
At that she streight reviv'd, and oh my Dear,
She claspt his neck, and hung a welcome burthen there.

Mean while Young *Tarquin* gathers lustfull Fire,
He burns and rages with a wild Desire;
Her Shape, her Lilie-white, and Yellow hair,
Her natural Beauty, and her gracefull Air,
Her words, her voice, and every thing does please,
And all agree to heighten the disease;
That she was Chast doth raise his wishes higher,

90   The less his hopes, the greater his Desire.
But now 'twas Morning, and the warlike Train
Return from *Rome*, and take the Field again:
His working Powers her absent Form restore,
The more he minds her, still he loves the more;
'Twas thus she sate, thus spun, and thus was drest,
And thus her Locks hung dangling o'er her Breast;
Such was her Mein, and such each Air and Grace,
And such the charming figure of her Face.

As when a furious storm is now blown o'er
100   The Sea still troubl'd, and the waters roar
And curle upon the Winds that blow before.

So he tho' gone the pleasing form retains
The Fire her present Beauty rais'd remains;
He burns, and hurry'd by resistless Charms,
Resolves to force, or fright her to his Arms.
I'll venture, let whatever fates attend,
The daring bold have fortune for their friend;

By daring I the *Gabii* did o'ercome;
This said, he takes his Horse, and speeds for *Rome*:
110 The sun was setting when he reach'd the place,
With more than Evening Blushes in his Face;
A Guest in shew, and Enemy in design
He reach'd the stately Court of *Collatine*,
And's welcom'd there, for he was nearly Kin.
How much are we deceiv'd? She makes a Feast,
And treats her Enemy as a Welcome Guest;
Now Supper's done, and sleep invites to Bed,
And all was husht, as Natures self lay dead.
The Lamps put out, and all for rest design'd
120 No fire in all the House, but in his mind:
He rose, and drew his Sword, with lustfull speed
Away he goes to chaste *Lucretia*'s Bed;
And when he came, *Lucretia*, not a word,
For look, *Lucretia*, here's my naked Sword;
My Name is *Tarquin*, I that Title own,
The King's young Son, his best beloved Son.
Half dead with fear, amaz'd *Lucretia* lay,
As harmless Lambs, their Mothers gone away,
Expos'd to ravenous Wolves an easie prey.
130 Her Speech, her Courage, Voice, and Mind did fail,
She trembled, and she breath'd, and that was all:
What could she doe? Ah! could she strive? with whom?
A Man! a Woman's easily o'ercome.
Should she cry out, and make Complaints of wrong,
His violent Sword had quickly stopt her tongue.
What should she strive to fly? that hope was gone,
Young *Tarquin* held her fast, and kept her down.
He prest her Bosome with a lustfull hand,
That chast, that charming Breast then first prophan'd.

---

108 *By daring . . . o'ercome*: Tarquin had conquered neighbouring Gabii through
treachery. *Fas.* 2.691–710 recounts his ruse fully.

140   The Loving Foe still sues, resolv'd to gain
       With promise, threats, and Bribes: but all in vain.
       At last 'tis Folly to resist, he cry'd,
       My Love will rise to Rage, if long deny'd;
       For I'll accuse thee of unlawfull Lust,
       Kill thee, and swear, tho' false, thy Death was Just.
       I'll stabb a Slave, and what's the worst of harms,
       Black Fame shall say I caught thee in his Arms.
       This Art prevail'd, she fear'd an injur'd name,
       And liv'd and suffer'd, to secure her Fame.
150   Why dost thou smile, Triumphant Ravisher?
       This shamefull Victory shall cost thee dear.
       Thy ruine pay for this thy forc'd delight,
       How great a price! a Kingdom for a Night!
       The guilty Night was gone, the day appears,
       She blusht, and rose, and double Mourning wears,
       As for her onely Son, she sits in Tears.
       And for her Father, and her Husband sends,
       Each quickly hears the message, and attends.
       But when they came, and saw her drown'd in Tears,
160   Amaz'd they askt the Cause, what violent Fears,
       What real ill did wound her tender mind;
       What Friend was dead, for whom this Grief design'd?
       But she sate silent still, still sadly cry'd,
       And hid her blushing Face, and wept, and sigh'd.
       Both strive to Comfort, both lament her Fate,
       And fear some deadly Ill, they know not what.
       Thrice she would speak, thrice stopt, again she tryes
       To speak her wrong, yet durst not raise her Eyes:
       This too on *Tarquin*'s score, she cry'd, I place;
170   I'll speak, I'll speak, ah me! my own disgrace,
       And what they could her modest words exprest,
       The last remain'd, her Blushes spoke the rest.
       Both weep, and both the forc't Offence forgive,
       In vain you pardon me, I can't receive
       The pity you bestow, nor can I live.

This said, her fatal Dagger pierc't her side,
And at her Father's feet she fell and dy'd.
Her Soul flew through the wound, and mounts above
As white, and Innocent as a Virgin Dove,
180   Not spotted with one thought of Lawless Love.
Yet as she fell, her dying thoughts contriv'd
The fall as modestly as she had liv'd.
The Father o'er the Corpse, and Husband fall,
And mourn, and both the common loss bewail.
While thus they mourn'd, the generous *Brutus* came
And shew'd his Soul ill-suited with his Name.
He graspt the Dagger reeking in her Gore,
And as he held it thus devoutly swore;
By thee, by this thy Chast and Innocent Bloud,
190   And by thy Ghost, which I'll esteem a God;
Tarquin, and all his Race shall be expell'd,
My Virtue long enough hath lain conceal'd.
At that she rais'd her Eyes, she seem'd to bow
Her head, and with her Nod approv'd the Vow.
The Pomp appears, and as it passes by
The gaping Wound expos'd to publick View,
Fill'd all the Crowd with rage, and Justly drew
Curses from every Heart, & Tears from every Eye.
Young *Brutus* heads the crowd, proclaims the wrong,
200   And tells them they endure the King too long:
The King's expell'd, and Consuls they create,
And thus the Kingdom chang'd into a State.

(1684)

JOHN WILMOT, EARL OF ROCHESTER (1647–1680)

During his short life, Rochester won notoriety as a stereotype of the Restoration court rake: educated, witty, brash, dissolute. His harsh satires and obscene verses helped fuel the reputation. In Ovid he found a more tempered role model. A slightly altered version of his *Amores* 2.9 – here taken from a manuscript version – appeared posthumously in the 1684 collection of Ovid's *Amours* that continued into numerous editions throughout the next century.

To Love [Am. 2.9]

O Love! how cold and slow to take my part,
Thou idle wanderer about my heart.
Why thy old faithful soldier wilt thou see
Oppressed in my own tents? They murder me.
Thy Flames consume, thy arrows pierce thy friends;
Rather, on foes pursue more noble ends.
   Achilles' sword would generously bestow
A cure as certain as it gave the blow.
Hunters who follow flying game give o'er
When the prey's caught; hope still leads on before.
We thine own slaves feel thy tyrannic blows,
Whilst thy tame hand's unmoved against thy foes.
On men disarmed how can you gallant prove?
And I was long ago disarmed by love.
Millions of dull men live, and scornful maids:
We'll own Love valiant when he these invades.

10

---

7 Achilles' *Sword*: Telephus, wounded by Achilles's sword, could be healed only by rust from the same weapon.

Rome from each corner of the wide world snatched
A laurel; else't had been to this day thatched.
    But the old soldier has his resting place,
20   And the good battered horse is turned to grass.
The harrassed whore, who lived a wretch to please,
Has leave to be a bawd and take her ease.
For me, then, who have freely spent my blood
Love, in thy service, and so boldly stood
In Celia's trenches, were't not wisely done
E'en to retire, and live in peace at home?

No! Might I gain a godhead to disclaim
My glorious title to my endless flame,
Divinity with scorn I would forswear,
30   Such sweet, dear, tempting mischiefs women are.
Whene'er those flames grow faint, I quickly find
A fierce black Storm pour down upon my mind.
Headlong I'm hurl'd, like horsemen who in vain
Their fury-forming coursers would restrain.
As ships, just when the harbour they attain,
By sudden blasts are snatched to sea again,
So Love's fantastic storms reduce my heart
Half-rescued, and the god resumes his dart.
    Strike here, this undefended bosom wound,
40   And for so brave a conquest be renowned.
Shafts fly so fast to me from every part,
You'll scarce discern your quiver from my heart.
What wretch can bear a live long night's dull rest,
Or think himself in lazy slumbers blest?
Fool! is not sleep the image of pale death?
There's time for rest when fate has stopped your breath.
Me may my soft deluding dear deceive:
I'm happy in my hopes whilst I believe.
Now let her flatter, then as fondly chide;
50   Often may I enjoy, oft be denied.

> With doubtful steps the god of war does move,
> By thy example led, ambiguous Love.
> Blown to and fro like down from thy own wing,
> Who knows when joy or anguish thou wilt bring?
> Yet at thy mother's and thy slave's request,
> Fix an eternal empire in my breast;
>   And let th' inconstant charming sex,
> Whose willful scorn does lovers vex,
> Submit their hearts before thy throne:
> 60   The vassal world is then thy own.   (1684)

ANNE KILLIGREW (1660–1685)

Anne Killigrew's celebrated career as poet, engraver and painter was cut short at the age of 25 by smallpox. The fragmentary, free translation of Ovid's first *Heroides* letter, 'found among her Papers', was printed posthumously in the 1686 collection of her poems.

Penelope to Ulysses [Her. 1.1–80]

> Return my dearest Lord, at length return,
> Let me no longer your sad absence mourn,
> *Ilium* in Dust, does no more work afford,
> No more Employment for your Wit or Sword.
>
>   Why did not the fore-seeing Gods destroy,
> *Helin* the Fire-brand both of *Greece* and *Troy*,
> E're yet the Fatal Youth her Face had seen,
> E're lov'd and born away the wanton Queen?
> Then had been stopt the mighty Floud of Woe,
> 10 Which now both *Greece* and *Phrygia* over-flow:
> Then I, these many Teares, should not have shed,
> Nor thou, the source of them, to War been led:

I should not then have trembled at the Fame
Of *Hectors* warlike and victorious Name.

Why did I wish the Noble *Hector* Slain?
Why *Ilium* ruin'd? Rise, O rise again!
Again great City flourish from thine Urne:
For though thou'rt burn'd, my Lord does not return.
Sometimes I think, (but O most Cruel Thought,)
20   That, for thy absence, th'art thy self in fault:
That thou art captiv'd by some captive Dame,
Who, when thou fired'st *Troy*, did thee inflame
And now with her thou lead'st thy am'rous Life,
Forgetful, and despising of thy Wife.

(1686)

CHARLES HOPKINS (*c.* 1664–1700)

A minor poet who spent his early years in Ireland, Charles Hopkins
eventually found his way into Dryden's London circle. His *Epistolary
Poems* appeared in 1694. The following year he published his *The History
of Love. A Poem: In a Letter to a Lady*, which incorporated a condensed
version of *Heroides* 18 into the epistle to his mistress, 'Delia'.

Leander's Epistle to Hero, In Imitation of Part of that of Ovid [Her. 18]

Read this; yet be not troubled when you read,
Your Lover comes not, in his Letters stead.
On you, all Health, all Happiness, attend,
Which I would much, much rather bring than send.
But now, these envious Storms obstruct my way,
And only this bold Bark, durst put to Sea.
I too had come, had not my Parents Spyes
Stood by to watch me with suspicious eyes.

How many tedious days and nights, are past
10   Since I was suffer'd to behold you last.
Ye spightful Gods, and Goddesses, who keep
Your wat'ry Courts within the spacious deep.
Why at this time, are all the Winds broke forth,
Why swell the Seas beneath the furious North.
'Tis Summer now, when all should be serene,
The Sky's unclouded, undisturb'd the Main,
Winter is yet unwilling to appear,
But you invert the Seasons of the Year.
Yet let me once attain the wish'd for Beach,
20   Out of the now Malicious *Neptune's* reach.
Then blow ye Winds; ye troubled Billows roar,
Roll on your angry Waves, and lash the Shore.
Ruffle the Seas, drive the Tempestuous Air,
Be one continued Storm to keep me there.
Ah! *Hero*, when to you my course is bent,
I seem to slide along a smooth descent.
But in returning thence, I clamber up,
And scale, methinks, some lofty Mountain's top.
Why, when our Souls by mutual Love are joyn'd,
30   Why are we sunder'd by the Sea and Wind?
Either, make my *Abidos* your retreat,
Or let your *Sestos* be my much–lov'd Seat.
This Plague of Absence, I can bear no more,
Come what can come, I'll shortly venture o'r.
Not all the rage of Seas, nor fource of Storms,
Nothing but Death shall keep me from thy Arms.
Yet may that Death, at least so friendly prove,
To float me to the Coast of her I love.
Let not the Thought occasion any fear,
40   Doubt not, I will be soon, and safely, there.
But till that time, let this employ your Hours,
And shew you, that I can be none but Yours.   (1695)

MARY, LADY CHUDLEIGH
(1656–1710)

Born Mary Lee, Lady Chudleigh came to win Dryden's praise for her accomplishments as a poet. Among the verses that appeared in her *Poems on Several Occasions* of 1703 is a slight lyric redaction of the Icarus myth, interesting especially for its reflection of an enduring tradition of 'moralized' Ovid.

Icarus [Met. 8.183–235]

Whilst *Icarus* his Wings prepar'd
His trembling Father for him fear'd:
And thus to him he sighing said,
O let paternal Love persuade:
With me, my dearest Son, comply,
And do not proudly soar too high:
For near, *Apollo's* scorching Heat,
Will on thy Wings too fiercely beat:
And soon dissolve the waxen Ties.
10   Nor loiter in the lower Skies,   ⎤
Least Steams should from the Land arise, ⎬
And damp thy Plumes, and check thy Flight,⎦
And plunge thee into gloomy Night.

   Th' ambitious Youth led on by Pride,
Did all this good Advice deride;
And smiling, rashly soar'd on high;
Too near the Source of Light did fly;
A while, well pleas'd, he wanton'd there;
Rejoicing breath'd Æthereal Air:

20   But ah! the Pleasure soon was past,
       The Transport was too great to last:
       His Wings dropt off, and down he came
       Into that Sea which keeps his Name.

       His grieving Father saw him drown'd,
       And sent loud moving Crys around:
       Ah! wretched Youth, he weeping said,
       Thou'rt now a dire Example made,
       Of those who with ungovern'd Heat
       Aspire to be supremely great;
30   Who from obscure Beginnings rise,
       And swoln with Pride, Advice despise;
       Mount up with hast above their Sphere,
       And no superior Pow'rs revere.

       O may thy Fall be useful made,
       May it to humbler Thoughts persuade:
       To Men th' avoidless Danger Show
       Of those who fly too high, or low;
       Who from the Paths of Virtue stray,
       And keep not in the middle Way:
40   Who singe their Wings with heav'nly Fire;
       Amidst their glorious Hopes expire:
       Or with a base and groveling Mind
       Are to the Clods of Earth confin'd.   (1703)

ALEXANDER POPE (1688–1744)

In addition to realizing the best modern imitation of the *Heroides'*
epistolary manner in his *Eloisa to Abelard*, the eighteenth century's
greatest English poet managed a splendid version of Sappho's letter to
her lover Phaon. Pope's treatment of the *Metamorphoses'* Dryope episode
would appear in 1717 in both his own *Works* and Garth's edition.

Sapho to Phaon [Her. 15]

Say, lovely Youth, that dost my Heart command,
Can *Phaon*'s Eyes forget his *Sapho*'s Hand?
Must then her Name the wretched Writer prove?
To thy Remembrance lost, as to thy Love!
Ask not the cause that I new Numbers chuse,
The Lute neglected, and the Lyric Muse;
Love taught my Tears in sadder Notes to flow,
And tun'd my Heart to Elegies of Woe.
I burn, I burn, as when thro' ripen'd Corn
10   By driving Winds the spreading Flames are born!
Phaon to *Ætna*'s scorching Fields retires,
While I consume with more than *Ætna*'s fires!
No more my Soul a Charm in Musick finds,
Musick has Charms alone for peaceful Minds:
Soft Scenes of Solitude no more can please,
Love enters there, and I'm my own Disease:
No more the *Lesbian* Dames my Passion move,
Once the dear Objects of my guilty Love;
All other Loves are lost in only thine,
20   Ah Youth ungrateful to a Flame like mine!
Whom wou'd not all those blooming Charms surprize,
Those heav'nly Looks, and dear deluding Eyes?
The Harp and Bow wou'd you like *Phœbus* bear,
A brighter *Phœbus*, *Phaon* might appear;

Wou'd you with Ivy wreath your flowing Hair,
Not *Bacchus*' self with *Phaon* cou'd compare:
Yet *Phœbus* lov'd, and *Bacchus* felt the Flame,
One *Daphne* warm'd, and one the *Cretan* Dame;
Nymphs that in Verse no more cou'd rival me,
30   Than ev'n those Gods contend in Charms with thee.
The Muses teach me all their softest Lays,
And the wide World resounds with *Sapho*'s Praise.
Tho' great *Alcæus* more sublimely sings,
And strikes with bolder Rage the sounding Strings,
No less Renown attends the moving Lyre,
Which *Venus* tunes, and all her Loves inspire.
To me what Nature has in Charms deny'd
Is well by Wit's more lasting Flames supply'd.
Tho' short my Stature, yet my Name extends
40   To Heav'n it self, and Earth's remotest Ends.
Brown as I am, an *Æthiopian* Dame
Inspir'd young *Perseus* with a gen'rous Flame.
Turtles and Doves of diff'ring Hues, unite,
And glossy Jett is pair'd with shining White.
If to no Charms thou wilt thy Heart resign,
But such as merit, such as equal thine,
By none alas! by none thou can'st be mov'd,
Phaon alone by *Phaon* must be lov'd!
Yet once thy *Sapho* cou'd thy Cares employ,
50   Once in her Arms you center'd all your Joy:
No Time the dear Remembrance can remove,
For oh! how vast a Memory has Love?
My Musick, then, you cou'd for ever hear,
And all my Words were Musick to your Ear.
You stop'd with Kisses my inchanting Tongue,
And found my Kisses sweeter than my Song.

---

28 Cretan *Dame*: Ariadne   **41** Æthiopian *Dame*: Andromeda

In all I pleas'd, but most in what was best;
And the last Joy was dearer than the rest.
Then with each Word, each Glance, each Motion fir'd,
60   You still enjoy'd, and yet you still desir'd,
Till all dissolving in the Trance we lay,
And in tumultuous Raptures dy'd away.
The fair *Sicilians* now thy Soul inflame;
Why was I born, ye Gods, a *Lesbian* Dame?
But ah beware, *Sicilian* Nymphs! nor boast
That wandring Heart which I so lately lost;
Nor be with all those tempting Words abus'd,
Those tempting Words were all to *Sapho* us'd.
And you that rule *Sicilia*'s happy Plains,
70   Have pity, *Venus*, on your Poet's Pains!
Shall Fortune still in one sad Tenor run,
And still increase the Woes so soon begun?
Enur'd Sorrow from my tender Years,
My Parent's Ashes drank my early Tears.
My Brother next, neglecting Wealth and Fame,
Ignobly burn'd in a destructive Flame.
An infant Daughter late my Griefs increast,
And all my Mother's Cares distract my Breast.
Alas, what more could Fate it self impose,
80   But Thee, the last and greatest of my Woes?
No more my Robes in waving Purple flow,
Nor on my Hand the sparkling Diamonds glow,
No more my Locks in Ringlets curl'd diffuse
The costly Sweetness of *Arabian* Dews,
Nor Braids of Gold the vary'd Tresses bind,
That fly disorder'd with the wanton Wind:
For whom shou'd *Sapho* use such Arts as these?
He's gone, whom only she desir'd to please!
Cupid's light Darts my tender Bosom move,
90   Still is there cause for *Sapho* to still to love:
So from my Birth the *Sisters* fix'd my Doom,
And gave to *Venus* all my life to come;

Or while my Muse in melting Notes complains,
My yielding Heart keeps Measure to my Strains.
By Charms like thine which all my Soul have won,
Who might not – ah! who wou'd not be undone?
For those, *Aurora Cephalus* might scorn,
And with fresh Blushes paint the conscious Morn.
For those might *Cynthia* lengthen *Phaon*'s Sleep,
100   And bid *Endymion* nightly tend his Sheep.
Venus for those had rapt thee to the Skies,
But *Mars* on thee might look with *Venus*' Eyes,
O scarce a Youth, yet scarce a tender Boy!
O useful Time for Lovers to employ!
Pride of thy Age, and Glory of thy Race,
Come to these Arms, and melt in this Embrace!
The Vows you never will return, receive;
And take at least the Love you will not give.
See, while I write, my Words are lost in Tears;
110   The less my Sense, the more my Love appears.
Sure 'twas not much to bid one kind Adieu,
(At least to feign was never hard to you.)
Farewel my Lesbian *Love!* you might have said,
Or coldly thus, *Farewel oh* Lesbian *Maid!*
No Tear did you, no parting Kiss receive,
Nor knew I then how much I was to grieve.
No Lover's Gift your *Sapho* cou'd confer,
And Wrongs and Woes were all you left with her.
No Charge I gave you, and no Charge cou'd give,
120   But this; *Be mindful of our Loves, and live.*
Now by the Nine, those Pow'rs ador'd by me,
And Love, the God that ever waits on thee,
When first I heard (from whom I hardly knew)
That you were fled, and all my Joys with you,

97ff. Sappho feels that Phaon could usurp the divine loves of Aurora (the dawn) for Cephalus, or Cynthia (Diana) for Endymion.

Like some sad Statue, speechless, pale, I stood;
Grief chill'd my Breast, and stop'd my freezing Blood;
No Sigh to rise, no Tear had pow'r to flow;
Fix'd in a stupid Lethargy of Woe.
But when its way th'impetuous Passion found,
130   I rend my Tresses, and my Breast I wound,
I rave, then weep, I curse, and then complain,
Now swell to Rage, now melt in Tears again.
Not fiercer Pangs distract the mournful Dame,
Whose first-born Infant feeds the Fun'ral Flame.
My scornful Brother with a Smile appears,
Insults my Woes, and triumphs in my Tears,
His hated Image ever haunts my Eyes,
And *why this Grief? thy Daughter lives*; he cries.
Stung with my Love, and furious with Despair,
140   All torn my Garments, and my Bosom bare,
My Woes, thy Crimes, I to the World proclaim;
Such inconsistent things are Love and Shame!
'Tis thou are all my Care and my Delight,
My daily Longing, and my Dream by Night:
Oh Night more pleasing than the brightest Day,
When Fancy gives what Absence takes away,
And drest in all its visionary Charms,
Restores my fair Deserter to my Arms!
Then round your Neck in wanton Wreaths I twine,
150   Then you, methinks, as fondly circle mine:
A thousand tender Words, I hear and speak;
A thousand melting Kisses, give, and take:
Then fiercer Joys – I blush to mention these,
Yet while I blush, confess how much they please!
But when with Day the sweet Delusions fly,
And all things wake to Life and Joy, but I,
As if once more forsaken, I complain,
And close my Eyes, to dream of you again.
Then frantick rise, and like some Fury rove
160   Thro' lonely Plains, and thro' the silent Grove,

As if the silent Grove, and lonely Plains
That knew my Pleasures, cou'd relieve my Pains.
I view the *Grotto*, once the Scene of Love,
The Rocks around, the hanging Roofs above,
That charm'd me more, with Native Moss o'ergrown,
Than *Phrygian* Marble or the *Parian* Stone.
I find the Shades that veil'd our Joys before,
But, *Phaon* gone, those Shades delight no more.
Here the prest Herbs with bending Tops betray
170 Where oft entwin'd in am'rous Folds we lay;
I kiss that Earth which once was prest by you,
And all with Tears the with'ring Herbs bedew.
For thee the fading Trees appear to mourn,
And Birds defer their Songs till thy Return:
Night shades the Groves, and all in Silence lye,
All, but the mournful *Philomel* and I:
With mournful *Philomel* I join my Strain,
Of *Tereus* she, of *Phaon* I complain.

    A Spring there is, whose silver Waters show,
180 Clear as a Glass the shining Sands below;
A flow'ry *Lotos* spreads its Arms above,
Shades all the Banks, and seems it self a Grove;
Eternal Greens the mossie Margin grace,
Watch'd by the Sylvan *Genius* of the Place.
Here as I lay, and swell'd with Tears the Flood,
Before my Sight a Watry Virgin stood,
She stood and cry'd, 'O you that love in vain!
Fly hence; and seek the fair *Leucadian* Main;
There stands a Rock from whose impending Steep
190 *Apollo*'s Fane surveys the rolling Deep;
There injur'd Lovers, leaping from above,
Their Flames extinguish, and forget to love.

---

176 *Philomel*: For the story of Philomela, Procne and Tereus, cf. *Met.* 6.424–674.

Deucalion once with hopeless Fury burn'd,
In vain he lov'd, relentless *Pyrrha* scorn'd;
But when from hence he plung'd into the Main,
Deucalion scorn'd, and *Pyrrha* lov'd in vain.
Haste *Sapho*, haste from high *Leucadia* throw
Thy wretched Weight, nor dread the Deeps below!'
She spoke, and vanish'd with the Voice−I rise,
200   And silent Tears fall trickling from my Eyes.
I go, ye Nymphs! those Rocks and Seas to prove;
How much I fear, but ah! how much I love?
I go, ye Nymphs! where furious Love inspires:
Let Female Fears submit to Female Fires!
To Rocks and Seas I fly from *Phaon*'s Hate,
And hope from Seas and Rocks a milder Fate.
Ye gentle Gales, beneath my Body blow,
And softly lay me on the Waves below!
And thou, kind *Love*, my sinking Limbs sustain, ⎫
210   Spread thy soft Wings, and waft me o'er the Main, ⎬
Nor let a Lover's Death the guiltless Flood profane! ⎭
On *Phœbus*' Shrine my Harp I'll then bestow,
And this Inscription shall be plac'd below.
'Here She who sung, to Him that did inspire,
Sapho to *Phœbus* consecrates her Lyre,
What suits with *Sapho*, *Phœbus*, suits with thee;
The Gift, the Giver, and the God agree.'
     But why alas, relentless Youth! ah why
To distant Seas must tender *Sapho* fly?
220   Thy Charms than those may far more pow'rful be,
And *Phœbus*' self is less a God to me.
Ah! canst thou doom me to the Rocks and Sea,
O far more faithless and more hard than they?
Ah! canst thou rather see this tender Breast
Dash'd on these Rocks, than to thy Bosom prest?

195f. a story not otherwise known: probably invented here by Ovid

This Breast which once, in vain! you lik'd so well;
Where the *Loves* play'd and where the *Muses* dwell. –
Alas! the *Muses* now no more inspire,
Untun'd my Lute, and silent is my Lyre,
230   My languid Numbers have forgot to flow,
And Fancy sinks beneath a Weight of Woe.
Ye *Lesbian* Virgins, and ye *Lesbian* Dames,
Themes of my Verse, and Objects of my Flames,
No more your Groves with my glad Songs shall ring,
No more these Hands shall touch the trembling String:
My *Phaon*'s fled, and I those Arts resign,
(Wretch that I am, to call that *Phaon* mine!)
Return fair Youth, return and bring along
Joy to my Soul, and Vigour to my Song:
240   Absent from thee, the Poet's Flame expires,
But ah! how fiercely burn the Lover's Fires?
Gods! can no Pray'rs, no Sighs, no Numbers move
One savage Heart, or teach it how to love?
The Winds my Pray'rs, my Sighs, my Numbers bear,
The flying Winds have lost them all in Air!
Oh when, alas! shall more auspicious Gales
To these fond Eyes restore thy welcome Sails?
If you return – ah why these long Delays?
Poor *Sapho* dies while careless *Phaon* stays.
250   O launch thy Bark, nor fear the watry Plain,
Venus for thee shall smooth her native Main.
O launch thy Bark, secure of prosp'rous Gales,
Cupid for thee shall spread the swelling Sails.
If you will fly – (yet ah! what Cause can be,
Too cruel Youth, that you shou'd fly from me?)
If not from *Phaon* I must hope for Ease,
Ah let me seek it from the raging Seas:
To raging Seas unpity'd I'll remove,
And either cease to live, or cease to love!   (1712)

The Fable of Dryope, 69–103 [Met. 9.371–93]

If to the wretched any faith be giv'n
I swear by all th'unpitying pow'rs of heav'n,
No wilful crime this heavy vengeance bred,
In mutual innocence our lives we led:
If this be false, let these new greens decay,
Let sounding axes lop my limbs away,
And crackling flames on all my honours prey.
But from my branching arms this infant bear,
Let some kind nurse supply a mother's care:
10 And to his mother let him oft' be led,
Sport in her shades, and in her shades be fed;
Teach him, when first his infant voice shall frame
Imperfect words, and lisp his mother's name,
To hail this tree; and say with weeping eyes,
Within this plant my hapless parent lies:
And when in youth he seeks the shady woods,
Oh, let him fly the crystal lakes and floods,
Nor touch the fatal flow'rs; but, warn'd by me,
Believe a Goddess shrin'd in ev'ry tree.
20 My sire, my sister, and my spouse farewell!
If in your breasts or love or pity dwell,
Protect your plant, not let my branches feel
The browzing cattle, or the piercing steel.
Farewell! and since I cannot bend to join
My lips to yours, advance at least to mine.
My son, thy mother's parting kiss receive,
While yet thy mother has a kiss to give.

---

3 *No wilful crime*: When Dryope comes with her son to worship at a sacred lake,
she plucks a water-lily to amuse the infant, unaware that the plant is actually the
transformed nymph Lotos. As a punishment for her unwitting crime, she is herself
transformed – the 'heavy vengeance'.

I can no more; the creeping rind invades
My closing lips, and hides my head in shades:
30   Remove your hands, the bark shall soon suffice
Without their aid, to seal these dying eyes.
    She ceas'd at once to speak, and ceas'd to be;
And all the nymph was lost within the tree;
Yet latent life thro' her new branches reign'd,
And long the plant a human heat retain'd.   (1717)

JOSEPH ADDISON (1672-1719)

Well known for his collaboration with Richard Steele on the *Spectator*
(1711–12) and famed in his own time for the popular tragedy *Cato*,
Joseph Addison contributed to Garth's *Metamorphoses* an excerpt from
Book 2 that first appeared in Tonson's fifth *Miscellany Poems* of 1705.
For Addison, the story of Phaeton's headstrong wish to confirm his
divine paternity by assuming command of the chariot of his father
(Helios or Apollo, in different constructions) was 'the most important
subject he treats of, except the deluge'.

The Story of PHAETON, from Ovid's Metamorphoses in Fifteen Books 2.177–248, 265–82, 318–88 [Met. 2.153–216, 227–40, 272–328]

    Meanwhile the restless Horses neigh'd aloud,
Breathing out Fire, and pawing where they stood.
Tethys, not knowing what had past, gave way,
And all the Waste of Heav'n before 'em lay.
They spring together out, and swiftly bear
The flying Youth through Clouds and yielding Air;

---

3 *Tethys*: Oceanus's wife

With wingy Speed outstrip the Eastern Wind,
And leave the Breezes of the Morn behind.
The Youth was light, nor cou'd he fill the seat,
10   Or poise the Chariot with its wonted Weight:
But as at Sea th' unballass'd Vessel rides,
Cast to and fro, the Sport of Winds and Tides;
So in the bounding Chariot toss'd on high,
The Youth is hurry'd headlong through the Sky.
Soon as the Steeds perceive it, they forsake
Their stated Course, and leave the beaten Track.
The Youth was in a Maze, nor did he know
Which way to turn the Reins, or where to go;
Nor wou'd the Horses, had he known, obey.
20   Then the Sev'n Stars first felt *Apollo*'s Ray,
And wish'd to dip in the forbidden Sea.
The folded Serpent next the frozen Pole,
Stiff and benum'd before, began to roll,
And raged with inward Heat, and threaten'd War,
And shot a redder Light from ev'ry Star;
Nay, and 'tis said *Bootes* too, that fain
Thou would'st have fled, tho' cumber'd with thy Wane.

    Th' unhappy Youth then, bending down his Head,
Saw Earth and Ocean far beneath him spread.
30   His Colour chang'd, he startled at the Sight,
And his Eyes Darken'd by too great a Light.
Now cou'd he wish the fiery Steeds untry'd,
His Birth obscure, and his Request deny'd:
Now would he *Merops* for his Father own,
And quit his boasted Kindred to the Sun.

    So fares the Pilot, when his Ship is tost
In troubled Seas, and all its Steerage lost,
He gives her to the Winds, and in Despair
Seeks his last Refuge in the Gods and Pray'r.

---

34 *Merops*: his mother's human spouse

40   What cou'd he do? his Eyes, if backward cast,
        Find a long Path he had already past;
        If forward, still a longer Path they find:
        Both he compares, and measures in his Mind;
        And sometimes casts an Eye upon the east,
        And sometimes looks on the forbidden West.
        The horses Names he knew not in the Fright,
        Nor wou'd he loose the Reins, nor cou'd he hold 'em right.
            Now all the Horrors of the Heav'ns he spies,
        And monstrous Shadows of prodigious Size,
50   That, deck'd with Stars, lye scatter'd o'er the Skies.
        There is a Place above, where *Scorpio* bent
        In Tail and Arms surrounds a vast Extent;
        In a wide Circuit of the Heav'ns he shines,
        And fills the Space of Two Cœlestial Signs.
        Soon as the Youth beheld him, vex'd with Heat
        Brandish his Sting, and in his Poison sweat,
        Half dead with sudden Fear he dropt the Reins;
        The Horses felt 'em loose upon their Mains,
        And, flying out through all the Plains above,
60   Ran uncontroul'd where-e'er their Fury drove;
        Rush'd on the Stars, and through a pathless Way
        Of unknown Regions hurry'd on the Day.
        And now above, and now below they flew,
        And near the Earth the burning Chariot drew.
            The Clouds disperse in Fumes, the wond'ring Moon
        Beholds her Brother's Steeds beneath her own;
        The Highlands smoak, cleft by the piercing Rays,
        Or, clad with Woods, in their own Fewel blaze.
        Next o'er the Plains, where ripen'd Harvests grow,
70   The running Conflagration spreads Below.
        But these are trivial Ills: whole Cities burn,
        And peopled Kingdoms into Ashes turn.

★

Th' astonisht Youth, where-e'er his Eyes cou'd turn,
Beheld the Universe around him burn:
The World was in a Blaze; nor cou'd he bear
The sultry Vapours and the scorching Air,
Which from below, as from a Furnace, flow'd;
And now the Axle-tree beneath him glow'd:
Lost in the whirling Clouds that round him broke,
80 And white with ashes, hov'ring in the Smoke.
He flew where-e'er the Horses drove, nor knew
Wither the Horses drove, or where he flew.
   'Twas then, they say, the swarthy Moor begun
To change his Hue, and Blacken in the Sun.
Then *Libya* first, of all her moisture drain'd,
Became a barren Waste, a Wild of Sand.
The Water-Nymphs lament their empty Urns,
Bœotia, robb'd of Silver *Dirce*, mourns,
Corinth Pyrene's wasted Spring bewails,
90 And *Argos* grieves whilst *Amymonè* fails.

★

   The Earth at length, on ev'ry Side embrac'd
With scalding Seas, that floated round her Waste,
When now she felt the Springs and Rivers come,
And crowd within the Hollow of her Womb,
Up-lifted to the Heav'ns her blasted Head,
And clapt her Hand upon her Brows, and said;
(But first, impatient of the sultry Heat,
Sunk deeper down, and sought a cooler Seat:)
'If you, great King of Gods, my Death approve,
100 'And I deserve it, let me die by *Jove*;
'If I must perish by the Force of Fire,
'Let me transfix'd with Thunderbolts expire.
'See, whilst I speak, my Breath the Vapours choak
(For now her Face lay wrapt in Clouds of Smoak),
'See my singe'd Hair, behold my faded Eye,
'And wither'd Face, where Heaps of Cinders lye!

'And does the Plow for This my Body tear?
'This the Reward for all the Fruits I bear,
'Tortur'd with Rakes, and harrass'd all the Year?

110 'That Herbs for Cattle daily I renew,
'And Food for Man, and Frankincense for You?
'But grant Me guilty; what has *Neptune* done?
'Why are his Waters boiling in the Sun?
'The wavy Empire, which by Lot was giv'n,
'Why does it waste, and further shrink from Heav'n?
'If I nor He your Pity can provoke,
'See your own Heav'ns, the Heav'ns begin to smoke!
'Shou'd once the Sparkles catch those bright Abodes,
'Destruction seizes on the Heav'ns and Gods;

120 '*Atlas* becomes unequal to his Freight,
'And almost faints beneath the glowing Weight.
'If Heav'n, and Earth, and Sea, together burn,
'All must again into their Chaos turn.
'Apply some speedy Cure, prevent our Fate,
'And succour Nature, ere it be too late.'
She ceas'd, for choak'd with Vapours round her spread,
Down to the deepest shades she sunk her Head.

  Jove call'd to witness ev'ry Pow'r above,
And ev'n the God, whose son the Chariot drove,

130 That what he acts he is compell'd to do,
Or universal Ruin must ensue.
Strait he ascends the high Ætherial Throne,
From whence he us'd to dart his Thunder down,
From whence his Show'rs and Storms he us'd to pour,
But now cou'd meet with neither Storm nor Show'r.
Then, aiming at the Youth, with lifted Hand,
Full at his Head he hurl'd the forky Brand,
In dreadful Thund'rings. Thus th' Almighty Sire
Suppress'd the Raging of the Fires with Fire.

---

120 *his Freight*: the heavens, which the god bore on his shoulders

140   At once from Life and from the Chariot driv'n,
       Th' ambitious Boy fell Thunder-struck from Heav'n.
       The horses started with a sudden Bound,
       And flung the Reins and chariot to the Ground:
       The studded Harness from their Necks they broke,
       Here fell a Wheel, and here a Silver Spoke,
       Here were the Beam and Axle torn away;
       And, scatter'd o'er the Earth, the shining Fragments lay.
       The breathless *Phæton*, with flaming Hair,
       Shot from the Chariot, like a falling Star,
150   That in a Summer's Ev'ning from the Top
       Of Heav'n drops down, or seems at least to drop;
       Till on the *Po* his Blasted Corps was hurl'd,
       Far from his Country, in the Western World.

       The *Latian* Nymphs came round him, and amaz'd
       On the dead Youth, transfix'd with Thunder, gaz'd;
       And, whilst yet smoking from the Bolt he lay,
       His shatter'd Body to a Tomb convey,
       And o'er the Tomb an Epitaph devise:
       'Here He who drove the Sun's bright Chariot lies;
160   'His Father's fiery Steeds he cou'd not guide,
       'But in the glorious Enterprize he dy'd.'

                                                        (1717)

NAHUM TATE (1652–1715)

By the time of his appointment as Poet Laureate in 1692 – successor
to Thomas Shadwell, the butt of Dryden's satire *Mac Flecknoe* – the
Irish-born Nahum Tate had established himself within London's literary
scene as a playwright, editor and translator. Nowadays Shakespeareans
remember him for his altered version of *King Lear*, which continued to

---

154 *The* Latian *Nymphs*: Phaeton's sisters

play well into the nineteenth century. Both of the following translations
place Tate in lasting proximity to Dryden: the *Remedy* was included in
the 1709 *Ars amatoria* volume for which Dryden had composed the first
book, and the Cephalus and Procris story was incorporated by Garth.

Ovid's Remedy of Love, 313–422 [Rem. 299–398]
The poet's own case

> Think, till the thought your indignation move,
> What damage you've receiv'd, by her you love:
> How she has drain'd your purse; nor yet content, ⎫
> Till your estate's in costly presents spent,   ⎬
> And you have mortgag'd your last tenement. ⎭
> How she did swear, and how she was forsworn;
> Not only false, but treated you with scorn:
> And, since her avarice has made you poor,
> Forc'd you to take your lodgings at the door:
> Reserv'd to you, but others she'll caress;
> The fore-man of a shop shall have access.
> Let these reflections on your reason win;
> From seeds of anger, hatred will begin.
> Your rhet'ric on these topics should be spent,
> Oh that your wrongs could make you eloquent!
> But grieve, and grief will teach you to enlarge,
> And, like an orator, draw up the charge.
>
>   A certain nymph once did my heart incline,
> Whose humour wholly disagreed with mine.
> (I, your physician, my disease confess)
> I from my own prescriptions found redress.
> Her still I represented to my mind,
> With what defects I cou'd suppose or find.
> Oh how ill-shap'd her legs, how thick and short!
> (Tho' neater limbs did never nymph support)

10

20

Her arms, said I, how tawny brown they are!
(Tho' never ivory statue had so fair.)
How low of stature! (yet the nymph was tall.)
Oh for what costly presents will she call!
30   What change of lovers! And, of all the rest,
I found this thought strike deepest in my breast,
Such thin partitions good and ill divide,
That one for t' other may be misapply'd.
Ev'n truth, and your own judgment, you must strain,
Those blemishes you cannot find, to feign:
Call her blackmoor, if she's but lovely brown;
Monster, if plump; if slender, skeleton.
Censure her free discourse as confidence;
Her silence, want of breeding, and good sense.
40   Discover her blind side, and put her still
Upon the task which she performs but ill.
Court her to sing, if she wants voice and ear;
To dance, if she has neither shape nor air:
If talking misbecomes her, make her talk;
If walking, then in malice make her walk.
Commend her skill when on the lute she plays,
Till vanity her want of skill betrays.
Take care, if her large breasts offend your eyes,
No dress do that deformity disguise.
50   Ply her with merry tales of what you will,
To keep her laughing, if her teeth are ill.
Or if blear-ey'd some tragic story find,
'Till she has read and wept herself quite blind.
But one effectual method you may take.
Enter her chamber, e'er she's well awake:
Her beauty's art, gems, gold, and rich attire,
Make up the pageant you so much admire;

34f. The advice tendered here inverts the reactions to which Ovid alludes in *Ars* 2.641–62 and *Amores* 2.4 (cf. Oldham's translation, above).

In all that spacious figure which you see,
The least, least part of her own self is she.
60 In vain for her you love, amidst such cost,
You search; the mistress in the dress is lost.
Take her disrob'd, her real self surprise,
I'll trust you then, for cure, to your own eyes.
(Yet have I known this very rule to fail,
And beauty most, when stript of art, prevail.)
Steal to her closet, her close-'tiring place,
While she makes up her artificial face.
All colours of the rainbow you'll discern,
Washes and paints, and what you're sick to learn.

70   I now should treat of what may pall desire,
And quench in love's own element, the fire,
(For all advantages you ought to make,
And arms from love's own magazine to take:)
But modesty forbids at full extent
To prosecute this luscious argument:
Which, to prevent your blushes, I shall leave
For your own fancy better to conceive.
For some of late censoriously accuse
My am'rous liberty, and wanton muse,
80 But envy did the wit of *Homer* blame,
Malice gave obscure *Zoilus* a name.
Thus sacrilegious censure would destroy ⎤
The pious muse, who did her art employ, ⎬
To settle here the banish'd gods of *Troy*. ⎦
But you who at my freedom take offence,
Distinguish right, before you speak your sense.

---

81 *Zoilus*: Cynic philosopher who built a career upon his harsh criticisms of Homer

Mæonian strains alone can war resound,
No place is there for love and dalliance found.
The tragic stile requires a tale distrest,
90   And comedy subsists of mirth and jest.
The tender elegy in love's delight,
Which to themselves pleas'd mistresses recite.
Callimachus would do Achilles wrong;
Cydippe were no theme for Homer's song.
What mortal patience could endure to see
Thais presenting chaste Andromache?
Kind Thais, (none of Vesta's nuns) supplies
My song; with Thais all my bus'ness lies:
The actress, if my muse performs with art,
100   You must commend, tho' you dislike the part.
Burst envy; I've already got a name;
And, writing more, shall more advance my fame.
Despair not then, for as I longer live,
Each day fresh fuel for your spleen shall give.
Thus fame's increasing gale bears me on high,
While tir'd and groveling on the ground you lie,
Soft elegy in such esteem I've plac'd,
Not Virgil more the Epic strain has grac'd.
Censure did us to this digression force;
110   Now, muse, pursue thy intercepted course.

(1709)

---

94 Cydippe: remembered as the maiden tricked into marriage by Acontius; her story would be deemed more appropriate to erotic poetry than to Homeric epic

96 Thais: famous prostitute who became a stock figure in Roman New Comedy

Ovid's Metamorphoses in Fifteen Books 7.1001– 1197 [Met. 7.661–865] *The Story of* Cephalus *and* Procis.

To th' inmost Courts the *Grecian* Youths were led,
And plac'd by *Phocus* on a *Tyrian* Bed;
Who, soon observing *Cephalus* to hold
A Dart of unknown Wood, but arm'd with Gold;
None better loves (said he) the Hunts-man's Sport,
Or does more often to the Woods resort;
Yet I that Jav'lin's Stem with Wonder view,
Too brown for Box, too smooth a Grain for Yew.
I cannot guess the Tree; but never Art
10   Did form, or eyes behold so fair a Dart!
The Guest then interrupts him – 'Twou'd produce
Still greater Wonder, if you knew its Use.
It never fails to strike the Game, and then
Comes bloody back into your Hand again.
Then *Phocus* each Particular desires,
And th' Author of the wond'rous Gift enquires.
To which the Owner thus, with weeping Eyes,
And Sorrow for his Wife's sad Fate, replies,
This Weapon here (O Prince!) can you believe
20   This Dart the Cause for which so much I grieve;
And shall continue to grieve on, 'till Fate
Afford such wretched Life no longer Date.
Would I this fatal Gift had ne'er enjoy'd,
This fatal Gift my tender Wife destroy'd:
Procris her Name, ally'd in Charms and Blood
To fair *Orythia* courted by a God.
Her father seal'd my Hopes with Rites Divine,

---

1 *the* Grecian *Youths*: Cephalus, on a mission to secure an alliance with Oenopia against Crete, is entertained here by Aeacus's son Phocus, whose question prompts the ensuing narrative.

But firmer Love before had made her mine.
Men call'd me blest, and blest I was indeed.
30   The second Month our Nuptials did succeed;
When (as upon *Hymettus'* dewy Head,
For Mountain Stags, my Net betimes I spread)
Aurora spy'd, and ravish'd me away,
With Rev'rence to the Goddess, I must say,
Against my Will, for *Procris* had my Heart,
Nor wou'd her Image from my Thoughts depart.
At last, in Rage she cry'd, Ingrateful Boy
Go to your *Procris*, take your fatal Joy;
And so dismiss'd me: Musing, as I went,
40   What those Expressions of the Goddess meant,
A thousand jealous Fears possess me now,
Lest *Procris* had prophan'd her Nuptial Vow:
Her Youth and Charms did to my Fancy paint
A lewd Adultress, but her Life a Saint.
Yet I was absent long, the Goddess too
Taught me how far a Woman cou'd be true.
Aurora's Treatment much Suspicion bred;
Besides, who truly love, ev'n Shadows dread.
I strait impatient for the Tryal grew,
50   What Courtship back'd with richest Gifts cou'd do.
Aurora's Envy aided my Design,
And lent me Features far unlike to mine.
In this Disguise to my own House I came,
But all was chaste, no conscious Sign of Blame:
With thousand Arts I scarce Admittance found,
And then beheld her weeping on the Ground
For her lost Husband; hardly I retain'd
My Purpose, scarce the wish'd Embrace refrain'd.
How charming was her Grief! Then, *Phocus*, guess
60   What killing Beauties waited on her Dress.
Her constant Answer, when my Suit I prest,
Forbear, my Lord's dear Image guards this Breast;

Where-e'er he is, whatever Cause detains,
Who-e'er has his, my Heart unmov'd remains.
What greater Proofs of Truth than these cou'd be?
Yet I persist, and urge my Destiny.
At length, she found, when my own Form return'd,
Her jealous Lover there, whose Loss she mourn'd.
Enrag'd with my Suspicion, swift as Wind,
70   She fled at once from me and all Mankind;
And so became, her Purpose to retain,
A Nymph, and Huntress in *Diana's* Train:
Forsaken thus, I found my Flames encrease,
I own'd my Folly, and I su'd for Peace.
It was a Fault, but not of Guilt, to move
Such Punishment, a Fault of too much Love.
Thus I retriev'd her to my longing Arms,
And many happy Days possess'd her Charms.
But with herself she kindly did confer,
80   What Gifts the Goddess had bestow'd on her;
The fleetest Grey-hound, with this lovely Dart,
And I of both have Wonders to impart.
Near *Thebes* a Savage Beast, of Race unknown,
Laid waste the Field, and bore the Vineyards down;
The Swains fled from him, and with one Consent
Our *Grecian* Youth to chace the Monster went;
More swift than Light'ning he the Toils surpast,
And in his Course Spears, Men, and Trees o'er-cast.
We slipt our Dogs, and last my *Lelaps* too,
90   When none of all the mortal Race woul'd do:
He long before was struggling from my Hands,
And, e'er we cou'd unloose him, broke his Bands.
That Minute where he was, we cou'd not find,
And only saw the Dust he left behind.
I climb'd a neighb'ring Hill to view the Chase,
While in the Plain they held an equal Race;
The Savage now seems caught, and now by Force
To quit himself, nor holds the same strait Course;

But running counter, from the Foe withdraws,
100 And with short Turning cheats his gaping Jaws:
Which he retrieves, and still so closely prest,
You'd fear at ev'ry Stretch he were possess'd;
Yet for the Gripe his Fangs in vain prepare;
The Game shoots from him, and he chops the Air.
To cast my Jav'lin then I took my Stand;
But as the Thongs were fitting to my Hand,
While to the Valley I o'er-look'd the Wood,
Before my Eyes two Marble Statues stood.
That, as pursu'd, appearing at full Stretch,
110 This barking after, and at point to catch.
Some God their Course did with this Wonder grace,
That neither might be conquer'd in the Chase;
A sudden Silence here his Tongue supprest,
He here stops short, and fain would wave the rest.
    The eager Prince then urg'd him to impart,
The Fortune that attended on the Dart.
First then (said he) past Joys let me relate,
For Bliss was the Foundation of my Fate.
No Language can those happy Hours express,
120 Did from our Nuptials me and *Procris* bless:
The kindest Pair! What more cou'd Heav'n confer?
For she was all to me, and I to her.
Had *Jove* made Love, great *Jove* had been despis'd;
And I my *Procris* more than *Venus* priz'd:
Thus while no other Joy we did aspire,
We grew at last one Soul, and one Desire.
Forth to the Woods I went at Break of Day
(The constant Practice of my Youth) for Prey:
Nor yet for Servant, Horse, or Dog did call,
130 I found this single Dart to serve for all.
With Slaughter tir'd, I sought the cooler Shade,
And Winds that from the Mountains pierc'd the Glade:
Come, gentle Air (so was I wont to say)
Come, gentle Air, sweet *Aura* come away.

This always was the Burden of my Song,
Come 'swage my Flames, sweet *Aura* come along.
Thou always art most welcome to my Breast;
I faint; approach, thou dearest, kindest Guest!
These Blandishments, and more than these, I said
140 (By Fate to unsuspected ruin led)
Thou art my Joy, for thy dear sake I love
Each desart Hill, and solitary Grove;
When (faint with Labour) I Refreshment need,
For Cordials on thy fragrant Breath I feed.
At last a wand'ring Swain in hearing came,
And cheated with the Sound of *Aura's* Name,
He thought I had some Assignation made;
And to my *Procris'* Ear the News convey'd.
Great Love is soonest with Suspicion fir'd,
150 She swoon'd, and with the Tale almost expir'd.
Ah! wretched Heart, (she cry'd) ah! faithless Man!
And then to curse th' imagin'd Nymph began:
Yet oft she doubts, oft hopes she is deceiv'd,
And chides herself, that ever she believ'd
Her Lord to such Injustice cou'd proceed,
Till she herself were Witness of the Deed.
Next Morn I to the Woods again repair,
And, weary with the Chase, invoke the Air:
Approach, dear *Aura*, and my Bosom chear:
160 At which a mournful Sound did strike my Ear;
Yet I proceeded, 'till the Thicket by,
With rustling Noise and Motion, drew my Eye:
I thought some Beast of Prey was shelter'd there,
And to the Covert threw my certain spear;
From whence a tender Sigh my Soul did wound,
Ah me! it cry'd, and did like *Procris* sound.
Procris was there, too well the Voice I knew,
And to the Place with headlong Horror flew;
Where I beheld her gasping on the Ground,
170 In vain attempting from the deadly Wound

To draw the Dart, her Love's dear fatal Gift!
My guilty Arms had scarce the Strength to lift
The beauteous Load; my Silks and Hair I tore
(If possible) to stanch the pressing Gore;
For Pity beg'd her keep her flitting Breath,
And not to leave me guilty of her Death.
While I intreat she fainted fast away,
And these few Words had only Strength to say;
By all the sacred Bonds of plighted Love,
180   By all your Rev'rence to the Pow'rs above,
By all the Truth for which you held me dear,
And last by Love, the Cause through which I bleed,
Let *Aura* never to my Bed succeed.
I then perceiv'd the Error of our Fate,
And told it her, but found and told too late!
I felt her lower to my Bosom fall,
And while her Eyes had any Sight at all,
On mine she fix'd them; in her Pangs still prest
My Hand, and sigh'd her Soul into my Breast;
190   Yet, being undeceiv'd, resign'd her Breath
Methought more chearfully, and smil'd in Death.
        With such Concern the weeping Heroe told
This Tale, that none who heard him cou'd with-hold
From melting into sympathizing Tears,
Till *Æacus* with his two Sons appears;
Whom he commits, with their new-levy'd Bands.
To Fortune's, and so brave a Gen'ral's Hands.

                                                        (1717)

JOHN GAY (1685–1732)

The poet and playwright John Gay, author of *The Beggar's Opera*, was
friend to Swift, Pope and Arbuthnot. Gay translates the bulk of Book
9 (from which the Alcmena passage comes) for the Garth edition,
holding his own admirably against Dryden's and Pope's contributions

to the same instalment. Handel found in him a worthy, witty librettist for his operatic rendition of the Acis and Galatea story. In both excerpts, Gay's skills as poet, dramatist and translator shine brilliantly. David Slavitt honours Gay's song of Polyphemus, interpolating part of it into his own 1994 translation of the *Metamorphoses*.

Ovid's Metamorphoses in Fifteen Books 9.356–405 [Met. 9.285–323] *The Transformation of Galanthis*

When now *Alcides'* mighty Birth drew nigh,
And the tenth Sign roll'd forward on the Sky,
My Womb extends with such a mighty Load,
As *Jove* the parent of the Burthen show'd.
I could no more th' encreasing Smart sustain,
My Horror kindles to recount the Pain;
Cold chills my Limbs while I the Tale pursue,
And now methinks I feel my Pangs anew.
Seven Days and Nights amidst incessant Throws,
10 Fatigu'd with ills I lay, nor knew Repose;
When lifting high my Hands, in Shrieks I pray'd,
Implor'd the Gods, and call'd *Lucina's* Aid.
She came, but prejudic'd, to give my Fate
A Sacrifice to vengeful *Juno's* Hate.
She hears the groaning Anguish of my Fits,
And on the Altar at my Door she sits.
O'er her left Knee her crossing Leg she cast,
Then knits her Fingers close, and wrings them fast:
This stay'd the Birth; in mutt'ring Verse she pray'd,
20 The mutt'ring Verse th' unfinish'd Birth delay'd.

---

1 Alcmena narrates   12 Lucina: goddess of childbirth
14 Juno's *Hate*: Since her husband Jupiter had fathered the child, Juno resentfully wishes to prevent the birth.

Now with fierce Struggles, raging with my Pain,
At *Jove's* Ingratitude I rave in vain.
How did I wish for Death! such Groans I sent,
As might have made the flinty Heart relent.
    Now the *Cadmeian* Matrons round me press,
Offer their Vows, and seek to bring Redress;
Among the *Theban* Dames *Galanthis* stands,
Strong limb'd, red hair'd, and just to my Commands:
She first perceiv'd that all these racking Woes
30   From the persisting Hate of *Juno* rose.
As here and there she pass'd, by chance she sees
The seated Goddess; on her close-press'd Knees
Her fast-knit Hands she leans; with chearful Voice
Galanthis cries, Whoe'er thou art, rejoyce,
Congratulate the Dame, she lies at Rest,
At length the Gods *Alcmena's* womb have blest.
Swift from her Seat the startled Goddess springs,
No more conceal'd, her hands abroad she flings;
The Charm unloos'd, the Birth my Pangs reliev'd;
40   *Galanthis'* Laughter vex'd the Pow'r deceiv'd.
Fame says, the Goddess dragg'd the laughing Maid
Fast by the Hair; in vain her Force essay'd
Her grov'ling Body from the Ground to rear;
Chang'd to Fore-feet her shrinking Arms appear:
Her hairy Back her former Hue retains,
The Form alone is lost: her Strength remains;
Who, since the Lye did from her Mouth proceed,
Shall from her pregnant Mouth bring forth her Breed;
Nor shall she quit her long-frequented Home,
50   But haunt those Houses where she lov'd to roam.   (1717)

---

48 origin of the popular belief that the weasel – Galanthis's new form – bears its
young from its mouth

Acis and Galatea, The Second Part, 9–48 [Met. 13.789–869] *Polyphemus's courtship song*

POLYPHEMUS.
RECITATIVO.
Polyphemus. I rage, I melt, I burn,
  The feeble God has stab'd me to the Heart.
  Thou trusty Pine, Prop of my Godlike Steps,
  I lay thee by.
  Bring me a hundred Reeds of decent growth,
  To make a Pipe for my capacious Mouth;
  In soft enchanting Accents let me breathe
  Sweet *Galatea*'s Beauty, and my Love.

  AIR.

  O ruddier than the Cherry!
10 *O sweeter than the Berry!*
    O Nymph, more bright
    Than Moonshine Night!
  Like Kidlings blithe And merry.

  Ripe as the melting Cluster,
  No Lilly has such Lustre;
    Yet hard to tame,
    As raging Flame,
  And fierce as Storms that bluster.

  O ruddier, &c.

POLYPHEMUS.
RECITATIVO.
20 *Polyphemus.* Wither, Fairest, art thou running?
    Still my warm Embraces shunning?

GALATEA.

Galatea. The Lion calls not to his Prey,
  Nor bids the Wolf the Lambkin stay.

POLYPHEMUS.
ARIOSO.

Polyphemus. Thee, *Polyphemus*, great as *Jove*,
  Calls to Empire and to Love,
  To his Palace in the Rock,
  To his Dairy, to his Flock,
  To the Grape of purple Hue,
  To the Plumb of Glossy Blue;
30 Wildings which expecting stand,
  Proud to be gather'd by thy Hand.
Galatea. Of Infant Limbs to make my Food,
  And swill full Draughts of Humane Blood!
  Go, Monster, bid some other Guest;
  I loath the Host, I loath the Feast.   [*Exit.*

POLYPHEMUS.
AIR.

Polyphemus. *Cease to Beauty to be suing,*
      Ever-whining Love disdaining,
      Let the Brave, their Aims pursuing,
        Still be conqu'ring, not complaining.
40   *Cease to,* &c.   (1732)

WILLIAM CONGREVE (1670–1729)

William Congreve's success as a playwright overshadows his non-dramatic work, of which his translation from Ovid is a superior example. In addition to the following version of the Orpheus and Eurydice narrative, included in Garth, he would add the third book to the *Ars amatoria* originally undertaken by Dryden and published in 1709.

The Story of ORPHEUS and EURYDICE, from Ovid's Metamorphoses in Fifteen Books 10.1–128 [Met. 10.1–77]

Thence, in his Saffron Robe, for distant *Thrace*,
Hymen departs, thro' Air's unmeasur'd Space;
By *Orpheus* call'd, the Nuptial Pow'r attends,
But with ill-omen'd Augury descends;
Nor chearful look'd the God, nor prosp'rous spoke,
Nor blaz'd his Torch, but wept in hissing Smoke.
In vain they whirl it round, in vain they shake,
No rapid motion can its Flames awake.

    With dread these inauspicious signs were view'd,
10 And soon a more disast'rous End ensu'd;
For as the Bride, amid the *Naiad* Train,
Ran joyful, sporting o'er the flow'ry plain,
A venom'd Viper bit her as she pass'd;
Instant she fell, and sudden breath'd her last.

    When long his Loss the *Thracian* had deplor'd,
Not by superior Pow'rs to be restor'd;
Inflam'd by love, and urg'd by deep Despair,
He leaves the Realms of Light, and upper Air;

Daring to tread the dark *Tenarian* road,
20   And tempt the Shades in their obscure Abode;
Thro' gliding Spectres of th' Interr'd to go,
And Phantom People of the World below:
Persephonè he seeks, and him who reigns
O'er Ghosts, and Hell's uncomfortable Plains.
Arriv'd, he, tuning to his Voice his Strings,
Thus to the King and Queen of Shadows sings.

Ye Pow'rs, who under Earth your Realms extend,
To whom all Mortals must one Day descend;
If here 'tis granted sacred Truth to tell:
30   I come not curious to explore your Hell;
Nor come to boast (by vain Ambition fir'd)
How *Cerberus* at my Approach retir'd.
My Wife alone I seek; for her lov'd sake
These Terrors I support, this Journey take.
She, luckless wandring, or by Fate mis-led,
Chanc'd on a lurking Viper's Crest to tread;
The vengeful Beast, enflam'd with Fury, starts,
And thro' her Heel his deathful Venom darts.
Thus was she snatch'd untimely to her Tomb;
40   Her growing Years cut short, and springing Bloom.
Long I my Loss endeavor'd to sustain,
And strongly strove, but strove, alas, in vain:
At length I yielded, won by mighty Love;
Well known is that Omnipotence above!
But here, I doubt, his unfelt Influence fails;
And yet a Hope within my Heart prevails.
That here, ev'n here, he has been known of old;
At least if Truth be by Tradition told;

---

19 Tenarian *road*: leading to Hades
23 *Persephonè*: raped by Pluto, whom she now serves as queen
32 *Cerberus*: recalling one of Hercules's earlier exploits

If Fame of former Rapes Belief may find,
50   You both by Love, and Love alone, were joyn'd.
Now, by the horrors which these realms surround;
By the vast chaos of these depths profound;
By the sad Silence which eternal reigns
O'er all the Waste of these wide-stretching Plains;
Let me again *Eurydice* receive,
Let Fate her quick-spun Thread of Life re-weave.
All our Possessions are but Loans from you,
And soon, or late, you must be paid your Due;
Hither we haste to Human-kind's last Seat,
60   Your endless Empire, and our sure Retreat.
She too, when ripen'd Years she shall attain,
Must, of avoidless Right, be yours again:
I but the transient use of that require,
Which soon, too soon, I must resign entire.
But if the Destinies refuse my Vow,
And no Remission of her Doom allow;
Know, I'm determined to return no more;
So both retain, or both to Life restore.

Thus, while the Bard melodiously complains,
70   And to his Lyre accords his vocal strains,
The very bloodless shades Attention keep,
And silent, seem compassionate to weep;
Ev'n *Tantalus* his Flood unthirsty views,
Nor flies the Stream, nor he the Stream pursues,
Ixïon's wondring Wheel its Whirl suspends;
And the voracious Vulture charm'd, attends;
No more the *Belides* their toil bemoan,
And *Sisiphus* reclin'd, sits list'ning on his Stone.

73ff. The infamous victims tormented in the underworld are sufficiently moved to find themselves distracted from their own suffering.

Then first ('tis said) by sacred Verse subdu'd,
80   The Furies felt their Cheeks with Tears bedew'd:
Nor could the rigid King or queen of Hell,
Th' Impulse of Pity in their Hearts, repell.

Now, from a Troop of Shades that last arriv'd,
Eurydice was call'd, and stood reviv'd.
Slow she advanc'd, and halting seem'd to feel
The fatal Wound, yet painful in her Heel.
Thus he obtains the Suit so much desir'd,
On strict Observance of the Terms requir'd:
For if, before he reach the Realms of Air,
90   He backward cast his Eyes to view the Fair,
The forfeit Grant, that Instant, void is made,
And she for ever left a lifeless Shade.

Now thro' the noiseless Throng their Way they bend,
And both with Pain the rugged Road ascend;
Dark was the Path, and difficult, and steep,
And thick with Vapours from the smoaky Deep.
They well-nigh now had pass'd the Bounds of Night,
And just approach'd the Margin of the Light,
When, he mistrusting, lest her Steps might stray,
100   And gladsom of the Glympse of fawning Day,
His longing Eyes, impatient, backward cast
To catch a Lover's Look, but look'd his last;
For, instant dying, she again descends,
While he to empty Air his Arms extends.
Again she dy'd, nor yet her Lord reprov'd;
What could she say, but that too well he lov'd?
One last Farewel she spoke, which scarce he heard;
So soon she drop'd, so suddain disappear'd.

    All stunn'd he stood, when thus his Wife he view'd
110 By second Fate, and double Death subdu'd:
Not more Amazement by that Wretch was shown,
Whom *Cerberus* beholding, turn'd to Stone;
Nor *Ollenus* cou'd more astonish'd look,
When on himself *Lethæa's* Fault he took,
His beauteous Wife, who too secure had dar'd
Her Face to vye with Goddesses compar'd:
Once join'd by Love, they stand united still,
Turn'd to contiguous Rocks on *Ida's* Hill.

    Now to repass the *Styx* in vain he tries,
120 *Charon* averse, his pressing Suit denies.
Sev'n Days entire, along th' infernal Shores,
Disconsolate, the Bard *Eurydice* deplores;
Defil'd with Filth his Robe, with Tears his Cheeks,
No Sustenance but Grief, and Cares he seeks:
Of rigid Fate incessant he complains,
And Hell's inexorable Gods arraigns.
This ended, to high *Rhodope* he hastes,
And *Hæmus'* Mountain, bleek with Northern Blasts.   (1717)

---

111 *that Wretch*: like the Olenos that follows, otherwise unknown

JONATHAN SWIFT (1667–1745)

Just as Ovid would inspire Pope's abilities as an epistolary poet, so would the Roman author afford Swift an opportunity to indulge his satiric talents. Swift's reworking of the *Metamorphoses'* Baucis and Philemon story is the best of the burlesques that had first become popular during the Restoration's outpouring of Ovidian translations. The poem, of which an autograph manuscript survives, was first published in the 1711 *Miscellanies*. The following corrected version comes from the *Poems* of 1735.

Baucis and Philemon Imitated, From the Eighth Book of OVID [Met. 8.594–721]

In antient Times, as Story tells,
The Saints would often leave their Cells,
And strole about, but hide their Quality,
To try good People's Hospitality.

    It happen'd on a Winter Night,
(As Authors of the Legend write;)
Two Brother Hermits, Saints by Trade,
Taking their *Tour* in Masquerade;
Disguis'd in tatter'd Habits, went
10   To a small Village down in *Kent*;

---

4 *Hospitality*: In Ovid's original, the disguised Jupiter and Mercury are refused lodging throughout their journeys; only the impoverished Baucis and Philemon treat them hospitably. The gods decide to spare the couple from the vengeful destruction wreaked upon the countryside, and also grant them anything they wish. They ask to serve as priests to the gods (hence the transformation of their hut into a temple), and for one partner not to outlive the other.

Where, in the Strolers Canting Strain,
They beg'd from Door to Door in vain;
Try'd ev'ry Tone might Pity win,
But not a Soul would let them in.

Our wand'ring Saints in woful State,
Treated at this ungodly Rate,
Having thro' all the Village pass'd,
To a small Cottage came at last;
Where dwelt a good and honest Yeoman,
20 Call'd in the Neighbourhood, *Philemon*.
Who kindly did the Saints invite
In his poor Hut to pass the Night;
And then the Hospitable Sire
Bid *Goody Baucis* mend the Fire;
While he from out the Chimney took
A Flitch of Bacon off the Hook;
And freely from the fattest Side
Cut out large Slices to be fry'd:
Then stept aside to fetch 'em Drink,
30 Fill'd a large Jug up to the Brink;
And saw it fairly twice go round;
Yet (what was wonderful) they found,
'Twas still replenished to the Top,
As if they ne'er had touched a Drop.
The good old Couple was amaz'd,
And often on each other gaz'd;
For both were frightened to the Heart,
And just began to cry; – What art!
Then softly turn'd aside to view,
40 Whether the Lights were burning blue.
The gentle *Pilgrims* soon aware on't,
Told 'em their Calling, and their Errant:

---

40 indicating a demonic presence

Good Folks, you need not be afraid,
We are but *Saints*, the Hermits said;
No Hurt shall come to You, or Yours;
But, for that Pack of churlish Boors,
Not fit to live on Christian Ground,
They and their Houses shall be drown'd:
Whilst you shall see your Cottage rise,
50   And grow a Church before your Eyes.

They scarce had Spoke; when, fair and soft,
The Roof began to mount aloft;
Aloft rose ev'ry Beam and Rafter,
The heavy Wall climb'd slowly after.

The Chimney widen'd, and grew higher,
Became a Steeple with a Spire.

The Kettle to the Top was hoist,
And there stood fast'ned to a Joist:
But with the Upside down, to shew
60   Its Inclination for below;
In vain; for some Superior Force
Apply'd at Bottom, stops its Course,
Doom'd ever in Suspence to dwell,
'Tis now no Kettle, but a Bell.

A wooden Jack, which had almost
Lost, by disuse, the Art to Roast,
A sudden Alteration feels,
Increas'd by new Intestine Wheels:
And what exalts the Wonder more,
70   The Number made the Motion slow'r:
The Flyer, tho't had Leaden Feet,
Turn'd round so quick, you scarce cou'd see't;
Now slacken'd by some secret Power,
Can hardly move an Inch an Hour.

The Jack and Chimney near ally'd,
Had never left each other's Side;
The Chimney to a Steeple grown,
The Jack wou'd not be left alone,
But up against the Steeple rear'd,
80   Became a Clock, and still adher'd:
And still its Love to Household Cares
By a shrill Voice at Noon declares,
Warning the Cook-maid, not to burn
That Roast-meat which it cannot turn.

   The Groaning Chair was seen to crawl
Like an huge Snail half up the Wall;
There stuck aloft, in Publick View,
And with small Change, a Pulpit grew.

   The Porringers, that in a Row
90   Hung high, and made a glitt'ring Show,
To a less Noble Substance chang'd,
Were now but Leathern Buckets rang'd.

   The Ballads pasted on the Wall,
Of *Joan* of *France*, and *English Moll*,
Fair *Rosamond*, and *Robin Hood*,
The *Little Children in the Wood*:
Now seem'd to look abundance better,
Improv'd in Picture, Size, and Letter;
And high in Order plac'd, describe
100   The Heraldry of ev'ry Tribe.

   A Bedstead of the Antique Mode,
Compact of Timber many a Load,
Such as our Grandsires wont to use,

---

92 *Leathern Buckets*: water buckets, hung as a precaution against fire

Was Metamorphos'd into Pews;
Which still their antient Nature keep;
By lodging Folks dispos'd to Sleep.

The Cottage by such Feats as these,
Grown to a Church by just Degrees,
The Hermits then desire their Host
110   To ask for what he fancy'd most:
Philemon, having paus'd a while,
Return'd 'em Thanks in Homely Stile;
Then said; my House is grown so Fine,
Methinks, I still wou'd call it mine:
I'm Old, and fain wou'd live at Ease,
Make me the *Parson*, if you please.

He spoke, and presently he feels,
His Grazier's Coat fall down his Heels;
He sees, yet hardly can believe,
120   About each Arm, a Pudding-sleeve;
His Wastcoat to a Cassock grew,
And both assum'd a Sable Hue;
But being Old, continu'd just
As Thread-bare, and as full of Dust.
His Talk was now of *Tythes* and *Dues*,
Could smoak his Pipe, and read the News;
Knew how to preach old Sermons next,
Vampt in the Preface and the Text;
At Christenings well could act his Part,
130   And had the Service all by Heart;
Wish'd Women might have Children fast,
And thought whose *Sow* had *farrow'd* last:
Against *Dissenters* would repine,

120ff. The sartorial changes that Swift's characters undergo mock the pseudo-fashionable garments (associated with the clergy) that replace their rustic clothes.

And stood up firm for *Right Divine*:
Found his Head fill'd with many a System,
But Classick Authors – he ne'er miss'd 'em.

Thus having furbish'd up a Parson,
Dame *Baucis* next, they play'd their Farce on:
Instead of Home-spun Coifs were seen,
140   Good Pinners edg'd with Colberteen:
Her Petticoat transform'd apace,
Became Black Sattin, Flounc'd with Lace.
Plain *Goody* would no longer down,
'Twas *Madam*, in her Grogram Gown.
Philemon was in great Surprize,
And hardly could believe his Eyes,
Amaz'd to see Her look so Prim,
And she admir'd as much at Him.

Thus, happy in their Change of Life,
150   Were several Years the Man and Wife,
When on a Day, which prov'd their last,
Discoursing o'er old Stories past,
They went by chance, amidst their Talk,
To the Church-yard, to fetch a walk;
When *Baucis* hastily cry'd out;
My Dear, I see your Forehead sprout:
Sprout, quoth the Man, What's this you tell us?
I hope you don't believe me Jealous:
But yet, methinks, I feel it true;
160   And really, Yours is budding too –
Nay, – now I cannot stir my Foot:
It feels as if 'twere taking Root.

Description would but tire my Muse:
In short, they both were turn'd to *Yews*.
Old Good-man *Dobson* of the Green
Remembers he the Trees has seen;

He'll talk of them from Noon to Night,
And goes with Folks to shew the Sight:
On *Sundays*, after Ev'ning Prayer,
170 He gathers all the Parish there;
Points out the Place of either *Yew*;
Here *Baucis*, there *Philemon* grew.
Till once, a Parson of our Town,
To mend his Barn, cut *Baucis* down;
At which, 'tis hard to be believ'd,
How much the other Tree was griev'd,
Grew Scrubby, dy'd a-top, was stunted:
So, the next Parson stub'd and burnt it.

(1735)

HENRY FIELDING (1707–1754)

One of our greatest novelists and prose stylists, Fielding issued his prose 'adaptation' of the *Ars amatoria*'s first book with a facing-page Latin text and notes in 1747. Five years after Fielding's death, it would reappear as *The Lovers Assistant, or New Art of Love*.

Ovid's Art of Love Paraphrased, And Adapted to the Present Time. Book I [Ars 1.525–68, 631–58, 679–706, 739–54]

[*Bacchus*]

But now *Bacchus* summons his Poet. He likewise assists Lovers, and favours the Flame which warms himself.

The *Cretan* Lady having jumped out of Bed in a raving fit, wandered on the foreign Shore of *Dia*. She had nothing on but a loose wrapping Gown, without Stockings or Cap; and her Hair

---

3 Cretan *Lady*: Ariadne

hung dishevelled over her Shoulders. She complained of the
Cruelty of *Theseus* to the deep Waves, whilst an unworthy Shower
of Tears ran down her Cheeks. She wept, and lamented aloud,
and both became her; nor did her Tears diminish her Beauty.
10   Once, and again, she beat her delicious Breasts with her Hands,
and cried aloud, *The perfidious Man hath abandoned me; what will
become of poor* Ariadne? *What will become of poor Ariadne?* On a
sudden a vast Multitude was heard, while many Kinds of strange
Instruments, like those of the miserable Masons, accompanied
the Voices. The poor Lady sunk with Fear, and suppressed her
last Words; nor did the least Blood remain in her Countenance.
And now behold the *Bacchanalian* Women, with their Hair about
their Ears, and the light Satyrs, who are always Forerunners of
the God. Behold old Master *Silenus* as drunk as a Piper, riding
20   on an Ass, which he is hardly able either to sit or guide. The old
Gentleman, endeavouring to follow the *Bacchanalians*, who fly
from him and towards him, sets Spurs to his Ass, which being a
vicious Beast, kicked up, and threw him over his Ears: upon
which all the Satyrs set up a loud Shout, crying out, *Rise, Father,
rise and be d——n'd to you.* And now the God himself, high mounted
on his Four-Wheel Chaise, the Top of which was adorned with
Grapes, and which he drove himself, flung his Golden Reins
over the Backs of his Pair of Tygers. Poor *Ariadne's* Colour
forsook her Cheeks, and *Theseus* and her Voice at once deserted
30   her Lips. Thrice she attempted to fly, and thrice being retained,
she grew stiff with Fear, and stood trembling as Corn waves in
the Field, or Reeds on the River Bank, when fanned by the
Wind. To whom the God; *Behold, Madam, a more faithful Lover
at your Feet: Fear nothing, Lady fair, you shall be the Wife of* Bacchus.
*The Sky shall be your Dowry, where shining in a bright Constellation,
by the Name of* Ariadne's *Crown, you shall often direct the doubtful
Mariner's Passage.* He said; and leaping from his Chariot, lest
Ariadne should be afraid of the Tygers, the Sand sunk under the
Weight of his Feet; and catching her instantly in his Arms, he
40   carried her, who was incapable of scratching, directly off; (for
every thing, we know, is in the power of a Deity:) And now, whilst

Part of his Train sing the *Hymenæum*, and others cry *Evie, Evoe*, two very mysterious Words, and full of Masonry, the God and his new-ravished Bride go together between a Pair of sacred Sheets.

Whenever therefore you happen to be in Company with a pretty Girl over a Bottle, pray heartily to *Bacchus*, and invoke his nocturnal Rites, that the Wine may not get into your Head.

★

[*Promises*]

Secondly, to Flattery, add Promises, and those not timorous nor sneaking ones. If a Girl insists upon a Promise of Marriage, give
50   it her, and bind it by many Oaths; for no Indictment lies for this sort of Perjury.

The Antients vented horrid Impieties on this Occasion, and introduced *Jupiter* shaking his Sides at the Perjuries of Lovers, and ordering the Winds to puff them away: Nay, he is said to have forsworn himself even by *Styx* to *Juno*; and therefore, say they, he encourages Men to follow his Example.

But though a *Christian* must not talk in this manner, yet I believe it may be one of those Sins which the Church of *Rome* holds to be venial, or rather venal.

60   I would here by no means be suspected of Infidelity or Profaneness. It is necessary there should be a God; and therefore we must believe there is; nay, we must worship him: for he doth not possess himself in that indolent State in which the Deities of *Epicurus* are depictured. If we live innocent Lives, we may depend on the Care of his Providence.

Restore faithfully whatever is deposited in your Hands: Be just in all your Contracts: Avoid all Kind of Fraud, and be not polluted with Blood. A wise Man will be a Rogue only among the Girls:

---

50 [Fielding's note]: This is the most exceptionable Passage in the whole Work. We have endeavoured to soften it as much as possible; but even as it now stands, we cannot help expressing Detestation of this Sentiment, which appears shocking even in a Heathen Writer.

For in all other Articles a Gentleman will be ashamed of breaking
70   his Word.

And what is this more than deceiving the Deceivers? The Sex
are for the greatest part Impostors; let them therefore fall in the
Snares which they have spread for others.

Perhaps you have never read the Justice of *Busiris;* when *Egypt*
was burnt up Nine Years together for want of Rain, one *Thrasius*
a Foreigner came to Court, and being introduced to the King by
Clementius Cotterelius, he acquainted his Majesty, that *Jupiter* was
to be propitiated by the Blood of a Stranger. The King answered
him, *Then thou thyself shalt be the first Victim, and with thy foreign*
80   *Blood shalt give Rain to* Egypt.

To the same Purpose is the Story of *Phalaris,* who roasted the
Limbs of *Perillus* in his own Bull: Thus making Proof of the
Goodness of the Work by the Torments of the unhappy Maker.

Now there was great Justice in both these Examples; for nothing
can be more equitable than that the Inventers of Cruelty should
perish by their own Art.

To apply this to our present Purpose: As there is no Deceit or
Perjury which Women will stick at putting in use against us, let
them lament the Consequence of their own Examples.

*

[Rape]

90   Ravishing is indeed out of fashion in this Age; and therefore
I am at a loss for modern Examples; but antient Story abounds
with them.

Miss *Phœbe* and her Sister were both ravished, and both were
well pleased with the Men who ravished them.

---

82 *Phalaris*: See p. 163, n. 47..

94 [Fielding's note]: *Phoebe* and *Ilaira* were two pretty Girls, the Daughters of
Leucippus, and by their Father betrothed to two Brothers *Idas* and *Lynceus;* but
before the Celebration of their Nuptials, were ravished by *Castor* and *Pollux.* This
ended in the Death of *Castor,* by the hands of *Lynceus;* and of *Lynceus,* by *Pollux,*
whose Death while *Idas* was attempting to revenge, he was struck dead by
Thunder at the Feet of *Pollux.*

Though the story of *Deidamia* was formerly in all the *Trojan News-Papers*, yet my Reader may be pleased to see it better told.

Venus had now kept her Word to *Paris*, and given him the Beauty she had promised, not as a Bribe, but as a Gratification for his having made an Award in her Favour, in the famous Cause between *Juno* and others against *Venus*, in *Trover* for a Golden Apple; which was referred to him at the Assizes at *Ida*.

Paris, every one knows, no sooner had received Mrs. *Helen*, than he immediately carried her off to his Father's Court.

Upon this the *Grecians* entered into an Association; and several Noblemen raised Regiments at their own Expence, out of their Regard to the Public: For Cuckoldom was a public Cause, no one knowing whose Turn it would be next.

Lieutenant-General *Achilles*, who was to command a large Body of Grenadiers, which the *Greeks* call *Myrmidons*, did not behave handsomely on that Occasion, though he got off afterwards at a Court-Martial by pleading, that his Mother (who had a great deal in her own power) had insisted on his acting the Part he did; for, I am ashamed to say, he dressed himself in Womens Clothes, and hid himself at the House of one *Lycomedes*, a Man of good Fortune in those parts.

Fie upon it, General, I am ashamed to see you sit quilting among the Girls; a Sword becomes your Hands much better than a Needle.

What can you mean by that Work-Basket in a Hand by which Count Hector is to fall? Do you carry that Basket with you to put his Head in?

For shame then, cast away your Huswife, and all those effeminate Trinkets from a Fist able to wield Harry *the Fifth's Sword.*

It happened, that at the same time when the General, at the House of 'Squire *Lycomedes*, performed this Feat, Miss *Deidamia*, one of the Maids of Honour, was visiting at the same Place. This young Lady soon discovered that the General was a Man; for indeed he got her Maidenhead.

He ravished her, that is the Truth on't; that a Gentleman ought to believe, in Favour of the Lady: but he may believe the Lady was willing enough to be ravished at the same time.

When the General threw away his Needle, and grasped the Armour, (you must remember the Story, for it was in the *Trojan Alamain*) the young Lady began to change her Note, and to hope he would not forsake her so.

Ah! little Mia! *is this the Violence you complained of? Is this the Ravisher you are afraid of? Why with that gentle Voice do you solicit the Author of your Dishonour to stay with you?*

To come at once to the Moral of my Story; as they are ashamed to make the first Advances, so they are ready to suffer whatever
140 a pushing Man can do unto them . . .

★

[Threats]

And here shall I lament the Wickedness of Mankind, or only simply observe it to you? But in reality all Friendship and Integrity are nothing more than Names.

Alas! It is dangerous to be too prodigal in the Praises of your Mistress, even to your Friend; for if he believes you, he becomes your Rival.

It is true, there are some old Stories of faithful Friends: *Patroclus* never made a Cuckold of *Achilles*; and *Phædra's* Chastity was never tempted by *Pirithous*.

150 *Pylades* loved *Hermiones*, who was his Friend's Wife; but it was with the pure Love of a Brother: And the same Fidelity did *Castor* preserve towards his Twin-Brother *Pollux*.

But if you expect to find such instances in these degenerate Days, you may as well have Faith enough to expect a Pine-Apple from a Pear-Tree, or hope to fill your Bottle with *Burgundy* from the River.

I am afraid we are grown so bad, that Iniquity itself gives a relish to our Pleasures; and every Man is not only addicted to his Pleasures, but those are the sweeter, when seasoned with another's
160 Pain.

---

149 *Pirithous*: friend to Theseus, Phaedra's husband

It is in short a terrible Case, that a Lover ought to fear his Friend more than his Enemy. Beware of the former, and you are safe.

Beware of your Cousin, and your Brother, and your dear and intimate Companions. These are the Sort of Gentry from whom you are to apprehend most Danger.   (1747)

ROBERT FORBES (*fl.* 1755)

Robert Forbes, *Gent.* – the 'R. F.' who penned the following translation from *Metamorphoses* 13 – is otherwise unknown. However, his Aberdeenshire dialect version ('Attempted in Broad *Buchans*', the original edition boasts) of Ajax's plea against Ulysses for the dead Achilles's armour, with the Latin text at the bottom of the page and a full glossary, enjoyed popularity well into the nineteenth century. All boldface annotations come from Forbes's own 'Key'.

Ajax's Speech to the Grecian Knabbs [Met. 13.1– 122]

The wight an' doughty Captains a'
     Upo their doups sat down;
A rangel o' the common fouk
     In bourachs a' stood roun.

AJAX bangs up, fase targe was shught
     In seven fald o' hide;
An' bein bouden'd up wi' wraith,
     Wi' atry face he ey'd

---

1 *wight*: brave   **3 rangel**: Croud, *omne-gatherum*   **4 bourachs**: Rings, circles
5 Ajax jumps up, whose shield was covered   **7 bouden'd**: swollen
8 atry: Stern, grim

The Trojan shore, an' a' the barks
10   That tedder'd fast did ly
Alang the coast; an' raxing out
        His gardies, loud did cry:

O JOVE! The cause we here do plead,
        An' unco great's the staik;
Bat sall that sleeth ULYSSES now
        Be said to be my maik?

Ye ken right well, fan HECTOR try'd
        Thir barks to burn an' scowder,
He took to speed o' fit, because
20   He cou'd na' bide the ewder.

Bat I, like birky, stood the brunt,
        An' slocken'd out that gleed,
Wi' muckle virr, an' syne I gar'd
        The limmers tak the speed.

'Tis better than, the cause we try
        Wi' the wind o' our wame,
Than for to come in hanny grips
        At sik a driry time.

At threeps I am na' sae perquire,
30   Nor auld-farren as he,
Bat at banes-brakin, it's well kent,
        He has na' maughts like me.

---

11 *raxing*: stretching   12 *gardies*: Arms   14 *unco*: uncommonly
15 *sleeth*: Sloven   16 *maik*: equal   17 *fan*: when   18 **scowder**: Set on fire
20 *ewder*: Blaze, scorching heat   21 *like birky*: more spirited
22 **slocken'd**: Quenched; *gleed*: fire   23 *gar'd*: made   24 *limmers*: scoundrels
26 *wame*: belly (i.e. with words)   27 **hanny grips**: Close grapple
29 **threeps**: Allegations, falsehoods   30 **auld-farren**: Sagacious
32 **maughts**: Might, strength

For as far as I him excel
   In toulzies fierce an' strong,
As far in chast-taak he exceeds
   Me, wi' his sleeked tongue.

My proticks an' my doughty deeds,
   O Greeks! I need na' tell,
For ther's nane here bat kens them well:
40   Lat him tell his himsel:

Which ay war done at glomin time,
   Or dead hour o' the night,
An' deil ane kens except himsel;
   For nae man saw the sight.

The staik indeed is unco great,
   I will confess alway,
Bat, name ULYSSES to it anes,
   The worth quite dwines away.

Great as it is, I need na' voust;
50   I'm seer I have nae neef
To get fat could be ettl'd at,
   By sik a mensless thief.

Yet routh o' honour he has got,
   Ev'n tho he gets the glaik,
Fan he's sae crous, that he would try
   To be brave AJAX' maik.

---

34 *toulzies*: Battles, engagements   35 *chast-taak*: Talking, prattling
37 *proticks*: Warlike deeds, atchievements   41 *glomin time*: Twilight
43 *deil ane kens*: devil one knows   49 *voust*: Brag, vaunt
50 *neef*: Difficulty, doubt   51 *ettl'd at*: Aimed at   52 *mensless*: shameless
53 *routh*: Plenty, wealth   54 *glaik*: Cheat   55 *crous*: Bold, stout

But gin my wightness doubted war,
   I wat my gentle bleed,
As being sin to TELAMON,
60   Right sickerly does plead:

Fa, under doughty HERCULES,
   Great Troy's walls down hurl'd,
An' in a tight Thessalian bark
   To Colchos' harbour swirl'd.

An' ÆACUS my gutcher was,
   Fa now in hell sits jidge,
Fare a fun-stane does SISYPHUS
   Down to the yerd sair gnidge.

Great JOVE himself owns ÆACHUS
70   To be his ain dear boy,
An' syne, without a' doubt, I am
   The neist chiel to his oye.

Bat thus in counting o' my etion
   I need na' mak sik din,
For it's well kent ACHILLES was
   My father's brither sin:

An' as we're cousins, there's nae scouth,
   To be in ony swidders;
I only seek fat is my due,
80   I mean fat was my brither's.

---

59 *sin*: son   **65** *gutcher*: Grand-father   **67** *fun-stane*: fool's-stone
68 *yerd*: Earth; *gnidge*: Squeeze, press down   **72** *oye*: Grand-child
73 *etion*: Kindred, geneaology   **77** *scouth*: Room
78 *swidders*: Doubt, hesitation

Bat why a thief, like SISYPHUS,
   That's nidder'd sae in hell,
Sud here tak fittininment,
   Is mair na' I can tell.

Sall then thes arms be deny'd
   To me, fa in this bruilzie
Was the first man that drew my durk,
   Came flaught-bred to the toulzie?

An' sall this sleeth come farrer ben,
90   Fa was sae dev'lish surly,
He scarce wou'd gae a fit frae hame,
   An' o' us a' was hurly?

An' frae the weir he did back hap,
   An' turn'd to us his fud;
An' gar'd the hale-ware o' us trow
   That he was gane clean wod.

Until the sin o' NAUPLIUS,
   Mair useless na' himsel,
His jouckry-pauckry finding out,
100   To weir did him compel.

Lat him than now tak will an' wile,
   Fa nane at first wou'd wear,
An' I get baith the skaith an' scorn,
   Twin'd o' my brither's gear!

---

82 nidder'd: Plagu'd, warmly handled   **83 fittininment**: Concern, footing in
86 bruilzie: Scuffle, quarrel   **88 flaught-bred**: Briskly, fiercely
89 come farrer ben: Be more favour'd   **92 hurly**: Last   **93 weir**: War
94 fud: Tail, back-side   **95 hale-ware**: Whole
97 sin o' NAUPLIUS: Palamedes, whom Ulysses would later charge falsely with treason
and see stoned to death (cf. lines 135ff., below)
99 jouckry-pauckry: Roguery, tricks   **104 Twin'd**: stripped

Because I was the foremaist man,
    An' steed the hettest fire,
Just like the man that aught the cow,
    Gade deepest i' the mire.

I wish the chiel he had been wod,
    Or that it had been trow'd;
That mither o' the mischief had not
    To Troy's town been row'd.

Syne PÆAN's son, thou'd not been left
    On Lemnos' isle to skirle,
Fare now thy granes in dowy dens
    The yerd-fast stanes do thirle:

An' on that sleeth ULYSSES' head
    Sad curses down does bicker,
If there be gods aboon, I'm seer
    He'll get them leel and sicker.

This doughty lad he was resolv'd
    Wi' me his fate to try,
Wi' poison'd stewgs o' HERCULES,
    Bat 'las! his bleed wis fey.

Wi' sickness now he's ferter like,
    Or like a water-wraith,
An' hirplin after the wil birds,
    Can scarce gat meat an' claith.

---

113 PÆAN's son: Philoctetes, wounded by a serpent and so (on Ulysses's counsel) abandoned on Lemnos   114 *skirle*: Howl, shreik   115 *dowy*: Dismal
116 *thirle*: Thrill, pierce   118 *bicker*: Rattle   120 *leel*: true
123 *stewgs*: Rusty darts   124 *fey*: Doom'd to die
125 *ferter like*: Like a little fairy   127 *hirplin*: Clenching, halting

An' now these darts that weerded were
130   To tak the town o' Troy,
To get meat for his gabb, he man
     Against the birds employ.

Yet he's alive, altho to gang
     Wi' him he was fu' laith;
If PALAMEDE had been sae wise,
     He had been free frae skaith:

For he'd been livin ti' this day,
     An' slept in a hale skin,
An' gotten fair play for his life,
140   An' stan'd he had nae been.

Because he prov'd he was nae wod,
     He was sae fu' o' fraud,
He slack'd na' till he gat the life
     O' this poor sakeless lad.

For to the Grecians he did swear,
     He had sae great envy,
That goud in goupens he had got,
     The army to betray.

An' wi' mischief he was sae gnib,
150   To get his ill intent,
He howk'd the goud which he himsel
     Had yerded in his tent.

---

129 weerded: Determined, foretold   **144 sakeless**: guiltless
147 goud in goupens: Gold in handfuls   **149 gnib**: Ready, quick
151 howk'd: Digg'd   **152 yerded**: buried

Thus wi' uncanny pranks he fights,
　　An' sae he did beguile,
An' twin'd us o' our kneefest men,
　　By death and by exile.

Altho' mair gabby he may be
　　Than NESTOR wise and true,
Yet few will say, it was nae fau't
160　　That he did him furhow.

Fan his poor glyde was sae mischiev'd,
　　He'd neither ca' nor drive,
The lyart lad, wi' years sair dwang'd,
　　The traitor thief did leave.

These are nae threeps o' mine, right well
　　Kens DIOMEDE the wight,
Fa' wi' snell words him sair did snib,
　　An' bann'd his cowardly flight.

The gods tho look on mortal men
170　　Wi' eyn baith just and gleg;
Lo he, fa NESTOR wou'd nae help,
　　For help himsel does beg!

Than as he did the auld man leave
　　Anon' sae fierce a menzie,
The law he made, lat him be paid
　　Back just in his ain cuinzie.

---

155 *kneefest*: Keenest, briskest   160 *furhow*: Forsake
161 *glyde*: An old horse   163 *lyart*: grey; **dwang'd**: Bow'd, decrepid
167 *snell*: sharp; **snib**: Chastised, frighted   170 *gleg*: bright, sharp
174 *menzie*: Croud, throng   176 *cuinzie*: Coin

Yet fan he cry'd, O neipers help!
    I ran to tak his part,
He look'd sae haw as gin a dwame
180   Had just o'ercast his heart.

For they had gi'en him sik a fleg,
    He look'd as he'd been doited,
For ilka' limb as' lith o' him
    'Gainst ane anithir knoited.

Syne wi' my targe I cover'd him,
    Fan on the yerd he lies,
An' sav'd his smeerless saul, I think,
    'Tis little to my praise.

Bat gin wi' Baite ye will bourd,
190   Come back, lad, to yon place;
Lat Trojans an' your wonted fears
    Stan glourin i' your face:

Syne slouch behind my doughty targe,
    That yon day your head happit;
There fight your fill, sin' ye are grown
    Sae unco crous an' cappit.

Fan I came to him, wi' sad wound
    He had nae maughts to gang,
Bat fan he saw that he was safe,
200   Right souple cou'd he spang.

---

177 *neipers*: Neighbours   179 *haw*: Pale; *dwame*: Qualm, fainting
181 *fleg*: Fright   182 *doited*: Stupified   184 *knoited*: Clash'd
187 *smeerless*: Senseless, thoughtless   194 *happit*: helped, saved
198 *maughts*: Might, strength   200 *souple*: Supple, agile; *spang*: Spring

Lo! HECTOR to the toulzie came,
　　An' gods baith fierce an' grim,
He flegged starker fouk na' you,
　　Sae sair they dreaded him.

Yet as he did o' slaughter voust,
　　I len'd him sik a dird,
As laid him arselins on his back,
　　To wamble o' the yerd.

Fan he spang'd out, rampag'd an' said
210　　That nane amon' us a'
Durst venture out upo the lone,
　　Wi' him to shak a fa';

I dacker'd wi' him by mysel,
　　Ye wish't it to my kavel,
An' gin ye speer fa got the day,
　　We parted on a nevel.

Lo! Trojans fetch baith fire an' sword
　　Amo' the Grecian barks:
Fare's eloquent ULYSSES now,
220　　Wi' a' his wily cracks?

I than a thousand ships did save,
　　An' muckle danger thol'd;
'Gin they 'ad brunt, deil ane had seen
　　Tha land fare he was soal'd.

---

203 *flegged*: Frighted   206 *dird*: Thump, box   207 *arselins*: Backwards
208 *wamble*: Tumble   212 *shak a fa'*: Wrestle, grapple
213 *dacker'd*: Engaged, grappled   214 *kavel*: Lot, share   215 *speer*: ask
216 *nevel*: A box, blow with the fist   222 *thol'd*: Suffered, endured
224 *soal'd*: born

Bat gin the truth I now durst tell,
　I think the honour's mair
To them, than fat it is to me,
　Tho' they come to my skair:

At least the honour equal is;
230　Than fat needs a' this din;
For AJAX them he does na' seek,
　Sae sair as they do him.

Than lat ULYSSES now compare
　RHÆSUS an' maughtless DOLON,
An' PRIAM's son, an' PALLAS phizz
　That i' the night was stoln.

For deil be-licket has he done,
　Fan it was fair-fuir days;
Nor without gaucy DIOMEDE,
240　Fa was his guide always.

Rather na' gi' him this propine,
　For deeds that feckless are,
Divide them, and lat DIOMEDE
　Come in for the best share.

Bat fat use will they be to him,
　Fa in hudge mudge wi' wiles,
Without a gully in his hand,
　The smeerless fae beguiles?

---

235 *phizz*: Image, the *Palladium*　**237** *be-licket*: Nothing
238 *fair-fuir*: Broad-day-light　**239** *gaucy*: Jolly, plump
241 *propine*: Gift, present　**242** *feckless*: Of no effect, value
246 *hudge mudge*: Secretly, underhandedly　**247** *gully*: Weapon

The gouden helmet will sae glance,
250   An blink wi' skyrin brinns,
That a' his wimples they'll find out
    Fan i' the mark he sheens.

Bat his weak head nae farrach has
    That helmet for to bear,
Nor has he mergh intil his banes,
    To wield ACHILLES' spear:

Nor his brae targe, on which is seen
    The yerd, the sin, and lift,
Can well agree wi' his cair cleuck,
260   That cleckit was for thift.

Fat gars you than, mischievous tyke!
    For this propine to prig,
That your sma banes wou'd langel sair,
    They are sae unco big?

An' gin the Greeks sud be sae blind,
    As gi' you sik a gift,
The Trojan lads right soon wou'd dight
    You like a futtle haft.

An' as you ay by speed o' fit
270   Perform ilk' doughty deed,
Fan laggert wi' this bouksome graith,
    You will tyne half your speed.

---

250 brinns: Rays, beams   **251 wimples**: Cunning, wiles
253 farrach: Strength, substance   **255 mergh**: Marrow
259 cleuck: Left hand   **260 cleckit**: Caught in the fire
262 prig: Importune, sue for   **263 langel**: Entangle
268 futtle haft: Handle of a knife
271 laggert: Encumber'd; **graith**: Bulky accoutrements   **272 tyne**: lose

Besides your targe, in battle keen,
  Bat little danger tholes,
While mine wi' mony a thudd is clour'd,
  An' thirl'd sair wi' holes.

Bat now, fat need's far a' this din?
  Lat deeds o' words tak' place,
An lat your stoutness now be try'd,
280 Just here before your face.

Lat the arms of ACHILLES brave
  Amon' our faes be laid,
An' the first chiel that brings them back,
  Lat him wi' them be clad.

                                        (1755)

WILLIAM MASSEY (1691–1764)

The eighteenth-century translator William Massey was inspired to undertake an English version of the *Fasti* out of regret 'that this most elaborate and learned of all Ovid's works, should be so little regarded', and by a firm conviction that John Gower's version of the previous century had not done justice to the poem ('The language and versification of that performance is such, that I could reap little or no help from it; and I flatter myself, that a comparison, made between his version and mine, would be no disadvantage to me'). Though he fails to live up to his brag, Massey does offer a good rendition of the dishonest merchant's prayer to Mercury from Book 5.

---

274 tholes: Suffers, endures

Ovid's Fasti, or the Romans Sacred Calendar
5.781–814 [Fas. 5.663–92] *15 May: Mercury's holiday*

    Now *Mercury* attend, thou son of *Jove*,
Whom *Maia* bore, the fruit of stolen love,
On some *Arcadian* hill; lo! wing'd thy feet,
From heav'n to hell must make thy passage fleet;
The gods swift messenger of peace and war!
The tuneful *lyre* thou dost with pleasure bear;
'Tis thou dost o'er the *wrestlers* ring preside,
And art the graceful orator's best guide;
Thy temple, that the *Circus* does survey,
10   Our fathers hallow'd on *the ides of May.*
And hence to thee we consecrate that day.
With insence ev'ry tradesman thee implores,
That he may get good profit by his wares.
Thy pool, O *Merc'ry*, near *Capena*'s gate,
Is holy, as experienc'd men relate;
Hither the *merchant*, with girt coat, repairs,
Well purify'd his hand a pitcher bears;
And water draws; in which a *laurel bough*,
He dips, and with it, like a sprinkling dew,
20   Does o'er his merchandize the droppings throw.
With which he also moistens his own hair,
And utters with a glossing tongue this pray'r:
    'My former *perjuries* purge thou away,
'And cleanse me from the frauds of yesterday;
'Whether I have by thee *false witness* born,
'Or by great *Jove* perfidiously have sworn;
'Or to deceive the sacred pow'rs design'd,
'May all those words be scatter'd with the wind;
'May I grow rich by perj'ry and deceit,
30   'Nor let the gods above regard the cheat;

'And when upon my *chapman* I impose,
'May my increase of gain increase my joys.'
   This pray'r the *god of theft* with smiles receives,
Conscious of how he once stole *Admetus'* beeves.   (1757)

PHILLIS WHEATLEY (c. 1753–1784)

African-born Phillis Wheatley was enslaved and brought to America
in 1761. Wheatley's prodigious literary talents became evident when
her masters made the uncommon move of granting her an education.
Her continued studies in the Latin and English poets inspired a volume
of poems published in 1773, the year she was also manumitted. The
following excerpt from that volume translates Ovid's story of Niobe
who, vain of her seven beautiful daughters and seven handsome sons,
has boasted of her superiority to the goddess Latona, mother of Apollo
and Diana. As a punishment, all of Niobe's children are struck down.

NIOBE in Distress for her Children slain by
APOLLO, from *Ovid*'s Metamorphoses, Book VI.,
161–212 [Met. 6.267–301]

  On the swift wings of ever-flying *Fame*
To *Cadmus'* palace soon the tidings came:
Niobe heard, and with indignant eyes
She thus express'd her anger and surprize:
'Why is such privilege to them allow'd?
'Why thus insulted by the *Delian* god?
'Dwells there such mischief in the pow'rs above?
'Why sleeps the vengeance of immortal *Jove?*'

---

34 Admetus' *beeves*: cf. *Met.* 2.676–707

For now *Amphion* too, with grief oppress'd,
10   Had plung'd the deadly dagger in his breast.
Niobe now, less haughty than before,
With lofty head directs her steps no more.
She, who late told her pedigree divine,
And drove the *Thebans* from *Latona's* shrine,
How strangely chang'd! – yet beautiful in woe,
She weeps, nor weeps unpity'd by the foe.
On each pale corse the wretched mother spread
Lay overwhelm'd with grief, and kiss'd her dead.
Then rais'd her arms, and thus, in accents slow,
20   'Be sated cruel *Goddess!* with my woe;
'If I've offended, let these streaming eyes,
'And let this sev'nfold funeral suffice:
'Ah! take this wretched life you deign'd to save,
'With them I too am carried to the grave.
'Rejoice triumphant, my victorious foe,
'But show the cause from whence your triumphs flow?
'Tho I unhappy mourn these children slain,
'Yet greater numbers to my lot remain.'
She ceas'd, the bow-string twang'd with awful sound,
30   Which struck with terror all th' assembly round,
Except the queen, who stood unmov'd alone,
By her distresses more presumptuous grown.
Near the pale corses stood their sisters fair
In sable vestures and dishevell'd hair;
One, while she draws the fatal shaft away,
Faints, falls, and sickens at the light of day.
To sooth her mother, lo! another flies,
And blames the fury of inclement skies,
And, while her words a filial pity show,
40   Struck dumb – indignant seeks the shades below.
Now from the fatal place another flies,
Falls in her flight, and languishes, and dies.

---

9 *Amphion*: Niobe's husband

Another on her sister drops in death;
A fifth in trembling terrors yields her breath;
While the sixth seeks some gloomy cave in vain,
Struck with the rest, and mingl'd with the slain.

One only daughter lives, and she the least;
The queen close clasp'd the daughter to her breast:
'Ye heav'nly pow'rs, ah spare me one,' she cry'd,
50   'Ah! spare me one,' the vocal hills reply'd:
In vain she begs, the Fates her suit deny,
In her embrace she sees her daughter die.

(1773)

ANNA LAETITIA BARBAULD
(1743–1825)

Born Anna Laetitia Aikin, Barbauld gained a reputation both for her work as an educator and for a literary career that would span the Neoclassical and Romantic periods. The following poem, a composite of passages translated from the *Tristia* and *Ex Ponto*, demonstrates her editorial tact. The outcome is a seamless lament that wonderfully preserves Ovid's mournful tone.

Ovid to his Wife: Imitated from different Parts of his Tristia

My aged head now stoops its honours low,
Bow'd with the load of fifty winters' snow;
And for the raven's glossy black assumes
The downy whiteness of the cygnet's plumes:
Loose scatter'd hairs around my temples stray,
And spread the mournful shade of sickly grey:

I bend beneath the weight of broken years,
Averse to change, and chill'd with causeless fears.
The season now invites me to retire
10   To the dear lares of my household fire;
To homely scenes of calm domestic peace,
A poet's leisure, and an old man's ease;
To wear the remnant of uncertain life
In the fond bosom of a faithful wife;
In safe repose my last few hours to spend,
Nor fearful nor impatient of their end.
Thus a safe port the wave-worn vessels gain,
Nor tempt again the dangers of the main;
Thus the proud steed, when youthful glory fades,
20   And creeping age his stiffening limbs invades,
Lies stretch'd at ease on the luxuriant plain,
And dreams his morning triumphs o'er again:
The hardy veteran from the camp retires,
His joints unstrung, and feeds his household fires,
Satiate with fame enjoys well-earn'd repose,
And sees his stormy day serenely close.
    Not such my lot! Severer fates decree
My shatter'd bark must plough an unknown sea.
Forc'd from my native seats and sacred home,
30   Friendless, alone, thro' Scythian wilds to roam;
With trembling knees o'er unknown hills I go,
Stiff with blue ice and heap'd with drifted snow:
Pale suns there strike their feeble rays in vain,
Which faintly glance against the marble plain;
Red Ister there, which madly lash'd the shore,
His idle urn seal'd up, forgets to roar;
Stern winter in eternal triumph reigns,
Shuts up the bounteous year and starves the plains.

---

10 *lares*: household gods   **35** *Ister*: lower portion of the Danube river

My failing eyes the weary waste explore,
40 The savage mountains and the dreary shore,
And vainly look for scenes of old delight;
No lov'd familiar objects meet my sight;
No long remember'd streams, nor conscious bowers,
Wake the gay memory of youthful hours.
I fondly hop'd, content with learned ease,
To walk amidst contemporary trees;
In every scene some fav'rite spot to trace,
And meet in all some kind domestic face;
To stretch my limbs upon my native soil,
50 With long vacation from unquiet toil;
Resign my breath where first that breath I drew,
And sink into the spot from whence I grew.
But if my feeble age is doom'd to try
Unusual seasons and a foreign sky,
To some more genial clime let me repair,
And taste the healing balm of milder air;
Near to the glowing sun's directer ray,
And pitch my tent beneath the eye of day.
Could not the winter in my veins suffice,
60 Without the added rage of Scythian skies?
The snow of time my vital heat exhaust,
And hoary age, without Sarmatian frost?
    Yet storm and tempest are of ills the least
Which this inhospitable land infest:
Society than solitude is worse,
And man to man is still the greatest curse.
A savage race my fearful steps surround,
Practis'd in blood and disciplin'd to wound;
Unknown alike to pity as to fear,
70 Hard as their soil, and as their skies severe.
Skill'd in each mystery of direst art,
They arm with double death the poison'd dart:
Uncomb'd and horrid grows their spiky hair;
Uncouth their vesture, terrible their air:

The lurking dagger at their side hung low,
Leaps in quick vengeance on the hapless foe:
No stedfast faith is here, no sure repose;
An armed truce is all this nation knows:
The rage of battle works, when battles cease;
80   And wars are brooding in the lap of peace.
Since CAESAR wills, and I a wretch must be,
Let me be safe at least in misery!
To my sad grave in calm oblivion steal,
Nor add the woes of fear to all I feel!
Ye tuneful maids! who once, in happier days,
Beneath the myrtle grove inspir'd my lays,
How shall I now your wonted aid implore;
Where seek your footsteps on this savage shore,
Whose ruder echoes ne'er were taught to bear
90   The poet's numbers or the lover's care?
     Yet here, forever here, your bard must dwell,
Who sung of sports and tender loves so well.
Here must he live: but when he yields his breath
O let him not be exil'd even in death!
Lest mix'd with Scythian shades, a Roman ghost
Wander on this inhospitable coast.
CAESAR no more shall urge a wretch's doom;
The bolt of JOVE pursues not in the tomb.
To thee, dear wife, some friend with pious care
100   All that of OVID then remains shall bear;
Then will thou weep to see me so return,
And with fond passion clasp my silent urn.
O check thy grief, that tender bosom spare,
Hurt not thy cheeks, nor soil thy flowing hair.
Press the pale marble with thy lips, and give
One precious tear, and bid my memory live:
The silent dust shall glow at thy command,
And the warm ashes feel thy pious hand.   (1773)

WILLIAM COWPER (1731–1800)

Plagued from an early age by debilitating fits of melancholy, and reduced to insanity towards the end of his life, William Cowper continued to write poetry throughout the course of his dark experiences. His works range from divine poems, to the epic-length *The Task* (1783), to a translation of Homer (1791). The contained despair haunting his best-known poem, 'The Castaway', also infuses his translation of Ovid's elegy, which appeared posthumously in John Johnson's edition of Cowper's works. Compare Catlin's earlier version of the poem, above.

TRIST. Lib V. Eleg. XII [Trist. 5.12]

You bid me write t' amuse the tedious hours,
And save from with'ring my poetic pow'rs.
Hard is the task, my friend, for verse should flow
From the free mind, not fetter'd down by woe;
Restless amidst unceasing tempests tost,
Whoe'er has cause for sorrow, I have most.
Would you bid Priam laugh, his sons all slain,
Or childless Niobe from tears refrain,
Join the gay dance, and lead the festive train?
Does grief or study most befit the mind,
To this remote, this barb'rous nook confin'd?
Could you impart to my unshaken breast
The fortitude by Socrates posses'd,
Soon would it sink beneath such woes as mine,
For what is human strength to wrath divine?
Wise as he was, and Heav'n pronounc'd him so,
My suff'rings would have laid that wisdom low.
Could I forget my country, thee and all,
And ev'n th' offence to which I owe my fall,

20   Yet fear alone would freeze the poet's vein,
      While hostile troops swarm o'er the dreary plain.
      And that the fatal rust of long disuse
      Unfits me for the service of the Muse.
      Thistles and weeds are all we can expect
      From the best soil impov'rish'd by neglect;
      Unexercis'd and to his stall confin'd,
      The fleetest racer would be left behind;
      The best built bark that cleaves the wat'ry way,
      Laid useless by, would moulder and decay –
30   No hope remains that time shall me restore,
      Mean as I was, to what I was before.
      Think how a series of desponding cares
      Benumbs the genius, and its force impairs.
      How oft, as now, on this devoted sheet,
      My verse constrain'd to move with measur'd feet,
      Reluctant and laborious limps along,
      And proves itself a wretched exile's song.
      What is it tunes the most melodious lays?
      'Tis emulation and the thirst of praise,
40   A noble thirst, and not unknown to me,
      While smoothly wafted on a calmer sea.
      But can a wretch like Ovid pant for fame?
      No, rather let the world forget my name.
      Is it because that world approv'd my strain,
      You prompt me to the same pursuit again?
      No, let the Nine th' ungrateful truth excuse,
      I charge my hopeless ruin on the Muse,
      And, like Perillus, meet my just desert,
      The victim of my own pernicious art.
50   Fool that I was to be so warn'd in vain,
      And shipwreck'd once, to tempt the deep again.

_____

49 See p. 163, n. 47.

Ill fares the bard in this unletter'd land,
None to consult, and none to understand.
The purest verse has no admirers here,
Their own rude language only suits their ear.
Rude as it is, at length familiar grown,
I learn it, and almost unlearn my own. –
Yet to say truth, ev'n here the Muse disdains
Confinement, and attempts her former strains,
60   But finds the strong desire is not the pow'r,
And what her taste condemns, the flames devour.
A part, perhaps, like this, escapes the doom,
And tho' unworthy, finds a friend at Rome;
But oh the cruel art, that could undo
Its vot'ry thus, would that could perish too!   (1815)

MARY WOLLSTONECRAFT
SHELLEY (1797–1851)

In *Frankenstein* (1818), Mary Shelley proposed to 'modernize' the Prometheus myth. The following excerpt is drawn from one of her lesser efforts to recast a mythological source. Journal references of April and May 1820 confirm that, before dramatizing the Midas story, she consulted the *Metamorphoses* directly. She departs freely from Ovid, inverting his narrative sequence to accommodate frequent references to the ass's ears that Midas sports. She also introduces as supporting characters various servants not mentioned in the original (among them, the Zopyrion who speaks in the following passage). Both this play and the *Proserpine* that served initially as a setting for her husband's Arethusa poem went unpublished until 1922.

Midas: A Drama in two acts 2.83–120 [Met. 11.106–30] *Midas's epiphany*

   Mid. (*lifting up the ewer*) This is to be a king! to touch pure
      gold!
Would that by touching thee, Zopyrion,
I could transmute thee to a golden man;
A crowd of golden slaves to wait on me!
                        (*Pours the water on his hands*)
But how is this? the water that I touch
Falls down a stream of yellow, liquid gold,
And hardens as it falls. I cannot wash –
Pray Bacchus, I may Drink! And the soft towel
With which I'd wipe my hands transmutes itself
10 Into a sheet of heavy gold. – No more!
I'll sit and eat: – I have not tasted food
For many hours, I have been so wrapt
In golden dreams of all that I possess,
I had not time to eat; now hunger calls
And makes me feel, though not remote in power
From the immortal Gods, that I need food,
The only remnant of mortality!
              (*In vain attempts to eat of several dishes*)
Alas! my fate! 'tis gold! this peach is gold!
This bread, these grapes, & all I touch! this meat
20 Which by its scent quickened my appetite
Has lost its scent, its taste, – 'tis useless gold.
   Zopyr. (*aside*) He'd better now have followed my advice
He starves by gold yet keeps his asse's ears.
   Mid. Asphalion, put that apple to my mouth;
If my hands touch it not perhaps I eat.
Alas! I cannot bite! as it approached
I felt its fragrance, thought it would be mine,
But by the touch of my life-killing lips
'Tis changed from a sweet fruit to tasteless gold.

30   Bacchus will not refresh me by his gifts,
     The liquid wine congeals and flies my taste.
     Go, miserable slaves! Oh, wretched king!
     Away with food! Its sight now makes me sick.
     Bring in my couch! I will sleep off my care,
     And when I wake I'll coin some remedy.
     I dare not bathe this sultry day, for fear
     I be enclosed in gold. Begone!
     I will to rest: – Oh, miserable king!   (1820; pub. 1922)

PERCY BYSSHE SHELLEY
(1792–1822)

Traits that distinguish Percy Shelley as one of English Romanticism's most accomplished and influential poets are evident in his contribution to Mary Shelley's mythological drama, particularly the dreamy lyricism of these 'murmurs as soft as sleep'. In the play, Arethusa's narrative is transformed into a musical interlude sung by Proserpine's maid Ino. Like his wife, Shelley drastically alters Ovid's version of the story, from Arethusa's descent to the ocean to her ultimate conciliation with Alpheus. The poem appeared, detached from its context, in the posthumous 1824 edition of Shelley's works. The breaks indicated by asterisks appear in the manuscript.

Mary Shelley's Proserpine: A Drama in Two Acts
1.82–171 [Met. 5.577–641] *Arethusa's tale*

     Arethusa arose
       From her couch of snows,
   In the Acroceraunian Mountains, –
       From cloud and from crag,
       With many a jag,
   Shepherding her bright fountains.

She leapt down the rocks
With her rainbow locks,
Streaming among the streams, –
10   Her steps paved with green
The downward ravine
Which slopes to the Western gleams: –
And sliding and springing,
She went, ever singing
In murmurs as soft as sleep;
The Earth seemed to love her
And Heaven smiled above her,
As she lingered towards the deep.

★

Then Alpheus bold
20   On his glacier cold,
With his trident the mountains strook;
And opened a chasm
In the rocks; – with a spasm
All Erymanthus shook.
And the black south wind
It unsealed behind
The Urns of the silent snow,
And earthquake and thunder
Did rend in sunder
30   The bars of the springs below: –
And the beard and the hair
Of the river God were
Seen through the torrent's sweep
As he followed the light
Of fleet nymph's flight
To the brink of the Dorian deep.

★

> Oh save me! oh, guide me!
>   And bid the deep hide me,
> For he grasps me now by the hair!
40   The loud ocean heard,
>   To its blue depth stirred,
> And divided at her prayer
>   And under the water
>   The earth's white daughter
> Fled like a sunny beam,
>   Behind her descended,
>   Her billows unblended
> With the brackish Dorian stream: –
>   Like a gloomy stain
50   On the Emerald main
> Alpheus rushed behind,
>   As an eagle pursueing
>   A dove to its ruin,
> Down the streams of the cloudy wind.
>   Under the bowers
>   Where the Ocean Powers
> Sit on their pearled thrones,
>   Through the coral woods
>   Of the weltering floods,
60   Over heaps of unvalued stones;
>   Through the dim beams,
>   Which amid the streams
> Weave a network of coloured light,
>   And under the caves,
>   Where the shadowy waves
> Are as green as the forest's night: –
>   Out speeding the shark,
>   And the sword fish dark,

---

42 In Ovid, it is Diana who comes to Arethusa's aid.

Under the Ocean's foam,
70   And up through the rifts
        Of the mountain clifts,
They passed to their Dorian Home.

★

        And now from their fountains
        In Enna's Mountains,
Down one vale where the morning basks,
        Like friends once parted,
        Grown single hearted
They ply their watery tasks.
        At sunrise they leap
80   From their cradles steep
In the cave of the shelving hill
        At noon-tide they flow
        Through the woods below
And the meadows of Asphodel, —
        And at night they sleep
        In the rocking deep
Beneath the Ortygian shore; —
        Like spirits that lie
        In the azure sky,
90 When they love, but live no more.   (1824)

EMMA GARLAND (*fl.* 1842)

What little we know of Emma Garland comes from the brief statement
prefacing her complete translation of the *Heroides*. Publication was, on
the one hand, encouraged by the clergyman Francis Wrangham (to
whom the volume is dedicated) and, on the other, coerced 'by the
most severe domestic trials'. Apprehensive of her peculiar status as a
female Latinist, Garland nevertheless states her ambitions with an elegant
surety: 'though Ovid has here and there "a few lines too luscious", or

a passage which his Translator of the nineteenth century would have fain dashed through by the ready help of a handful of *asterisks;* yet, rather than offer, *knowingly,* an imperfect version to the Public, she e'en determined to hesitate at none, but rather endeavour to give the most pure and delicate English that strict fidelity to her Author would allow, to every idea and line contained in his matchless Love Letters; and yet hopes these productions of the "tuneful Ovid" may have been so far modernized by her hand, as to be agreeable to many of her own sex.' She realizes the task she sets for herself with considerable vigour.

Deianira to Hercules [Her. 9]

GRATEFUL, I would have heard Œchalia's name
Was added to thy victories' list and fame;
'T is dire to learn, that he who should have reigned,
Submits e'en by his victim to be chained!
Oh, 't was a bitter hour, when first I heard
All that report through Grecian states averred;
Foul was the scandal, and I well might sigh,
And wish the story I might dare deny!
That he whom Juno's self could never bend,
10   Though thousand labours their assistance lend,
That he whom war and hardship never harms,
Bows slavish to the yoke of Beauty's charms!
Surely Eurystheus planned this work for thee —
Juno, the thunderer's sister, smiles to see
How base, how low her rival's son can be!
But he to whom thou owest thy wondrous birth,
Views with lamenting eye thy waning worth.

---

1 *Œchalia*: kingdom of Iole's father Eurytus, conquered by Hercules
13 *Eurystheus*: architect of the twelve labours that Hercules had to endure at Juno's behest, to expiate the deaths of his own children

Venus hath triumphed high where Juno failed!
When she oppressed, thy mighty power prevailed;
20   But Venus, she who holds the captive now,
Treads on the haughty neck she taught to bow!

Look round thee, and behold each smiling land
From terrors freed by thine avenging hand;
Look out upon the blue encircling sea,
And own their peacefulness is due to thee.
Far from the glowing east to crimson west,
See every nation by thy valour blest!
He who the skies upon his shoulders bore,
Might well amid those skies prepare to soar;
30   But what avails it now these deeds to name,
If to the list thou addst thy present shame?
Thou once wast worthy of thy sire; they say,
E'en in thy cradle, serpents thou couldst slay!
Hast thou continued as thou hadst began?
Oh no, thine infant deeds disgrace the man.
He whom a thousand monsters could not move,
Nor earthly foe, nor enemies above,
Sinks softly down beneath the power of Love!

The world congratulates and envies me,
40   Because the fates united me to thee;
Not as the wife of Hercules alone,
But, as my father, Jupiter I own.
Ah, why to me such gratulations yield?
How ill the ummatched oxen plough the field!
So she who's wedded to a lofty spouse,
No honour, but humiliation knows!
If thou wert wedded, as thou shouldst have been,
It should not be to mortal bride, I ween. –
Far from his home my valiant husband dwells,
50   While to his wife his deeds the stranger tells;
While after direful monsters he must roam,
She stays in anguish at her widowed home.

For him the victims burn, and her chaste tears
Flow for the object of her anxious fears;
Not only man, but monsters too I dread,
Not in the day alone, but on my bed;
Oft I behold thee in that lonely hour,
With boars and lions eager to devour!
The gaping hell-dog, with his three mouths wide,
60   Is barking savage at my hero's side!
Thus in the night; — and through the lingering day,
I search the entrails of the beasts we slay.

   And so the day rolls on; mysterious night,
With flitting phantoms, then renews my fright;
Each wild report invites my anxious ear,
When fear must yield to hope, and hope to fear.
I am alone amid these numerous woes,
No mother's love to soothe, my bosom knows;
Thy parents are not here, and they deplore
70   That e'er such hero-son Alcmena bore.
And not one consolation left to bless —
I am deprived of e'en my son's caress —
Instead of these, Eurystheus haunts my mind,
And Juno's ire, too long to thee unkind.

   'T was not enough — all this I could have borne,
Had not my bosom by thine hand been torn!
Each foreign land not only owns thy fame,
But tells some amorous story of thy shame;
It is not of the wronged Arcadian maid,
80   Nor of Ormenus' daughter only said —
The fifty Thespian sisters won by thee —
Though now no offspring of their race we see!

77f. Deianira's succeeding catalogue of Hercules's sexual conquests will contrast
the list of martial victories at lines 97ff.

Such are thy deeds! 't is not of them I'd speak,
A later crime, a newer theme, I'd seek;
They told me lately of a Lydian queen,
'T is Lamus' mother; at her side is seen,
(Where wild Meander, in his wanderings slow,
Turns and returns, and seems averse to flow;)
They told me – but methinks they must deceive,
90   Who could such wondrous spectacle believe?
My god-like husband, decked with female pride,
In amorous dalliance lingers at her side!
That he who on his neck the heavens bore,
Contented now the light gold necklace wore!
Was not ashamed upon his arms to bind
Bracelets of gold, with many a gem confined!
Strong arms and nervous, which the lion slew,
And o'er thy shoulder oft his rough hide threw!
He who the wreath of poplar leaves should wear,
100   With barbarous ornaments now decks his hair!
Dost thou not blush with very shame to own,
Thou, like a girl, couldst wear the Lydian zone?
Say, while thou 'rt lost amid this vile disguise,
E'er meets the shade of Diomed thine eyes?
He, who to feed his horses, men would slay, –
The king thou conquer'dst in a former day.
If Egypt's monarch this could wondering see,
He well might blush to yield to such as thee!
Antœus would undeck his former foe,
110   Ashamed his conqueror's disgrace to know!
They tell me too (a smile I can't repress),
That, not contented with thy woman's dress,
Oft, 'mid the maidens of the Lydian queen,
The spinning basket in thine hands is seen!
The hand that thousand victories could win,
Does not disdain at last to learn to spin!
With clumsy diligence, and fingers strong,
Twines the thick thread with care, and labour long!

Oft must thy manly hand have broke the thread,
120 And made thee e'en thy mistress' wrath to dread;
And thy stiff fingers, all unused t' engage
In girlish work, have felt perchance her rage;
It might be so, for it is said that thou,
In supplication, at her feet would bow.

Great were thy trophies; I remember well –
But now methinks thou 'dst be ashamed to tell,
How, strangled, even by thine infant arm,
The direful serpents failed to do thee harm!
How the Arcadian boar hath ceased from ill,
130 And lies in death upon his wooded hill!
The cypress trees of Erymanthus wave
Now o'er the savage creature's monstrous grave!
How fell at last, by thee, the king of Thrace,
Who on his walls his victims' heads would place!
Or how the threefold monster, king of Spain,
Enriched thee with his flocks when he was slain!
And how the triple, snake-haired dog of hell
Into thy chains and power quickly fell!
How the Lernœan hydra, that which bled
140 Only to multiply each serpent head,
Mighty in wounds – not e'en in death surpassed,
Fell by thy conquering arm and art at last!
Or how Antœus, born of mother earth,
Sunk crouching down on her who gave him birth;
The ponderous wrestler, of her aid bereft,
Was vanquished by thine arm, though 't was the left!
Or how the troop of monster horsemen fled
O'er the Thessalian hills in mighty dread!
They who believed none could their track pursue,
150 Found Hercules was strong and speedy too!

Such feats as these, say, can thy lip now tell?
Suits not thy purple garb such stories well?
'T is said that Lydia's foreign arms thou 'st worn,
When thy known trophies from thine hands were torn!
By Lydian Omphale! (this all exceeds;
Cheer up, and tell once more thy warlike deeds!)
She was no woman, as *thou* fain wouldst be,
Or surely never had she conquered thee!
Great are thy victories, but 't was greater far
160   To vanquish him who'd never failed in war!
And to thy victor now belongs the praise,
Which thou hadst dearly earned in former days.
'T is as it should be – merit to the brave!
The mistress owns the glory of her slave!
Shameful to tell! the hide the lion wore,
The Lydian queen upon her shoulders bore!
'T was not to show her lover's valiant pride,
She clothed her in the shaggy monster's hide;
No – rather that the world might look, and say,
170   'Such are the spoils of him she would not slay!'
And now the hydra's blood-empoisoned brand
Is wielded by a woman's feeble hand,
Which erst the distaff's weight could scarce withstand!
Nor yet content with thy Lernœan spears,
In her soft hand the conquering club appears!
And in the mirror, when she looks by chance,
She sees her lover's trophies at a glance!

Thus far I've heard, fain would I not believe,
But ah, report can wound, and yet deceive!
180   'T was not enough to hear, mine eyes must see
The foreign favourite, when brought home by thee;
Not for one instant parted from thy side,
Oh say, how could I my emotions hide?
All through the city my unwilling eyes
Pursued, with jealous glance, thine envied prize;

Not in a captive's fashion walked she there,
With downcast look or with dishevelled hair;
But, all conspicuous with glittering gold,
She looked around her, with a front so bold,
190 One might have thought her in Œchalia still,
And at her father's side some place to fill!
So looked she scornful on thy subjects down,
Proud of the conquest of their master grown!
And next, perhaps, from mine Œtolia driven,
My name and place to Iole is given;
And Hymen's self be pray'd to tie the bands,
Which will unite your base, adulterous hands.
I shudder at the words – such thoughts as these
The very blood within my heart would freeze;
200 And the right hand, that ne'er refused before,
Turns cold and languid, and would write no more!

That thou *hast* loved me, is not much to boast,
Me among others, of a numerous host!
Thine was an honourable love for me,
No guilt, no shame it brought, though war to thee!
Achelous, weeping, sought along the shore
For broken horns which he had worn before –
Rushed to conceal within his turbid tide
The scanty relics of his former pride!
210 The Centaur Nessus, too, who hidden lay
In dark Evenus, thy strong arm did slay;
The savage monster's blood entinged the wave,
Which served him for an ambush and a grave!
Why write I thus? report – but ah, too late,
Has whispered something of my bitter fate;
Speaks of infection from the Centaur's dress,
Which I, unguarded, sent in my distress.

216f. For the origin of the poisoned robe with which Deianira unwittingly kills her husband, cf. *Met.* 9.101–33.

Ah, wretched me, was it for this I raved?
Shall jealous love destroy, when 't would have saved?
220   Say, when the hero breathes his parting sigh,
Will Deianira hesitate to die?
How could the wife survive, when burns the while,
On Œtna's hill, her husband's funeral pile?
When o'er his corpse the curling smoke shall rise,
How shall she live, who sent him to the skies?
Ah, if in life thou wert not wholly mine,
In death, at least, I'll prove that I was thine!
And Meleager shall his sister own,
In love and courage such as he had shown!
230   When her lost hero breathes his parting sigh,
Deianira will not hesitate to die!

Alas, doomed daughter of a fated race,
Why dost thou hope from fortune aught of grace?
Another fills thy father's lofty throne –
Oppressed, he lingers out his days alone;
Worn out with age, neglected, in despair,
No filial love attempts to soothe his care;
One son, a wanderer in some unknown land;
The other, perished by that fated brand!
240   And his own mother, when the deed she'd done,
Died to avange her lost, lamented son!
Say, when the hero breathes his latest sigh,
Can Deianira hesitate to die?
One thing I would entreat, by all that's dear,
Let me not guilty of thy death appear!
The amorous Centaur, when he dying bled, –
'This flowing gore hath passion's power,' he said

---

228 *Meleager*. For her brother Meleager's tragic story, cf. *Met.* 8.260–544.

I luckless sent the blood empoisoned vest –
It spreads infection to my husband's breast!
250   And when her hero breathes his latest sigh,
Can Deianira hesitate to die?

Farewell, my venerable sire, to thee,
And sister sweet, whom I no more shall see!
Farewell, Œtolia dear, where I was born!
Farewell, my brother, from Œtolia torn!
Last, to my dying eyes, sweet day, farewell!
Grant it, ye gods! – my child, my spouse, farewell!   (1842)

ARTHUR HUGH CLOUGH
(1819–1861)

Clough, who died before his fuller promise as poet and scholar was
realized, forged close friendships with two of the leading intellectuals
of his day, on both sides of the Atlantic: Arnold in England, Emerson
in America. This brief passage from the *Ars amatoria*, left among Clough's
manuscript translations from the classics, marks his only foray into Ovid.
Though he manages to convey the richness of this peculiar set piece in
quantitative metre, the performance strains beneath the weight of its
own lushness. It appeared only in 1974, in the second Oxford edition
of his works.

Ars Amatoria iii. 687–90, 695–8 [Ars 3.687–90, 695–98]

Near to the empurpled and flowery mountain Hymettus,
    Where grass grows freshest, riseth a holy river.
Arbutus and other low shrubs o'ershadow the greensward,
    Dark myrtle, cytisus, rosemary scatter odours.

Here toil-worn Cephalus, deserting dogs and attendants,
  Found often grateful rest from his early labour.
'Aura,' he would cry then, 'delicious Aura, I pray thee,
  'Come cool this fervour, come to my weary bosom!'

(unknown; pub. 1974)

MATTHEW ARNOLD (1822–1888)

One of the Victorian era's foremost intellectuals and poets, Arnold in his critical essays both articulated and significantly shaped the literary tastes of his day. While Ovid would not find a comfortable place amid the cultural aesthetic of 'high seriousness' that Arnold pursued, the song of Callichles from *Empedocles on Etna* displays the kind of inspiration that the Latin author still could offer. Arnold beautifully embellishes Ovid's compressed, stark account of the contest between Marsyas and Apollo and its grim outcome, to emphasize the god's cruelty and the consequent heartbreak of the satyr's companion Olympus. Arnold liked the passage sufficiently to have it published separately in 1855.

Empedocles on Etna, Act II.121–90 [Met. 6.382–400] *Marsyas*

As the sky-brightening south-wind clears the day,
And makes the massed clouds roll,
The music of the lyre blows away
The clouds which wrap the soul.
Oh! that Fate had let me see
That triumph of the sweet persuasive lyre,
That famous, final victory,
When jealous Pan with Marsyas did conspire;

When, from far Parnassus' side,
Young Apollo, all the pride
Of the Phrygian flutes to tame,
To the Phrygian highlands came;
Where the long green reed-beds sway
In the rippled waters grey
Of that solitary lake
Where Mæander's springs are born;
Whence the ridged pine-wooded roots
Of Messogis westward break,
Mounting westward, high and higher.
There was held the famous strife;
There the Phrygian brought his flutes,
And Apollo brought his lyre;
And, when now the westering sun
Touched the hills, the strife was done,
And the attentive Muses said:
'Marsyas, thou art vanquished!'
Then Apollo's minister
Hanged upon a branching fir
Marsyas, that unhappy Faun,
And began to whet his knife.
But the Mænads, who were there,
Left their friend, and with robes flowing
In the wind, and loose dark hair
O'er their polished bosoms blowing,
Each her ribboned tambourine
Flinging on the mountain-sod,
With a lovely frightened mien
Came about the youthful God.
But he turned his beauteous face
Haughtily another way,
From the grassy sun-warmed place
Where in proud repose he lay,
With one arm over his head,
Watching how the whetting sped.

But aloof on the lake-strand,
Did the young Olympus stand,
Weeping at his master's end;
For the Faun had been his friend.
For he taught him how to sing,
50   And he taught him flute-playing.
Many a morning had they gone
To the glimmering mountain-lakes,
And had torn up by the roots
The tall crested water-reeds
With long plumes and soft brown seeds,
And had carved them into flutes,
Sitting on a tabled stone
Where the shoreward ripple breaks.
And he taught him how to please
60   The red-snooded Phrygian girls,
Whom the summer evening sees
Flashing in the dance's whirls
Underneath the starlit trees
In the mountain-villages.
Therefore now Olympus stands,
At his master's piteous cries
Pressing fast with both his hands
His white garment to his eyes,
Not to see Apollo's scorn;
70   Ah, poor Faun, poor Faun! ah, poor Faun!   (1852)

F. H. HUMMEL   (*fl.* 1876)

Lays from Latin Lyres, the 1876 volume of translations by F. H. Hummel
and A. A. Brodribb, stands out as something of a Victorian anomaly: a
collection of verse imitations, parodies and epitomes of the classical
Roman poets that carries its learning with a delightful levity. Not
since the early seventeenth century had translators taken such obvious

enjoyment in their task as Hummel and Brodribb. The good–humoured irreverence they bring to all the major Latin poets represented in this anthology works best with Ovid, who recovers his sheer entertainment value in their versions.

The Poet's Master [Am. 1.1]

HIGH deeds of heroes to rehearse
    I thought, in grave heroic measure,
When Cupid, laughing, clipped my verse,
    And bade me sing of love and pleasure.

Usurping boy! what right has he
    To deal with poets as he chooses?
I'll start afresh, and let him see
    I'm not his servant, but the Muse's.

Alas! unnerved by shafts of love,
10   To frame heroics I am ill able;
In lighter measures I must move,
    I cannot rhyme in decasyllable.

(1876)

A. A. BRODRIBB (*fl.* 1876)

The Wooing O' It [Am. 1.3]

The girl who bound me as her slave,
Ne'er let her scorn the heart I gave;
Or let me only love her still;
Venus, my modest prayer fulfil.
Take me, I will guard thee surely,
Take me, I will love thee purely.

Though no great ancestry I claim,
(A knight the author of my name,)
Though scarce ten oxen plough my land,
10   And parents give with frugal hand,
Let Phœbus and the Muses nine
Suffice, and love that makes me thine,
And honour, and a life unblamed,
Truth, and a conscience never shamed.
I am not fickle; thou shalt be
(If vows are aught) the world to me,
While the kind Fates prolong thy thread
To love me living, mourn me dead:
And let my happy verses prove
20   Not all unworthy of my love.   (1876)

The Tablets [Am. 1.12]

CONDOLE with me; my slave has brought
    The unwelcome, melancholy message,
'She cannot come.' I hardly thought
    My scheme would prosper: I'd a presage,

An omen, of my dreary fate;
    For, when I sent the note this morning,
The servant stumbled at the gate,
    And foolishly ignored the warning.

But you, that make my woe complete,
10   My tablets, bringing her refusal,
Go hence, I fling you in the street,
    Lie there, for every knave's perusal.

---

7 *stumbled at the gate*: a bad omen

Lie there, let every passing wheel
    Your form and features bruise and batter;
Lie there, let every booted heel
    Each last surviving fragment shatter.

My malison on your parent tree,
    Apt, doubtless, for the hangman's uses;
My malison on the pirate bee
20   That culled your wax from hemlock juices.

Your waxen face, as if for shame,
    Blushed, by some poisonous dye made ruddy;
Or did your maker's evil name –
    Some murderer – make his work seem bloody?

You would have served extremely well
    For some prosaic legal process;
Or you would very fitly tell
    A greedy gambler's gains and losses:

But I was mad to trust to you
30   A letter fervid with affection,
Well-phrased my mistress' heart to woo;
    What was it but to court rejection?

Ill-omened tablets, all unmeet,
    Ill-omened in your double number,
Be lost or broken in the street,
    Or kept (who cares?) with mouldy lumber.   (1876)

17ff. Roman tablets were hinged wooden panels, coated with wax to receive the
writer's inscriptions.

HENRY WADSWORTH LONGFELLOW (1807–1882)

In his own day Henry Wadsworth Longfellow enjoyed international respect as one of America's preeminent literary figures. A professor of foreign languages at Harvard from 1836 to 1854, Longfellow augmented his voluminous poetic output with a well-received verse translation of Dante's *Divine Comedy*. Though his attempts at Ovid's *Tristia* 3.10 and 3.12 are hampered by a formal stuffiness absent from the original, Longfellow does have a better go at the elusive quantitative metre than anyone else in his century.

Ovid in Exile: At Tomis, in Bessarabia, near the mouths of the Danube [Trist. 3.12]

Now the zephyrs diminish the cold, and the year being ended,
    Winter Mæotian seems longer than ever before;

And the Ram that bore unsafely the burden of Helle,
    Now makes the hours of the day equal with those of the
        night.

Now the boys and the laughing girls the violet gather,
    Which the fields bring forth, nobody sowing the seed.

Now the meadows are blooming with flowers of various
        colors,
    And with untaught throats carol the garrulous birds.

Now the swallow, to shun the crime of her merciless mother,
10   Under the rafters builds cradles and dear little homes;

And the blade that lay hid, covered up in the furrows of Ceres,
    Now from the tepid ground raises its delicate head.

Where there is ever a vine, the bud shoots forth from the
        tendrils,
    But from the Getic shore distant afar is the vine!

Where there is ever a tree, on the tree the branches are
        swelling,
    But from the Getic land distant afar is the tree!

Now it is holiday there in Rome, and to games in due order
    Give place the windy wars of the vociferous bar.

Now they are riding the horses; with light arms now they are
        playing,
    Now with the ball, and now round rolls the swift-flying
20   hoop:

Now, when the young athlete with flowing oil is annointed,
    He in the Virgin's Fount bathes, overwearied, his limbs.

Thrives the stage; and applause, with voices at variance,
        thunders,
    And the Theatres three for the three Forums resound.

Four times happy is he, and times without number is happy,
    Who the city of Rome, uninterdicted, enjoys.

But all I see is the snow in the vernal sunshine dissolving,
    And the waters no more delved from the indurate lake.

Nor is the sea now frozen, nor as before o'er the Ister
30   Comes the Sarmatian boor driving his stridulous cart.

Hitherward, nevertheless, some keels already are steering,
    And on this Pontic shore alien vessels will be.

---

30 *stridulous*: noisy

Eagerly shall I run to the sailor, and, having saluted,
   Who he may be, I shall ask; wherefore and whence he hath
      come.

Strange indeed will it be, if he come not from regions adjacent,
   And incautious unless ploughing the neighboring sea.

Rarely a mariner over the deep from Italy passes,
   Rarely he comes to these shores, wholly of harbors devoid.

Whether he knoweth Greek, or whether in Latin he speaketh,
40   Surely on this account he the more welcome will be.

Also perchance from the mouth of the Strait and the waters
      Propontic,
   Unto the steady South-wind, some one is spreading his sails.

Whosoever he is, the news he can faithfully tell me,
   Which may become a part and an approach to the truth.

He, I pray, may be able to tell me the triumphs of Cæsar,
   Which he has heard of, and vows paid to the Latian Jove;

And that thy sorrowful head, Germania, thou, the rebellious,
   Under the feet, at last, of the Great Captain hast laid.

Whoso shall tell me these things, that not to have seen will
      afflict me,
50   Forthwith unto my house welcomed as guest shall he be.

Woe is me! Is the house of Ovid in Scythian lands now?
   And doth punishment now give me its place for a home?

---

48 reference to the German expedition undertaken by Tiberius after AD 9

> Grant, ye gods, that Cæsar make this not my house and my
>   homestead,
>   But decree it to be only the inn of my pain.   (1878)

F. A. WRIGHT (1869–1946)

A classical scholar and prolific translator, F. A. Wright brought together
an interesting collection of excerpts from across the Ovidian canon in
his 1925 anthology *A Mirror of Venus*. Although he would dismiss the
Fasti therein as little more than 'a gallant attempt to extract material for
poetry from the barren ore of the Roman calendar', Wright excavated
two of his best poems from this source. The paired hymns to Minerva
and Venus derive much of their strength from the unassuming rhetorical
and metrical simplicity that they share. Together, they effectively capture
the spirit of 'festivity' so vital to the work.

In praise of Minerva [Fas. 3.815–34]

Come now, ye lads and lasses all,
   And sing Minerva's praise.
For those who on Minerva call
   With hymns and tuneful lays
In every art will dextrous be
And trained in all housewifery.

From her, ye maidens, learn to fill
   The distaff with soft wool,
The shuttle use and loom with skill,
10   And close your weaving pull,
To cleanse your spotted robes from stain
And dye them in the vat again.

No cobbler can make a shoe
   Unless Minerva aid.
Doctors and humble ushers too
   Give to the virgin maid
Share of your fees and she will bring
New pupils for your offering.

The painter's and the sculptor's art,
20   The astronomer's belong
To her: in each she has a part
   And most of all in song.
If I have earned her help, I pray
She guide me still upon my way.   (1925)

In praise of Venus [Fas. 4.91–113]

Venus is queen: to her is given
Power over land and sea and heaven.
To her the gods their lineage owe
And we all things on earth that grow.
'Twas she who peopled wood and grove.
'Twas she who taught the world to love.

Ram against ram his horn will press,
Yet woo the sheep with soft caress;
The bull, whom all the forest fears,
10   Complacent to his cows appears;
And e'en the fish beneath the sea
Acknowledge Venus' mastery.

Venus is queen: she did remove
Men's savage ways and gave them love.
A thousand arts from her derive;
For when to please a maid men strive
They have to show a craftsman's skill
If they would mould her to their will.

A lover first, his suit refused,
20   The power of plaintive music used.
A lover first on some stern maid
The pleader's cunning art essayed.
It is with Venus songs commence,
And Venus lends us eloquence.

                                                    (1925)

ROBERT GRAVES (1895–1985)

Despite his expertise as classicist, mythographer and translator, Robert
Graves chose not to engage Ovid explicitly in his own poetry. 'Ovid
in Defeat' – published originally under the title 'Ovid's Breeches' in
the 1925 volume *Welchman's Hose* – stands rather alone in this regard,
and Graves did not care enough for the poem to see it reprinted beyond
the collected *Poems* of 1927. Whatever we make of its curious distillation
of the *Ars amatoria*'s counsels, poised against the Blakean cast of its
climactic final stanzas, the poem subtly diagnoses the sexual conflict
staked out by Ovid's plan to 'arm' both male and female camps in the
three books of his manual. In addition, the poem illustrates the continued
allure of Ovid's image as poet in exile.

Ovid in Defeat

The grammar of Love's Art
    Ovid still teaches,
Grotesque in Pontic snows
    And bearskin breeches.

'Let man be ploughshare,
    Woman his field;
Flatter, beguile, assault,
    And she must yield.'

'Snatch the morning rose
10   Fresh from the wayside,
Deflower it in haste
    Ere the dew be dried.'

Ovid instructs you how
    Neighbours' lands to plough;
'Love smacks the sweeter
    For a broken vow.'

Follows his conclusion
    Of which the gist is
The cold 'post coitum
20   Homo tristis.'

Thereat despairing,
    Other Ovids hallow
Ploughshare in rust
    And field left fallow,

Or, since in Logic books
    Proposed they find,
'Where two ride together,
    One rides behind,'

This newer vision
30   Of love's revealed,
Woman as the ploughshare,
    Man, her field.

Man as the plucked flower
    Trampled in mire,
When his unfair fair
    Has eased desire.

19f. *post coitum Homo tristis*: after sex, man is sad

One sort of error
   Being no worse than other,
O, hug this news awhile,
40   My amorous brother,

That the wheel of Fortune
   May be turned complete,
Conflict, domination,
   Due defeat.

Afterwards, when you weary
   Of false analogy,
Offending both philosophy
   And physiology,

You shall see in woman
50   Neither more nor less
Than you yourself demand
   As your soul's dress.

Thought, though not man's thought,
   Deeds, but her own,
Art, by no comparisons
   Shaken or thrown.

Plough then salutes plough
   And rose greets rose:
While Ovid in toothache goes
60   Stamping through old snows.

                                   (1927)

SIR JAMES GEORGE FRAZER
(1854–1941)

Sir James George Frazer's four-volume commentary to his translation of the *Fasti* stands worthily alongside his influential masterpiece *The Golden Bough*. Ovid's poem provided a rich field for Frazer's anthropological studies, and all scholars of the poem owe him a lasting debt. Although his prose trot is by and large unexceptional – its language antiquated by an academic formality held over from nineteenth-century practice – it does settle into a quiet grace such as we find in the following passage, commemorating the assassination of Julius Caesar on 15 March 44 BC.

Fasti 3.697–710 *The assassination of Julius Caesar*

I was about to pass by in silence the swords that stabbed the prince, when Vesta spoke thus from her chaste hearth: 'Doubt not to recall them: he was my priest, it was at me these sacrilegious hands struck with the steel. I myself carried the man away, and left naught but his wraith behind; what fell by the sword was Caesar's shade.' Transported to the sky he saw the halls of Jupiter, and in the great Forum he owns a temple dedicated to him. But all the daring sinners who, in defiance of the gods' will, profaned the pontiff's head, lie low in death, the death they merited. Witness Philippi and they whose scattered bones whiten the ground. This, this was Caesar's work, his duty, his first task by righteous arms to avenge his father.   (1929)

B. P. MOORE (1877–1955)

B. P. Moore's 1935 translation of the *Ars amatoria* confirms that the couplet remains a standard form for rendering Ovid in the twentieth century. A. D. Melville thinks enough of Moore's version to reprint it (with some adjustment of its more quaint features) in his 1990 Oxford Classics volume of Ovid's love poems. The following passage comes from early in the third book, where Ovid directs his erotic counsels to a female audience.

The Art of Love 3.27–58 [Ars 3.27–58]

Light loves shall be my teaching's sole concern,
How to be loved from me shall woman learn.
'Tis not with fire and sword that women arm;
Through these I rarely see men come to harm.
Men oft deceive, less often womankind,
They're seldom charged with perfidy, you'll find.
False Jason took to bed another bride,
And cast the mother of his babes aside.
For aught that Theseus cared, his spouse left lone
10 Had fed the sea-birds on a shore unknown.
Who asks why one way's known as 'Nineways' hears
How woods o'er Phyllis shed their leaves for tears.
Though famed as pious, Dido's guest supplied
Both sword and motive for her suicide.
This damned you all: in love you had no tact;
Art keeps love constant and 'twas art you lacked:
And still you'd lack it, but before my sight
Stood Venus' self and bade me teach you right.

11f. reference to the legend that Phyllis had paced this roadway nine times before committing suicide over her abandonment by Demophoon

'Poor sex,' she said, 'why treat them in such sort?
20   An unarmed mob to be an army's sport!
Two books to make men expert have been writ,
'Tis our turn now to profit by thy wit.
Who first reviled the bride from Therapnæ
Soon sang her praises in a happier key.
Thou'lt ne'er (I know thee) hurt the dainty fair,
Throughout your life thou'lt look for favour there.'
A myrtle leaf and berries as she spake
– For myrtle wreathed her hair – she bade me take;
I took and felt her power; serener glowed
30   The heavens and my spirit shed its load.
While she inspires me, learn the code, ye dames,
That law, propriety and right proclaims.   (1935)

A. E. WATTS

Published in 1954 and re-issued in 1981, Watts's *Metamorphoses* is
remarkable both for the Picasso line drawings accompanying his text
and for its titanic effort to cast Ovid's poem once more into heroic
couplets. Select passages of his version hold up well, as the following
self-contained narrative illustrates.

Metamorphoses 4.723–62 [Met. 4.631–62] *Perseus and Atlas*

On earth's far edge, where dips the sun to sea
With panting steeds and wearied axletree,
Atlas was monarch, who with stature vast
All make of mortal giants far surpassed.

23f. Simonides was supposedly struck blind after composing a poem vilifying
Helen, but regained his vision when he recanted.

A thousand flocks, a thousand herds were his,
On pastures with no cramping boundaries;
And trees, whose leaves of golden sheen enfold
On golden boughs the fruits of living gold.
   Of him the traveler, needing roof and rest,
Asked entertainment, as a worthy guest:
'If birth allures you, know that Jove's my sire:
If deeds impress, you shall my deeds admire.'
Atlas bethought him what the doom foretold,
That Themis on Parnassus spoke of old:
'The time will come, a son of Jove shall seize
The gold of Atlas, ravaged from his trees.'
The king had ringed his orchards, in alarm,
With walls of stone, to keep his gold from harm;
A dragon, vast of bulk, was set on guard,
And every stranger from his borders barred.
So now to Perseus: 'Get you gone,' he cried,
And added to his words brute force beside;
'Lest the great father and the glorious deed
You falsely boast of, fail you in your need.'
   Then Perseus, backing slowly, tried at first
To speak him fair, then bade him do his worst;
And found himself (as who would not?) surpassed
In strength by Atlas; and exclaimed at last:
'Well, since you think my rank and worth to be
Of slight importance, take this gift of me.'
And on his left, while turning right about,
He held Medusa's ghastly visage out.
Atlas, transformed in every part, became
A mountain mass, that matched his mighty frame.
That peak was once his head; those ridges bare
His arms and hands; those woods, his beard and hair;

31f. After decapitating the gorgon Medusa, Perseus kept the head – which had not lost its petrifying capabilities – as a potent weapon.

That flint, his bones: by heaven's decrees he grew
To cosmic scale, with augmentation new
In length and breadth and height, and on his crest
40   The sky, with all its stars, was made to rest.   (1954)

ROLFE HUMPHRIES (1894–1969)

Certainly for American audiences, Rolfe Humphries's translations of
Ovid, Virgil and Juvenal rank among the best-known modern versions.
The virtues of his functional and unobtrusive blank verse – instanced
here in one of the poem's most gripping descriptive passages, Aeacus's
account of the plague that has depopulated his city – stand out, over-
shadowing the pentameter couplets of Watts's translation, published
only the year before. Even more impressive are his approximations of
quantitative metre in his line-for-line translations of the elegies. With
Humphries's work, Ovid's twentieth-century renaissance in English
reached a new level of technical sophistication.

Metamorphoses 7.568–627 [Met. 7.501–613]
The plague at Aegina

A dreadful plague came on our people. Juno
Hated our land, named for a rival of hers,
But this we did not know; we thought the cause
Was mortal, and we fought with every resource
Of medicine against it, but the evil
Had too much strength for us. In the beginning
Was darkness, and a murk that kept the summer
Shut in the sullen clouds, four months of summer,
Four months of hot south wind, and deadly airs.
10   Fountains and lakes went dry, serpents came crawling
Over deserted fields, thousands on thousands,
Tainting our streams with poison. The animals

Went first, the dogs and birds, the sheep and cattle,
The beasts of the wild woods. The unlucky farmer
Stood in dumb wonder as the strong bulls stumbled,
Fell, in the furrow, and the wool fell off
The feebly bleating sheep, with wasted bodies.
The race-horse, whose proud spirit used to bring him
Home winner over the dust of the track, trains off,
20   Trails off, to nothing, droops and sags in his stall.
The boar forgets his raging, and the deer
No longer trusts his swiftness, and the bear
Lets the weak herds alone. A life in death
Seizes them all. In woods and fields and highways
Lie bodies rotting, and the air is all
One smell of death. Even the very buzzards,
Jackals, gray wolves, refused to touch this carrion.
Contagion thickens, and the plague, grown stronger,
Fastens on men, on the walls of the great city.
30   Men's vitals seem to burn: the proof is given
By a red flush and difficult breath; the tongue
Thickens, and lips are cracked and dry; the sick
Can not lie still in bed, they cannot bear
The weight of covers over them; they try
To get some coolness from the ground, and lie there,
And get no coolness from the ground, which burns,
Itself, from the heat of their fever. Even our doctors
Fare as the others do, or worse; the nearer
One comes to the sick, the greater his devotion
40   In looking after others, the more quickly
He comes to the share of death. As hope of safety
Departs, men see no end, or one end only
To suffering; abandoned, they care for nothing,
There is nothing to care for. So, with no compunction,
They lie in the spring, the streams, any basin of water,
In rabid thirst, cured only by death, not drinking.
And many, too feeble to rise, die in the water
And others drink that water. In delirium

Many poor souls leap from their beds, and stagger
50   Too weak to stand, and others, too weak for leaping,
Roll out on the ground. They flee their household gods,
Since no man's home is sacred. Each man's home
Seems to him Death's abode. Since no man knows
The cause, he blames his little habitation.
You could see them walking along the roads, half lifeless,
As long as they could totter; you could see them
Sobbing, and lying on the ground, and rolling
Their dull eyes upward with a last weak effort;
You could see them holding out their arms to heaven,
60   Breathing their last wherever death had seized them.   (1955)

The Art of Love 3.577–610 [Ars 3.577–610]

Might as well open the gates, admit the foe, in our treason,
    In our faithlessness keep faith, in our renegade way.
Gifts too easily made encourage no permanent passion –
    Mix in a little rebuff, once in a while, with your fun.
Let him lie on the stone, complain that the door is too cruel,
    Let him be meek as a mouse, then let him threaten and rave.
Sweetness we cannot stand: refresh us with juice that is bitter.
    Often a boat goes down sunk by a favoring wind.
That is what keeps some wives from being loved by their
        husbands:
10   It's all too easy for him, coming whenever he will.
Put a door in his way, and have a doorkeeper tell him
    'No admittance: keep out!' – then he will burn with desire.
Put your blunt swords down, and take up deadlier weapons,
    Turn them on me (I suppose that's what I'll get for my
        pains).
When he falls into the snare, your lover, just recently captured,
    Ought to be made to feel he is the only one there.
Later on, let him know you go to bed with a rival:
    Fail in this, you will find ardor beginning to wane.

Your true thoroughbred, when the starting gate is thrown
    open,
    Runs his best race in a field where he must come from
20   behind.
Fires that are burning low are fanned into flame by an outrage.
    Look at me! I ought to know; I can love only when
        wronged.
Still, let the cause of the grief be not unduly apparent,
    Let him worry, suspect more than he actually knows.
It will arouse him to hear of a slave (whom you may have
        invented)
    Glumly on guard, or the dour stare of a husband, that pest.
Pleasure too safely enjoyed is that much less of a pleasure:
    Though you are perfectly free, freer than Thais, act scared.
When you might let him in by the door, let him in by a
        window,
30   Let your features assume every expression of fright,
Have your maid rush in (she will have to be clever about it)
    Crying, 'My God, we're sunk!'; hide the poor frightened
        young man.
Yet, in spite of the fear, you must give him some genuine
        pleasure;
    Don't let him get the idea nights in your house aren't worth
        while.

                                                        (1957)

The Remedies for Love, 609–54 [Rem. 609–54]

Once a young patient of mine, obeying my Muse's
    prescription,
    Found himself almost cured, almost recovered and well,
Then he had a relapse, met up with some lovers, all eager,
    Love resuming, once more, arms that were hidden away.

---

28 *Thais*: a famous prostitute

If you don't want to love, don't expose yourself to contagion;
    Even the beasts of the field often can come to this harm.
Looking at those who are sick, you also may suffer infection;
    Just from a casual glimpse, frequently, damage is done.
Sometimes to fields that are dry, to clods that are parching and
        arid
10   Water comes creeping in, sly, from the neighboring stream.
So love creeps in, sly, if you stay at the side of the loved one.
    We are ingenious folk, cunning to fool ourselves so.
I knew another man who was perfectly cured, but he lingered
    In the old neighborhood, meeting the lady again.
That was too much for him: ill-healed, the scarified tissue
    Rankled, a festering wound, one more defeat for my art.
If the house next door is on fire, your own is in danger;
    You can insure yourself best rapidly running away.
Also, don't go for a walk on the streets she is apt to be
        strolling,
    Keep from the set and the round where she is apt to be
20   found.
How does it make any sense to heat yourself up by
        remembrance?
    What do you have to do? – Live in a different world.
It is not easy to fast when you sit at an opulent table;
    It is not easy to thirst, watching the cool of a spring.
Try to hold back a bull when he has a chance at the heifer,
    Try to hold back a stud hearing the nickering mare!
Nor does it always suffice to reach the shore that you long for,
    Simply to be on your way, shutting her out of your mind.
No! You must banish the rest, her mother, her nurse, and her
        sister,
30   Every companion of hers, every close friend that she knew.
Don't let her slave come around, or her maid, with some
        fanciful story,
    Spilling her crocodile tears, saying she misses you so.
Much as you may want to know, don't ever ask what she's
        doing.
    Patience and fortitude! Keep your tongue in your head.

Furthermore, when you state the reasons you had for
    complaining,
  Make it perfectly clear this is the absolute end.   .
Cease to complain: you will gain a better vengeance by silence;
  If you indulge in regrets, she will remain in your mind.
Silence is better, too, than saying, 'Of course I don't love her!'
40   Saying I *don't* too much really implies that I *do*.
Let the fire die out, gradually, little by little,
  Take it easy, don't rush; better be safe, and be slow.
Does not a flash-flood race with wilder rage than a river?
  One is a burst of spate, one a continual flow.
Let love falter and fade, into thin air disappearing;
  Dying by slow degrees, let love falter and fade.   (1957)

HORACE GREGORY (1898–1982)

The third English translation of the *Metamorphoses* to appear in the
1950s was that of the scholar and poet Horace Gregory, who would
follow up in 1964 with a selection from Ovid's love poetry. Though
more congested than Humphries', Gregory's blank verse rendition soon
became a classroom text of choice, and was for a time after its publication
more widely recognized than his predecessor's. The following passage
offers the Cumaean Sibyl's reply to Aeneas, who upon their exit from
the underworld asks if she is a goddess.

Metamorphoses 14.171–205 [Met. 14.101–53]
The sibyl

    The sibyl glanced at him, then drew her breath:
'No, I'm no goddess, nor should sacred fires
Be lit for you to praise mortality.
There's some mistake, for what you do not know
Is that an immortality came near me –

Or if my innocent chastity had yielded
In early moments of Apollo's favour.
And while his hopes ran high, he tempted me;
He said, "My dear, my little friend of Cumae,
10   I'll give you anything your heart desires,
Or anything or all." I pointed at
A swirling hill of sand (O, I was stupid!).
"Give me as many years as grains of dust
Are there," but I forgot the best of it:
That I should be as young as I was then.
He promised me the years — and if I'd sleep
With him, I'd be forever then as now,
A girlish goddess resting in his arms.
But I said no, and took the years unmarried;
20   Summer is gone, and trembling old age follows,
And years to follow these, and more, and more,
Seven centuries gone by, nor sands nor dust
Is counted end of years; yet I must see
Three hundred seasons of the harvest moon,
Three hundred autumns of the purple vine.
So as my years increase, I shall grow less,
Withering beyond old age to small, then smaller,
Limbs, branches in the wind, then twigs, then feathers,
So dry, so small, so next to nothingness
30   It shall seem strange that I was someone loved,
Loved at first sight and cherished by a god.
Even Phoebus shall glance past me, seeing nothing,
And then say that he never looked at me.
Myself, almost invisible or vanished,
Shall be a voice, the last poor gift of fate.'

(1958)

GUY LEE (1918–   )

Guy Lee, who has also translated Catullus and Tibullus, presents a fresh rethinking of the *Amores* in his 1968 version, one that attends respectfully to the subtlety of Ovidian nuance. His streamlined translation of the elegy mourning Ovid's friend and fellow poet Tibullus, who died in 19 BC, expertly captures the original's barely restrained emotion. Lee's trim lines at once convey a slow recalcitrance and an impatient drive to reach their inevitable, sombre conclusion. It is a sterling performance that does full justice to Ovid's (often underrated) tragic sensibility.

Amores 3.9 *The Tibullus elegy*

If Thetis and Aurora
Shed tears for their dead sons,
If goddesses feel grief,
Loosen your hair and weep,
Gentle Elegia,
Sorrow's true namesake.
For the spent body of Tibullus
Your poet laureate
Is burning on the tall pyre,
10   And Cupid's bow is broken,
His quiver reversed,
His torch burnt out.
See how sadly he walks
With wings drooping,
Beating his breast.
And the tears fall
On his wild hair
And he sobs aloud,
As when he left Iulus' palace
20   Long ago

To follow his brother to the grave.
Venus too grieves for Tibullus
As she grieved for Adonis
When the wild boar ripped his groin.
'Dedicated poet',
'In God's keeping',
'Divinely inspired' – so run the phrases,
But Death mocks dedication
With the laying on
30   Of invisible hands.
What help were Phoebus and the Muse
To their son Orpheus?
What help the song that tamed wild beasts?
And did not Phoebus in the forest
Sing *Linos ailinos*
To the broken strings of his lyre?
Even Maeonian Homer,
Spring of the water of life
On the lips of poets,
40   Drowned at last
In black Avernus.
Only his verse evades the pyre,
A rumour of heroic war,
A deceiving web unravelled at night.
His megalith.
So Nemesis and Delia,
Last longing and first love,
Shall be live names,
Though Isis failed them

---

21 *his brother:* Aeneas   **32** *Orpheus:* dismembered by the Maenads
35 Linos ailinos: 'woe for Linus', Apollo's lament for Orpheus's brother Linus
41 *Avernus:* lake near Cumae, regarded as the entrance to Hades
46 *Nemesis and Delia:* mistresses celebrated in Tibullus's poetry
49 *Isis:* regarded as a goddess of healing

50   In a clacking of rattles,
        An emptiness of lonely nights.
        When evil overtakes the good,
        To disbelieve in God
        Can be forgiven.
        The decent life is death,
        The decent worship – death,
        Dragging you from high altar to hollow tomb.
        Some trust in verse –
        Let them look at Tibullus,
60   A little ash in a little urn.
        Flames inspired
        And flames destroyed him,
        Eating his heart
        In desecration
        Worse than the gutting
        Of a gilded shrine.
        And Venus on the heights of Eryx
        Looked away –
        Hiding the tears perhaps.
70   But better to die in Rome
        Than a stranger on Corfu
        Thrust in a cheap grave.
        Here at least his mother
        Could close the blank eyes
        And offer farewell gifts.
        His sister could take part
        In the ritual of grief,
        Tearing dishevelled hair.
        Nemesis and his first love
80   Could attend the pyre

---

71 *Corfu*: reference to a near-fatal illness Tibullus had suffered on the Mediterranean island, and remarked in the third poem of his first book

And add their kisses.
'I was the lucky one'
Delia whispered at parting –
'My love gave you life.'
But Nemesis replied
'Not yours the loss.
He died with his hand in mine.'
And yet, if human survival
Is more than a haunting name,
90 Tibullus lives in Elysium,
Welcomed there by Calvus
And Catullus the scholar-poet,
Young men, ivy-garlanded –
By Gallus too, if the charge
Of friendship betrayed is false,
Gallus who flung away life and love.
To these rare spirits,
If the spirit lives,
Tibullus brings grace.
100 May his bones rest in peace,
Undisturbed in the urn,
And earth be no burden to his ashes.   (1968)

91ff. Ovid provides here a list of the deceased lyric poets that he and Tibullus both honoured.

C. H. SISSON (1914–   )

The poet C. H. Sisson has translated widely from modern and classical sources, and in 1990 compiled his reflections on the practice in *Two Minds: Guesses at Other Writers*. In the title poem to his 1968 volume *Metamorphoses*, Sisson turns a series of Ovid's myths into an extended lyric meditation on sexuality. His version of Actaeon's story forms the first movement.

Metamorphoses, 1–22 [Met. 3. 143–252] *Actaeon*

Actaeon was a foolish hind
To run from what he had not seen.

He was a hunter, and had called
An end to slaughter for that day

And laid his weapons by a well.
Diana knew the man he was

But took her kirtle from her waist.
She gave her arrows to her maids

Then dropped her short and flimsy dress.
10   There was some muscle on the girl.

I think she knew the hunt was up
But set the hounds upon the man

To show her bitter virgin spite.
There was some blood but not her own.

Actaeon sped, his friends hallo'ed,
The forest rang but not with tears.

His favourite whippet bit his flank:
His friends hallo'ed him to the kill

Which they were sure he would enjoy.
20 Diana by the fountain still

Shuddered like the water on her flesh
And after that there came the night.   (1968)

PETER GREEN (1924–   )

The classicist, novelist and translator Peter Green presses beyond Lee's earlier experiments to arrive at one of the most deft and enjoyable versions of Ovid to date. His 1982 translation of the love poetry, beautifully rendered and copiously annotated, is a landmark for English readers of Ovid. He has followed up with a similar treatment of the exile poems.

Amores 1.4

'So your man's going to be present at this dinner-party?
    I hope he drops down dead before the dessert!
Does this mean no hands, just eyes (any chance guest's
        privilege) –
    Just to *look* at my darling, while *he*
Lies there with you beside him, in licensed embracement
    And paws your bosom or neck as he feels inclined?
I'm no longer surprised at those Centaurs for horsing around
        over
    Some cute little filly when they were full of wine –

---

7 *Centaurs*: For the story of the centaurs' conduct at the wedding of Pirithous and Hippodame, cf. *Met.* 12.210–535.

I may not live in the forest, or be semi-equipped as a stallion,
10   But still *I* can hardly keep my hands to myself
When you're around. Now listen, I've got some instructions
          for you,
     And don't let the first breeze blow them out of your head!
Arrive before your escort. I don't see what can be managed
     If you do – but anyway, get there first.
When he pats the couch, put on your Respectable Wife
          expression,
     And take your place beside him – but nudge my foot
As you're passing by. Watch out for my nods and eye-talk,
     Pick up my stealthy messages, send replies.
I shall speak whole silent volumes with one raised eyebrow,
20   Words will spring from my fingers, words traced in wine.
When you're thinking about the last time we made love
          together,
     Touch your rosy cheek with one elegant thumb.
If you're cross with me, and can't say so, then pinch the
          bottom
     Of your earlobe. But when I do or say
Something that gives you especial pleasure, my darling,
     Keep turning the ring on your finger to and fro.
When you yearn for your man to suffer some well-merited
          misfortune
     Place your hands on the table as though in prayer.
If he mixes wine specially for you, watch out, make him drink it
30   Himself. Ask the waiter for what *you* want
As you hand back the goblet. I'll be the first to seize it
     And drink from the place your lips have touched.
If *he* offers you tit-bits out of some dish he's tasted,
     Refuse what's been near his mouth.
Don't let him put his arms round your neck, and oh, don't lay
          that
     Darling head of yours on *his* coarse breast.
Don't let his fingers roam down your dress to touch up
     Those responsive nipples. Above all, don't you dare

Kiss him, not once. If you do, I'll proclaim myself your lover,
40   Lay hand upon you, claim those kisses as mine.
So much for what I can see. But there's plenty goes on under
        A long evening wrap. The mere thought worries me stiff.
Don't start rubbing your thigh against his, don't go playing
        Footsy under the table, keep smooth from rough.'
(I'm scared all right, and no wonder − I've been too successful
        An operator myself, it's my own
Example I find so unnerving. I've often petted to climax
        With my darling at a party, hand hidden under her cloak −)
'− Well, *you* won't do *that*. But still, to avoid the least
        suspicion,
50   Remove such natural protection when you sit down.
Keep pressing fresh drinks − but no kisses − on your husband,
        Slip neat wine in his glass if you get the chance,
If he passes out comfortably, drowned in sleep and liquor,
        We must improvise as occasion dictates.
When we all (you too) get up and leave, remember
        To stick in the middle of the crowd −
That's where you'll find me, or I you: whenever
        There's a chance to touch me, please do!'
(Yet the most I can win myself is a few hours' respite:
60   At nightfall my mistress and I must part.)
'At nightfall he'll lock you inside, and I'll be left weeping
        On that cold front doorstep − the nearest I can come
To your longed-for embraces, while *he's* enjoying, under
        licence,
        The kisses, and more, that you give me on the sly.
What you *can* do is show unwilling, behave as though you're
        frigid,
        Begrudge him endearments, make sex a dead loss.'
(Grant my prayer, Venus. Don't let either of them get pleasure
        Out of the act − *and certainly not her!*)
'But whatever the outcome tonight, when you see me
        tomorrow
70   Just swear, through thick and thin, that you told him No!' (I.iv.982)

The Art of Love 2.233−54, 273−80, 641−62, 733−44 [Ars 2.233−54, 273−80, 641−62, 733−44]

Love is a species of warfare. Slack troopers, go elsewhere!
   It takes more than cowards to guard
These standards. Night-duty in winter, long route-marches, every
   Hardship, all forms of suffering: these await
The recruit who expects a soft option. You'll often be out in
   Cloudbursts, and bivouack on the bare
Ground. We know how Apollo pastured Admetus' cattle,
   Dossed down in a herdsman's hut. What mere
Mortal's too good for conditions a god accepted? Is lasting
10   Love your ambition? Then put away all pride.
The simple, straightforward way in may be denied you,
   Doors bolted, shut in your face −
So be ready to slip down from the roof through a lightwell,
   Or sneak in by an upper-floor window. She'll be glad
To know you're risking your neck, and for her sake: that will offer
   Any mistress sure proof of your love.
Leander might, often enough, have endured Hero's absence −
   But swam over to show her how he felt.
Don't think it beneath you to cultivate madam's houseboys
20   And her more important maids:
Greet each one by name (the gesture costs you nothing),
   Clasp their coarse hands in yours − all part of the game.

*

Would you be well advised to send her love-poems?
   Poetry, I fear, is held in small esteem.
Girls praise a poem, but go for expensive presents:

---

7 *Admetus' cattle*: Apollo sufferes this indignity as a penalty imposed by Jupiter.

Any illiterate oaf can catch their eye
    Provided he's rich. Today is truly the Golden
      Age: gold buys honours, gold
Procures love. If Homer dropped by – with all the Muses,
30   But empty-handed – he'd be shown the door.

★

Take care not to criticize girls for their shortcomings: many
    Have found it advantageous to pretend
Such things don't exist. Andromeda's dusky complexion
    Left wing-footed Perseus silent. Although
Everyone else thought Andromache too large a woman,
    To Hector alone she looked
Just the right size. Habit breeds tolerance: a long-established
    Love will condone much, whereas
At first it's all-sensitive. While a new graft's growing
40   In the green cortex, a light
Breeze can detach it; but soon, time-strengthened, the tree will
    Outface all winds, hold firm,
Bear adopted fruit. Time heals each physical blemish,
    The erstwhile flaw will fade:
Young nostrils cannot abide the stink of tanning leather,
    But age inures them to it, after a while
They don't even notice the smell. Labels minimize feelings –
    She's blacker than pitch? Try 'brunette'.
If she squints, compare her to Venus. She croaks? She's
    Minerva!
50   A living skeleton? 'Svelte' is the word. Call her 'trim'
When she's minuscule, or 'plumpish' when she's a Fat Lady –
    Use proximate virtues to camouflage each fault.

★

My task is ended: give me the palm, you grateful
    Young lovers, wreathe myrtle in my scented hair!
As great as Podalirius was among the Achaeans
    For his healing arts, or Achilles for his strength,

Or Nestor in counsel, or Calchas as prophet, or Ajax
    In arms, or Automedon as charioteer,
So great am I at the love-game. Sing my praises, declare me
60   Your prophet and poet, young men: let my name
Be broadcast world-wide. As Vulcan made arms for Achilles,
    So have I done for you: then use
My gift, as he did, to conquer! And when you've brought
    down your
    Amazon, write on the trophy *Ovid was my guide.*   (1982)

Black Sea Letters 3.1.1–30

Sea first manstruck by the oars of Jason's rowers,
    land never free of wild enemies and snow,
will a time ever come when I, Ovid, will leave you,
    bidden to exile in some less hostile place?
Or must I live for ever among these barbarous natives,
    be buried in Tomis' soil? Saving your grace –
if there's grace, or peace, to be found in you, land of Pontus,
    ever chafed by the swift steeds of your border foes –
saving your grace, I'd term you the most unpleasant
10   element in my exile, you increase
the weight of my ills. You know not flower-wreathed
      springtime,
    you never see brown bare reapers, nor for you
does autumn provide vine-tendrils, grapes in clusters:
    all seasons freeze in the grip of biting cold.
You hold the sea ice-bound, so that fishes not seldom
    swim envaulted, a glacial roof overhead.
You boast no fresh springs: your water's brackish, saline –
    drink it, and wonder whether thirst's been slaked

---

1 *Jason's rowers*: Jason, the first mariner, had explored the world's outer reaches
– where Ovid now finds himself.

or sharpened! Your open fields have few trees, and those
    sterile,
20   your coast's a no-man's-land, more sea than soil.
There's no birdsong, save for odd stragglers from the distant
    forest, raucously calling, throats made harsh by brine;
across the vacant plains grim wormwood bristles –
    a bitter crop, well suited to its site.
Then there's the fear – attackers battering at the ramparts,
    arrows fresh-smeared with lethal filth,
the site's remoteness, far distant from all traffic,
    providing no safe approach by land or sea.
Small wonder, then, if I seek an end to these horrors,
30   and plead, incessantly, for a change of venue; . . .   (1994)

FLORENCE VERDUCCI (1940–)

Florence Verducci is professor in the Classics department at the University of California, Berkeley. *Ovid's Toyshop of the Heart*, her scholarly study of the *Heroides*, offers skilled and faithful translations of letters 3, 6, 10, 11, 12 and 15. Compare her version of the Sappho poem to Pope's famous rendition, above.

Heroides 15 *Sappho to Phaon*

Tell me: with your first glance at this learned and passionate
    hand,
    did your eyes instantly tell you it was mine?
Or if you had not read the name of the writer, Sappho's name,
    would you fail to know from whose hand this brief letter
      came?

And perhaps you will ask why I write in elegy's rhythms
    when my sure gifts lie in the lyric mode.
This love of mine demands tears: elegy is the music for pain.
    No lyre can fit its intervals to my grieving.

I burn, I burn like the rich field ablaze with its harvest of fire,
10   while the winds from the East, masterless, fan the flames.
Far away are the fields of Aetna: your presence there assigns
    them to fame:
    but a heat no less intense than Aetna's devours me here.
And no poems come to me, come to life, no songs I can marry
    to harmony
    with the strings of the lyre: poetry is work for a mind at rest.
And no, not the girls of Pyrrha, nor the maidens of Methymna,
    nor the whole throng of Lesbos' children: none please me,
    none.
Anactorië is nothing to me; incandescent Cydro, nothing.
    I take no pleasure in the sight of Atthis, as once I did, none
    in the sight
of the hundred others I loved – and by loving earned some
    reproach.
    What many women claimed for their own, you, in your
20   cruelty, possess alone.
You are beautiful; your years are ripe for the pleasures of love –
    Your treacherous beauty! It has ensnared my sight –
Take up a lyre and quiver: you are Apollo embodied and alive.
    Let horns appear above your brow, and Bacchus appears: he
    is you!

And Phoebus loved Daphne, and Bacchus loved the maiden of
    Cnossos.
    Yet neither of them, neither, was one who wrote lyric
    poems.

---

25 *maiden of Cnossos*: Ariadne

But the daughters of Pegasus speak to me, speak songs utterly
      sweet,
   and even now the whole world is alive with the sound of
      my name.
And not even my countryman, Alcaeus, the comrade of my
      lyre, is granted more fame
   than I, although his poetry resounds to strains far grander
30   than mine.

If stubborn nature has refused me beauty,
   then weigh my measure of genius against beauty's default.
I am small, yet I have a name to fill all the world;
    the measure of my stature is my fame.
If I am not fair, yet Perseus found Cepheus' Andromeda fair to
      look on,
   and tawny-dark, with the dusk color of her home.
And doves of white are sometimes mated with others of
      different hue,
   and the green bird loves the black turtle-dove.
If, unless her beauty appears worthy of your own, no woman
40   will belong to you, then not one will ever be yours.

But once I seemed beautiful enough, when I read my poems
      to you.
   You swore that – alone among women – I took grace
      always from the words I spoke.
I would sing, I remember . . . lovers remember it all . . .
   As I sang, you returned me my kisses, kisses stolen while I
      sang.
You would praise them, too, and in all ways I was pleasing to
      you,
   but specially then, when we practiced the art of our love.

---

27 *daughters of Pegasus*: the Muses

Then, more than ever, my wanton play delighted you,
    my constant motion, my observances of delight,
and, with the body's exhaustion, that languor beyond languor
    in us both,
50   after that final, fine confusion of our desire.

But now new victims come to you: the girls of Sicily.
    What is Lesbos to me? I wish Sicily were my home.
O dismiss the truant from your land,
    Nisaean mothers, and Nisaean maids;
do not be deceived by the lies of his beguiling tongue:
    what he now says to you, he said before, to me.
And you, too, Erycina, you who haunt the mountains of
        Sicily –
    for I am yours – protect, O goddess, your own poet!

Must my life's fortune hold to the grim course on which it
        began
60   and pursue in bitterness its inexorable direction forever?
I was not yet seven years old when the bed that held the body
        of my father,
    dead before his time, drank the water of my tears.
My misguided brother, trapped in infatuate passion for a
        whore,
    at once lost his wealth at the cost of disgrace and shame.
Reduced to poverty, he plies the blue ocean with his agile oar
    and seeks
    by shameful means the wealth that by shameful means he
        lost.
And I, who loyally offered him good and frequent warning,
    am the object of his hatred.
    This has my candor brought me, this the reward for dutiful
        speech.

---

57 *Erycina*: Venus   **66** *shameful means*: piracy

And, as if there were any lack of things to wear me out
    endlessly,
70   my small daughter fills my cup of sorrows to the brim.
And now you come, too, the last of my causes for complaint.
    My ship is driven by an ill wind, and in the wrong direction.

Look! My hair falls, unkempt, about my shoulders:
    my fingers do not suffer the weight of one translucent stone.
The dress I wear is shabby, I wear no gold in my hair,
    my curls accept no tribute from scented Araby.
For whom should my misery adorn itself? Whom should I try
    to please?
    He, the one agent of my elegance, has gone from me.
My heart is fragile, and easily pierced by weapons that are light,
80   and there is always a reason why I should always be in love –
either because the fates bound me by this condition at my birth
    and spun my life without a single sturdy thread
or because what you do love turns into who you *are* and
    becomes your *life* and Thalia,
    who commands my art, has made my nature subtle, and
    matched me to my poems.
What wonder then, if the downy cheek of adolescence and
    that time of life
    in which boys storm the captive heart of manhood have
    captured me?

I used to fear you, Aurora, afraid you would steal him to fill
    Cephalus' place –
    and you would, but that your first conquest still occupies
    your soul.
If Diana, who looks on all things, should look upon him,
90   it would be Phaon whose eternal slumber she would devise.

---

83 *Thalia*: muse of comic verse

Venus would have carried him to heaven in her ivory car, but
        that she does
    look on him, and sees that he would win the love of Mars,
        who is hers.
O you, not yet a man, no longer a boy – the perfect years,
    your time's chief ornament and the glory of your age,
come to me, my lovely, sail back into the havens of my
        embrace.
    I beg you, not begging for your love, but that you permit
        my loving you.
Even as I write, tears spring to my eyes, and fall;
    See: this part of my letter is everywhere blurred.

If you were so determined to leave me, you might have left
        more kindly,
    and you might at least have said 'My lady of Lesbos,
100   farewell.'
You took with you no tears, none of my kisses;
    to the last I had no thought of the pain I was to endure.
You have left me nothing, nothing but your cruelty,
    and you have no keepsake, no token of my love reminding
        you of me.
I asked nothing of you, nor would I have asked for anything
    except your consent simply to remember me.

I swear by my love for you – may my love stay close forever –
    and by the nine goddesses whose will is my own,
I swear that when someone said to me 'Your happiness is
        escaping'
110   for a long time I was unable either to cry or to speak.
My eyes had no tears, my tongue no words,
    a clear chill gripped my heart.
When my grief had discovered itself, I was lost to shame:
    I beat my breast, tore my hair, and I wailed aloud, violently,
much like a loving mother whose son has been taken from her
    when she carries his vacant form to the tall pyre.

My brother, Charaxus, takes pleasure in my grief and, swollen
    with joy of it, walks back and forth before me, and then,
in order to degrade its cause, says
120   'Why should she cry? Her daughter is still alive.'
There is no agreement between modesty and love. The entire
    town was watching;
    I tore open my dress, and I tore my naked breasts.

I can only think of you, Phaon. My dreams bring you back to
    me –
    dreams more intense and dazzling than radiant day.
I find you in those dreams, although you are worlds away.
    But sleep offers pleasures too brief to satisfy.
Often it seems that your arms are holding the weight of my
    neck,
    often I seem to be holding your head in my arms;
the kisses are familiar, those kisses, tongue to tongue, I
    recognize them,
130   the kisses you used to take and give back to me.
Sometimes I caress you, and say words that seem utterly real,
    and my lips are awake, responsive to all that I feel.
I hesitate to say what happens next, but it all happens,
    there's no choice, just joy, and I'm inundated with it.

But when Titan reveals himself, his presence exposing all
    things,
    I can only grieve that my dreams have left me so soon.
I seek out the caves and the woods, as though they were any
    use –
    but woods and caves shared in the secret of my delights.
I rush there wildly, maddened, like one whom frantic Bellona
    has touched,
140   my hair loosened, falling about my shoulders.
I look at the caves, at the coarse stone of their arches,
    that had once seemed like Lydian marble to me;
I come upon the forest that offered us many times

the bed we lay upon, and whose abundant boughs covered
   us in darkness.
But I do not find the master, the forest's lord, and mine. The
      place
   is only impoverished earth; his presence was the grace that
      endowed it.

I recognized the grass, pressed down, of the familiar hollow
   our bodies made in the blades on the green remembered
      bank.
I lay down and touched the place, the part in which you lay.
   The earth that once delighted me was thirsty and drank in
150   my tears.
Even the branches have cast off their leaves; they seem to
      mourn;
   the birds are quiet; none make their dear lament.
Only the nightingale, only Philomel, whose terrible grief took
      vengeance
   most terrible against her husband, laments for Itys her son.
The nightingale sings of Itys, her abandoned love is Sappho's
      song:
   Only that; all else is as silent as the dead of night.

There is a shining spring there, its water clearer than any glass.
   There are many who think a spirit lives within.
Above the spring a water-lotos opens wide its branches –
   a single tree: a whole grove. The delicate mosses make the
160   earth there green.
Tired, and in tears, I lay down here at last to take my rest
   when before my eyes, a Naiad appeared, and stopped.
Standing before me she spoke: 'You must seek out Ambracia's
      land,
   for you burn in the fire of a love that is not returned.

153f. cf. *Met.* 6.424–674.

From his temple above, Apollo looks down on the open sea
   — Actium, the people call it, and Leucadian.
From here Deucalion, aflame with love for Pyrrha,
   hurled himself down and struck the water unharmed.
Instantly that love for Pyrrha escaped his stubborn heart:
170   Deucalion was released from the fire of love.
It is the law of that place. Go now, find the cliff
   of high Leucas, and do not be afraid to leap.'

She had spoken, and was gone. I rose in terror
   and could not contain my tears.
I shall go, nymph, I shall find the cliff you spoke of.
   Let my fear leave me, banished by maddened love.
Whatever happens will be better than this is now. Breeze,
   come quickly. My body is not heavy at all.
You too, soft Love, place your wings beneath me as I fall
180   so that I do not die, a reproach to Leucady's wave.
Then my lyre, our common gift, I'll dedicate to Apollo
   and below it shall be one verse, then another:
SAPPHO THE POET, APOLLO, HAS GRATEFULLY GIVEN
   HER LYRE TO YOU:
   IT SUITS ME WELL: FOR YOU IT IS FITTING TOO.

But why do you send me grieving to the shores of Actium
   when you yourself might turn back your escaping steps?
You can heal me more than Leucady's wave.
   By your beauty, and by your kindness, you will be Apollo to
   me.
Or can you, fiercer than any cliff or wave, if I die,
190   bear to be known as the one who caused my death?
How much better that my breast be pressed to your breast
   than to be hurled from those cliffs headlong
   — the breast, Phaon, which you used to praise, and which
   so often seemed to you to have genius within it.

I wish I were eloquent now! Sorrow checks my art
   and all my genius is halted by my grief.
My old power for poetry will not come at my call;
   my plectrum is sorrowing and silent, sorrow has hushed my
      lyre.
Daughters of the island of Lesbos, children married and soon to
   be wed,
200   daughters of Lesbos, your names sung to the Aeolian lyre,
Lesbian women I have loved, and in loving hurt my fame,
   do not come crowding any longer to hear my music.
Phaon has stolen everything that once was pleasing to you,
   Phaon, alas, I came close to calling him mine.
Bring him back; your singer too will return.
   He gives power to my genius: he takes it away.

But do my prayers do anything at all? Do they move his
    country heart?
   Or is it frozen, and do the Zephyrs carry off my fallen
    words?
I wish the winds that carry my words away might return your
    sails.
210   To return, stubborn one, would be fitting, if you could feel.
Or if you are preparing the votive gifts for your stern,
   why then do you tear my heart with your delay?
Weigh anchor. Venus, born from the sea, smoothes the waves
   for a lover.
   The wind will speed your course. Only weigh anchor!
Cupid himself will sit as pilot at your stern. With delicate hand
   he will himself furl and unfurl the sail.
But if it is your desire to flee from Pelasgian Sappho
   — although you will find no reason to flee from me —
at least let a cruel letter tell me this is my pain:
220   that I may look in Leucadia's waters for my fate.   (1985)

A. D. MELVILLE

After distinguishing himself as a classicist at Cambridge, A. D. Melville took up a career as solicitor. He returned to his earlier work with a complete translation of the *Metamorphoses* in 1986, followed by a volume of the love poems in 1990 and the *Tristia* in 1995. His version of the flood that Jupiter decrees in order to punish human transgression, and the underworld *tableau* from Book 4, represent well his supple blank verse rendition of Ovid's hexameters. His translations of the erotic poems affect a 'typographical' accommodation of elegiac verse's uneven couplets.

Metamorphoses 1.304–60 [Met. 1.262–312] *The flood*

Swiftly within the Wind-god's cave he locked
The north wind and the gales that drive away
The gathered clouds, and sent the south wind forth;
And out on soaking wings the south wind flew,
His ghastly features veiled in deepest gloom.
His beard was sodden with rain, his white hair drenched;
Mists wreathed his brow and streaming water fell
From wings and chest; and when in giant hands
He crushed the hanging clouds, the thunder crashed
10   And storms of blinding rain poured down from heaven.
Iris, great Juno's envoy, rainbow-clad,
Gathered the waters and refilled the clouds.
The crops lay flat; the farmer mourned his hopes;
The long year's labour died, vain labour lost.

    Nor was Jove's wrath content with heaven above;
His sea-blue brother brings his water's aid,
And summons all the rivers to attend
Their master's palace. 'Now time will not wait
For many words', he says; 'pour out your strength –
20   The need is great! Unbar your doors! Away

With dykes and dams and give your floods free rein!'
The streams returned and freed their fountains' flow
And rolled in course unbridled to the sea.
Then with his trident Neptune struck the earth,
Which quaked and moved to give the waters way.
In vast expanse across the open plains
The rivers spread and swept away together
Crops, orchards, vineyards, cattle, houses, men,
Temples and shrines with all their holy things.
30   If any home is left and, undestroyed,
Resists the huge disaster, over its roof,
The waters meet and in their whirling flood
High towers sink from sight; now land and sea
Had no distinction; over the whole earth
All things were sea, a sea without a shore.
Some gained the hilltops, others took to boats
And rowed where late they ploughed; some steered a course
Above the cornfields and the farmhouse roofs,
And some caught fishes in the lofty elms.
40   Perchance in the green meads an anchor dropped
And curving keels brushed through the rows of vines,
And where but now the graceful goats had browsed
Gross clumsy seals hauled their ungainly bulk.
The Nereids see with awe beneath the waves
Cities and homes and groves, and in the woods
The dolphins live and high among the branches
Dash to and fro and shake the oaks in play.
Wolves swim among the sheep, and on the waters
Tigers are borne along and tawny lions.
50   No more his lightning stroke avails the boar
Nor his swift legs the stag – both borne away.
The wandering birds long seek a resting place
And drop with weary wings into the sea.

---

44 *Nereids*: sea goddesses

The waters' boundless licence overwhelmed
The hills, and strange waves lashed the mountain peaks.
The world was drowned; those few the deluge spared
For dearth of food in lingering famine died.   (1986)

Metamorphoses 4.513–76 [Met. 4.432–80]
Juno's descent into Dis

    There is a dropping path in twilight gloom
Of deadly yews; it leads through silent slopes
Down to the Underworld, where sluggish Styx
Exhales his misty vapours. By that path
New ghosts, the duly buried dead, descend.
There in a wan and wintry wilderness
The new wraiths grope to find the way that leads
To Hades' city and the cruel court
Of swarthy Dis. Countless broad entrances
10 That city has and portals everywhere
Open, and, as the sea from every land
Receives the rivers, so that place receives
The spirits, every one; no multitude
Finds it too small; it never knows a crowd.
There the shades wander without flesh or blood
Or bones; some gather in the central square;
Some throng the courts of Hell's infernal king;
Some busy with their skills that mimic life,
And some enduring their due punishment.
20   Hither Queen Juno forced herself to go
(So huge her hate and anger) from her home
In heaven. She entered and the threshold groaned
Under her holy tread. Immediately
Cerberus sprang at her with his three heads
And gave three barks together. Juno called

The Sisters born of Night, divinities
Implacable, doom-laden. There they sat,
Guarding the dungeon's adamantine doors,
And combed the black snakes hanging in their hair;
30   And when they recognized her through the gloom,
The Sisters rose. 'The Dungeon of the Damned'
That place is called. There giant Tityus
Lies stretched across nine acres and provides
His vitals for the vultures; Tantalus
Can never catch the water, never grasp
The overhanging branches; Sisyphus
Chases and heaves the boulder doomed to roll
For ever back; Ixion's wheel revolves,
Always behind himself, always ahead.
40   The Danaids who dared to do to death
Their cousin-husbands carry endlessly
The water that their sieves can never hold.
    At all of them, but chiefly at Ixion,
The child of Saturn glared, then turned her gaze
To Sisyphus and 'Why should he', she said,
'Of all the brothers suffer punishment
For ever, while proud Athamas resides
In a rich palace, he who with his wife
Has always held me in contempt?' She explained
50   Her hatred's cause, and why she came, and what
She wanted. What she wanted was the fall
Of Cadmus' house and Athamas dragged down
To crime and horror by those Sisters three.
Prayers, promises and orders, all in one,
She poured and begged their aid. When she had done,
Tisiphone, dishevelled as she was,
Shook her white hair and tossed aside the snakes

---

26 *Sisters born of Night*: the Furies
47 *Athamas*: Sisyphus's brother, husband to Ino   **56** *Tisiphone*: one of the Furies

That masked her face. 'There is no need', she said,
'Of rigmaroles. Count your commands as done.
60   Leave this unlovely realm and make your way
Back home to the more wholesome airs of heaven.'
Juno went blithely back and Thaumas' child,
The Rainbow, as she entered heaven again,
Purged her with sprinkled drops of cleansing rain.   (1986)

Amores 1.9

Lovers are soldiers, Atticus. Believe me,
    Lovers are soldiers, Cupid has his corps.
The age that's fit for fighting's fine for Venus;
    Old men are shamed in loving, shamed in war.

The spirit captains look for in a soldier
    A pretty girl will look for in her man.
Both keep night watches, on the hard ground resting,
    Each for his girl, or captain, guardian.

Long marches are a soldier's job: a lover
10   After his girl to the world's end will go.
High mountain barriers, rain-doubled rivers
    He'll cross and trudge his way through drifts of snow.
At sailing time he'll not plead dirty weather,
    Or wait for stars to tell him when to row.

Soldier or lover, who but they'd put up with
    The rain, the sleet, the snow, the cold of night?
One's sent to spy upon a dangerous enemy,

---

63 *The Rainbow*: Iris
1 *Atticus*: friend to Ovid, also addressed at *Pont.* 2.4

One keeps his rival, like a foe, in sight.
Besieging cities, or a hard girl's threshold,
20   On barbicans – or doors – they spend their might.

It often pays to catch the enemy sleeping,
    And rank and file unarmed with arms to slay.
Thus fell the fierce brigade of Thracian Rhesus;
    The captured horses left their lord that day.

And likewise lovers use a husband's slumber
    And launch their weapons on a sleeping foe.
Soldier and wretched lover, it's their business
    To foil the watch and past the sentries go.
Venus is chancy, Mars unsure; the vanquished
30   Rise, those you thought could never fall, lie low.

So chuck it, anyone who thinks love's lazy!
    Love's for a dashing soul who dares the most.
Achilles was aflame for lost Briseis –
    Take your chance, Trojans, smash the great Greek host!

When Hector left Andromache's embraces
    To fight, his wife gave him his casque to tie;
When Agamemnon saw wild-haired Cassandra
    They say that great commander's heart leapt high.
Mars too was caught and felt the blacksmith's meshes;
40   No tale in heaven had more publicity.

I was born idle, for unbuttoned leisure,
    Just lying languid with the shade above.
A pretty girl spurred me from my slack habits
    And bade me in her camp my service prove.
So now you see me brisk, a brave night-fighter:
    Yes, if you'd not be lazy, you should love.

(1990)

23f. cf. *Iliad* 10.   **36** *casque*: helmet

Cosmetics for Ladies, 43–50 [Med. 43–50] *Probity*.

Your first thought, girls, should be for your behaviour;
   A face will please when character is fine.
Love lasts for character: age ruins beauty
   And looks that charmed are ploughed with many a line.
The time will come when you will loathe your mirror
   And grief a second cause of wrinkles sends.
Goodness suffices and endures for ever;
   On this throughout its years true love depends.   (1990)

DAVID R. SLAVITT (1935–   )

David R. Slavitt's beautiful translations bring Ovid's exile poems finally into their own for the contemporary English audience, capturing the poignancy of these often difficult laments in sturdy couplets of six and five stresses. The elegies offered here – two of Ovid's letters to his wife, who had stayed behind in Rome to plead his case – are among the best in the collection. Seldom has autobiographical verse worked so well as the *Tristia*'s, or been so successfully turned into English. Slavitt – a widely published poet, novelist, critic and translator of Virgil, Tibullus and Seneca – has also brought his metrical skills to bear on the *Metamorphoses*, providing the latest 'free' translation of the poem. (For the full context of the passage from the Actaeon episode, see Sandys's version, above.)

Tristia 1, 6

Let us imagine a ruin – say, of some small Greek temple
   in an out of the way place, where the god happened
to speak or spare or warn or simply to show herself,
   nearly leveled, say by an earthquake, but one

single column left, still holding up its corner
   by which we can imagine the rest of the structure.
Which is the more affecting, the ruined part of the building,
   or that surviving piece of it, forlorn,
bereaved of the rest? My life is the ruin; yours, dear wife,
   is that still-standing beautiful pillar, vessel
for the spirit that yet abides. How else to declare
   my love for you, who deserve a less wretched
though not a better or more adoring husband? My powers
   are not what they were. Clumsy sincerity
must speak with its thick tongue, stammering out thanks
   and affection, unadorned but still heartfelt.
I know how you've been besieged, from the very day I left.
   Here the wolves creep close and the vultures circle,
eager for easy pickings. Back in Rome, gallants
   came with offers of comfort no less rapacious
than predator or scavenger would have been.
   Another Penelope, you fended them off –
for which your fame should exceed hers. At any moment,
   her husband might have reappeared, but you
have no such comforting hope, not even as idle fancy.
   But I'm no Homer. I never was,
even when I was a poet good enough to offend
   the august powers. Now I'm a picturesque
ruin, a possible asset to Tomis for the tourists
   I might attract to inspect my bleak wreck
and picnic here. Let them come and take the tour.
   As guide, I shall recite to them the marvel
Of your faith and love to which I am monument.
   No triumphal arch that looms in Rome
stands prouder. Let the world come to admire,
   as I have learned to do, now and forever.

                              (1990)

Tristia 4, 3

It is one of those clear nights when the stars appear to shine
    just out of reach. There is, of course, no moon,
and that's fine: the fickle moon is always changing,
    while the stars remain the same, and the two bears,
wheeling about forever but never deigning to touch
    even their paws in the restless sea, are constants
sailors trust with their lives. To them I make my appeal,
    for in their ample orbit the wide world
is embraced at once. They shine on me, here in Tomis
10   and also upon those walls that Remus vaulted
before his brother killed him. They can look down on Rome
    on a night like this to beam into my window . . .
Is my wife there? Is she looking out, thinking of me?
    What, if the stars could speak, would they report?
Would I really want to know? Or dare? I swear I would.
    One must have faith in unwavering faith. Polaris
would be less likely to wander than she. I don't need
    the testimony of stars to what I already
know in the depths of my heart to be certain and true. She
20   thinks of me and says her name aloud,
which is my name too, and gazes at my portrait
    to speak to me of her love. Providing only
that she is alive tonight, her love is alive.
    And if those stars could speak to her, they'd say,
when her heart is heavy, having braved its griefs all day,
    and woe sneaks up at night when she lays her head
on the pillow we used to share, that I love her still
    and wish I could reach out my hand to comfort
her tossing body. Our love expresses itself in aches
30   instead of pleasures; morning's weary bones
are a parody of past mornings when, after passion,
    we'd drag ourselves from bed. The torture is all

we have left these days. It's what Andromache felt,
  watching Hector's body hauled in the dust.
I can't imagine what to pray for or what to want.
  Should I want you sad? Could I bear to be the cause
of your unhappiness? Do I want you not to be sad?
  But what kind of wife would you be then?
I wish a bearable grief for my misfortunes rather
  than yours. Weep for my woes. There's pleasure in it,
sweet release and relief. If you had been mourning my death
  you would have known that comfort, and my spirit
could have sailed forth, free, into the open air,
  while your tears wet my lifeless breast. The sky
on which my eyes had closed, gazing and then glazing,
  would have held your face like a constellation.
My ashes could then have been laid to rest in the family tomb,
  in native ground. This life I lead is worse
than any such death, for you are an exile's wife,
  and you look away and blush to be so called,
as I blush now. It is a misery, your shame.
  A misery, for you to regret our marriage!
Where is the time you boasted that you were married to me?
  Where is the time when you were proud to be seen
beside me in public? You don't hate to have such moments
  recalled, do you? I think of little else . . .
How happy we were then! And how you graced my life!
  You must never let your grief curdle to shame,
for which you have no cause. I could rehearse the stories
  of gods and heroes — Euadne and Capaneus,
or Semele and Cadmus. The fall of a husband or father
  is not contagious, carries no dreadful taint.
Indeed, the reverse is true — that there is a kind of challenge
  catastrophe brings. The old stories are clear:
glory is never the fruit of a happy and tranquil life.
  Without the Greek invasion, Troy would have been
better off, no doubt, but who would have heard of Hector?
  Without the raging storms to batter the Argo,

(line numbers 40, 50, 60 in margin)

how could the strength and skill of Tiphys have been made
    known?
70   Apollo's arts of healing would never merit
our admiration if men and women were always healthy.
    It's up to you, my dear, how you respond
to this dire occasion. I'm sure your greatness of spirit
    will shine as a beacon, guiding the lives of others
for years to come. That you speak out in my behalf
    does you credit, whatever people may think
of me and my sad case. Adversity is the only
    test by which virtue can prove itself
in action. Nothing else we say or sincerely intend
80   is worth a damn. My exile here is your
fame, now and forever, a pedestal for your lofty
    monument, and a field of honor for love.
These waste expanses before me will bud and I'll watch them
    bloom
    in bouquets of your richly deserved praise.   (1990)

Metamorphoses 3.218–48 [Met. 3.225–52]
The death of Actaeon

This enormous pack has roamed these woods and highlands for
    years,
the best collection of hunting dogs in the world, and Actaeon
runs for his life, fleeing his old and adoring friends,
sprinting on rocky ground that isn't likely to hold
much of a scent, or splashing upstream and then crossing back
the way he came to try to confuse the leaders, who know
all the tricks of the wiliest quarry. He's spent his life
teaching these dogs their art, which he realizes will be
the death of him now. He wants to turn back, stand, and call
    out
10   to let them all know: 'I am Actaeon, your master!
You recognize my voice!' But there is no voice, and words

are gone, have abandoned his spirit, and the woods are loud
    with the baying
of those excellent, relentless, and splendid — those dreadful —
    dogs.
They are closing, are on him. The first, Ebony, leaps on his
    back,
bites, and holds on; and Butcher is there, sinking his fangs
into the meat of his haunch. It's agony. He feels another
searing pain as Montagnard mounts to his shoulder and mauls
    him
pitilessly. These three had taken a kind of shortcut,
were ahead of the pack, but they held him as the other dogs
    approached,
20   belling and barking, to bury their teeth in the gory flesh.
He groans aloud with a sound no deer has ever produced.
It fills the hills and valleys, which echo with grief and the pain
of how things are. He is down, his legs have given way,
and he looks with shock and love at his best friends in the
    world,
which are turning back to look for their master, him whom
    they love
and would willingly die for, even as he knows he's going to
    die.
They're barking now, their signal for him to come and
    dispatch
the beast they've brought down. They're puzzled that he is not
    here, as he
is puzzled himself to be here in this terrible guise, and they
    harry
30   and wound him further and even to death in Diana's wrath,
of which they are unaware. At last, she is pacified.   (1994)

DEREK MAHON (1941–)

The Irish poet, journalist, screenwriter and critic Derek Mahon has displayed an ongoing intimacy with the workings of Ovidian verse, contributing most recently a fine reworking of the Pygmalion story to the 1994 collection *After Ovid*. The following piece is drawn from his *Selected Poems* (1991). Mahon's mastery of the octosyllabic couplet lends the verse a playfulness especially well fitted to the original Latin. The poem is a *propempticon*, a conventional expression of anxiety at the departure of a loved one for a foreign land.

Ovid in Love 2. (*Am.* 2. 11)

This strange sea-going craze began
with Jason. Pine from Pelion,
weathered and shaped, was first to brave
the whirlpool and the whistling wave.
I wish the *Argo* had gone down
and seafaring remained unknown;
for now Corinna, scornful of
her safety and my vigilant love,
intends to tempt the winds and go
10   cruising upon the treacherous blue
waters where no shade-giving ilex,
temple or marble pavement breaks
with its enlightened artistry
the harsh monotony of the sea.
Walk on the beach where you may hear
the whorled conch whisper in your ear;
dance in the foam, but never trust
the water higher than your waist.
I'm serious. Listen to those with real
20   experience of life under sail;
believe their frightening anecdotes

of rocks and gales and splintered boats.
You won't be able to change your mind
when once your ship is far from land
and the most sanguine seamen cease
their banter as the waves increase.
How pale you'd grow if Triton made
the waters crash around your head –
so much more comfortable ashore
30   reading, or practising the lyre!
Still, if you're quite determined, God
preserve you from a watery bed:
Nereus' nymphs would be disgraced
if my Corinna should be lost.
Think of me when your shrinking craft
is a poignant pinpoint in the afternoon, and again when homeward bound
with canvas straining in the wind.
I'll be the first one at the dock
40   to meet the ship that brings you back.
I'll carry you ashore and burn
thank-offerings for your safe return.
Right there we'll make a bed of sand,
a table of a sand-dune, and
over the wine you'll give a vivid
sketch of the perils you survived –
how, faced with a tempestuous sea,
you hung on tight and thought of me!
Make it up if you like, as I
50   invent this pleasant fantasy . . .

(1991)

DARYL HINE (1936–)

The poet Daryl Hine is well known for his translations of Theocritus,
and has also published a version of the Homeric Hymns. Hine reinforces
his more comic, irreverent reading of the *Heroides* with a return to the
heroic couplet, and in so doing comes up with pieces that resemble
some of the lighter Restoration imitations. The translator's ironic
approach lends a particularly interesting slant to Medea's letter to Jason
– a work Hine regards as 'the most dramatic of [Ovid's] monologues'.

Heroines 12 *Medea to Jason*

While queen of Colchis, I believe, I made
Available to you my magic aid.
That was the period at which the dread
Sisters should have cut my mortal thread
Short, for then I could have died content:
Existence since seems one long punishment.

Cursed be the day the gilded youth of Greece
Aboard the Argo sought the golden fleece!
When we in Colchis saw this foreign ship
10   Crowded with heroes in our Phasis dip
Oar! just why your beauty charmed me so,
Fair hair and fair, false tongue, I do not know.
O why, when that strange ship had come to land
And had discharged its brash, adventurous band,
Didn't heartless Jason meet his death
Unarmed against the bronze bulls' fiery breath?
Or plant a fatal foe with every seed

---

10 *Phasis*: a river in Colchis

And therefore reap what he had sown indeed?
What bad faith would have perished, rogue, with you!
20   How many woes would have been spared me too!

There is a certain pleasure – is there not? –
In bringing up old benefits forgot?
And I intend to savour what may be
The only pleasure you can give to me.
Untried, obedient to some command,
You trespassed in my happy fatherland.
Medea in that country occupied
The same position as your newest bride
In this; in father's wealth I too took pride:
30   Hers rules the shores of Corinth; my papa
Reigns from the Hellespont to Scythia.
Aeetes welcomed you; your shipmates made
Themselves at home upon our rich brocade.
I saw you; even though you were unknown
To me, my peace of mind was overthrown.
I looked and was lost, I burned with strange, divine
Fire, like a pine torch blazing in a shrine.
Irresistible as destiny.
And handsome, with a look you ravished me.
40   I think you guessed, you wretch! for there's no way
Of hiding love; it gives itself away.

Then you were told our laws: that you somehow
Must break two untamed oxen to the plough.
(The bulls belonged to Mars, their igneous
Breath as well as horns were dangerous.
Their feet were solid brass, each brazen snout
Was blackened by the flames that they breathed out.)
You were commanded furthermore to sow

---

32 *Aeetes*: Medea's father, king of Colchis

The fields with seeds from which a host would grow
50   To attack you, earthborn men at arms,
A disconcerting crop for one who farms!
Your final task: by any means you can
To dupe the fleece's sleepless guardian.
So said the king. You Argonauts in woe
From your purple couches rose to go.
How far away Creusa seemed to you
Then, her father and her dowry too!
Sadly you left. A tear bedimmed my eye,
Seeing you depart; I sighed, 'Goodbye!'

60   Smitten, I sought my bed, then – not to sleep
But all night long to lie awake and weep.
The bulls – the watchful snake – the dreadful crop
Plagued my imagination without stop,
Whence fear, then love – but love was fed by fear.
Next morning, entering my room, my dear
Sister perceived my pitiable case
From my disheveled hair and tear-stained face.
She begged me anyway I could to save
The Argonauts . . . the aid she asked I gave.

70   Pines and oaks obscure a certain glade
So sunbeams rarely penetrate its shade:
There is – or was – a temple in that wood
Where chaste Diana's golden statue stood:
Have you forgotten that as well as me?
For there you first committed perjury!
'Yours to decree what destiny demands:
Henceforth my life and death are in your hands.
Great as appears your power to hurt at will,
My preservation would be greater still.
80   Since you can solve my problems I implore

You, by your family's solar ancestor,
And by the rites of great Diana, and
Whatever gods are honored in this land,
O maiden, pity me and mine, and make
Me yours eternally, for pity's sake.
But if you will not deign to wed a Greek –
Dare I such heavenly condescension seek? –
May my spirit melt into thin air
Before another bride than you shall share
90   My bed! Witness Juno who presides
Over the vows of bridegrooms and of brides,
Also the goddess in whose marble fane
We're standing, that I do not swear in vain!'
The speech of which these words are but a part,
Your handclasp, touched a simple maiden's heart.
I even saw you weep – is there a way
Of feigning tears? The things you had to say
Thus quickly stole my maidenhead away.

You brought the brazen bulls beneath the yoke
100   Unscathed, and then the hard-packed ploughland broke,
Using that plough of which my father spoke.
With deadly dragons' teeth you sowed the earth,
And soldiers sprang up, fully armed from birth,
And even I, who'd lent my magic aid,
Paled to see so suddenly arrayed
That miraculously earth-born band
In fratricidal combat hand to hand.
Behold the sleepless, giant loathly worm
Hiss and on his scaly belly squirm!
110   Where was the dowry of your royal bride,
The isthmus with the sea on either side,

---

81 *solar ancestor*: Aeetes' father is Helios, the sun.
108 *worm*: the dragon that guarded the golden fleece

When I, outlandish as I seem to you
Nowadays, and poor, and baleful too,
Cast on those blazing eyes a drowsy spell
And helped you safely snatch the fleece as well?

My father I betrayed, his realm forsook:
Exile as my just deserts I took.
I left my sister and my mother, gave
Myself, a virgin, to an errant knave.

120   I sacrificed my brother to our flight
Ruthlessly, but more I cannot write,
The deed I dared to do defies my pen:
I too should have been torn in pieces then!
Nor did I fear the sea — why, after all,
Should I, a woman and a criminal?

Where's the heavenly retribution we
So thoroughly deserved to meet at sea —
You for deceit, I for credulity?
Why didn't the Symplegades collide
130   To mash our bones together side by side?
Why did rapacious Scylla, who must loathe
All ingrates, not make mincemeat of us both?
Or Charybdis' whirlpool drag us down
Under the Sicilian sea to drown?

In triumph, safe returned against all odds,
You laid the golden fleece before your gods.
Why mention Pelias' pious daughters, who

---

122 *deed*: Medea had dismembered her brother, Absyrtus, and cast the parts into
the sea to delay the pursuers.

129 *Symplegades*: the mythic Wandering Rocks which jeopardize voyages through
the Bosphorus

137 *Pelias' pious daughters*: Pelias had usurped Jason's family's throne. In revenge,
Medea deluded his daughters into thinking they could restore the old man's
youth by dismembering him. The exploit would lead to Jason's and Medea's
expulsion from Iolcos.

Were hoodwinked by my demonstration to
Chop their father up to make a stew?
140   To you I'll praise myself, since others blame
The crimes that I committed in your name.
But then you dared — words fail me, yes, I grieve
To say — you dared to order me to leave!
I left, and took our children with me, and
That love that drives me over sea and land.

Too soon I seemed to hear the marriage choir
As torches blazed with hymeneal fire
And flutes poured forth your wedding melody,
Alas! more doleful than a dirge to me!
150   I had not known there was such wickedness,
But I turned cold with horror nonetheless,
And still the crowd's enthusiastic cheers,
Drawing ever nearer, hurt my ears.
Covertly my slaves were all in tears
On every side, for nobody could choose
To be the messenger of such bad news.
Whatever it was, I did not want to know;
My heart was sore with knowing even so.
My younger son, agog to see the show,
160   Called me to the window, 'Mummy, see
Daddy's leading the parade — there he
Goes in all his golden finery!'
At that I beat my breast and tore my dress
And even scratched my face in my distress.
My fury prompted me to rush outside
And snatch the wedding garland off your bride;
Beside myself, I almost could have thrown
My arms about you, claimed you as my own.

Father, rejoice! Forsaken and betrayed,
170   Thus I propitiate my brother's shade!
Having lost my home and native land,

I find myself at last abandoned and
Humiliated by my husband – he
Who hitherto was all in all to me.
Wild bulls and serpents I could subjugate,
One creature I could not subdue: my mate.
Although my spells protected him from fire,
I can't escape the ardours of desire;
My magic arts are gone, enchantment fails,
180   Not even mighty Hecate avails.
Daylight I loathe, I lie awake all night,
Uncomforted by sleep however slight,
And I, who could a dragon hypnotize,
Cannot induce myself to close my eyes
With drugs that proved so potent otherwise.
The limbs I saved another's limbs entwine:
The prize is hers, the effort all was mine.

Perhaps when boasting to your foolish wife
You will find something in my way of life
190   Or appearance possibly to blame?
Well, let her laugh and vilify my name,
Let her exult in purple! Soon she will
Weep, and burn with fiercer passions still.
As long as there is poison, steel, or fire,
Medea's enemies shall feel her ire!
Listen, if prayer can touch a breast of steel,
To words that fall far short of all I feel.
Today I come as supplicant to you,
And kneel at your feet, just as you used to do
200   At mine in supplication – often, too!
Think of our sons, though you think ill of me;
Protect them from Creusa's savagery.
They trouble me – how like you they appear!
Each time I look at them I shed a tear.
By the gods and my forebear, the sun,
By our babes and everything I've done

For you, give back your love, which I was mad
Enough to buy with everything I had!
Be true to your word, remembering your vow,
210 And if I ever helped you, help me now.
I do not seek your aid with man or bull
Or to make a snake insensible,
It's you I seek, I have deserved your love
Which you yourself made me a present of.

You ask, where is my dowry? Need you ask?
Did I not assist you in your task?
My dowry is the golden fleece, which I
Know, if I asked it back, you would deny.
My dowry is your safety and the health
220 Of all your crew. Has Creon's girl such wealth?
Your life, your marriage, your prosperity –
And your ingratitude! – you owe to me,
And soon enough . . . but why should I say more?
My anger has enormities in store,
Which I'll pursue. Perhaps I shall repent
In time the manner of your punishment,
Yet what is worthier repentance than
Having cared for such a callous man?
Let that deity see to the rest
230 Who causes such a turmoil in my breast,
As I elaborate I don't know what
Awful scheme too terrible for thought!

(1991)

ALLEN MANDELBAUM (1926–)

Allen Mandelbaum earns distinction as one of the most prolific and
ambitious English translators now at work. He has so far taken up the
Aeneid (1971), the *Divine Comedy* (1980–84), the *Odyssey* (1990) and,
most recently, the *Metamorphoses*, from which the following passage

comes. The anecdote of the newt's origin is one of the narrative inserts adorning the larger story of Ceres' search for her daughter Proserpine, carried off to Hades by Pluto.

Metamorphoses 5.664–97 [Met. 5.438–61] *The newt*

Meanwhile, the heartsick Ceres seeks her daughter:
she searches every land, all waves and waters.
No one – not Dawn with her dew-laden hair,
nor Hesperus – saw Ceres pause. She kindled
two pinewood torches in the flames of Etna.
Through nights of frost, a torch in either hand,
she wandered. Ceres never rested. When
the gracious day had dimmed the stars, again
the goddess searched from west to east, from where
10   the sun would set to where the sun ascends.

Worn out and racked by thirst – she had not wet
her lips at any spring along her path –
she chanced to see a hut whose roof was thatched
with straw. And Ceres knocked at that poor door,
which an old woman opened. When she saw
the goddess there and heard her ask for water,
she gave her a sweet drink in which she'd soaked
roast barley. While the goddess drank this brew,
a boy came up to her; and scornful, rude,
20   he laughed and said she drank too greedily.
Offended, Ceres stopped her sipping, threw
the brew and all of its pearl-barley grains
full in his face. So – soaked – his face soon showed
those grains as spots; his arms were changed to claws;
a tail was added to his altered limbs.
And that his form might not inflict much harm,
the goddess shrank him, left him small – much like
a lizard, and yet tinier in size.

This wonderous change was watched by the old woman,
30 who wept to see it, even as she tried
to touch the transformed shape: he scurried off
to find a place to hide. The name he got
is suited to his skin: the starry newt –
a beast that glitters with his starlike spots.

(1993)

TED HUGHES (1930–)

Ted Hughes, Britain's Poet Laureate since 1984, confirmed his status
as one of the century's foremost English poets with the publication of
Crow in 1970. In 1997, Hughes released his *Tales from Ovid*, which
renders 24 episodes from the *Metamorphoses*. The following lines from
Book 1 come from his contribution to 1994's *After Ovid: New Metamor-*
phoses, a bold reworking of Ovid's myths by some of the best contemporary talents. Contrast Chaucer's version, above.

Creation/Four Ages/Flood, 160–283 [Met. 1.89–150] *The four ages*

And the first age was gold.
Without laws, without law's enforcers,
This age understood and obeyed
What had created it.
Listening deeply, man kept faith with the source.

None dreaded judgement.
For no table of crimes measured out
The degrees of torture allotted
Between dismissal and death.
10 No plaintiff
Prayed in panic to the tyrant's puppet.
Undefended all felt safe and were happy.

Then the great conifers
Ruffled at home on the high hills.
They had no premonition of the axe
Hurtling towards them on its parabola.
Or of the shipyards. Or of what other lands
They would glimpse from the lift of the ocean swell.
No man had crossed salt water.

20   Cities had not dug themselves in
Behind deep moats, guarded by towers.
No sword had bitten at its own
Reflection in the shield. No trumpets
Amplified the battle-cries
Of lions and bulls
Out through the mouth-holes in helmets.

Men needed no weapons.
Nations loved one another.

And the earth, unbroken by plough or by hoe,
30   Piled the table high. Mankind
Was content to gather the abundance
Of whatever ripened.
Blackberry or strawberry, mushroom or truffle,
Every kind of nut, figs, apples, cherries,
Apricots and pears, and, ankle deep,
Acorns under the tree of the Thunderer.
Spring weather, the airs of spring,
All year long brought blossom.
The unworked earth
40   Whitened beneath the bowed wealth of the corn.
Rivers of milk mingled with rivers of nectar.
And out of the black oak oozed amber honey.

After Jove had castrated Saturn,
Under the new reign the Age of Silver –
(Lower than the Gold, but better
Than the coming Age of Brass) –
Fell into four seasons.

Now, as never before,
All colour burnt out of it, the air
50 Wavered into flame. Or icicles
Strummed in the wind that made them.
Not in a cave, not in a half-snug thicket,
Not behind a windbreak of wattles,
For the first time
Man crouched under a roof, at a fire.
Now every single grain
Had to be planted
By hand, in a furrow
That had been opened in earth by groaning oxen.

60 After this, third in order,
The Age of Brass
Brought a brazen people,
Souls fashioned on the same anvil
As the blades their hands snatched up
Before they cooled. But still
Mankind listened deeply
To the harmony of the whole creation,
And aligned
Every action to the greater order
70 And not
To the blind opportunity of the moment.

Last comes the Age of Iron.
And the day of Evil dawns.
Modesty

Truth
Loyalty
Go up like a mist – a morning sigh off a graveyard.

Snares, tricks, plots come hurrying
Out of their dens in the atom.
80 Violence is an extrapolation
Of the cutting edge
Into the orbit of the smile.
Now comes the love of gain – a new god
Made out of the shadow
Of all the others. A god who peers
Grinning from the roots of the eye-teeth.

Now sails bulged and the cordage cracked
In winds that still bewildered the pilots.
And the long trunks of trees
90 That had never shifted in their lives
From some mountain fastness
Leapt in their coffins
From wavetop to wavetop
Then out over the rim of the unknown.

Meanwhile the ground, formerly free to all
As the air or sunlight,
Was portioned by surveyors into patches,
Between boundary markers, fences, ditches.
Earth's natural plenty no longer sufficed.
100 Man tore open the earth, and rummaged in her bowels.
Precious ores the Creator had concealed
As close to hell as possible
Were dug up – a new drug
For the criminal. So now iron comes
With its cruel ideas. And gold
With crueller. Combined, they bring war –
War, insatiable for the one,

With bloody hands employing the other.
Now man lives only by plunder. The guest
110 Is booty for the host. The bride's father,
Her heirloom, is a windfall piggybank
For the groom to shatter. Brothers
Who ought to love each other
Prefer to loathe. The husband longs
To bury his wife and she him.
Stepmothers, for the sake of their stepsons,
Study poisons. And sons grieve
Over their father's obdurate good health.
The inward ear, attuned to the Creator,
120 Is underfoot like a dog's turd. Astraea,
The Virgin
Of Justice – the incorruptible
Last of the immortals –
Abandons the blood-fouled earth.

                                                            (1994)

CHRISTOPHER REID (1949–   )

The poet and editor Christopher Reid follows up the narrative of the
flood in *After Ovid* with a terse epitome of the Deucalion and Pyrrha
story. He manages here a beautiful distillation of the sentiment contained
in Ovid's account of our dubious regeneration after mythic catastrophe.

Deucalion and Pyrrha [Met. 1.313–415]

                              Only
two survived the flood.
We are not of their blood,
springing instead from the bones
of the great mother: stones,
what have you – rocks, boulders –

hurled over their shoulders
by that pious pair
and becoming people, where
10   and as they hit the ground.
Since when, we have always found
something hard, ungracious,
    obdurate in our natures,
a strain of the very earth
that gave us our abrupt birth;
but a pang, too, at the back
of the mind: a loss . . . a lack . . .   (1994)

SEAMUS HEANEY (1939–)

Winner of the 1995 Nobel Prize for literature, the Irish poet Seamus
Heaney contributes to the *After Ovid* volume his version of one of the
Metamorphoses' most frightening and haunting moments. Orpheus's
withdrawal to the forest following his abortive attempt to rescue Eurydice from Hades (a passage Heaney also reworks earlier in the collection)
comes to an abrupt, violent end. It is a high point in Ovid's narrative,
and retains its power in Heaney's skilled transformation.

Death of Orpheus [Met. 11.1–84]

The songs of Orpheus held the woods entranced.
The animals were hushed, the field-stones danced
Until a band of crazed Ciconian women,
A maenad band dressed up in wild beasts' skins,
Spied him from a hilltop with his lyre.
As he tuned his voice to it and cocked his ear,
One of them whose hair streamed in the breeze
Began to shout, 'Look, look, it's Orpheus,
Orpheus the misogynist,' and flung

10   Her staff straight at the bard's mouth while he sang.
     But the staff being twined with leaves just left a bruise
     And did no injury. So another throws
     A stone that his singing spellbinds in the air,
     Making it drop like a shamed petitioner
     At his affronted feet. But even so,
     There could be no stop to the violence now.
     The furies were unleashed. And his magic note
     That should have stalled their weapons was drowned out
     By blaring horns and drums, beatings and yells
20   And the pandemonium of those bacchanals
     So that at last his red blood wet the rocks.
     But first the maenads ripped apart the snakes
     And the flocks of birds he'd charmed out of the sky
     And the dreambound beasts that formed his retinue.
     Orpheus then, torn by their blood-filled nails,
     Was like an owl in daytime when it falls
     Prey to the hawks of light; or a stag that stands
     In the amphitheatre early, before the hounds
     Have savaged it to pieces on the sand.
30   They circled him, still using as their weapons
     Staffs they had twined with leaves and tipped with cones
     That were never meant for duty such as this.
     Some pelted him with clods, some stripped the branches
     To scourge him raw, some stoned him with flintstones.
     But as their frenzy peaked, they chanced upon
     Far deadlier implements.

                    Near at hand
     Oxen in yokes pulled ploughshares through the ground
     And sturdy farmers sweated as they dug –
     Only to flee across their drills and rigs
40   When they saw the horde advancing. They downed tools
     So there for the taking on the empty fields
     Lay hoes and heavy mattocks and long spades.
     The oxen lowered their horns, the squealing maenads

Cut them to pieces, then turned to rend the bard,
Committing sacrilege when they ignored
His hands stretched out to plead and the extreme
Pitch of his song that now for the first time
Failed to enchant. And so, alas, the breath
Of life streamed out of him, out of that mouth
50   Whose songs had tamed the beasts and made stones dance,
And was blown away on the indiscriminate winds.

For Orpheus then the birds in cheeping flocks,
The animals in packs, the flint-veined rocks
And woods that had listened, straining every leaf,
Wept and kept weeping. For it seemed as if
The trees were mourners tearing at their hair
As the leaves streamed off them and the branch went bare.
And rivers too, they say, rose up in floods
Of their own tears, and all the nymphs and naiads
60   Went dishevelled in drab mourning gowns.
Meanwhile, the poet's mangled flesh and bones
Lay scattered and exposed. But his head and lyre
Were saved by miracle: the Hebrus River
Rose for them, ran with them, bore them out midstream
Where the lyre trembled and the dead mouth swam
Lapping the ripples that lipped the muddy shore
And a fluent humming sadness filled the air.
As they rode the current downstream, they were swept
On out to sea off Lesbos and washed up
70   On the strand there, unprotected. Then a snake
Unleashed itself like a slick whip to attack
The head in its tangled web of sopping locks
But Phoebus intervened. Just as its bite
Gaped at its widest, it solidified.
The jaws' hinge hardened and the open yawn
Of the empty vicious mouth was set in stone.

The poet's shade fled underneath the earth
Past landmarks that he recognized, down paths
He'd travelled on the first time, desperately
80 Scouring the blessed fields for Eurydice.
And when he found her, wound her in his arms
And moved with her, and she with him, two forms
Of the one love, restored and mutual –
For Orpheus now walks free, is free to fall
Out of step, into step, follow, go in front
And look behind him to his heart's content.

But Bacchus was unwilling to forget
The atrocities against his sacred poet,
So, there and then, in a web of roots, he wound
90 And bound the offending women to the ground.
However deftly they would try to go,
Earth's grip and traction clutched them from below.
They felt it latch them, load them heal and toe.
And, as a caught bird struggles to get free
From a cunningly set snare, but still can only
Tighten the mesh around its feet still tighter
The more it strains its wings and frets and flutters,
So each of the landlogged women heaved and hauled
In vain, in agony, as the roots took hold
100 And bark began to thicken the smooth skin.
It gripped them and crept up above their knees.
They struggled like a storm in storm-tossed trees.
Then, as each finger twigged and toe dug in,
Arms turned to oak boughs, thighs to oak, oak leaves
Matted their breasts and camouflaged their moves
So that you couldn't tell if the whole strange growth
Were a wood or women in distress or both.

(1994)

BETTY ROSE NAGLE

Though the *Fasti* remains a neglected corner of Ovid's work, the 1990s have witnessed a scholarly revival of the calendar poem. The appearance of a fresh translation by the classicist Betty Rose Nagle should help to keep the interest of its English audience alive. In addition to the more substantial passages, two representations of the 'epigrammatic' moments that frequently separate the poem's narratives are featured here.

Roman Holidays 1.457–60 [Fas. 1.457–60]
Dolphin epigram

Meanwhile the Dolphin constellation rises above the sea,
    and pokes his snout from the waters of his origin.

The next day marks the turning point of winter.
    What remains will equal what has passed.   (1995)

Roman Holidays 3.523–40 [Fas. 3.523–40]
Anna Perenna festivities

On the Ides the merry festival of Anna Perenna takes place,
    not far from the banks of the wandering Tiber.
The common people come and drink scattered about on the
       grass,
    each man stretched out with his partner.
Some rough it out in the open, a few pitch tents;
    some have leafy lean-to's made of branches;
some set up cane poles instead of sturdy pillars,
    and spread their togas out on top.
But they still warm up from the sun and the wine, and pray for
10   as many years as they drink toasts.
There you'll find a man who drinks up Nestor's years

and a woman whose cups have made her a Sibyl.
There they sing whatever they've learned at the shows
  and wave their hands nimbly along with the words.
They set the punchbowl aside and perform crude reels, and a
    stylish
  girlfriend lets down her hair and dances.
They come back home staggering, a spectacle for the masses,
  and the crowd they run into calls them lucky.   (1995)

Roman Holidays 4.85–132 [Fas. 4.85–132] *Venus*

Does envy spare no one? Some begrudge you the tribute
  of your month, Venus, and want to rob you of it.
Because all things appear in spring and the freezing sharpness
  of the cold departs and the fertile earth relaxes,
they say that April was named for this season of appearance,
  but kindly Venus formally claims it as hers.
She indeed quite rightfully regulates the entire world,
  no god has greater jurisdiction than she,
she lays down the law for heaven, earth and her native sea;
10   her approach perpetuates every species.
She produced all the gods (too numerous to mention),
  she provided crops and trees with their origin,
she brought together the hearts of primitive men
  and taught each to be joined with his partner.
What but seductive pleasure produces every species of bird?
  Cattle would not mate, in the absence of gentle love.
The belligerent ram locks horns with other males, but refrains
  from hurting his beloved ewe's forehead.
In pursuit of a heifer the bull sheds his ferocity, the bull,
20   terror of every glade and every grove.
The same drive preserves everything living beneath broad
    ocean
  and fills the waters with countless fish.
Venus was the first to rid man of his savage customs;

from her came elegance and concern for style.
They say a lover denied admission sang the first song
    while keeping watch at the barred door,
and rhetoric arose to plead with a hard-hearted girl,
    and everyone was eloquent on his own behalf.
She inspired a thousand skills; eagerness to be attractive
30   supposedly discovered many things hidden before.
Who would dare plunder her of the distinction of the second
      month?
    Keep that crazy idea far away from me!
And while she's powerful everywhere, glorified in crowded
      temples,
    in Rome the goddess holds still greater sway.
Romans, Venus took up arms in defense of your Troy, and
      groaned
    when a spear injured her delicate hand.
When Trojan Paris was judge, she defeated two heavenly
      goddesses
    (how I wish the defeated goddesses had forgotten this).
She became the mother of a Trojan son, plainly in order
40   that one day great Augustus might have Julian ancestors.
No other season is better suited to Venus than spring:
    in spring the land glistens and the fields are thawed;
now the grasses break through the ground and push up their
      blades,
    now the vine forces buds through the swollen bark.
Lovely Venus deserves a lovely season, and now,
    as usual, she comes right after her beloved Mars.
In spring she advises curved ships to cross her native seas,
    and no longer fear the threats of winter.   (1995)

Roman Holidays 6.771–72 [Fas. 6.771–72]
Couplet on time

Time slips away and we grow old in the course of the noiseless
years, and the days, unbridled, run away.   (1995)

LIST OF EDITIONS

Joseph Addison. In *Ovid's* Metamorphoses *in Fifteen Books. Translated by the most Eminent Hands*, London, 1717.

Anonymous. *The fable of Ouid treting of Narcissus*, London, 1560.

Matthew Arnold. *The Poems of Matthew Arnold*, ed. Kenneth Allott, London: Longmans, 1965.

Anna Laetitia Barbauld. *The Poems of Anna Laetitia Barbauld*, ed. William McCarthy and Elizabeth Kraft, Athens: University of Georgia Press, 1994.

Francis Beaumont. In *Elizabethan Minor Epics*, ed. Elizabeth Storey Donno, New York: Columbia University Press, 1963.

A. A. Brodribb and F. H. Hummel. *Lays from Latin Lyres*, London, 1876.

Zachary Catlin. *De Tristibus: or Mournefull Elegies, in Five Bookes*, London, 1639.

William Caxton. *The Metamorphoses of Ovid*, 2 vols, New York: George Braziller, 1968.

Sir Thomas Chaloner. In Sir John Harington *et al.*, *Nugæ Antiquæ*, London, 1804. Reprinted New York: AMS, 1966.

Geoffrey Chaucer. *The Riverside Chaucer*, ed. Larry D. Benson, third edition, Boston: Houghton Mifflin, 1987.

Mary, Lady Chudleigh. *The Poems and Prose of Mary, Lady Chudleigh*, ed. Margaret J. M. Ezell, New York: Oxford University Press, 1993.

Thomas Churchyard. *The Three first Bookes of Ouid de Tristibus*, London, 1578.

Arthur Hugh Clough. *Poems*, ed. F. L. Mulhauser and Jane Turner, second edition, Oxford: Clarendon Press, 1974.

William Congreve. *The Complete Works of William Congreve*, ed. Montague Summers, 4 vols., London: Nonesuch Press, 1923.

William Cowper. *Poetical Works*, ed. H. S. Milford, revised fourth edition, London: Oxford University Press, 1967.

Thomas Creech. In *Miscellany Poems*, London, 1684.

John Dryden. *The Poems of John Dryden*, ed. James Kinsley, 4 vols, Oxford: Clarendon Press, 1958.

Henry Fielding. *Ovid's Art of Love Paraphrased, And Adapted to the Present Time. Book I*, London, 1747.

Robert Forbes. *Ajax's Speech to the Grecian Knabbs, From Ovid's Metam. Lib. XIII.*, Glasgow, 1755.

Abraham Fraunce. *The Third part of the Countesse of Pembrokes Yuychurch: Entituled, Amintas Dale*, London, 1592. Reprinted New York: Garland, 1976.

Sir James George Frazer. *The* Fasti *of Ovid*, 5 vols, London: Macmillan, 1929.

Emma Garland. *Ovid's Epistles*, London, 1842.

John Gay. *Dramatic Works*, ed. John Fuller, 2 vols, Oxford: Clarendon Press, 1983. *Poetry and Prose*, ed. Vinton A. Dearing and Charles E. Beckwith, 2 vols, Oxford: Clarendon Press, 1974.

Arthur Golding. *Shakespeare's Ovid, Being Arthur Golding's Translation of the Metamorphoses*, ed. W. H. D. Rouse, Carbondale: Southern Illinois University Press, 1961.

John Gower. *The English Works of John Gower*, ed. G. C. Macaulay, 2 vols., London: Early English Text Society, 1900–1901.

John Gower. *Ovids Festivalls, Or Romane Calendar*, London, 1640.

Robert Graves. *Poems (1914–1926)*, London: Heinemann, 1927.

Peter Green. *Ovid: The Erotic Poems*, Harmondsworth: Penguin, 1982. *Ovid: The Poems of Exile*, Harmondsworth: Penguin, 1994.

Horace Gregory. *Ovid: The Metamorphoses*, New York: Viking, 1958.

Seamus Heaney. In *After Ovid*, ed. Michael Hoffmann and James Lasdun, New York: Farrar, Straus and Giroux, 1994.

Robert Herrick. *The Poetical Works of Robert Herrick*, ed. L. C. Martin, Oxford: Clarendon Press, 1956.

Thomas Heywood. *Publii Ouidii Nasonis De Arte Amandi or, The Art of Love*, n.p. [Amsterdam?], n.d. [1600–1625?]. *Pleasant Dialogues and Dramma's*, London, 1637. *Troia Britanica: Or, Great Britaines Troy*, London, 1609.

Daryl Hine. *Ovid's Heroines: A Verse Translation of the* Heroides, New Haven: Yale University Press, 1991.

Charles Hopkins. *The History of Love. A Poem: In a Letter to a Lady*. London, 1695.

Ted Hughes. In *After Ovid* (see Seamus Heaney).

F. H. Hummel. See A. A. Brodribb.

Rolfe Humphries. *Ovid's Metamorphoses*, Bloomington: University of Indiana Press, 1955. *The Art of Love*, Bloomington: University of Indiana Press, 1957.

Ben Jonson. *Ben Jonson*, ed. C. H. Herford, Percy Simpson, and Evelyn Simpson, 11 vols, Oxford: Clarendon Press, 1925–52.

Anne Killigrew. *Poems (1686)*, Gainesville: Scholars' Facsimiles & Reprints, 1967.

F. L. *Ouidius Naso His Remedie of Loue*, London, 1600.

Guy Lee. *Ovid's Amores*, New York: Viking, 1968.

Henry Wadsworth Longfellow. *The Complete Poetical Works of Henry Wadsworth Longfellow*, Boston: Houghton Mifflin, 1922.

Derek Mahon. *Selected Poems*. London: Viking, 1991.

Allen Mandelbaum. *The Metamorphoses of Ovid*, New York: Harcourt Brace, 1993.

Christopher Marlowe. *The Complete Works of Christopher Marlowe*, ed. Roma Gill, 4 vols., Oxford: Clarendon Press, 1987.

John Marston. In *Elizabethan Minor Epics* (see Francis Beaumont).

William Massey. *Ovid's Fasti, or the Romans Sacred Calendar*, London, 1757.

A. D. Melville. *Ovid: Metamorphoses*, Oxford: Oxford University Press, 1986. *Ovid: The Love Poems*, Oxford: Oxford University Press, 1990.

B. P. Moore. *The Art of Love: Ovid's Ars amatoria*, Glasgow: Blackie, 1935.

Betty Rose Nagle. *Ovid's Fasti: Roman Holidays*, Bloomington: University of Indiana Press, 1995.

John Oldham. *The Poems of John Oldham*, ed. Harold F. Brooks and Raman Selden, Oxford: Clarendon Press, 1987.

Sir Thomas Overbury. *The First and Second part of The Remedy of Loue*, London, 1620.

Alexander Pope. *The Poems of Alexander Pope*, ed. John Butt, New Haven: Yale University Press, 1963.

Christopher Reid. In *After Ovid* (see Seamus Heaney).

Wye Saltonstall. *Ovids Tristia Containinge fiue Bookes of mournefull Elegies*, London, 1633. *Ovid De Ponto. Containing foure books of Elegies*, London, 1639.

George Sandys. *Ovid's Metamorphosis Englished, Mythologized, and Represented in Figures*, ed. Karl K. Hulley and Stanley T. Vandersall, Lincoln: University of Nebraska Press, 1970.

William Shakespeare. *The Tempest*, ed. Horace Howard Furness, seventh edition, Philadelphia, 1892.

Mary Wollstonecraft Shelley. In vol. 10 of *The Bodleian Shelley Manuscripts*, ed. Charles E. Robinson, New York: Garland, 1992.

Percy Bysshe Shelley. In vol. 10 of *The Bodleian Shelley Manuscripts* (see Mary Wollstonecraft Shelley).

John Sherburne. *Ovids Heroical Epistles*, London, 1639.

James Shirley. In *Elizabethan Minor Epics* (see Francis Beaumont).

C. H. Sisson. *Metamorphoses*, London: Methuen, 1968.

David R. Slavitt. *Ovid's Poetry of Exile*, Baltimore: Johns Hopkins University Press, 1990. *The Metamorphoses of Ovid*, Baltimore: Johns Hopkins University Press, 1994.

Edmund Spenser. *Poetical Works*, ed. J. C. Smith and E. de Selincourt, London: Oxford University Press, 1912.

Jonathan Swift. *Poetical Works*, ed. Herbert Davis, London: Oxford University Press, 1967.

Nahum Tate. In *Ovid's Art of Love In Three Books. Together With His Remedy of Love*, London, 1776. Reprinted New York: AMS, 1977. In *Ovid's Metamorphoses in Fifteen Books* (see Joseph Addison).

George Turbervile. *The Heroycall Epistles of the Learned Poet Publius Ovidius Naso*, ed. Frederick Boas, London: Cresset Press, 1928.

Thomas Underdowne. *Ouid his inuectiue against Ibis*. London, 1569.

Henry Vaughan. *The Works of Henry Vaughan*, ed. L. C. Martin, 2 vols., Oxford: Clarendon Press, 1914.

Florence Verducci. *Ovid's Toyshop of the Heart:* Epistulae Heroidum, Princeton: Princeton University Press, 1985.

A. E. Watts. *The Metamorphoses of Ovid*, San Francisco: North Point Press, 1980.

Phillis Wheatley. *The Collected Works of Phillis Wheatley*, ed. John C. Shields, New York: Oxford University Press, 1988.

John Wilmot, Earl of Rochester. *The Complete Poems of John Wilmot, Earl of Rochester*, ed. David M. Vieth, New Haven: Yale University Press, 1968.

F. A. Wright. *The Mirror of Venus: Love Poems and Stories from Ovid's Amores etc.*, London: Routledge, 1925.

INDEX OF TRANSLATED PASSAGES

INDEX OF TRANSLATORS

READ MORE IN PENGUIN

READ MORE IN PENGUIN

A CHOICE OF CLASSICS

Aeschylus	**The Oresteian Trilogy**
	Prometheus Bound/The Suppliants/Seven against Thebes/The Persians
Aesop	**Fables**
Ammianus Marcellinus	**The Later Roman Empire (AD 354–378)**
Apollonius of Rhodes	**The Voyage of Argo**
Apuleius	**The Golden Ass**
Aristophanes	**The Knights/Peace/The Birds/The Assemblywomen/Wealth**
	Lysistrata/The Acharnians/The Clouds
	The Wasps/The Poet and the Women/ The Frogs
Aristotle	**The Art of Rhetoric**
	The Athenian Constitution
	De Anima
	Ethics
	Poetics
Arrian	**The Campaigns of Alexander**
Marcus Aurelius	**Meditations**
Boethius	**The Consolation of Philosophy**
Caesar	**The Civil War**
	The Conquest of Gaul
Catullus	**Poems**
Cicero	**Murder Trials**
	The Nature of the Gods
	On the Good Life
	Selected Letters
	Selected Political Speeches
	Selected Works
Euripides	**Alcestis/Iphigenia in Tauris/Hippolytus**
	The Bacchae/Ion/The Women of Troy/ Helen
	Medea/Hecabe/Electra/Heracles
	Orestes and Other Plays

READ MORE IN PENGUIN

A CHOICE OF CLASSICS

READ MORE IN PENGUIN

A CHOICE OF CLASSICS

Plautus	**The Pot of Gold and Other Plays**
	The Rope and Other Plays
Pliny	**The Letters of the Younger Pliny**
Pliny the Elder	**Natural History**
Plotinus	**The Enneads**
Plutarch	**The Age of Alexander** (Nine Greek Lives)
	The Fall of the Roman Republic (Six Lives)
	The Makers of Rome (Nine Lives)
	Plutarch on Sparta
	The Rise and Fall of Athens (Nine Greek Lives)
Polybius	**The Rise of the Roman Empire**
Procopius	**The Secret History**
Propertius	**The Poems**
Quintus Curtius Rufus	**The History of Alexander**
Sallust	**The Jugurthine War/The Conspiracy of Cataline**
Seneca	**Four Tragedies/Octavia**
	Letters from a Stoic
Sophocles	**Electra/Women of Trachis/Philoctetes/Ajax**
	The Theban Plays
Suetonius	**The Twelve Caesars**
Tacitus	**The Agricola/The Germania**
	The Annals of Imperial Rome
	The Histories
Terence	**The Comedies (The Girl from Andros/The Self-Tormentor/The Eunuch/Phormio/The Mother-in-Law/The Brothers)**
Thucydides	**History of the Peloponnesian War**
Virgil	**The Aeneid**
	The Eclogues
	The Georgics
Xenophon	**Conversations of Socrates**
	A History of My Times
	The Persian Expedition

READ MORE IN PENGUIN

A CHOICE OF CLASSICS

Adomnan of Iona	**Life of St Columba**
St Anselm	**The Prayers and Meditations**
St Augustine	**Confessions**
	The City of God
Bede	**Ecclesiastical History of the English People**
Geoffrey Chaucer	**The Canterbury Tales**
	Love Visions
	Troilus and Criseyde
Marie de France	**The Lais of Marie de France**
Jean Froissart	**The Chronicles**
Geoffrey of Monmouth	**The History of the Kings of Britain**
Gerald of Wales	**History and Topography of Ireland**
	The Journey through Wales and **The Description of Wales**
Gregory of Tours	**The History of the Franks**
Robert Henryson	**The Testament of Cresseid and Other Poems**
Walter Hilton	**The Ladder of Perfection**
St Ignatius	**Personal Writings**
Julian of Norwich	**Revelations of Divine Love**
Thomas à Kempis	**The Imitation of Christ**
William Langland	**Piers the Ploughman**
Sir John Mandeville	**The Travels of Sir John Mandeville**
Marguerite de Navarre	**The Heptameron**
Christine de Pisan	**The Treasure of the City of Ladies**
Chrétien de Troyes	**Arthurian Romances**
Marco Polo	**The Travels**
Richard Rolle	**The Fire of Love**
François Villon	**Selected Poems**

READ MORE IN PENGUIN

A CHOICE OF CLASSICS

ANTHOLOGIES AND ANONYMOUS WORKS

The Age of Bede
Alfred the Great
Beowulf
A Celtic Miscellany
The Cloud of Unknowing and Other Works
The Death of King Arthur
The Earliest English Poems
Early Irish Myths and Sagas
Egil's Saga
English Mystery Plays
Eyrbyggja Saga
Hrafnkel's Saga and Other Stories
The Letters of Abelard and Heloise
Medieval English Lyrics
Medieval English Verse
Njal's Saga
Roman Poets of the Early Empire
Seven Viking Romances
Sir Gawain and the Green Knight

READ MORE IN PENGUIN

POETRY LIBRARY

Blake	Selected by W. H. Stevenson
Browning	Selected by Daniel Karlin
Burns	Selected by Angus Calder and William Donnelly
Byron	Selected by A. S. B. Glover
Clare	Selected by Geoffrey Summerfield
Coleridge	Selected by Richard Holmes
Donne	Selected by John Hayward
Dryden	Selected by Douglas Grant
Hardy	Selected by David Wright
Housman	Introduced by John Sparrow
Keats	Selected by John Barnard
Kipling	Selected by Craig Raine
Lawrence	Selected by Keith Sagar
Milton	Selected by Laurence D. Lerner
Pope	Selected by Douglas Grant
Rubáiyát of Omar Khayyám	Translated by Edward FitzGerald
Shelley	Selected by Isabel Quigly
Tennyson	Selected by W. E. Williams
Wordsworth	Selected by Nicholas Roe
Yeats	Selected by Timothy Webb

READ MORE IN PENGUIN

A SELECTION OF POETRY

James Fenton Out of Danger

A collection wonderfully open to experience – of foreign places, differences, feelings and languages.

U. A. Fanthorpe Selected Poems

'She is an erudite poet, rich in experience and haunted by the classical past ... fully at home in the world of the turbulent NHS, the decaying academies, and all the draughty corners of the abandoned Welfare State' – *Observer*

Craig Raine Clay. Whereabouts Unknown

'I cannot think of anyone else writing today whose every line is so unfailingly exciting' – *Sunday Times*

Marge Piercy Eight Chambers of the Heart

Marge Piercy's poetry is written to be read and spoken aloud, to move, provoke and entertain, on every subject under the sun from ecology to cats and cookery, to political, sexual and family relationships.

Joseph Brodsky To Urania
Winner of the 1987 Nobel Prize for Literature

Exiled from the Soviet Union in 1972, Joseph Brodsky has been universally acclaimed as the most talented Russian poet of his generation.

Paul Celan Selected Poems
Winner of the first European Translation Prize, 1990

'The English reader can now enter the hermetic universe of a German–Jewish poet who made out of the anguish of his people, things of terror and beauty' – *The Times Literary Supplement*

Geoffrey Hill Canaan

'Among our finest poets, Geoffrey Hill is at present the most European – in his Latinity, in his dramatization of the Christian condition, in his political intensity' – *Sunday Times*

READ MORE IN PENGUIN

A SELECTION OF POETRY

Octavio Paz Selected Poems

'His poetry allows us to glimpse a different and future place ... liberating and affirming' – *Guardian*

Fernando Pessoa Selected Poems

'I have sought for his shade in those Edwardian cafés in Lisbon which he haunted, for he was Lisbon's Cavafy or Verlaine' – *Sunday Times*

Allen Ginsberg Collected Poems 1947–1985

'Ginsberg is responsible for loosening the breath of American poetry at mid-century' – *New Yorker*

Carol Ann Duffy Selected Poems

'Carol Ann Duffy is one of the freshest and bravest talents to emerge in British poetry – any poetry – for years' – *Independent on Sunday*

John Updike Collected Poems 1953–1993

'Updike's eye comes up very close ... yet eschews the gruesome, keeps life vivid and slippery and erotic' – *Observer*

Frank O'Hara Selected Poems

With his unpremeditated, fresh style, O'Hara broke with the academic traditions of the 1950s and became the life and soul of the New York school of poets.

Dannie Abse Selected Poems

Medicine, music, the myths of Judaism, the cities of London and Cardiff – all recur in poems composed in a spare and witty style.

Penguin Modern Poets

A new series celebrating, in ten volumes, the best and most innovative of today's poetic voices.

READ MORE IN PENGUIN

A SELECTION OF POETRY

American Verse
British Poetry since 1945
Caribbean Verse in English
Chinese Love Poetry
A Choice of Comic and Curious Verse
Contemporary American Poetry
Contemporary British Poetry
Contemporary Irish Poetry
English Poetry 1918–60
English Romantic Verse
English Verse
First World War Poetry
German Verse
Greek Verse
Homosexual Verse
Imagist Poetry
Irish Verse
Japanese Verse
The Metaphysical Poets
Modern African Poetry
New Poetry
Poetry of the Thirties
Scottish Verse
Surrealist Poetry in English
Spanish Verse
Victorian Verse
Women Poets
Zen Poetry